MW00355487

SHADOW OF THE WINTER KING

Book One of the World of Ruin

Erik Scott de Bie

DRAGON
MOON
PRESS

SHADOW OF THE WINTER KING

"The World of Ruin:
A dying world—an inevitable end.
Much and many have been lost,
All must pass to Ruin."

This book is dedicated to my wife Shelley, for helping me along this epic journey, smoothing the path ahead and behind, and always being there with an extra sword when I needed it. She is my Blood and my Bond, my Master and my Goddess.

I also want to acknowledge the hard work and support of my own Circle of Writers, without whom this book would not have been possible, particularly my exacting editor Gabrielle Harbowy, the wise Gwen Gades at Dragon Moon Press, the legendary Ed Greenwood, the superheroic Nathan Crowder, and the irrepressible Rosemary Jones.

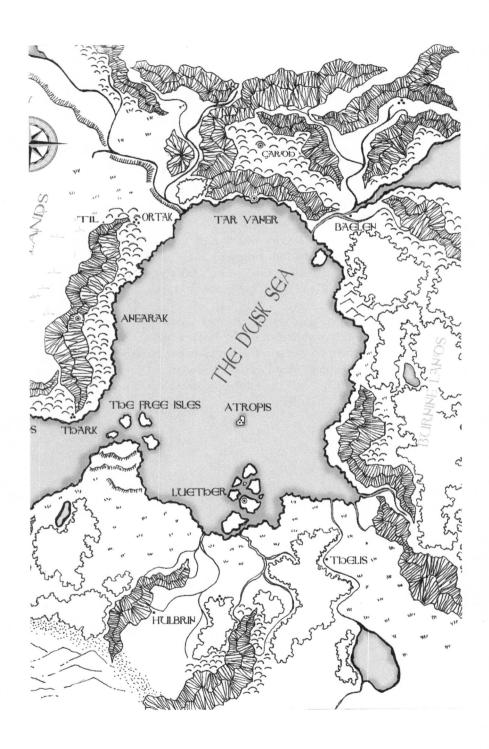

PROLOGUE

THE LORD OF TEARS tried very hard not to kill her.

It would have been so easy. As she sat there, he could have slipped his blade between her ribs or looped a garrote around her neck. He could have commanded a servant to lace her mead with poison or sprinkle broken glass into her food. He could have put a casterbolt through her belly from under the table and watched her explode backward from the force.

He had planned this. The Lord of Tears would stand in this place, in view of all, and take her life with a single swipe of his blade. None would challenge him here, even as he stood over her bloody corpse. All knew this was his tavern, where he killed with impunity. His Tears surrounded him in this place: any one of his sworn servants would kill or die for him. This was his place of power.

And who was she? Friendless and alone. The great Bloodbreaker, who had slain the last heir of the Blood Denerre and wiped the Kings of Winter from the World of Ruin forever. The sheer enormity of her crime was known by all. He could have cut her throat in the street and all would cheer him.

Instead, he sat and listened to her plea. Her hand lay upon his, her skin against his skin.

"I need your help, Regel."

She used his old name. The one he had almost forgotten.

The problem, Regel thought, was that Ovelia spoke the truth. Now, after five years, she had walked back into his life and offered him nothing but truth.

He laid a finger along his nose, tracing the black teardrop etched beneath his left eye. The tattoo had hurt, but it had been nothing compared to the pain she had caused with a swipe of her sword.

"And why should I help you?" he asked, though he meant to ask, *Why haven't I killed you?*

"Because you loved the Winter King." Ovelia's eyes glittered. "And you loved me, once."

Regel drew his hand away from hers. Ovelia's eyes fell to where her fingers curled ineffectually on the table, nails scratching against years of accumulated wax. She sat, quiescent and waiting.

Why tonight, of all nights? The night he'd returned to the city after two years away, and the night he meant to kill her? The coincidence seemed impossible.

He concentrated on the carving in his hand: a rough-hewn dove, more useful than artistic. Rubbing its smooth surface let his mind focus and relax while his

7

senses expanded, like sharpening his perception on a whetstone. He'd learned this trick as a boy, and honed it in the forty years since.

With his spiraling awareness, Regel took in the smoky, breath-stealing interior of the common room of the Burned Man, noting the surreptitious gazes of the other patrons. He saw the hilt of a knife under the ale-bearer's skirts and met her eye, marked with the painted tear they all wore in the Burned Man. She stood ready for his move. His snare was set.

Ovelia had sealed her own fate by entering the tavern. And yet the Lord of Tears hesitated.

Ovelia watched Regel levelly, not a hint of guile on her face. "That's beautiful." She indicated the carving. "You always had a way with carving. Such hands you have."

Wordlessly, he set the carved dove on the table and focused on Ovelia instead.

Ovelia Dracaris didn't look like a murderer, let alone a traitor and regicide. Hers was neither the haughty demeanor of the courts of High Blood nor the charm of a rustic beauty, but rather something altogether unique and hers. He knew her features well: the little fishhook scar at the left edge of her mouth, the hazel eyes always a touch wet, the brow inclined to worry. He thought her nose had been broken again since he'd last seen her, but it had knit well. The tiny wrinkles spreading like wings from the corners of her eyes had deepened. He remembered Ovelia's face wreathed in crimson curls, but now she wore white-blonde hair, cropped just below her ears. The color made her older, but that was not its purpose. Instead, he knew she had dyed her hair that she might resemble another woman he had known—a woman he had loved far more than he ever had her.

He did not want to remember. That life was far behind him. Who was she to revive it?

"You are staring," she said. "As though I were a woman returned from the grave?"

Her demure smile made his stomach churn, and not with anger. He wondered if she knew her effect on him, and suspected that she did.

"You dyed your hair to hide your identity and to distract me with thoughts of a woman long dead," Regel said. "It will not serve."

Though she hid her reaction well, the hope in her eyes dimmed somewhat. She had heard his message clearly. He would grant her no sway over his heart. Never again.

"Surely you know I want you dead," he said. "You betrayed me. Betrayed all of us."

"Straight to it—I see you've not changed overmuch. I did not come to speak of the past. It is too late for us, but not—" Ovelia closed her eyes. "Not for one last task. A last homage to the Winter King."

That caught his attention. What possible service could they pay a dead man?

The Lord of Tears searched for a lie in her face and in her throat, but he found none. He should have killed her quickly, rather than allowed her to speak. He *would* have, had the contract on her life been less than strictly clear: *One thrust through the heart—the heart she swore to another and yet betrayed.*

"I need a man loyal to the Blood of Denerre, the true rulers of Tar Vangr," she said. "More than that, I need the Frostburn, the blade so fast it could—"

"That man died alongside his king," Regel said. "You slew them both, Bloodbreaker."

He remembered that night well. And from the pall that passed over Ovelia's face, so did she. Ovelia shivered, and for the first time, her seeming vulnerability slipped into something else: sorrow.

Why should she have that reaction? Should she not revel in her ignobility? If she yet lived—had not ended her life in shame as honor demanded—then surely she was a worse monster than the most loathsome Child of Ruin. And yet Ovelia reacted to the name "Bloodbreaker" with real pain, and not for herself. She truly regretted her treachery.

Her distress made him want her. He pictured seizing her wrist with a sudden creak of leather that would bite through the silence. He would pull her closer and run his fingers through her silver-dyed hair. He would draw her face to his and breathe deep. Perhaps she smelled like the woman he resembled.

But much as he itched to, he would do none of these things. Now was hardly the time to be a besotted idiot.

"I am Oathbreaker," he said. "I am the Lord of Tears. I have no other name."

Ovelia's eyes said she didn't believe him for a heartbeat. "What passes now, then?"

"We are a man and a woman seated at table, negotiating business. Offer me coin." He looked her over, then fixed on her eyes once more. "Or was it my lust you would use?"

That struck at her. Ovelia's sorrowful affect darkened into anger. "I did not come to whore myself, if that is what you mean."

"It was not." Regel shrugged. "But it is an answer."

Finally he had struck her temper. From her Luethaar father, Ovelia had the hot blood of the southland, where smoldering nights turned women and men into beasts with blades in their hands and fierce desires in their beds. She tempered her rage with the cool honor of her Vangryur mother, though, and it made her deadly. A child of two kingdoms, she was fire and cold steel both at once.

"That is all?" she asked. "Will you say nothing else? You will insult me and leave it to the wind?"

"So I have." Stand, he thought. Walk away, that I might kill you with no regrets. Let us put the old world behind us.

"Do I waste my time?" she asked.

"Clearly." And yet, she had spoken of a last homage...

She frowned. "It pains me to see you become such a coward."

Ovelia rose, but he caught her arm before she could walk away. She looked down at his hand. He had touched her without thinking. He'd not wanted her to go. Now he released her.

"I did not say no," he said. "Tell me of this task of yours, and we shall see."

"Very well. It will take me a moment."

"Take your time," Regel said. She had the rest of her life to explain, but that was not long.

9

They sat again, the moment tempered by the tavern smoke. The ale-bearer appeared and poured fresh drink for them both. While Ovelia was distracted, Regel glanced to his squire at the nearest table and nodded slightly. The nod was returned.

"I did not call for ale." Ovelia sniffed warily at her drink.

Regel waved. "You need fear no poison."

"I appreciate the reassurance." She set her tankard, untasted, on the table.

Regel sipped his ale. The movement revealed the hilt of one of the falcata sheathed at his belt. The curved blades were hardly a match for a knight's sword, but he favored them. He nodded to her empty swordbelt. "You are certainly brave, Bloodbreaker, to come to me unarmed."

"A wise man once told me," she said, "that a blade is only as sharp as its reverse edge."

Regel tried not to wince. The Winter King had said that, and the words from her lips—her damned, filthy lips—filled him with a hot storm that raged in his veins.

Of course she did not wear her family's Bloodsword, with its flamed blade and crossbar shaped like a dragon of myth. Draca, as the sword was called, bore the crest of Ovelia's family—of her father Norlest, Sworn Shield before her—and they in turn bore the name of the blade. *Draca* meant "guardian" in the Imperial tongue, for the dragons that had defended the world before Ruin fell and the time of darkness began. It was an ancient name for an ancient family, with its last heir sitting before him.

In truth, he supposed calling her "Dracaris" was not right after all. She only truly earned that name by wielding the family sword, and she certainly did not have it now. This Regel knew because he himself held Draca sheathed below the table, his right hand on its hilt. The Bloodsword would speak better to Ovelia, of course, but it held more than enough power even in Regel's hands: plenty enough to kill its former master. The sword had arrived two days before, along with a missive offering the price of her blood. It specified in detail how Ovelia was to die: spitted on her own treacherous sword, the end of her bloodline spilled upon the steel that had birthed it. Whoever sought her death had a sense of irony, it seemed, and hated her enough to risk the loss of a priceless weapon to do it.

A single thrust through the heart—the heart she swore to another and yet betrayed.

Regel wondered if that referred to the king's heart or his own.

"I need your help," Ovelia said. "And if I must fill your pockets with gold or offer you my body, I will. I believe, however, that once I name the task, payment will be unnecessary."

"You would appeal to my honor, then." Regel could barely contain his rage at the thought. "You, who have no honor. You would make such demands of me."

"Yes." Her gaze was sharpened steel. "I have more honor than you could imagine."

Under the table, Draca felt warm against his skin. It bore an old magic that alerted the bearer to imminent danger, and even painted images with smoke of a coming attack. With the blade in her hand, Ovelia would be impossible to surprise, but across the table from him, she was unarmed and helpless. A perfect mark. Ovelia's eyes searched him in his reverie, but she did not look ready to attack. He had never known the sword to err, but it was old—perhaps its magic had unraveled over the years. He would know if danger lurked around them if he could use his carving again, but he'd left it on the table. Instead, he hid his disquiet behind his tankard.

Regel should have killed her immediately, but now he was intrigued. What posed a greater danger to her than Regel himself? "Who is it you wish me to kill?"

"You misunderstand," Ovelia said. "I cannot do this alone. You will accompany me."

"An obvious trap. I should simply kill you here and now. No doubt the Ravalis would pay a fine proscription price."

"No doubt," she said. "But you will not kill me—not until we complete this task. Then I shall offer no resistance."

"And you thought I would agree to such terms?"

"Perhaps I trust you."

Regel's hands grew slick with sweat. The candles on the table burned low—soon, the attack would come, as he had planned it. His squire would strike, Ovelia would block, and Regel would have an opening to drive the sword home. But her words gave him pause. Could she not see the trap closing around her, sword or no sword? She had admitted—to him, a known slayer—that there was a contract for her blood. Had Ovelia lost her wits since he had seen her last, or was she truly desperate?

He was missing something, and he had to know what it was. "Time passes. Speak plainly."

"I offer that which you most desire," she said. "Vengeance. Yours and mine."

Draca's warning magic practically scalded his hand. Danger was coming, but he could not see it. Perhaps it meant the impending attack upon Ovelia, or perhaps Regel himself drew close to a precipice. Whence the ambush?

She leaned halfway across the table. Her red lips parted gently. "Through her heart," she whispered, so only he could hear. "The heart she swore to another, and yet betrayed."

As she spoke the words from the contract, Regel understood. This trap was not for her, but for him. He raised his right hand a fraction from the table—the signal to hold. His squire sat back, and Regel saw yellow eyes glimmer at him with a frustrated question he ignored. Regel had bought himself and Ovelia a momentary respite from the impending strike. Stay too long, however, and his Tears might decide she had ensnared him in some way and attack anyway. Ovelia had mere heartbeats to live.

"Is this an attack?" Regel asked. "Tell me that, and perhaps no one need die."

"Time to place all our knives on the table, I see." Ovelia stared at him directly, ignoring the threat gathering around her. "This is not a trap. I am the one who hired you, so that you would meet with me, alone. It was a risk, but I need you to give me what I want."

"Is that death?" Regel clasped the sword under the table. "Because I will gladly give you that."

Her eyes burned bright in the candlelight. "Another's death—one we both want."

"Whose?" Regel hissed. "Who could you possibly hate so much you'd risk facing me? Whose death would I want more than *yours*?"

"*Mask.*"

The name froze him where he sat.

"Semana," Regel said. "You mean to avenge Princess Semana."

Ovelia nodded slowly, seeming to hear his thoughts. "Regel, I need you. *She* needs you. Please."

Sudden movement stole Regel's attention. He saw the glint of a casterbolt amongst the crowd, though the casterman took care to hide it. The weapon's discharge cracked the uneasy silence.

Regel's mind went silent and his body moved. With his left hand, he drew one of his falcat and cut the bolt from the air a thumb's breadth from Ovelia's face. His left arm shrieked in protest at the exertion. The bolt splintered off the scythe-sword, and Ovelia took cover like the trained warrior she was. She had always been fast to react, even without her sword, but without Regel's block, that would have killed her.

Regel released Draca, palmed a dagger into his right hand, and threw even as he fell to one knee. The fang streaked across the smoky tavern and buried itself in the shooter's forearm. The man cursed and fell back.

That man was not one of his Tears. What was happening?

Two more castermen appeared to the right. Regel dove to the floor next to Ovelia as she pushed the table over for a shield. With a sharp *crack*, the tabletop splintered, sending wood chips spraying. A casterbolt tented the underside of the table like a blade through canvas.

"They've come for me." Ovelia's cool voice hardly sounded surprised, much less anxious.

"You knew they were following you," Regel said.

"I suspected." Ovelia glanced at her family sword sheathed at Regel's side. "I can fight."

"No doubt that was your plan all along." Regel switched his curved sword to his right hand and flexed his strained left arm. "Two swords cannot defeat four casters. We flee."

She nodded, conceding the point. "Together."

He nodded. How easy it was to fall into the familiar matching rhythm of war beside her—how easy it would be to trust her again.

Regel peered around the table. The castermen had vanished into a chaotic jumble of bodies. There were screams and curses, and brawls broke out. He saw his carved dove lying on the floor a pace away from the table, but he could not reach for it without exposure. He would need a new one.

A caster appeared on the other side of the room. Regel palmed a second knife and threw. It stabbed into the caster, sending it wide and setting the weapon off with a crack. The opposite window shattered outward.

"Go." Regel pointed to the new exit, but Ovelia seemed frozen, eyes wide. "What passes—?"

He heard a click behind him.

The slayer wore plain black leather and a hauberk of rings, well-oiled to keep silence. Unlike the others—amateurs all, to have burned their own attack by being spotted—this one was a veteran. He had waited for his moment, then crept close to catch them unawares. His plain, gutter-born face was not one Regel knew, but he had the red hair and deep gold skin of a summerblood from Luether.

The slayer carried a double-caster, neither bolt of which had been fired. It was a cold, ugly weapon—two bows mounted on a shaft of metal, either or both of which could be fired in quick succession. A caster required neither strength nor much skill, and thus was fit only for a coward.

"You're fast, old man. I've never seen anyone parry a casterbolt." The man aimed his caster at Regel's face from a hand's span away. "Can you block this one, I wonder?"

"Yes," Regel said.

That startled the slayer long enough for a shadow to move behind him.

Regel's squire stepped to the man's side, put steel to flesh, and opened his throat in a crimson waterfall. Regel stood up to catch the slayer as he fell, knocking the caster arm wide. With a splitting crack, the bolts discharged: one jammed, and the other flashed toward Ovelia. She spun aside and down, struck. Fear seized Regel's throat, even as the choking man struggled in his arms.

Kneeling, Ovelia touched her cheek with her bare fingers, where a line of blood dripped down her face. The shot had slashed past her head, just close enough to cut open her skin. A hair to the left, and it would have torn away her face. She stared at her bloody fingers in confusion.

Then—as though she suddenly remembered how to move—Ovelia drew her bloodsword from Regel's belt, the light dancing off its flame-like folds, and rammed it through the dying slayer's chest with a cry. The steel wrenched the man into a statue, its wavy edge tearing his flesh apart. He slumped to the floor, his strings cut.

"Well struck—" Regel started.

Ovelia faced him, the blood-smeared Draca low and deadly at her side. In her hands, the blade blazed with crimson fire, its ancient magic awakened at her touch. There was anger in her eyes, and the assurance of more violence to come. Regel tightened his grip on his sword, ready to move.

Fingers touched his hand. "I think your guest's ire is for *me*, Lord of Tears."

A wiry woman in a spattered dress stood beside him: his squire Serris, who had cut their would-be slayer's throat. She had the build of a hunting cat—all angular, dangerous lines—and a hard expression to match. The candlelight made the long scar on her cheek glow.

Serris directed her bloody knife at Ovelia in warning but looked to Regel for guidance. "M'lord?"

"Hold," he said.

That she had not attacked meant Serris hadn't recognized Ovelia. With her most distinctive feature—her fiery corona of hair—hidden under a beaker of silvery dye, Ovelia became a winterborn commoner, not the infamous Bloodbreaker. If his squire had known her true identity, Regel suspected Serris wouldn't have saved her at all.

Heedless of the battle near her, Serris knelt over the body of the casterman. "Summerborn," Serris said with disgust. "Poorly trained. Else I'd think Demetrus had decided to take his vengeance after all."

"Vengeance for what?" Ovelia asked.

"This is the mark." Serris glared at Ovelia, her expression unimpressed, then looked to Regel. "Why not kill her and have done?"

Ovelia lowered the sword. "Woman after your own heart."

Fresh casterbolts shot toward them, and the three crouched behind the battered table. The chaos in the Burned Man had reached a new furor, and steel shrieked in the night.

"I'll handle the slaying, Serris," Regel said. "Return to the fight. Take one alive if possible."

Serris gave them both an uncertain look. "Very well. Flee while you can." She nodded toward the window, then sprang back into the brawl.

Regel crouched against Ovelia behind cover. Now that she held her bloodsword again, Ovelia's limbs were tightly corded and her head up, eyes open and confident. They pressed close behind cover. He breathed in the smell of her hair, and felt momentarily dizzy. She *did* smell like he remembered.

His mind drifted, for a mere instant, to the last time he had seen her, and he'd seen the image over and over in his dreams. He watched as she stood amongst a dozen foes, gleaming in the moonlight like a blood-stained goddess with hair of flame. She looked so sad.

He remembered also this same tavern—remembered rage and blood and justice. He remembered the feel of another carving in his hands—a beast to slay a beast. He remembered the power in his arm, the righteous fury in his heart. His great mistake.

"Regel, we have to go now," Ovelia said.

Regel nodded. His Tears would win the day, but the Ravalis Guard would soon arrive. He heard watch horns in the distance outside, and from the sound of creaking metal down the street, they would be bringing at least one ironclad. They had to end the fight now, and Regel and Ovelia could not be here when the Ravalis arrived.

"It is true, then?" he asked. "This quest of yours?"

"Will you trust me?" Ovelia put out her hand.

No, he thought. "We do what we must," he said as he took her hand.

14

Keeping low, they scurried across the open common room. Two more casters fired, but the shots went wide: one split a chair, the other cracked a wall. Regel and Ovelia tumbled out the window into the darkened alley behind the Burned Man amid crunching glass and mud.

Burning rain fell heavily, cutting into them like knives.

ACT ONE: SHADOWS

Five Years Previous—the Burning Man Tavern—
Ruin's Eve, 976 Sorcerus Annis

SIZZLING RAIN CUT INTO the Burned Man's roof. The corroded metal held for now, but in time it would buckle under the acidic rain and collapse in a great sigh of surrender. Such was the way of Ruin.

At the table in the corner, the King's Shadow sheltered under his gray cloak and cut a ribbon of golden wood from a carved jackal that fit in his palm. The artistry that went into such a delicate piece was impressive, honed over decades of service to the City of Winter. Its snout curled almost in a smile, after the fashion of that beast, but he did not share its mirth. The figure was nearly finished, as was the task for which he had made it. He focused upon its rough fangs and let his mind and senses wander free.

Paeter Ravalis sat across the way, flushed and swollen, bristling with the red hair that marked his Blood. Around the crown prince sat four of his boon companions, lesser lordlings of weaker Bloods allied with the Ravalis: Saras, Rolan, Vortusk, and one he did not recognize. They had employed about a dozen fresh-faced lads and lasses for hire to blanket their laps and table in young, smooth flesh. It was hardly strange on a fate-cursed Ruin's Night to spend the darkness in revelry and celebration of continuing life. In hiding from Ruin on its own night, the living indulged in all those things that the Children of Ruin feared, and love was one such. The lordlings were pleased, one and all, but for Paeter Ravalis.

His smile once had commanded legions, but Paeter scowled more these days than he smiled. Perhaps a part of his once keen mind recognized how far he had fallen: a warrior prince become a beast, lounging among slaves and ale. The wrinkles edging his eyes that many had once thought intriguing had become sagging folds of weathered skin. Beneath his jaw, a livid ridge of scar glowed in the ruddy candlelight along the left side of his throat. Paeter would find no love this night, and from his face, perhaps he knew it. Outwardly, he cared nothing for his crumbling world, but inwardly, he was in pain.

Good.

Regel Frostburn—the King's Shadow—nursed a tankard of ale and watched through his expanded awareness. He took in the minutiae of Paeter's presence: his appearance, his depth of drink, which saleable flesh he eyed most. No—this was not even honest prostitution. The Ravalis had introduced slavery to Tar Vangr, and treated all who lacked a name as bodies they either owned or had yet to purchase. Even those who had bought a name through good works or earned

16

one through bold action meant little in the Ravalis' eyes, and Paeter was the most contemptuous of the Blood. He insulted, belittled, and took anyone he wanted without consequence.

Regel's hands trembled, and he told himself he had come not to kill a man so much as put down an animal. A rabid jackal.

It was not long before the red-haired lordling selected one of the slaves to take upstairs: a blonde stickling who wore childish timidity like a mantle. She had a forgettable peasant's face, but her pale hair and her age reminded Regel of his beloved Lenalin—as she had been when Paeter murdered her.

Ten years, Regel thought. *Ten years, and so he honors her.*

Pity for the slave coiled in Regel's heart but he forced it away so he could focus. He counted their steps: twenty on the stairs, eight on the landing above. Regel heard the slave's nervous voice, and Paeter's deeper, commanding reply. A door opened and closed.

The memory came to him of Ovelia from not three hours earlier. He saw her, naked and pleading, her taut body framed against the sweaty, black-sheeted bed. He hated her, yes, but also—far more—he hated what this man had done to her.

"How many, Prince?" he asked under his breath. "How many must you take from me?"

He closed his hand around the jackal figurine and put it back in his belt pouch. He had needed it to feel out the room for a waiting snare. Now, he needed to feel nothing at all.

Regel counted to one hundred before he made his way up the stairs. The other powder-nosed noble scions were too interested in their wine and company to notice an old man shambling off to bed.

As he reached the floor above, he put his hand on the hilt of his ancient sword, shaped in the scythe-curved falcat style. The tales named the blade Frostburn, forged of steel so cold it seared flesh from bone. The magic was real enough: he felt the familiar chill within, drinking life from his flesh. Crafted for harvest, the Deathless called this blade—for reaping the yield of Summer. And that was exactly what it would do this night.

"Let this be the last life this steel ends," he prayed. "Let *his* be the last."

～

Upstairs, Regel could hear the slave weeping loudly enough to fill the hall. He slipped a dagger through the jamb of Paeter's latched door and lifted. The door creaked open.

Paeter stood over the slave in the middle of the room. In the years since Lenalin's death, much of the lordling's once impressive collection of muscles had gone to fat and wild red hair bristled in patches along his limbs. He was mostly nude, and Regel could see—with some satisfaction—that the brutish prince could not stand to the task at hand. He would be impotent in life and in death.

Instead, Paeter held aloft a weapon far more dangerous: his dueling sword, which he dangled over the cowering slave. A red slash cut across her cheek, dripping blood.

"Here's coin for you," he slurred. "Coin for all of you!"

There was no time for a proper challenge, and in truth, Regel was grateful. Letting his mind fall still, he darted across the room and smashed his elbow into the side of Paeter's head. The bigger man reeled three paces and collapsed to the floor.

Regel thought he had never stuck such a satisfying blow.

A whimpering sound reminded him of the slave Paeter had brought into that room. Blood streaked down her face from where the prince had cut it open, but her gray eyes were wide and attentive. There was power in those eyes. Fire. Her thin-lipped mouth seemed drawn inward in thought as she watched him, fascinated.

"No fear." Regel dropped to one knee and reached for the slave, but she cringed. He looked down at his black-gloved hand, a touch of sadness in his heart. He withdrew.

"Kill you..." Paeter half-rose, eyes red with drink and anger. "Kill..." His eyes rolled and he slumped back to the floor.

"Unlikely," Regel said.

The wounded slave drew in a sharp breath when Regel looked at her but did not otherwise flee. There was fear in her eyes, but strength too. Perhaps, as Paeter would be his blade's last victim... perhaps he could find a new path. They both could.

Regel's leather gloves creaked as he released the hilt of his blade. He held up two fingers. "There are two moments where a man is weakest. The first is when he takes a lover. You will remember?"

Her face showed first confusion, then a wary understanding. She nodded slightly.

"I am not here to free you," Regel said, "but you may free yourself if you will it so."

She nodded again, wide-eyed.

"You will say nothing of this." Regel knelt and put a pouch of coins into her left hand. "Walk out of this place and do not return. Do you understand?"

"What if—?" Her voice was soft but steady. "What if someone stops me?"

"None will stop you. You'll not let them." He drew a short knife from his belt, put it in her right hand, and curled her fingers around it. "Do you have a name, child?"

Marveling at the beautiful steel in her hand, she shook her head. Of course she had no name. Most of the poor of Tar Vangr had not earned one. She looked up, expectant, but he shook his head.

"It is not for me to name you. If you would have a name, you must name yourself."

"Serris," she said, her voice soft and crackling like embers. "For the angel."

Paeter moaned and swore. His wits were returning, and Regel knew the time had come for him to conclude his night's business.

"A fitting name," he said. "I will see you marked as well."

"I... I already have a mark." She reached up to the slash on her cheek. "Given me by a prince. You have a greater name than his?"

"No." Regel noted her obvious wits: to know the Crown Prince of Tar Vangr was no mean feat for a slave who had likely never set foot outside low-city. "Then you are named and marked. I take you for my Squire, Angel Serris, and I will be your Master, if you will have me."

She looked surprised, but not displeased. What he had proposed to this girl he had just met was a great intimacy and responsibility. She would be his Blood in all but name, and her life would be his responsibility until such time as she broke with him. He asked as much of her as he offered, but he knew he had not erred.

"You may not have a greater name." Her eyes locked on his. "But you are a greater man."

Regel nodded. "Now walk away. If the Old Gods smile, we shall meet again."

Silently, Serris disappeared out the door, glancing back over her shoulder at the last.

"How... *dare* you."

Regel turned slowly, watching Paeter Ravalis trying to climb to his knees. Slowly, Regel touched the hilt of his curved blade. It was a weapon of another world—of another time.

The man spat and mewled, his eyes wild. "You have no right to touch me, Denerre's dog!" His mouth frothed. "Beg forgiveness and I'll kill you before my father hears of this. Count it a mercy."

Regel drew Frostburn, bathing the room in the weird light of its wavy blue steel. His hand prickled as the blade sucked at the warmth from his arm. "Get up," he said.

"You think you have the advantage, don't you?" Paeter felt at the blood running from his face, and it made him smile. He tore open his tunic, revealing a red jackal tattooed across his flabby flesh, through which ran three scratches. "You've drawn my blood, and now it will prove your end."

Regel stiffened, but he sensed no attack coming. Had pain and drink driven Paeter mad?

Nothing happened for a long moment, and Paeter blinked down at the blood on his hand. Realization dawned on his face, then turned to anger. "That treacherous filth. He *lied* to me."

Regel didn't know what Paeter meant and didn't care. "Get up," he said again.

"You think you frighten me, old man? You and your fairy steel?" Paeter wiped his mouth, then tapped the scar on his left throat. "You didn't kill me ten years ago, and you won't kill me now. And how well that blade will look on my trophy wall—beside the portrait of that whore, Lenalin. Even after I shoved the whore through a mirror—and oh, she made a hideous corpse!" Paeter grinned wide. "Even then, you didn't kill me. You are a coward, Frostburn."

Regel held his sword high, cutting the space between them. The torchlight shimmered along its ever-sharp edge, which stood along the inside of the curve. He had to kill Paeter, if only to stop him speaking of Lenalin. The monster did not even bother to deny his guilt in her death.

"Get up," he said for a third time. "There is no honor in killing a man on his knees."

"You are ardent. You *truly* mean to kill me?" Paeter laughed and ran his fingers through his sweaty red hair. He got to his feet and drew his sword up clumsily from the floor. "You are a fool, then, if you think you are a match for the finest swordsman in Tar Vangr—in Luether—in all of Old Calatan."

Regel called upon the Old Gods to bless Frostburn's aim. He was not the sword's first wielder, and neither would he be the last. The strength of centuries filled him, burning fit to match his hatred.

"And even if you could kill me, you *would* not," Paeter said. "I am the heir of Ravalis, and the future king of Tar Vangr. Touch me, and you destroy all you love. I am the man you cannot kill."

"You are not a man but a beast." Heart thudding in his throat, Regel held his hand firm. "No man would do what you did to... *her*." He could not speak her name, for then he would lose all control.

"I see." A cloud passed over Paeter's eyes, and a wicked smile curled his face. He raised his sword. "Whose honor do you avenge, King's Shadow? Is it Lenalin or Ovelia—my whore or yours?" He snickered. "Do not answer. They are *both* my—"

Regel lunged forward and blew the life from Paeter in a single blow.

The strike cut open Paeter's neck so deeply it almost took off the man's head. Paeter's body slammed into the wall. It spun and seemed as if it might stay standing, then slumped to the floor. The corpse jerked and twitched in a widening crimson pool.

Paeter Ravalis died pitifully, just as Regel had wanted.

"Make it swift and ignoble," the Winter King had said earlier that eve, when he'd sent forth his Shadow. "Though do not be cruel. Despite his works, he is a prince of the realm."

Paeter Ravalis had become a corpse now, and held as little relevance as a haunch of meat. He had begun his path to Ruin long before he had ever met the King's Shadow, long before he had murdered his wife, and long before that lonely, sad night in the Burned Man, as his lifeblood ceased to flow.

Regel looked down at the chill blade balanced lazily in his hand. "Let this be the last life I take by this blade," he prayed. "No more King's Shadow—no more Regel Frostburn. Let me take a new name."

Cold teased up his arm from the hungry sword. He fought it back with a firm purpose.

"For you, Lena," he murmured. "For you."

Even as he said it, he found himself thinking not of Lenalin—his perfect, silver-haired princess, dead these ten years—but of Ovelia. He saw again her pleading eyes, her rough fingers, and her warm lips. He felt again his heart squeezing as though it would break under the strain.

Footsteps on the stairs broke his reverie. Paeter's lordlings, come to investigate the sound of their master crashing to the floor. Regel sighed. He drew the figurine from his pouch—a jackal for a jackal—and dropped it onto the corpse that had been Paeter Ravalis.

He was out the window of the Burned Man before the door burst open.

~

As cries of "Murder!" rang in his ears, Regel skittered spider-like up the mountain wall of the palace, trying to slow his raging heart. He could no longer hear the accusations, but only the wind that sang of his victory, so long overdue.

He drove his fingers into a handhold and pulled himself to the next, shoulders corded with effort. Breath came hard as he worked, so he found a perching dragon, wedged his calves inside, and leaned back to rest and gulp down the cold mountain air that rushed through his hair, chapped hands hanging. Thirty years had passed since he had first made this climb, and he had grown no younger in that time.

A thousand feet below him, low-city sparkled with a night sky's worth of candles burning in thousands of windows. From this distance, Tar Vangr looked peaceful, even though he knew the watch would be storming house to house, searching for the murderer of Paeter Ravalis. Fitting, he supposed, that he had dealt Paeter's death on this night of all nights. Doom stalked the streets on Ruin's Night, the last night of the year, visiting death and destruction where it wished.

He had ridden a skylift most of the way up to the palace, but ultimately he'd had to duck Ravalis guards at the gates. They were out in force, and had even rounded up ironclads to guard high-city for Ruin's Night. Any other route—even killing the guards, regardless of armament—would have been easier than the climb, but the effort quieted the fierce joy and anger that warred in his heart. Scaling the mountain gave him a chance to be alone and think.

Regel felt it before he heard it: stone trembled and cracked under his feet. He lunged out and caught himself on the dragon's wing, then leaped from there to the carved slit of a window. The dragon itself broke away from the mountain and tumbled down over low-city. Regel remembered the jackal figurine, falling on Paeter's body. The stone beast shattered into rubble on a lower ridge.

The whole city was falling apart, as Ruin encroached outside the walls.

Regel flexed his arms, swung about, and alighted on a high balcony that looked out over low-city and the bay. As a nameless child climbing and skulking in the passages beneath the palace, he had delighted in his skill. The palace had been his world, and these stones his kingdom. Now, as a man, he was tired and wanted nothing more than to find a warm place to rest.

He thought of the king. "We are all of us old men," he said to no one.

The darkness of Ruin's Night whispered in reply, but he thought that just the wind. Either way, it chilled him.

Before that night, Regel had expected to feel righteous or at least *justified*. Finally, Orbrin had loosed his hand, and Regel had avenged the only woman he had ever loved. Finally, Princess Semana was old enough to rule on her own without Paeter, and depriving her of her wretch of a father seemed like a service. Finally, the Blood of Winter could break free of these damned Ravalis of the summerblood.

So why did he feel no warm elation, but only cold dread?

Then Regel saw something afire in the ice-choked harbor. Ships were making their way toward burning hunks of metal that lay strewn across the harbor: the wreck of a crashed skyship.

Regel's stomach lurched. This very eve, Princess Semana had been returning to the city by skyship.

It took a moment for the horror to strike him—a moment wherein his chest heaved in increasing panic and he almost lost his grip on the window. He knew, with a frenzied, mad certainty, that something had gone terribly wrong this night, in part by his own hand.

Then he saw it: a dark shape framed against the moon, flying toward the king's balcony above. Not a bird, he thought—a *man*.

Heedless of the deadly drop below, Regel leaped up the outside wall and caught one of the nearly invisible handholds he'd cut years ago. He climbed, racing the flying man, and swung up over the banister onto the main balcony just as he landed. Inner light through the stained glass of the palace window cast scintillating colors over the two figures.

Before Regel stood a spindly creature wrapped toe to crown in black leather. Its arms and legs—the latter trailing smoke in the wake of the flight—looked more like black-swathed bones than the limbs of a living thing. It wore mismatched gauntlets: one of fire-blasted metal with talons, one a more elegant construction of silver and iron. Its face hid behind a leather mask that covered its head entirely, leaving only small slits for eyes and mouth. Regel might have thought the creature a manikin, but for the way its eyes flicked to him beneath the mask. The moonlight made the eyes seem blood red.

Regel knew this creature and his murderous powers. Frostburn was instantly in his hands, filling him with a cold hunger. "Mask," he said.

The sorcerer considered him a moment, as though pondering his presence. In his left hand, he held what looked like a hempen rope soaked in blood. "Regel, King's Shadow," he said, his voice both sibilant and rough-shod, like a snake slithering through jagged glass. "I always knew it would be you."

Regel found the words odd, but a surge of anger drowned out all thought. The ravings of a lunatic could not be credited. "What are you doing here?"

Mask hesitated a moment. "I slay the Blood of Winter this night—what of you?"

He thought of the destroyed skyship he'd seen in the harbor. "It was you," he said. "You crashed the *Heiress*. You..." He raised Frostburn. "You killed Semana."

He could not read Mask's expression, of course, but the sorcerer hesitated. "Why would you care? Were you not here to kill the king, slayer? Do you not kill all that you swear to love, by your hand or another's?"

Then Mask tossed the gory rope to the stone between them, and Regel knew it for what it was: a sticky mass of hair. It was Semana's silver-white braid, smeared with half-congealed blood.

Rage welling, Regel tensed to spring, but a cry from the throne room broke his concentration. His eyes flickered to the window for an instant, and something struck him from Mask's direction—sickly green magic that flared around the slayer's mask and surged forth to saturate him like a flood. His body felt hard as bone under Mask's power, every muscle afire. His insides churned and air would not come. He coughed, spattering the stones with blackish blood. He fell, nerveless beyond his inner agony, face turned so he could see into the throne room.

A score of guardsmen stood in a circle, weapons drawn, frozen. There, in the center of the ring, knelt King Orbrin, leaning against Ovelia. Regel thought at first that they were embracing, and found it strange. She was devoted to him, yes, but that embrace was too intimate—like that of a child and parent, or even that of lovers. Then she pulled away, and her sword wrenched free of Orbrin's chest. Blood smeared across her face. For a moment, her hazel eyes wet and gleaming, she gazed out at them—at him. Then she saluted with her bloody sword.

The guardsmen roared a chorus of anger and charged her.

Regel heard a sound like a choked gasp. Mask was looking into the throne room, hand at his obscured mouth. Was that laughter?

Then the creature strode away and leaped from the balcony to take flight.

The magic wracking Regel's body subsided, but he was too weak to move, too weak to defend his king or even himself.

The scalding rain returned, sliding across his face like burning tears as he lay helpless as a corpse.

23

ONE

S TEAM RISING FROM THEIR clothes, Regel and Ovelia plunged out of the
Burned Man into the night. The scything rain fell like acid on their exposed
skin and their blood burned inside. Behind them, Ravalis slayers fought against
the Circle of Tears, who bought them time to flee.

Three hundred feet above them, balanced gracefully on mage-glass and curling
buttresses, high-city sparkled in the rain light, pouring down waterfall streams of
liquid fire. The great palace of Tar Vangr rose on a mountain through the center
of the city, standing like a petrified god in judgment as they plunged into the
labyrinth of ancient streets, putting as much cobblestone between them and their
pursuers as possible. Ovelia had left her cloak back at the embattled tavern, so
Regel held his over her head as they ran past suspicious tradesmen and ducked
gazes from behind the soot-stained windows of wine taverns. He kept his eyes up
for Ravalis patrols, and they steered away from the echoing watch horns.

Around them, the rain sizzled on ground heated from the silver forge-fires of
the Nar deep below. In their time in Tar Vangr, the Ravalis had stoked the Narfire
to turn out blades and armor by the wagonload to gird an army of soldiers. The
power armor they constructed was a threat, though it had its weaknesses, and
their swords were all inferior pieces, of course—hardly a one of them could stand
against the ancient art of Tar Vangr swordsmithing. But the Ravalis commanded
enough soldiers that the dwindling noble bloods of the city stood little chance of
rising against their summerblood masters.

And, of course, the Ravalis had their war machines to tip the balance and
keep the people in line. Some of the monstrosities were salvaged from the fields
of Echvarr, others freshly built in the caverns below Tar Vangr. Regel shuddered
to think what other devices the southern princes—with their blood of metal and
thoughts of gears—might be forging in those caves.

Around Hangman's Crook, half a mile from the Burned Man, they finally
halted to catch their breath at the edge of the Square of the Fallen, nestled near
one of the towering, cloud-wreathed columns that held up high-city. The watch
horns had receded in the distance, and they would be safe for the moment.
Regel cursed the loss of his carved dove back at the tavern, as it would have let
him see without seeing. Instead, he hid against the corner and glanced back.
No pursuit—good.

As on most nights, the Square of the Fallen lay fallow, barren of visitors.
Vangryur rarely frequented the place except on Ruin's Night, when they paid

24

their respects at the black obelisk that rose from its heart. Tar Vangr's calamitous history was carved into its surface in just a few words: a list of years, and names of those Ruin had claimed on the final, fatal night of that year. The monument to Ruin's Night made the square a sacred place, and under the rule of the godless Ravalis, Tar Vangr had little room left for the sacred.

"Still as fast as ever," Ovelia said breathlessly. Her warm body pressed against his side felt entirely too good. "Deflecting a casterbolt with a blade? Not many could do that."

"Luck." He broke away from her to step toward the obelisk.

"Ha... *luck*." Ovelia gazed at him piercingly. "Only Regel the Frostburn could do that."

"As you say."

Regel examined the weathered obelisk, carved with a list of deaths, losses, and blood-breakings that reached halfway up from the ground. Each entry was simply a year and one or more names, all of whom that fallen to Ruin in one way or another. Many runes rose from the time since the Ravalis had come to the city—almost as many as the rest of Tar Vangr's centuries-long history. Though Regel had been present at many of the assassinations, only a few of the dates and names meant anything to him. "961—Luether," when the Ravalis had come to Tar Vangr. "966—Lenalin Denerre," murdered by her monstrous husband Paeter. "971—Darak Ravalis nô Denerre," sent into exile for a crime Regel could not prove he did not commit. And, of course, five years past: "976—Orbrin Denerre, Paeter Ravalis, Semana Denerre nô Ravalis," all of them gone in one bloody night of treachery. *Ovelia's* treachery.

"What is it?" Ovelia pointedly did not look at the obelisk.

"How simple that makes it all seem," Regel said. "As if those nights were merely history."

"We know better." Ovelia nodded back the way they had come. "Who were those folk back at the tavern? You had an *army* in that place."

"Tears," Regel said. "Courtesans, spies—little passes in this city that I don't know."

"You are a spymaster in your own right, then," Ovelia said. "Did you know about me all along?"

"No." Regel peered around the edge once more, but the street had yet to clear. "The only one who knows more than I do about the goings-on of Tar Vangr is the Shroud, whoever he is. I've never been able to reason it out. I believe those were his men. If the Ravalis know of you, we have to move quickly."

"Agreed." Ovelia nodded slightly, her face unreadable.

"I've a safehouse for the night," Regel said. "But we should leave the city as soon as possible."

"I have a ship waiting at the dock," she said.

"I should have known you'd have a plan."

Ovelia stiffened at Regel's side. Before he could react, she tackled him against the obelisk.

"Ovelia," Regel said, warning in his voice.

"Just—" She pressed herself against him and kissed him hard. Her lips were warm and soft.

He reached for her shoulders, but belatedly he saw warning shadows leaking from the sword sheathed at her belt. He relaxed and put his arms up around her. Above him, he was accutely aware of Lenalin's name, traced in acid rain, burning at the edge of his senses.

Metal crunched on stone as something huge ground its way toward them. Over his shoulder, Regel glimpsed the massive silhouette of a Lancer striding into the Square of the Fallen, a mechanized suit of armor the size of a dire bear. It bore the standard armament the Ravalis bestowed on their war machines: a heavy caster installed in its right arm, while its left boasted a crackling butcher's sword that could cut through solid stone walls at a single blow. That single war machine could kill a dozen men in less time than it took a trained swordsman to draw steel.

Trailing behind the ironclad, two Ravalis foot soldiers appeared at the mouth of the alley, searing rain dripping off their wide-brimmed hats to sizzle off their powered armor. In the night, their eyes gleamed, making them resemble wolves more than men. They saw the two lovers, leered a few seconds, then walked on, grumbling about crazy Vangryur and the rain as they followed the ironclad south down the Path of Dustweavers out of the square.

"You could have simply warned me." Regel broke their embrace. "You didn't have to *kiss* me."

Ovelia refused to meet his eye. "As you say."

They paused in the alley to collect their breath. Regel watched the soldiers disappear in the haze, then considered the rivulets of searing rain on the ground. He would do anything to avoid looking at Ovelia, or Lenalin's name on the obelisk. "What if I had refused?"

"Refused the kiss?" Ovelia asked. "We could have killed them, I suppose. Perhaps not the ironclad, but we could have fled."

"I meant your desperate scheme," Regel said. "If I had said no, what would you have done then?"

"Ah." Ovelia's expression cooled. "Then we would have dueled. And even if you hadn't called in what is apparently a small army of agents, I would likely be dead now."

"Why take such a risk?"

"I—" Ovelia looked at her feet. "I have made mistakes, Regel—unforgivable mistakes."

"Yes," he said.

He saw tension ripple through Ovelia as the last vestiges of her once-fearsome pride made war against her will. Finally, she sank to one knee, there in the Square of the Fallen. "Please," she said.

Regel regarded her silently, unable to muster a reply.

"Please aid me." She laid her hands on his calves—the old gesture of supplication.

"I know I have no right to ask it of you, but I do as I must. 'Eternal, Unyielding'—those are the words of my house, but I will yield unto you. Promise me."

He looked up at Lenalin's name, and at that of her daughter Semana. The injustice burned him.

"Ovelia, I am a man of honor."

"Yes, but you doubt me. I can see it in your eyes." She clutched him hard. "Please help me. Take my gold, my body, my life—only do this. *Please*."

Regel wanted to touch her face. He wanted to reassure her. He did neither.

"I will not play you false," Regel repeated. "Get up."

Ovelia shook her head. "Say it again—give me your word."

"I give it. I will aid you." Regel looked away from her, up at the obelisk. When he gave his word, it was less to Ovelia than to Lenalin's name, graven in the stone. "We will kill Mask." He looked back to Ovelia, with her blonde hair like Lenalin's. "Get up—you shame me."

She did so, standing with her familiar, easy grace. She touched her lips with two fingers.

"What is it?" Regel asked. "We need to move."

She drew her fingers away and closed her hand into a fist. "Nothing," she said. "Let's away."

～

As they rounded a corner along the Path of Spidercatchers, Regel and Ovelia passed by the worn feet of the outer wall that marked Tar Vangr's northern edge. The monstrous presence dominated the maze of alleys below, offering shelter but also a dire promise: Ruin lay beyond this wall. Outside those stones, Regel thought, the world went mad.

Since the Ravalis had come to power five years ago, the northern kingdom had eroded to little beyond the city wall. Thus had Tar Vangr—the last city-state remaining of the old Empire of Calatan, born a thousand years ago and fallen before its eight hundredth year—entered its final dotage. Beyond the old stones lay fallow plains where once had stood farms and homesteads that became endless snowfields in the winter. Since ascending the throne, the Ravalis had made no effort to expand Tar Vangr's power or lands. It was only a matter of time, some said, before the Ravalis let Tar Vangr itself fall to Ruin just as they had lost their ancestral homeland of Luether. Some even believed the ancient Prophecy of Return was being fulfilled, and the passing of King Orbrin—the last unifying force in Tar Vangr—heralded the final triumph of Ruin a thousand years after the birth of Calatan. Nineteen years had yet to pass before the roll of Sorcerius Annis came to a thousand, but with each year, the world seemed a little darker—and a little madder.

Ovelia had made herself harbinger of that self-same Ruin by slaying Orbrin. For this alone, Regel might have killed her, but he needed her for now. For Mask.

Regel paused at the Aleisaar, the wide main road that ran north to south.

They would have to cross to reach the safehouse. Here, he hesitated. Across the road stood an empty commune that had held perhaps fifty families in ages past. Now it was condemned and wholly unoccupied, its every window dark. By all accounts it looked safe, but Regel was cautious. He drew one of his falcata and focused on the plain steel pommel, letting his senses drift. Sure enough, Regel saw without seeing—knew without knowing—that foes waited.

"The way is watched," he said. "Ravalis soldiers."

"I feel it too." Ovelia had one hand on her sword hilt. "Draca does not lie."

Sure enough, her bloodsword glimmered with crimson fire and cast devious shadows all around them. Regel had used the warning sword to some effect in the Burning Man, but it awoke to its true power in the hands of an heir of Dracaris. Few in the World of Ruin bore true magic in these latter days, with the noble lines all but exhausted, but some wielded ensorcelled heirlooms that spoke to their blood. For Ovelia, the sword conjured portentious images of swordsmen that came at them in a rush. The flame-wrought semblances burst away into the air as they struck, leaving only a warning.

Regel and Ovelia shared a nod, eyes deadly. They were prepared. Regel drew his second sword and took a single step into the street to announce their presence.

The attack came suddenly. Regel raised his falcata as a slayer rushed from hiding. No casters—whoever had come to kill them wanted to keep it quiet. Ovelia's sword had warned him of the direction of the man's attack, so he could block easily. He caught the slash high, locked blades, and twisted to slash his other blade across the man's belly. Steel screeched against power armor, shedding sparks as its fine edge gouged the imbued iron. The man staggered back, surprised at Regel's perfect block and counterstroke, and his gray cloak swirled in the night air.

"Dusters," Regel said. Neither of them had known the identity of their foe, and it gave him pause.

Three more power armored men—elite Dust Knights of the Ravalis— appeared then, their gray cloaks parting as they moved. Hooked swords glittered and armor hummed, imbued with destructive magic. Thaumaturgy or "dust magic" was not real magic—not like the Frostfire of Denerre, the metal sculpting of Ravalis, the warding of Dracaris, or the power certain heirs of another noble blood might wield. A thamaturgical charge could be used up unlike a true relic, but it could slay just the same.

" 'Ware sorcery!" Regel cried even as one of the swords blasted into his defense with a roar. The cacophony blew him through the air three paces, and he fell to one knee, magic ensnaring and binding him like a man trapped in a net. Eyes swimming, he looked back to the duel.

Ovelia was holding all four at bay, cutting red lines through the air with Draca. One of the ensorcelled blades slashed toward her but she caught it and—with a whine of fizzling magic—the Duster's sword rebounded, its power drained away. That was Draca's other power: it devoured magic, the better to defend its chosen ward. The wavy shape of the steel gave Ovelia a further advantage, because it made swords she parried vibrate painfully in their wielders' hands. Regel felt a surge of hope.

Blades sang in the gloomy alley and artificial magic withered away to nothing. Ovelia hissed aloud as she fought, sacrificing accuracy for speed, and the ferocity of her defense surprised and impressed Regel. At length, the four Dusters fought defensively to reassess the situation. They showed no fear, only an evolving strategy. They gave up hope of overwhelming her and instead sought to tire her.

Regel knew he had to help Ovelia, or they would be lost. "Get up, old man," Regel said despite his heaving lungs. His body wouldn't obey. "Get up."

As if he'd heard, one of the Dusters broke from Ovelia and rushed Regel, sword high. Weariness giving way to the thrill of combat, Regel felt his limbs throw off the binding magic. He waited until she was two paces from him, than sprang forward in a roll. The Duster tripped and went down with a crash, and Regel hooked his falcat like a scythe under the Duster's faceplate, beheading her as she fell.

A war cry alerted Regel, and he wrenched the blade free to parry another rushing Duster. He slammed his elbow into the back of the man's neck and ran for Ovelia and her two foes, who had maneuvered to either side of her. He saw the truth of the duel in a heartbeat: Ovelia was a great swordswoman but she could not win. Her foes wore armor that she lacked, and though their inferior swords had chipped against Draca, the weapons yet held. Their plates would weaken her strikes, but the first blow they landed—her first mistake—would end the duel.

Regel charged, silent as looming death.

Sensing him, the nearest Duster began to turn—too late. Regel kicked off the ground, shattered the weaker sword with a vicious cross, stepped on the near alley wall, and slashed out the Duster's throat with his second sword. The knight tumbled aside, blood sailing, as Regel spun and landed just behind his the last of their attackers, blades crossed and ready.

This one seemed more capable than the others, but the impossible move still took him by surprise. "Silver Fire!" he cried as he turned on Regel.

He slammed his sword wildly into Regel's defenses, and though it was a poor blow, the dust magic exploded with enough force to send Regel back a step. The Duster spun back and managed to bat the Bloodsword wide and strike Ovelia in the chest with the pommel of his sword. She fell back, gasping, but before the Duster could launch a killing blow, he had to defend against Regel's assault. The older man's twin falcat spun around his hacking blade, kissing the steel but seemingly unable to stop it.

"You're dead, traitors!" the Duster said. "You're dead!"

Then Regel locked the off-balance Duster's sword between his two weapons and held it wide. "Not likely," he said.

The Duster's eyes widened in realization of his mistake. Regel had lured him in, and now he couldn't disengage. He might have managed to rip the sword free with a heartbeat's effort, but Ovelia only needed that long to rise and put her sword through his back with a grunt. The point burst out his chest, parting the steel plate with ease. As the Duster choked on rising blood, Draca slid out of him as smoothly as a knife through water. Regel had known only one other sword so efficient and deadly, but the days of wielding it lay far behind him.

Dropping his blades to stab into the refuse-covered ground, Regel caught the dying Duster, covered his mouth, and lowered him to the cobblestones. The man stared up at him, confused and terrified, so Regel put a blade through his heart. Mercifully, the man's gasps choked off. From his face, the Duster was little more than a boy—perhaps half Regel's age—and northern-born by his pale skin and black hair. What a waste.

"Dust and shadow." Regel murmured as much in mourning as in benediction.

Ovelia was staring at him, Regel realized. "Frostburn is gone, and yet you wield the falcat." She gestured to Regel's swords, hooked like a scythe and sharpened on the inside of the curve. It was an ancient design, hard to wield but deadly. "You are still a reaper of men."

To that, he refused to respond.,

Ovelia wiped Draca on one of the gray cloaks. Blood steamed off the blade. "You never did tell me where you learned to move with such grace."

"No." Regel closed the Duster's dead eyes. "I did not."

He accepted Ovelia's proffered hand to get to his feet, and it was only then he recognized the shape in the shadows flowing from Draca's blade: a casterman.

There came the great *crack* of a caster firing and blood spattered Regel's face. Ovelia's fingers splayed out in shock, her hand just short of Regel's own. Her face went white.

Regel's eyes shot to the man who had risen behind them. It was the Duster Regel had merely stunned with a blow to the neck and—in his haste to defend Ovelia—forgotten entirely. Now he stood behind Ovelia, a caster in his hand.

Then blood bubbled out of the man's helmet, and he toppled. A bolt had driven a hole through his middle. His caster—unfired—landed on the ground with a wet thud.

"Stand away from him!" A slim woman in dark leather and a cloak the color of fog appeared. She tossed one expended caster aside and pointed a second at Ovelia's face. "Right burning *now!*"

TWO

Draca's shadows never lied, but they were not always clear. Ovelia had sensed the danger, but she had thought it would come from the last Duster, so she had shifted her weight to dodge an attack from that direction. Thus, Regel's squire had a perfect shot lined up at her head, and there was not a burning thing she could do about it. Keeping her right hand on the hilt of Draca, she raised her left hand peaceably.

"Don't even move, traitor," Serris said. "I will put this bolt in your throat. I'm a remarkable shot."

Ovelia believed her.

"Serris," Regel said warily, his blue-black eyes burning.

"Shut up, by the bleeding Narfire! And you shut your mouth, too, old man." Serris inclined her head to Regel. "You blind as well as stupid? This woman has led you into two traps this night, graybeard—and I'm rescuing you. *Again.*"

Ovelia's heart raced. She focused on the sword's shadows, preparing her body for an attack. She would have to be fast. She doubted she could draw Draca in time, let alone move fast enough to block a casterbolt, even if she knew exactly how Serris would aim. That was Regel's skill, and she had never known another who could do it. Still, she had to try. She could not fail now.

"Stand down, Squire," Regel said.

"Can't do that, Master." The scar on Serris's cheek glowed red in the moonlight with a fury to match that of her eyes. "This is for you and me both."

Keep her talking, Regel. The shadows flowed uncertainly. Ovelia studied Serris's stance, trying to predict which way she should leap to dodge the woman's cast. If she picked wrong...

"You saw her slay men of the Ravalis," Regel said. "She is their enemy."

"She is *our* enemy." Serris tightened her finger on the caster's trigger. "The Ravalis have been following her all along. Either she's one of them, or she's dangerously stupid. Either way." She adjusted her aim at Ovelia. "We've a contract to kill her, whoever she is."

"Except that she's the one who gave us the contract," Regel said.

Serris blinked. "What?"

Ovelia bit her lip. Regel was playing a dangerous game, but perhaps it would serve and they could talk Serris down after all. After she'd taken so much from Regel in her life, Ovelia would hate to have to kill his squire without cause.

"He speaks true," Ovelia said, speaking for the first time. "Through the heart—the one she—"

"Swore to another," Serris said. She looked to Regel, eyes narrow. "M'lord? This true?"

He nodded.

"Old Gods!" Serris lowered the caster. "That's the greatest idiocy I've ever heard."

"Thanks?" Ovelia relaxed, removing her hand from the hilt of her sword.

"Misjudged you, m'lady," Serris said.

"How——?" Ovelia gasped as Serris slammed a foot into her belly. She sank to one knee, clutching herself.

"Didn't expect such a ninny," Serris said. "Lowering your guard—*honestly*." She put the caster anew to Ovelia's temple. "Can I kill her now, Master?"

Regel waved. "Put it away, Squire," he said.

It was no use—Serris's hand was true. Ovelia saw death coming and made a choice.

"Do it." She leaned her head against the caster. "I deserve it, after all I've done."

"What you've—wait. Who is she?" Serris's eyes widened at Ovelia. "Who are you?"

Ovelia was confused. Did Serris not know her?

"No one." Regel rose slowly, making no threatening moves. "She's no one of consequence."

That said much. Regel must have hidden her true identity when the contract arrived, but why? Was it to preserve her life? Few would hesitate to slay the great Bloodbreaker of Denerre. But more importantly, *why?* Regel hated her. He had almost killed her before he knew of their quest. And now?

Ovelia glanced at Regel, took a deep breath, and looked Serris straight in the face. "If I am to die, I'll die in honor, not deception. I am Ovelia Dracaris, First Shield to Orbrin Denerre the Winter King."

"The Bloodbreaker!" Serris grasped the caster in both hands. "I thought you *dead*."

"Thank you," Ovelia murmured with a bitter smile. "I give myself to your justice, if that is what you will give me. Do it. Cast."

Serris was overwhelmed, her hands trembling ever so slightly. Death waited only heartbeats away, but in truth Ovelia watched the master, not the squire. Regel's was the judgment she sought, not that of Serris, and his face might have been carved of stone. Had Ovelia erred in her hope?

Finally, Regel put his hand on Serris's arm. "Stand down," he said. "She is no threat to me, and we have made a bargain. I am honor bound to protect her."

"But she's the Bloodbreaker." Serris's teeth clenched and she stood trembling. "She's the enemy of Tar Vangr... *your* enemy, most of all! You *hate* her."

"Stand down," Regel said again, his voice deeper.

"But——" Her eyes burned at Ovelia. "Master, what you've told me of this... this *creature*."

"I know what I've told you."

Ovelia was curious, but she knew when to stay silent.

"She used you—lied to you," Serris argued. "Betrayed you and everything she swore to protect. She's an oathbreaker, Lord of Tears! Worse than——"

"Worse than I?" he interrupted. "Has she broken more oaths than I have?"

Lightning crackled, but the rain had abated and the skies were clearing. Ovelia drew in a breath, not trusting herself to speak.

Serris's eyes narrowed. "She broke your heart, master."

Ovelia could see in Regel's eyes that she'd broken far more than that.

"Put the caster away," he said.

Serris hesitated, then withdrew the weapon.

The tension passed, and all breathed easier. Without the caster threatening her, Ovelia could rise unhindered. Her middle hurt, and she put a hand to rub at the ache.

Serris saw the gesture and frowned. "Not sorry for that."

"I am," Ovelia murmured. "She's clearly your student, Regel."

"Indeed." Regel drew Serris around. "You've my thanks for following us."

Serris brightened. "You bring Ruin to my tavern and expect me *not* to follow?"

"I think you mean *my* tavern."

"As you say. Seems to me I've been the one running it these past two years, and you aren't in the city a day before a proscription letter arrives. Knew it was a trap."

She wound her arms around Regel's neck in an intimate, even amorous gesture. Ovelia was startled at the girl's forwardness. A squire and master grew close, sometimes even closer than blood, but that was not the look of a daughter embracing a father.

"Meant to throttle you until you choked out the silver for repairs, Master." Serris looked to Ovelia. "Your fortune we happened upon these corpses when we did, Bloodbreaker. Had my fill of blood tonight." She knelt over one of the Dusters and swore a quiet oath. "Winterborn. Damn Ravalis." She offered a prayer to the Old Gods to honor the dead knight.

"We have to move," Regel said. "This safehouse is known to the Ravalis."

"True enough." Serris nodded. "Help you hide the corpses?" Watch horns sounded from nearby in the rainy night. "Too late anyway."

They headed back up the Aleisaar away from the exposed safehouse and took refuge beneath the overhang of a long-abandoned smithy. Half a dozen Dusters and a Lancer searching the spot they had left, and shouts rose as they inspected the bodies. Ovelia knew they had to move quickly.

"Need a good hiding place," Serris said. "The Doxy Dive, or under the boards at the wharf—"

"We're leaving Tar Vangr tonight," Regel said.

"But..." Serris paled slightly. "You just returned. We haven't had time to talk—"

"Serris." Regel touched her arm to make her focus. "Is the Rat Cellar clean?"

"Should be," Serris said. "But why do you have to go so quickly?"

Ovelia knew they had no time for this. "We need supplies—weapons, food, clothes. Preferably something richly made or at least modest."

The young woman's vulnerable voice transmuted into cold steel at Ovelia's voice, as though she just remembered she and Regel were not alone. "Your pet

Bloodbreaker looks a fright, Master. Few clothes for a woman at the Cellar, but some of my things are still there from last time. Should fit her well enough." She looked anxious. "Let's move."

"No. Ovelia and I have business—solitary business." He took her by the shoulders. "You will shed the Tears. Whisper promises, spill blood, share beds. Find out what words will be spoken this night of the attack on our home. Find a name for our betrayer."

Serris's eyes narrowed. "Beware, Master," she said. "I spared her at your will, but I'll be burned before I trust the Bloodbreaker. You should do the same."

"Disobedience ill suits you, squire."

"Nor foolishness you, Master." She leaned close, but Ovelia could still hear her faintly. "She's a danger. You know this."

"Tonight," he reiterated. "Yours is the command in my absence."

Serris cast Ovelia a suspicious glance. "Master—"

"You've heard my will."

Serris sighed. "You're well?" She put her hand on Regel's chest. "For certain?"

Regel nodded. Something that Ovelia could not name passed between them. It made her feel like an unwelcome spectator.

"Return soon." Serris smiled awkwardly. "Something I need to talk to you about."

"Soon," Regel agreed without meeting her eye.

The woman disappeared into the night. Freed of her threat, Ovelia slapped at the mud on her trousers. "Deadly lass," she said. "Shame about the scar."

Regel's face darkened slightly. "She has earned better than your judgment."

"Granted." He was very protective of his squire. Ovelia waved that away. "You finally took a squire, then. I never would have expected it of you."

"We grow older, if not wiser."

"True." Regel's face was certainly older—the lines around his eyes darker, the crags on his cheeks deeper—but his eyes held as much darkness as ever. Unnerving but also magnetic. Ovelia looked after Serris, who had vanished into the hazy street. "She obviously cares for you deeply."

"She is my squire," Regel said.

"Nothing more?"

"Once."

Ovelia waited, but Regel did not continue. He never wasted three words when one would do. How she had once loathed his terse manner, and missed it in the years since.

The relation he invoked between master and squire was an ancient tradition of Tar Vangr. In most cases, a master was closer to a squire than even a father or a mother. Ovelia had known two masters in her time, one who actually *was* her father. But both of them were long gone now.

Ovelia sighed. "My thanks for talking her down. She might have slain me."

"It wasn't for you," Regel turned and started up the street in the direction Serris had gone.

"It was for Lenalin," Ovelia said. "Wasn't it? That's why you agreed to this. For her sake."

Regel hesitated.

"She is dead, Regel," Ovelia said.

His eyes might have stabbed her in that moment. Then he nodded and they walked on.

~

Shivering in the cold night, Serris almost wished the acidic rain would return in force to suit her mood. "Silver Fire!" she muttered. "That woman!"

But—as ever—Regel surely knew what he was about and she would have to trust him.

"Haven't failed me yet, Lord of Tears," she said, and took comfort in it.

Rain dripped from an eave above, and she recoiled beneath shelter. Magic had long ago scoured the sky, leading to this rain of fire. She knew little about magic, and it certainly wasn't her place to do anything about the rain or the smog. She wished someone would, though. Her eyes watered, and she told herself it was the fumes stinging her eyes, as they always had.

She gazed up into the night sky, up the mountain crowned with the palace of Tar Vangr. Lights burned on the great height to mark the residences of the rich and powerful, and great skyships moved in the night to carry those who could afford freedom. Meanwhile, down here in the slums, the poor fought and shed blood in the muddy streets. The sight never failed to anger her, even more so when Ovelia Dracaris—the Ruin-burned Bloodbreaker herself—had descended like a raven of death to pull her master back into that world. A sour feeling twisted her gut, but she had to trust in the Lord of Tears. He had saved her five years ago, and she had never known him to make a mistake. Serris, on the other hand, had made enough mistakes for the both of them.

Why hadn't she told him? She could have just blurted it out, but with that woman there—the damned Bloodbreaker, of all people!—somehow she'd been unable to speak of it, and now she did not know when she would get another chance. If ever.

"Damn." Serris turned to head back to the Burned Man when something struck the back of her head and the world shattered in a burst of white light. Vision swimming, Serris staggered back, grasped at her face with one hand, and tried to pull her blade with the other. Steel kissed her throat, and she froze.

"Now now, Serris, First of the Circle of Tears," a barely human voice said in her ear. "Why do you weep, I wonder? Is it for your master?"

Why hadn't she heard him approach? Had she been so stupid as to let her doubts distract her, at the cost of her life? She gazed into where her attacker's face should be and saw only a mask of interlaced bones over boiled black leather. The eyes were different colors: one vivid blue and the other bare white—blind, she thought, until she saw it scanning her features. Her stomach gave a wrench, and she felt her gorge rise into her throat.

35

"Who are you?" she asked through the shaking fear. Perhaps she could reach her dagger—

"A friend, if you will make it so." The mask mostly hid the speaker's lips, but sharp teeth glinted in the moonlight. "You saw how easily I could take you unawares, and now you are under my knife. If you want the Lord of Tears to live, listen and do as I say."

"That's your play, threatening my master?" Serris smiled crookedly, her fears easing a bit. "You might catch me, but you think you're a threat to him? You, a man afraid to show his face? I hope you try."

Her attacker tensed at the barb, and Serris heard his teeth grind. Then the bones of the mask drew upward in a smile. "Perhaps you have no fear for him, or for yourself, but there are others you care for just as deeply. Hidden where all can see but none suspect…"

He drew something from a pouch at his belt, and Serris's stomach lurched. She recognized the tiny straw doll, with its distinct, ratty yellow fabric topping its head to represent a mane of blonde hair. She had made that doll herself, and knew well the hands from which this man had taken it.

Slowly, Serris took her hand from the hilt of her dagger. She put her shoulders back and met the masked man's eye. "What do you want?"

∾

They passed the next half hour mostly in silence.

Regel led the way to the Rat Cellar, a bolthole beneath the Mangy Page tavern. He'd considered blindfolding Ovelia so she wouldn't learn the location, but saw little purpose in it. Whether they failed or succeeded, she wouldn't return, and if this was a trap, they would both be dead before morning.

Rat Cellar had a single, cramped room—more a root burrow than anything else, with two filthy windows above their heads that peeked out onto the cobbled alley. The cellar gave the Tears a place to stash ill-gotten gains, store supplies for quick missions, or hide from Ravalis hounds. With its few customers and uninspired fare, the tavern above did not stand out in any way. The owner owed eternal loyalty to the memory of Blood Denerre, and she would never betray the Tears to the Ravalis. It was a kind of courage rare in the World of Ruin in these latter years.

"Mask is in the Burning City." Ovelia splashed water on her face from the basin in the corner. "Luether."

"The City of Pyres." Regel nodded grimly. "You really *do* need me."

"You don't fancy." Ovelia gave him a wry look. "With barbarians in the streets, traitors on the throne, and Ravalis slayers close behind? Nay, I'm sure I'd be very well alone."

Regel had to smile. Ovelia had not lost her sense of humor. "Luether, the city that burns without being consumed. It is the best place for Mask to hide."

"And the worst." Ovelia shivered. "I was there once, twenty years ago."

36

"I remember," Regel said. "The day Prince Darak was born and Luether died." Ovelia scowled, and the subject fell away for the moment.

Once, Luether had been a powerful mage-city, a place of mechanical wonder and innovation. Lenalin had given birth to Prince Darak there, the first child of the rival Bloods Denerre and Ravalis, a light in the darkness on Ruin's Night. Ruin would not be denied, however. That very night treachery had befallen, barbarians had stormed Luether's high walls, and only half the Denerre delegation and a few of the Blood Ravalis had escaped. Regel had sworn never to return. On that day, he would never have expected his path would lead him this way

Regel let the past burn away and focused on the present. He drew his falcata and placed them on the brick oven for consideration. He'd sheathed them bloody, which was a dishonor to the blades. He slicked them clean with water, whispered a prayer to the Old Gods, and begged forgiveness of the steel for his haste. It had been needful, and he prayed the gods understood.

For her part, Ovelia honored Draca in a similar way: she washed the blade in sacred water to purify it and whispered prayers over the ancient steel. If anything, her ritual was longer, and Regel was surprised to see the tenderness with which she handled the sword. After so many years thinking her a horrible traitor to Tar Vangr, seeing her honor the ways of Winter was...soothing.

Once the rituals were done, they set to the practical task of making ready to depart.

"Tonight. We need to hurry," Ovelia said as they rifled the cellar's stores. "My ship will not wait forever. The *White Dart*. Mage-caravel: immediate, hard to track, and easy to hide among the crew."

"Solid men?"

"Smugglers." She withdrew a rolled scroll from her mud-spattered breeches. "I've chartered passage with the captain—a Free Island man called Fersi."

"You certainly plan ahead." Regel sifted through the secreted equipment in the lockers: weapons, coin set aside in pouches, spare clothing—some for himself, and some of Serris's things for Ovelia. Not rich clothes, but they would serve. "A skyship would be faster. We could stow away on a noble's jaunt."

"Few jaunts are launched these days, and the next skyship sails for Luether in at least a quarter-moon's time. Already the Ravalis have attacked us twice. We need to leave as soon as possible."

"Fair." Regel offered her the clothes. "Try these."

Ovelia raised her hands to the laces of her tunic, then looked at the floor. It was damned strange that she should be shy now when she had kissed him so hungrily less than an hour before—doubly damned, for how much it made him want her. He turned.

They undressed, back to back in the small room. Regel changed his spattered shirt, a matter of a moment, but he had not been sprayed with as much blood as Ovelia had. He doffed his spattered tunic and found, in the process, a hunk of wood that had lodged in its folds. With one hand, he held it up for inspection while the other hand rubbed at the sore spot on his side where it had chafed him. It was a piece of table, probably attached to him when they'd taken cover from the casterbolts. He hadn't even noticed in his haste to escape with Ovelia. An image suggested itself to him, and he drew out a small, sharp knife and set to work to distract himself.

"I see you still whittle," Ovelia said.

"Sometimes," he said.

As he worked, his active mind fell silent, and Regel spread his senses. He was aware of the whole room, and the building above. He counted the patrons and listened to their converse. Most of them spoke of the mundane matters of the day, or took part in the persistent grousing about a coming war. A few complained of the politics of the city, of the Vangruyr Council that resisted King Ravalis's edicts with ever greater insubordination. Tensions in the City of Winter grew hotter every year—it was a wonder the city's eternal snows had not melted.

Regel wondered how this night's events would affect matters. Serris could handle the Ravalis, of that he had no doubt. Despite all the madness of the last hour, she was still solid. Regel realized he hadn't actually bade Serris farewell, but he knew she would be waiting when he returned. She'd claimed she had something to tell him, but why hadn't she said it in the alley? Perhaps it was not important.

Regel cut a deep gouge in the chunk of wood and paused. He glanced over his shoulder.

Ovelia knelt by the ewer in the corner, praying over Draca. It had taken her a few moments to honor the sword, and now the time had come to cleanse her body, as was her family's ritual. She'd disrobed to the waist, and her white-blonde hair was slicked to her neck. There, inked in her bare skin, was a familiar image: a dragon that rose from her waist and reached to her shoulders. The furrows of a whip distorted the image, but the serpentine beast—the Dracaris crest—was clear enough.

What shame her back must bear, Regel thought, and yet it was so proud.

With his expanded senses, Regel noted how the water dripped over her neck and shoulders, running along her smooth muscles. Ovelia laid her head on the lip of the bowl to scrub her short hair, which darkened almost imperceptibly as her ministrations eroded the dye. Her raised arms looked slim and strong, and her fingers moved delicately in the water. She seemed motherly, as though she was washing not her own hair in the copper tub, but that of a child.

"I am nearly finished," she said, looking at him under her arm.

Regel narrowed his gaze back to his carving. "Whence the scars? I do not remember those."

If the question rattled her, she hid it well. "The Ravalis are not the most gracious of hosts."

Regel nodded. "There is wine if you want it." Water dripped into the basin.

"Revenge does make for thirsty work." She shook the last drops of water from her hair and reached for a towel.

Setting his carving aside for the moment, Regel turned to the supplies. He made a show of setting out two ceramic bowls, while at the same time his left hand found a tiny green vial secreted away between two bricks. He ran his fingers over it, considering, then looked to where Ovelia was securing one of Serris's dresses around her muscular body.

She turned to face him and stood up straight to model the dress. "Well?" she asked awkwardly.

Regel considered. Dressed in women's clothes she seemed softer. Serris's things fit well enough, Regel thought, though the fabric stretched tight across Ovelia's chest and at her hips. The Bloodbreaker had always had a robust build. "It serves," he said.

"How flattering." Ovelia made a face and looked away. "What of that wine?"

He drew a bowl of wine from the Cellar stores and—with his back to her so she couldn't see—he poured a thimble's volume of clear, odorless liquid from the green vial into the wine. She looked up when he turned back to her, and her expression turned shrewd when he held out the doctored bowl.

"I would hardly kill you *tonight*." Regel offered what he hoped was a reassuring smile. "Not before we even begin."

Ovelia considered, then accepted the wine but lingered over it, her brow furrowed in thought.

"What is it?" Regel asked.

"It has been a long time," Ovelia said. "That is all."

She drained the bowl. As she did so, Regel's back prickled, and he thought for a moment someone was watching at the windows of the Rat Cellar. He looked and saw no one.

Part of this task was already complete, then: a slow poison in the Bloodbreaker's belly, which he could delay with regular doses of the antidote. There was comfort in knowing that his business with her would be done, however she betrayed him, as well as something like shame.

"Prepared?" Ovelia asked.

Regel nodded, and they left for the docks.

THREE

As the night wore on toward dawn, a cold mist rolled across Tar Vangr's low-city docks, where less than half a dozen ships rocked uneasily in the chilly waters of the Dusk Sea. With conditions on the sea and land so cold and inhospitable, only the most daring and desperate captains dared venture north to do trade in the coldest season. Nestled between craggy, impassable ridges of icy rock and perpetual, shifting icy floes, the docks defied an invasion in the best of seasons, and avalanches had been known to seal it off during the nearly constant winter. Spending too much time in Tar Vangr was never a good choice for any captain, as green-tinged mist crept up from the cloudy waters in any season, discoloring sails and enfusing wooden hulls with a persistent stench worse than that of salt or rotting fish.

Regel and Ovelia paused at the edge of the docks beneath the shadow of the Cathedral of Amanul. A relic of the long-dead Calatan Empire, the mighty building towered up to high-city and beyond. No ritual had passed there since the coronation of King Demetrus Ravalis, whose reign had proved anything but godly. Now the Cathedral served as a communal home for the impoverished, tended by weary priests. The Winter God Amanul was dead or gone, and his church had lost its majesty.

"Much and many have been lost," Ovelia said at his side.

"All things pass to Ruin," Regel finished.

He realized that Ovelia had not spoken of the temple, but was instead gazing at a building on the north side of the street: a marking hall called Nefeti's Art of the Flesh. The crest bore a sigil of a fearsome crimson phoenix painted on an upright palm. Located in low-city, Nefeti's was not a particularly prestigious or wealthy establishment, and it looked like it did little business these days. Highborn Vangryur often employed master flesh artists to come straight to their holdfasts, and in these latter years smallfolk rarely earned names and marks, much less could they afford to pay real artists. Things had not always been thus. Once, when mystic arts had shaped the mage-cities, even smallfolk had worn the images of beasts that could come to life at command or even spring forth from their wearer's bodies.

"Did I ever tell you the story of my dragon?" Ovelia nodded over her shoulder. Regel shook his head.

"Lenalin and I," Ovelia said. "When we were girls, named but not marked, she—she came up with this plan. We sneaked away from the palace. Perhaps Nefeti did not know us, or else he wished not to offend us. Either way, he gave us the matching marks we asked for."

"In one night?" Regel touched his simple teardrop tattoo, which had taken an hour to craft.

"Several nights," Ovelia said. "For a moon, we came to this place whenever we could get away unnoticed. We'd sneak out and make our way here, hand-in-hand. It was my duty to protect her, you understand, but I'd have gone anyway." She touched the back of her neck.

"It was painful," Regel said.

"Very." Ovelia winced. "I held my silence throughout, as best I could. I..." She looked at her empty fingers. "I held Lena's hand when she cried out. She clutched my hand so tightly."

"You wanted to have your own marks of your own making," Regel said. "Brave."

"We were foolish," Ovelia said. "The king was furious, of course, but Lena soothed him. She... she had a gift with words, and he forgave us. I was punished for my indiscretion, of course, but then, I deserved it. Honor would have permitted no less." Ovelia smiled wanly.

"Indeed." Regel had been there, secretly following Ovelia and Lenalin, and he himself had told the king of their childish rebellion. Orbrin had commanded Regel to follow them every time they slipped away—a lurking shadow to ensure their safety. "We should make haste."

"Yes." Ovelia pointed to one of the ships in particular, where hooded lanterns burned faintly. "If we tarry, Captain Fersi will sail without us, and it is a long swim to the Summerlands."

Ships groaned gently in their low-city moorings, shifting with the dawn tide. The lanterns led them to a merchant caravel with white and red sails, the words *White Dart* emblazoned on the keel. Next to the script ran the likeness of a white bird of prey on a silver field. Regel conceived respect for this Fersi's courage, to bear a crest with Denerre's colors, subtle as it might be. In a world where the art of words faded year by year, symbols had great power.

A cry rose aboard the *Dart*. Crewmen appeared at the banister, displeased faces peering down at them shrewdly. The ship must have been waiting for some time. Then one of them spoke.

"Ah, Lady Aniset!" The boisterous voice seemed to address Ovelia with this name that did not belong to her. A thick-set man pushed between the sailors and bowed to them from the top of the boarding plank. "I was beginning to fear you would not come."

The man had a thick accent that made his words awkward. His deeply tanned skin and bleached white hair marked him for a Free Islander, and the many gold rings and jewels in his ears and nose spoke of the Islands' exotic traditions. The islands had not fallen to Ruin, but sages debated whether they'd ever been civilized in the first place. Pirates and deserters lived there, hidden from the mage-cities' flying seekers in endless networks of caves and secluded coves.

"Captain Fersi," Ovelia said, inclining her head. "Circumstances have been... difficult." For the first time, Regel noted spotted blood from the battle on one of Ovelia's boots. "May we board?"

"First, the passing words, if you please," Fersi said, "or my men bolt you to the docks, m'lady."

Regel saw that most of the crewmen had drawn and aimed casters.

"We are who we claim to be, Captain," Ovelia said. "By Winter's fall."

"Until it should rise anew," Fersi intoned, then nodded. "It's about time, lady. We almost missed the tide." He held up a hand, and the casters disappeared back into weather cloaks.

Ovelia took the captain's arm while Regel looked around at the crewmen. Two dozen hard faces confronted him, their eyes daring him to reach for a weapon. He understood the suspicion, considering the significance of the passing words. Clearly, these were Denerre loyalists, which implied that they didn't know Ovelia's identity as the Bloodbreaker. If they puzzled it out, this would be a short voyage. The woman had lost none of her nerve, he had to admit.

"You seem unwell, Lady. Have you been mishandled this night?" Fersi's eyes flicked to Regel.

"No," Ovelia said in a tone that brooked no question. "This is my manservant, Norlest."

The men nodded. For a man to bear the name Norlest—the old king's First Shield and best friend—meant he was no friend to the Ravalis. Regel said nothing. "Men shut their eyes when they open their mouths," Orbrin had told him once, and the words had proved true many times. Regel could not tell if Fersi accepted their tale as quickly. He had a distrustful face and suspicious eyes that scrutinized them to minute detail. He may appear casual, but beneath his exterior hid a cunning, scrupulous pirate.

"I have only one cabin to offer," the captain said. "Your man could take a hammock in the commons if you wish. Unless—" Fersi passed appraising eyes over Regel, no doubt assessing whether he warmed his mistress's bed. After all, "Lady Aniset" had no ladies in waiting. But weathered Regel hardly looked like a lady's doxy. Perhaps a consort?

"Show me the cabin, Good Captain," Ovelia said, without answering Fersi's speculation.

While the crew eyed Ovelia, the captain led them to a cabin opposite his own in the aftcastle. It was a simple, curved room, perhaps five paces at the longest. It bore a single bed, at the foot of which sat a strongchest without a lock. A copper basin rested on a table in one corner.

"The door locks from the inside and out." Fersi handed Ovelia a long, three-toothed key. "I have the only other. You are welcome to this cabin and the upper deck. Meals are in my cabin, unless you wish to dine with the crew." Fersi shrugged. "This I do not advise. The men have a crude view of your sex. Best not to start conflicts among them."

Regel saw Ovelia's jaw tighten, but she had the sense to hold her tongue. Among the civilized Tar Vangyur, a warrior carried his worth in his sword, not in his breeches. Some of the barbarian Free Islanders did not even allow women on their ships. Foolish, in Regel's opinion, but he supposed if a man thought of a woman only as a pleasure to be had, her presence would make such a man forget his work. Such a man was a coward and an idiot, but he would keep such thoughts to himself in this place.

When Fersi looked at Ovelia, the same desire burned there, but he was refined enough to attempt to disguise it. "As to the discussed payment—?"

"Have my thanks, Captain." Ovelia handed him a pouch that clinked with coin. "The rest awaits you at our destination, as we agreed."

Fersi hesitated a bit too long, looking at her, pondering. Ovelia met that gaze, then looked away. She did not smile, but Regel could sense her body warming a touch.

"Of course, Lady." Fersi inclined his head. "And so I leave you in peace." Then, with his palms pressed together, he bowed them farewell and shut the door behind him.

"A pleasant leavetaking," Ovelia said. "After I delayed his voyage so long."

"Don't take it to heart," Regel said. "Pirates of the Free Isles say those same words over enemy ships they have scuttled—usually with the crew still aboard."

"So I have heard." Ovelia gripped the key tighter.

Watching Ovelia, Regel pondered the look that had passed between her and the captain. Had Ovelia made another arrangement about which Regel did not know?

Seemingly oblivious to his scrutiny, Ovelia crossed to the bed. She traced her fingers along its blankets, gazing at them longingly. She must have been exhausted.

"I'll take first watch," Regel said, "in case Fersi crosses us."

"If he does, it won't be within sight of the shore. We should be safe this night." Ovelia shrugged off her cloak. "Shall I use the bed, or would you have me on the floor?"

Regel tried to ignore her choice of words. He would certainly not be *having* her anywhere. He turned his back so she could disrobe with privacy. "Before the crew," he asked at length, "why did you name me *Norlest*?"

He heard Ovelia's borrowed leathers creak. "Why not?"

"This name is not mine," Regel said. "It belonged to the Winter King's First Shield, before you."

"Norlest is the most common name taken by worthy boys of our generation."

"*Our generation*, indeed." Once, the six winters he had over Ovelia had seemed so long. Now, they had both grown old, and they seemed not so different.

"What boy would not want to honor such a champion of Tar Vangr?" Ovelia shrugged. "Norlest, the hero. Norlest, the noble."

"Norlest, your father."

She said nothing as she stripped off her tunic and laid it on the bed. "You do not remind me of him, if that is what you are asking," she said. "You never did. He was a man of honor."

Regel let that slight flow past him. "And who is Aniset?"

"My mother. She—" Ovelia's words cut off in a groan and she touched her belly.

"What ails?" he asked, though he knew well. The green vial. The poison acted fast.

"Not to worry," she said. "The sea, mayhap. I've never had a sailor's stomach."

"Would you take tea to settle it?" He drew a tin from his pack. "Jasmine, your favorite?"

"Of course you remembered tea." The tiniest of smiles crossed Ovelia's face.

Regel set the kettle to boil and took a ceramic tankard from the shelf. Into it, shielding his work with his body, he slipped a small measure of sweet-soul powder to delay the venom in her belly. As the tea brewed, he poured some of the antidote into the tin and shook it to mix the grains.

When he turned back, Ovelia wore a blanket wrapped about herself, her hair ringing her head in a silvery corona. Their fingers touched as he gave her the tankard.

"What now?" Ovelia ran her fingers along the bottom of the tankard with a soft whisper of skin on clay. "Will you sleep in here with me?" Her eyes widened. "I meant—"

"I know what you meant," he said. "I think a hammock among the servants is best."

Ovelia nodded, though he saw disappointment flicker briefly in her eyes. What did she expect?

Regel shut the cabin door behind him. The coming morn dawned chill and dark, its gloom splitting around the few lanterns on the *Dart's* deck. As the smugglers went about their duties, Regel tried to force the image of Ovelia's naked back out of his mind.

He climbed down into the common area, where two dozen sailors eyed him. They were working men, stained with the salty winds and callused from years spent doing the mundane duties of a ship. Some could carry themselves well in a fight, he knew, and they sized him up immediately as a potential threat.

Regel did nothing to allay or confirm their suspicions. He looked around for the empty hammock Fersi had promised, and found it strung haphazardly in a corner near a particularly foul-smelling sailor and what looked like the ship's commode. Not that it functioned, of course—its purpose these days seemed to be to collect as much filth as possible.

This would be a long voyage indeed.

~

Not too far from the docks, a man grunted as he worked his will upon hired flesh that writhed and feigned excitement. Their efforts steamed the grimy windows of the rented room.

The Necromancer sighed and tried to put such cynical waste of life from his mind.

Outside, the rain relented in its assault on low-city Tar Vangr, but thunder roiled in the distance and lightning split the gray clouds that shrouded the moon.

They cast the soaring mountain that formed the center of the last remaining mage-city into sharp relief, making it loom over the lice-ridden docks like an eternal specter. It seemed, on such nights, that the World of Ruin actively sought to wipe away the last remnants of the Empire of Calatan.

But what would spring up in its place? When the bickering noble bloods were ground into the dirt where they belonged, what would rise in a world purified of the weak? Would anyone at all?

Such thoughts consumed Vhaerynn, Necromancer and Court Wizard of Tar Vangr, on nights when he had to forsake his comfortable chambers in the palace in favor of some lice-ridden hole in low-city. It happened more often than he might have liked, but such was his duty to the crown and the Blood Ravalis that wore it. He tried to touch nothing.

The Prince must have his diversions.

The grimy city outside the window pane was starting to disgust him, and he focused instead on the reflection of his aged face. His eyes seemed to be shrinking in place as his flesh withered and contracted around them, skin collecting in thick pads that hung over his once-strong cheekbones. It made his nose seem very large and his mouth thin. His cheeks had hollowed out to leave only hanging sinews. It was a half-skeletal face for a man half dead.

Vhaerynn shut his eyes and touched the source of his power: the golden dagger he wore in a sheath around his neck. The blade was older by far than he was—older than Tar Vangr itself—and meant for the hand of a god, not a man. It was a relic from a long dead age, which had escaped the first Ruin of the world—or perhaps caused it. Vhaerynn let its power fill him, breathed easier, and reached out to the blood of those nearby.

From his place in the antechamber, he felt the coursing blood of the prince and his coin-woman in the next room beating in his head, and he expanded his reach elsewhere. All around him, more prostitutes practiced their trade for their clients, Ravalis loyalists one and all. He felt them—knew them—could take their bodies if he wanted with little or no resistance. In this place, men did crude things to women or other men, and hired smallfolk danced and rutted for the pleasure of any who foisted copper coins upon them. Vhaerynn found it pathetic, if only because none of them had the slightest knowledge of true pleasure.

Vhaerynn expanded his reach to taste the beating blood of smallfolk in the street. Down at the docks, only three blocks away, a merchant caravel was preparing to make way across the Dusk Sea. It amazed him that folk actually continued the business of trade in these latter days. Did they seek profit in a crumbling world, or was this merely man's audacity to hope in the face of encroaching Ruin?

Someone was coming, he realized. Someone he had not seen was even now stalking toward him down the hall, the hilt of a blade grasped in one hand. He had come closer than most would-be slayers, but Vhaerynn had detected him before he posed any real threat.

"If you mean to speak, you might as well do it," the sorcerer said.

The slayer paused, no doubt trying to determine if the words had been for him. His heartbeat quickened slightly in his anxiety. It excited Vhaerynn.

Vhaerynn reached out with his power and caressed the would-be slayer. The man stood more fully upright, his skin erupting with stimulated nerves. That was just a taste of what the Golden Blade of the Aza could do in the hands of Vhaerynn the Necromancer.

"Speak," Vhaerynn said again. "The Prince is... indisposed. I will hear you."

The man stepped out of the shadows, though it was unnecessary. He wore a mask covered with bones: fingerbones, toes, shards of ribs. Vhaerynn could tell at a glance that they were all human bones. "Your ambuscades have failed," the man said in a gravel-shredded voice. "Your men are dead."

"I felt this," Vhaerynn said, unconcerned. The deaths had felt perfectly ordinary—mere soldiers and none of noteworthy Blood. "Your point?"

"Shame, is what it is," said the man. "It's almost like your Shroud has betrayed you."

"Almost."

"Fortunately, I know where the two traitors have gone and by what means they travel."

"And you want something for the secret, I imagine."

"An audience with the prince."

"Hrm." Vhaerynn thumbed his thick nose. "I could force the secret from you. I would enjoy it."

He drew upon the power of the dagger, and felt the blood quicken in the slayer's veins.

"Perhaps," the slayer said slowly. "But if I were you, I'd look to set my own house in order. Find any other traitors before they act, rather than going off to hunt those two."

"My own house." Vhaerynn finally opened his eyes and saw a man in a death's head mask, sculpted of leather and bone. "We both know that those of us who possess power have no true houses. Not anymore. Blood is what we have—power in the Blood."

The masked man returned his words with silence. The mask made his face a barren graveyard, its earth despoiled and the bones revealed. Such a barbaric thing these northern winterborn did, burying the bodies of their dead. In Luether, at least they had the decency to burn corpses so they could not be put to such garish display.

"Unless when you speak of my 'house,' you mean the Blood Ravalis," Vhaerynn said. "Do you mean that traitors yet surround the great King Demetrus? Blood-thieves and slayers?" He stifled a yawn.

"Surely you love your king and country, and will do this tiny thing to protect them," the slayer said. "More I'll say to your prince, and only to him."

Vhaerynn smiled cryptically. He knew what the masked man had to say. Intriguing. This could work to his advantage. "Enter, then."

He pushed open the door to the brothel chamber. Though the slayer hid it well, Vhaerynn observed the man walking with a slight limp—an awkward gait borne of a crippling injury, perhaps? Or was it a mistake of birth? Vhaerynn wondered at the identity of the slayer. He longed to taste the man's blood and know him. He caressed the golden dagger idly.

Inside, Prince Lan Ravalis glistened in the firelight, tough and well-muscled and built like the bear that was his sigil. His was an angular head with a lean, predatory's face and very little neck, and his mouth stood perpetually open just wide enough to offer a glint of yellowed teeth. He had a woman on all fours and busied himself rutting her like an animal. She was, Vhaerynn guessed, nameless—a peasant who had not earned a name and could not afford to buy one. When Lan saw Vhaerynn and the man in the bone mask, he grunted and waved them inside. He didn't stop for the interruption.

"You know what I hate about this city?" he asked between thrusts. "The cold. The damn winter never ends, and the twice-damned cold seeps into my bones. I can't get warm." He grasped his hired woman by the hair and wrenched her against him with a gasp. "Even the whores are cold."

"As ice, m'lord." The woman panted. "Shall I bring you a boy, next? They're warmer."

"Wretch." He shoved her into the rumpled bed and stood. "Bow to your king."

She crawled toward him and went about her business, face in his lap. Lan put one hand on her head and turned to regard his visitors like a king.

"What rabble have you brought me, Vhaerynn?" he asked. "Does this man have no face?"

"My Lord Ravalis," said the slayer, but Lan spoke over him.

"You are just like this cursed city," he said. "Savages, all of you. Everywhere I step in this awful place, there's a chamberpot, or a pile of horse dung, or a firepit. In Luether, we use machines to do these things, but here you can barely work an anvil, much less an alchemy lab. By the Narfire, your rutting council's full of jumped-up beggars prattling on about honor and tradition."

Vhaerynn nodded. "Noble concepts, Your Highness."

"Noble, *ha*. All I see is a horde of unwashed vermin, so stupid it's a wonder you even have a high-city, much less a skyship port. Ugh. At least sex for coin requires little training." He gestured to the prostitute who murmured halfheartedly. "Speak quickly, masked thing, 'ere I lose my strength."

The masked man spread his hands. "I would speak to you of the Bloodbreaker."

That drew Lan's attention like a polished-bright sword drawn from a sheath, and pushed him over the edge. The coin-woman moaned and tried to escape, but he grasped her hair to hold her in place. He spent himself in her mouth and only let her go, gasping, when he was done. She glared at him, but he seemed to have forgotten her entirely.

"You've found her?" Lan reached for his clothes and sword. "Ovelia Dracaris?"

"The same," the masked man said. "She took passage on a mage-craft caravel this very night. If I'm not mistaken, it will be leaving within the hour."

47

"Why do we wait?" Lan slid into his breeches. "Let us go and slay the whore right now."

The slayer held up a hand. "I have not said all, Your Highness."

"What more is there to say?" Lan bared his teeth as he fumbled with his shirt. "She killed my brother. She is a traitor and a whore and we must——"

Lan might have meant to impress with his bravado, but Vhaerynn only found it tedious. He could go after the Bloodbreaker himself and slay her with his magic before the prince even finished donning his clothes, but another possibility occurred to him. A chance to make a change in the World of Ruin.

"Will you accept my council or not?" Vhaerynn asked.

"Speak, then." Lan turned to the coin-woman, who'd gathered up her clothes. "And you—don't you dare put those on. I'm not finished with you."

The woman tensed in rage but dropped her robe back to the floor. "As m'lord commands."

The masked man continued. "The Lord of Tears goes with her."

"Regel the Oathbreaker, he who was Shadow to the Winter King? He is just a useless old man, one with more reason than any of us to hate her." Lan looked to Vhaerynn. "Is this true, wizard?"

The necromancer nodded. Hearing the beat of a man's heart was the easiest of all his magic, and the slayer's had not fluctuated. "All the more reason to wait," Vhaerynn said. "We must know what they seek. Whatever cause unites them, it must be a powerful one. Let this one follow them. In the meantime, we watch the Burned Man, and we wait for a sign."

Lan looked displeased, but he nodded at length. "Very well." He looked to the slayer in the bone mask. "What is your business in this? Did you come for coin, or is there more?"

The slayer bowed. "I have business of my own with the Lord of Tears and the Bloodbreaker."

Lan scowled. "You northerners and your intrigues," he said in disgust as he shrugged into his doublet. "You scheme and you plot but you *do* nothing while the world slips into Ruin around us. You are no better than the barbarians who took my home. The Children that will slay you in your beds one day."

A shadow loomed behind Lan, and he flinched away. Even the slayer in his bone-mask seemed too surprised to react. For Vhaerynn, who had felt the coin-woman move and draw the hidden dagger from the bedside table, stopping her was simple. He reached out to her blood and seized her limbs, so she froze in place like a statue. Her chest heaved and her eyes were wild.

Lan looked at the knife she held over him, then at Vhaerynn, then back to the woman. "Found your courage, did you, whore?"

"No." She spoke through gritted teeth. "I can stomach your mongrel insults to my people, but you called us Children of Ruin. I'll see you dead for that."

Lan took the dagger from her frozen hand and put it to her throat. He pressed it into her skin, and delicious blood trickled down the blade. "I might have rutted you once more and sent you on your way, but now I'll take my time. With this blade instead of the one Ruin gave me."

"It'll be an improvement," she said. Fearless, even as Vhaerynn squeezed her with his magic.

Lan's smile became a grimace. He held the dagger before her eyes. "Open your mouth."

The masked slayer stepped forward, hand going for a blade. This, Vhaerynn found interesting. Lan's callous treatment of the coin-woman was to be expected—even among the chauvenist Ravalis, Lan's disdain for women was legendary—but why would it bother the slayer so, that he would stand against his would-be employer? The man *was* winterborn, of a people with a misguided sense of honor.

"Your Highness," Vhaerynn said. "The woman is nameless. Nobody. Surely it would be a waste of a fine doublet to spill her blood upon it."

Lan hesitated. He cut a little more, and the coin-woman could not even flinch. "You and your wisdom, necromancer." He looked to the slayer, who had noticeably calmed. "And what is your name, if you have one? I would know those who claim to be in my service."

"I made no such claim—our interests simply align in this matter. I will do as you wish. My name is Davargorn, but you may call me *Mask*." He turned to the window. "Now if you'll pardon me—I've a caravel to catch."

He stepped out the window of the brothel and fell into the night. There was a rush of air, and then a black form swooped away through the darkness like a raven. Vhaerynn tasted the dull smoke of magic.

Vhaerynn breathed deeply of the sweet scent left by his guest. Now that he had tasted it, Vhaerynn would recognize that particular blood anywhere.

"Patience, Prince," Vhaerynn said. "You will have your prize—your brother's whore, and his worst foe. Both to do with as you wish."

"Very well." Lan grunted at the coin-woman. "What of this one? My desire is gone."

Vhaerynn released his blood hold. The woman collapsed to the bed, writhing in pain from the blood magic. "Rest easy," he said. "Your offense is easily forgiven."

Even in the midst of her agony, she looked at him defiantly. She reached for her robe, sat up, and brushed past them. She laid a finger against her cheek—the sign of the Circle of Tears. Damn. Word returning to the Burned Man was the last thing Vhaerynn needed tonight.

Heedless of the sign—if he'd seen it, he'd not recognized it—Lan caught the woman by the arm. "I don't pay if you don't finish your job."

She slapped Lan, which made him smile. He returned her a punch to the stomach, and she doubled over. Still, that Vangryur honor rose in her, and she would not make a sound of discomfort. Instead, she rose and limped toward the door.

Vhaerynn grasped her wrist with a strength that belied his aged body. She struggled to no avail. "Alas," he said. "You've heard far more than you should."

He drew the golden dagger with a ring of steel and scratched the woman's hand, then released her. The woman looked to him, confused, then stepped away. She made for the door, but shivered and fell to one knee after the second step. Her hand had turned gray and dead, and the corruption was creeping up her arm from the slight wound.

She made it two more shaky steps before the gray shrouded her skin entirely. She aged on the spot, purple veins pulsing across her flesh, and her eyes sinking into their sockets. She collapsed, falling apart into a skeleton on the floor, and billowed away to dust within a heartbeat.

Vhaerynn breathed in deeply as new life—her life—flooded through the dagger and into his body. It poured strength into his muscles, relieved his grinding bones, and filled his mind with a lifetime of memories not his own. These he pushed away like a bit of cobweb—troublesome but irrelevant. How he loved his golden dagger, the finest gift he had ever received.

The sorcerer glanced at the window where the masked slayer had disappeared. The man had the temerity to claim a name that was not his to wear, but no matter. He saw, in his reflection, that he looked different: his skin brighter, his cheeks fuller, his eyes more vibrant. He looked younger.

The blessing of the Red God.

Vhaerynn turned his gaze to Lan, intrigued to see his reaction. The necromancer knew some of the Bloodbreaker's plans, of course, but he'd purposefully not revealed any of them to Lan. The junior Ravalis Prince could be...unpredictable.

The prince was looking out the window toward the docks. "Ovelia Dracaris," he said. "How long I have waited for you."

FOUR

The Dusk Sea

A DAY HAD PASSED and Tar Vangr had long since faded to invisibility astern when Ovelia decided to make the first move.

All around the *White Dart* placid water reached to the distant horizons, slowly shifting between shades of gray. The seeming peace was a trap, though: just that morn, Ovelia had watched an unfortunate sailor lose his footing and slip over the side. The water darkened around him, nearly to black, and he slipped beneath the waves within heartbeats, before anyone could do more than cry for help. Though they might let a ship pass in peace, the corrupted creatures that dwelt in the Dusk Sea were not to be denied.

Mustering herself, Ovelia joined Regel at the rail where he stood watching the deadly waters pass around them. He wore simple leathern breeches and a loose black shirt that allowed him mobility. A thick cast of gray covered his chin and throat as well—he'd not shaved since leaving Tar Vangr.

"Do you think they're following us?" Ovelia nodded northward. "Will those clouds part and reveal Dusters in an ornithopter, do you think?"

Silently, Regel looked into the waves spreading in the *White Dart*'s wake. He held his fledgling sculpture in his hands, sending chips of it into the sea.

Ovelia ran her hands up her arms, fighting a chill. "Fersi claims to have a trick to elude pursuit. But what if I chose wrongly, and he is in league with the Ravalis? I feel... Something is amiss. I know it."

Paranoia, her father had told her, was a skill rather than a curse. It was a blade to be sharpened, and a shield to be polished. "Many will find your suspicion tedious," Norlest had told her, "but they will thank you when your caution saves their lives."

Regardless, if Regel had something to say, he kept it to himself.

At least they were making good time. The mage-wrought caravel would take three more days to cross the sea, assuming they had to stop only once more for the ship's mage to do maintenance. The lost time could not be avoided: a brand new dust-magic engine could operate unmanned for fifty days without stopping, but Ovelia could not remember the last time she had seen anything *new*. Growling and clanking, the engine propelled them at a speed of fifteen knots without wind, leaving a trail of sickly gray smoke that lingered over the sea. Like all magic, the ship left its mark on the world.

Ovelia looked across at Regel, the silent conflict between them stealing her words. Since Tar Vangr, Ovelia slept behind a locked door, listening to the

51

deckboards creak under Regel's footfalls as he watched outside. They rarely spoke, even when they took meals with Captain Fersi. *Especially* not then. Adept at reading folk as she could be, she could never say what Regel was thinking.

"Enough," she said.

Regel looked at her.

"This silence between us cannot stand," she said. "If we're to do this, we need to know each other again. Learn each other's styles. Trust each other."

Regel gazed off into the morning sea, his expression unreadable. "Steel then?"

"Steel." She nodded.

"We will draw a few eyes," Regel said. "Are you so eager to shed your pretense as a refined noblewoman?"

"Let them watch—they have been watching us enough already." Ovelia ignored the eyes that lingered on her whenever she stepped out of her cabin, but she had noticed them, of course. The captain in particular watched her, though he was subtler than the others. She tried not to think about that. "And besides, all women of Tar Vangr fight, do they not?"

The answer seemed to please Regel. "I'll get practice blades."

Waiting at the rail for him to return, Ovelia watched the crew haul lines, mend sails, and perform the countless other tasks required of a ship at sea. Morning wind and spray caught at her cropped hair, and her weather-cloak pressed tight against her wiry frame. Idly, she ran her fingers through a curl of her hair. The crimson roots had shown in the mirror just that morn: she could conceal her mingled heritage, but the Blood of Summer would never truly leave her. Dracaris was a southern blood, so its folk had red hair, sun-kissed skin, and hazel eyes, though her mingled blood left Ovelia paler than most southerners.

The only other feature Ovelia bore of the winterlands—her sharp nose—came from her northern mother, a lowly maid in the winter palace, unnamed and unmarked. To hear Norlest speak of her, on one of the rare occasions he'd done so, she'd had an unbreakable spirit, which had attracted him with irresistible force. The honorable Norlest had named the maid—Aniset—and wanted to tie her to his Blood, but the Old Gods of the Nar did not give him the chance. The newly named Aniset had died bringing their child into the world, and Ruin had made Ovelia a murderer from her birth: a Bloodbreaker too, if Aniset (the first and only of her name) could be called the last of her own Blood.

A cursed child, marked by ill fortune—was it any surprise she sowed Ruin in her wake?

Ovelia had loved her father dearly, and she remembered many nights crying herself to sleep after seeing the wistful way he looked at her. Ovelia thought of Orbrin the Winter King, his own sad look and his blood on her hands. She remembered what she had done to Lenalin's son Darak the day of his birth, and what she had done in Lenalin's own bed that tenth anniversary of her passing. And lastly, she thought of Regel, and how badly she had hurt him. Was she doomed to betray everyone she ever loved?

She sensed Regel and had more than enough time to settle herself before he offered her a practice sword. He held up a wooden shield. "Do you still hide behind one of these?"

"A swordsman has to be an idiot not to, unless he wishes to die." Ovelia seized the shield and strapped it to her left arm. "What's your excuse?"

"Confidence." Regel tested the balance of his blunt sword: straight, unlike his favored falcat.

More of the crew were watching them, suspicious and expectant. Half of them suspected "Lady Aniset" was more than she seemed, and half only wanted to leer. Ovelia would give them a show.

Ovelia stepped away and loosed the ties of her weathercloak. The bulky garment slid from her shoulders to the deck. Beneath, she wore a red vest laced over a half-shirt that left her shoulders bare. It was one of Serris's outfits, and far less modest than anything Ovelia might have chosen for herself.

Regel nodded approvingly. "Serris has such...*dramatic* taste."

Ovelia rolled her eyes. "It will serve well enough."

Too well, Ovelia thought, by the looks of one sailor who threw her an obscene gesture. In another lifetime, she might have taken the offending fingers for his insolence, but this was not Tar Vangr where such things were not tolerated. And she was the Bloodbreaker now—she had no honor left.

Ovelia saluted and took a defensive stance, sword low.

Regel held his sword high, hanging toward Ovelia like a spear.

"You still take a high guard?" Ovelia asked.

Regel considered her coolly. "Fight low only when you have a shield. When you are a coward."

"Trying to rattle me already?" Ovelia turned her buckler slightly, both to emphasize it and to prepare her move. "You can surrender now if you're so scared."

"Hmm." Regel stood still as a statue, practice sword in hand.

"Well?" Ovelia pursed her lips. "What stays you?"

The first attack came fast. One instant Regel stood like stone, the next his sharp steel sparked off Ovelia's sword and shield. They stood locked together, weapons high. Ovelia twisted the sword aside and thrust back, matching speed for speed. Regel parried and dodged a step back, casting her attack wide.

Gasps and fire-curses rose from the crew of the *Dart*: none would expect such speed from a man past his fortieth winter or a noblewoman. They had suspected anyway, of course, but now they knew without doubt: it would not do to trifle with their passengers.

"I thought we were merely sparring," Regel observed, his voice and face blank.

"Say on, turncloak." Ovelia swashed her blade against her dented shield with a hollow ring of steel. "Your first cut would have taken my head."

Regel brushed back an errant spike of hair from his face. "You blocked it."

"And if I hadn't?"

He shrugged.

Ovelia understood well enough the warning he'd delivered with that blow. Regel had never been one to give easy tests, be they of steel or anything else. "I'll start with Rising Heron," she said.

Regel nodded, his face blank.

She struck with the technique Norlest had taught them: an upward cut at the sword arm. Regel parried perfectly, dropping his blade point-down to deflect her slash up into his cross-guard. He could have locked the sword wide, but instead he stepped forward in a counter and laid the flat of his sword against her throat.

"Well?" she asked.

"Dancing Deer," he said, and pulled away.

He struck once, twice, then feinted the third strike to her left ear. She anticipated the real cut—the fourth of the deer's steps, a reverse strike at her right cheek—and raised her blade alongside her face to block it next to her head.

"Good," Regel murmured. "Now—"

Ovelia thrust her shield at his nose, and he narrowly dodged. His eyes gleamed.

Warning received, she thought, and returned.

They traded blows under the rising sun, and the crew of the *Dart* put their work aside to watch in silence. The sea air was still but for the shriek of steel, the groan of a gouged wood buckler, and the heavy breath of the duelists.

After a time, Ovelia and Regel stopped calling out the moves they would perform and fought without pause. Their duel became a fluid thing, and individual exchanges melted into unconscious movements. Their minds fell silent and they communicated with their bodies. Ovelia could not say how much time passed in this familiar dance. The years fell away and they were once again young, each full of the other's pain, each the answer to the other's need.

Regel was excellent. Though his age might split forty and fifty, he had the strength and speed of a much younger man. Ovelia used feint after twisting strike—some Norlest had taught her and more she'd devised herself. She tried forthright attacks and deceptive turns, then jabs and slices, then thrusts in varied time. Regel dodged or parried every one, even when Ovelia thought for certain he would falter. He was the faster, she the stronger, but they fought with equal skill, and neither could touch the other.

Then, inevitably, the delicate balance cracked.

Toward the aftcastle, Ovelia saw Fersi emerge from his cabin, fingers working at his laces. His eyes found the duel and burned into Ovelia. He smiled knowingly.

Ovelia tried to lose herself again in the swordplay, but the distraction broke her rhythm. She and Regel could not match each other, and he surpassed her. Regel had already won.

A particularly strong blow rang off her buckler. He struck her shield over and over, his blows falling harder and harder until her arm trembled.

She fell to one knee under his assault. "I yield," she said.

Heedless of her surrender, Regel hacked at her buckler-guarded arm like a woodsman worrying a log. The shield groaned and shuddered as he pulled back to strike again.

"I yield!" Ovelia said.

Regel's sword struck her shield squarely, and it splintered. Her arm fell limp and burning at her side, and she got her sword up in time to deflect Regel's next strike barely wide of her face. It rustled her hair and cut through the left shoulder of her vest, biting into the skin beneath. Had Regel's practice sword been sharper, it would have taken her sword arm clean off.

Blood spattered the deck, and she exhaled sharply—in pain and a sickly sort of euphoria. "Stop," she cried, her voice delirious. "I yield!"

Regel's ears seemed deaf and his eyes clouded. He did not hear her—did not know her. He was death, she realized, and his rising sword would bring hers.

And oh, how she *loved* him for it.

Something groaned deep within her, a dam swollen nigh to bursting. Deep within, sickness and fury warred with one another. She wanted to die, and she wanted so very badly for him to be the one to kill her. But not yet, by the Old Gods. She needed to make amends. She needed justice.

Ovelia planted her feet beneath her and lunged forward. Her whole body shivered as her cut shoulder crunched into Regel's midsection, but—thank the Nar—he fell backward. Ovelia felt his blade skip along her back, tearing her vest. Dizzy with pain, she straddled him and lifted her useless sword—nicked and dented and, Old Gods, *bent*—only to toss it clattering to the deck.

"Regel." She gasped for breath, heart beating in her throat. "Regel!"

His body trembled and she could feel his muscles clenching between her thighs. He opened his mouth to speak—a vow of love or a malediction, she did not know.

Ovelia kissed him.

All her thoughts fled as Regel returned the kiss in full. Need blazed within her, and she could not touch enough of him at once. She had to be part of him. All the weariness and the pain of her wounds built to a rising tide of fire that—

"Lenalin."

The name between Regel's lips shook her. Lenalin, he called her—the woman he had loved and the woman she had so desperately wanted to be.

Instantly, the heat between them went out like an extinguished torch. Ovelia found Regel's eyes and saw a question there. He had many questions, none of which she could answer. He had never truly known her, because he had never hurt her so badly. She drew away, feeling cold and small. Regel's blow had split her vest, and she wore blood rather than cloth over her right arm and chest. Against the pulsating pain, the left side of her body felt foreign to her, like a withered vestige and not her own flesh. She shivered in delight and loathing.

Fumbling the torn vest up, Ovelia saw the shocked and hungry gazes of the men, could read the lust on their sweaty faces. "Gods," one of them whispered. "What just passed?"

Why bother trying to explain it? If Regel had never known her, as close as he had been to her, how could these men comprehend her for what she was?

Of them all, Fersi understood. From across the deck, the captain gazed at her, his face cool but his eyes hot. It set her insides to squirming, with desire as much as fear. As long as she could remember, Ovelia had always wanted those she should not, because of her curse.

"Good," she said to Regel, who was still staring up at her, dumbfounded. "Good, I—"

With the blood flowing from her shoulder, she could say nothing else, so she rose and staggered away, toward the aftcastle. Regel did not call after her, or if he did, she did not hear.

~

Davargorn watched the increasingly vicious duel from the crow's nest above.

They fought well. The woman's prowess, he had expected, as she had once championed the Winter King. But Regel... The years withered away as the Lord of Tears fought. With each hammering blow upon his opponent's shield, he moved faster. Anger gave him strength.

Then something truly surprising came to pass: the bout ended in a fearsome kiss. Davargorn had expected hatred between them—not passion, and certainly not *fire*. He did not understand it, but still he longed for it and feared it in equal measure. When Davargorn recovered, he realized that Ovelia had run back to the guest cabin. Soon enough, Regel followed Ovelia, murderous purpose written on his face.

Davargorn drew a caster from his cloak and took aim at Regel. The sight on the caster, crafted by the finest mage-smiths in Luether, let him see across that distance as though he stood just behind the Lord of Tears. With that sight, he could not miss.

At the forecastle, Regel paused, hand raised to knock on Ovelia's door. Even from behind, through the magic of the sight, Davargorn could see the hesitation in the set of his jaw.

One black-wrapped finger caressed the weapon's trigger.

The old man pushed the door open and paused—a dark silhouette upon the threshold.

"Crack." Davargorn imitated the caster's recoil.

The door closed behind Regel. Davargorn reclined in the crow's nest and smiled.

Potent or not, accomplished swordsman or not, Regel had met his match in Davargorn. He would learn in time—when all was in readiness.

"You seek Mask, Oathbreaker," Davargorn said. "And you will find him—to your peril."

~

When she was safely behind the cabin door, Ovelia slumped to the floor and loosed a moan of pain. Her heart thudded fit to burst her chest, and its every beat felt like clenching agony in her wounded shoulder. Regel had dealt so very harshly with her, and she wanted him to be harsher still.

Wetness flowed down her arm from the gash, staining her sleeve a deep red-black. On the deck, she hadn't thought the wound so bad. A washbasin and towels sat on the table. She climbed to her feet, reeled dizzily, and caught the bulkhead to keep from falling. Her legs bumped painfully against the bed. Her strength and grace was gone. Her body wanted her to collapse and her vision grew blurry—

Forcing her mind into line against the haze of pain and blood loss, Ovelia disrobed to her breeches and tossed her blood-slick shirt and vest in the corner. She wet a cloth in the basin and raised it to her sweaty forehead. Her hands shook as she pressed the cloth to her shoulder.

The door thrust open and Ovelia whirled, barely catching herself on the table. In her delirium, Ovelia thought Regel stood like a conquering god in the doorway.

"R-Regel..." Ovelia grasped the hilt of her practice sword. There was no way she could fight, of course, but she longed to do it anyway. "I don't... I don't need you."

He strode mutely forward and caught her up in his arms. The sudden pain in her shoulder choked off her words, and she stood, letting him hold her. Her heart pounded and she feared—*hoped*—he would hurt her, but instead he inspected her wound. "This is not so bad," he said, guiding her to the bed. "Sit."

As they sat together, Ovelia grew acutely and warmly aware of her bare skin from the waist up. It embarrassed her, but Regel hardly seemed to notice. He cleaned her wound with stinging rum, then put a cloth on her bleeding shoulder and pressed her hand over it. She nodded and pressed hard. Regel rooted through the pockets of his pack, then drew forth a package rolled in leather. He unwrapped it as he returned to her side and leaned over her shoulder. He withdrew what looked like a bundle of black hair.

"Whur—" Ovelia said, meaning to ask what he was doing.

Regel drew out a thread and strung it through a hooked needle of silver. He bent over Ovelia and slid it into her flesh with a tiny sting. "Sorry," he said.

Despite the pain, Ovelia chuckled. "You nearly cut my arm off in a bout, then... apologize for stabbing me with a needle?"

Regel's hands worked quickly. He stitched back and forth and drew the skin tightly closed with each turn. His cold fingers soothed her angry, inflamed flesh.

"Your hands," she murmured. "You always had... a healer's hands." Her head lolled against his arm. "Ironic... for a slayer."

He rubbed ointment from the leather pouch over her wound. It stung but she let him bind her shoulder in silence.

As Regel started to draw away, Ovelia reached up, caught his hand, and pressed his palm tight to her cheek. She turned her face into his fingers and kissed them. She felt his body tremble against hers—or maybe it was she that trembled.

"I am sorry," she said. "I am so sorry..."

Regel pushed her gently to the bed. "Rest. I'll stay right here."

Ovelia relaxed. She saw a half-molded hunk of wood sitting on the near table. Regel's carving stood over her like a warding charm.

As sleep took her, she tried not to think about Regel's fingers on her naked skin or his eyes that threatened to swallow her whole. She had no right to want him, after what she had done.

Instead, darker dreams awaited—dreams of searing heat and of falling winter.

FIVE

Tar Vangr

A RESONANT MOAN ROSE from Serris as she lay on her stomach in her bed. Snow flurried outside the steamed window, but the sizzling brazier kept the room warm. It was just the two of them, and only thoughts of pleasure. "By the Fire, Vidia," she said. "That's exactly right. Just there. Just—*unhh.*"

Her fellow Tear smiled. "Here?"

Vidia dug her fingers deeper into Serris's bare foot, prompting a deeper moan.

By the Old Gods, Serris needed this. With the council in a frenzy, the Ravalis locked down tight in the palace, and Dusters patrolling in force, Serris had plenty to worry about. She'd hardly stopped moving in the two days since Regel had departed for Luether, and her feet ached fiercely. One of Vidia's massages was just what she craved.

Self-named and recruited into the Circle of Tears not long after Serris herself, Vidia had been a baker in her nameless life. Once accustomed to kneading the infamously dense and rich bread of Tar Vangr's bakeries, her fingers held both strength and grace. Sometimes—like tonight—her Nar-blessed touch seemed to be all that kept the Circle together.

Even the massage couldn't ease Serris's mind entirely. Regel was gone again, after such a short time in the city, and she couldn't help but fear he wouldn't return this time. She'd almost given him up for dead before, and this time he had left in the company of the horrid Bloodbreaker of Denerre herself. Ordinarily, she'd have trusted Regel, but the attack weighed on her mind as well. And the threat...

Serris felt again the masked slayer's hands on her, smelled the foul breath hot on her face. He'd barely touched her—he'd used words more than steel—and yet she'd felt helpless under his knife as she'd not felt since Paeter Ravalis had scarred her. Even now, just *thinking* about that awful feeling—about his threat—she wanted to weep. But weakness did not befit the center of the Circle of Tears.

Vidia had moved up to her backside. "Are you well, Serris?"

"Well enough," she said. "Sorry I can't return the favor. I've matters to attend this eve."

"Matters more pressing than your own pleasure?" Vidia pressed the palm of her hand hard into Serris's lower back, releasing waves of delight through her tight muscles. "I pity you."

That made Serris smile despite her misgivings. "You always seem to know the right thing to say."

The door to Serris's chamber opened suddenly, and a diminutive figure came in. The child stopped short and looked upon the two women with wide eyes.

"Child!" Clutching the coverlets to her chest, Serris sat up and pulled free of Vidia. "What have I told you about knocking?"

The child looked chastened but said nothing. She had a mess of blonde hair, a pert face, and almost black eyes that had gone big and watery. She would not cry, though—Serris had taught her better than that. She had no name, of course— she was only a child, and as such only bore the name "Child" until she came of age or earned her own name. She might not even remain a girl: if she took a man's name, then to all Vangryur she would be a man, as she chose. The child tightened her grip on the towels she bore in her arms, as though fearful of dropping them and provoking another scolding.

"Tsch, do not sling your discomfort at the child." Vidia stood up and patted the spot she had been sitting. "Come, Child. Set those down. Would you like to look at the cards?"

The child brightened at Vidia's softer tone. She hurried over to lay the towels carefully on the bed, then joined Vidia at the room's lone table. The former baker took from Serris's shelf a stack of bone playing cards bound up with string, which she unwound with such delicate grace Sarelle was transfixed. Amazing. Those hands could choke the life from a man or handle an axe with the best of warriors, and yet Vidia had such a gentle touch with this child or any other. It was the same with her massages: Vidia could dispense life or death with equal ease, a talent Serris wished she possessed. Death was her forte, and she'd grown quite good at dealing it over the years.

As the two played their game, Serris turned instead to preparations for her liaison of the evening. She shrugged into a dress of blue-black damask pulled over her leather underthings. The Vangryur Councilor she would see tonight loved the contrast, and she could oblige such fantasies. The scar across her cheek had once made her self-conscious, but she had come to see it as a source of strength, not weakness. It reminded her of what she had overcome, and of the vengeance she had yet to exact. Besides, if she did her job well, her lover would not be looking at the scar.

As she worked, Serris watched the blonde child through the mirror. The girl stared at the colorful design on each card Vidia laid out on the bed with delight, her mind whirring despite her tender years. Ruin's Night would see the beginning of her third year of life, and she'd been an autumn birth. Despite using words so rarely, the girl seemed an intelligent, perceptive girl. Serris often thought Vidia made an excellent mother for her, far better than the one Ruin had chosen.

All the Tears were orphans, however young or old they might be, and the Circle provided all the family they would ever need. They were servants of secrets and blades of vengeance, to be wielded as their master directed. It was not Serris's place to make demands of Regel, even if he would in all likelihood do as she asked. He was a good man, but there were certain things she could not ask of him.

Serris couldn't help thinking of the masked slayer again: the threat he had made, and what he had commanded her to do...

Vidia saw Serris watching and smiled sadly at her. "You didn't tell him, did you?" she asked. "Before he left?"

Serris straightened up and steeled her expression against any sign of emotion. "Pass well, and I'll see you on the morrow."

~

They coursed together rhythmically in the roaring firelight. The lord grunted with each thrust that slapped her hindquarters against his belly. His hands cupped her breasts and squeezed urgently but not painfully. He made love to her as firmly and as well as he could. All the while, his eye lay fixed upon their naked bodies in the mirror.

Kiereth of the Blood Yaela always did like to watch himself.

For her part, Serris moaned and panted because he expected that, while in truth she felt like sighing. Her heart was far from this, even if Kiereth worked with passion and enthusiasm. To her, his well-meaning efforts were little more than sound.

Kiereth spent himself before she reached fulfillment, but that was not surprising. With all that had passed over the last days—with all her worries, fears, and rages—Serris would have got down on her knees and praised the heir of Blood Yaela as an Old God reborn if he could have pleased her. He went on for a time, caught up in a desperate need to share the gift she had given him, and she obliged him by feigning release herself.

Finally, Kiereth sagged against her and laid his cheek on her back. They knelt together on his bed for a moment, breathing in unison, before he pulled away and laid his shivering body down. His arm offered a snug place to curl up, and she took advantage of the invitation. He felt sweaty, muscular, and warm. He shut his eyes and smiled at her, drifting off into shallow dreams surrounded by her perfume.

This, she liked: the exhausted intimacy that came right after sex, one of the times a man was at his weakest. She liked Kiereth—liked dining with him, lying with him, and rutting with him—but she held no illusions. If this night's business called for his death, she would plant a knife in his ribs and walk away with no compunction or regret.

Fortunately, it did not.

"My Winter Angel." He traced his finger along her brow. "How I have missed you."

"Really." Serris gave him a wry smile. "I hadn't noticed."

He smiled drowsily and pressed his face into her forehead.

As one of the most powerful voices on the Tar Vangr council, Kiereth was one of the Circle's most potent assets. That Serris held him on such a short leash should have made him biddable, but the headstrong heir of Blood Yaela all-too-often found ways to skirt the Circle's wishes and go his own way, regardless of the consequences. It was one of the things Serris liked about him: Kiereth certainly could never be called boring or predictable.

Also, the Blood Yaela was a steadfast enemy of the Ravalis, which she liked even more.

The Yaela Bloodsword, namesake of Kiereth's blood, hung in a place of honor before the hearth. Serris had heard it said otherwise, but she knew the Yaela sword was a mundane if richly-crafted blade that bore no ancient enchantments. Kiereth seemed uninterested in wielding it outside of ceremony and ritual. He was a nobleman, not a warrior—Serris had never seen him so much as lift a dagger—and that ultimately made him enjoyable to rut but easy to forget.

Serris wondered why she felt so judgmental toward Kiereth. She'd been in a foul mood for days, and he deserved none of her wrath. The one who did slept far away to the south, on his way to a tortured city across the Dusk Sea. If he even still breathed. She prayed Regel would finish his damned quest quickly and return safely.

Time passed, and ultimately Kiereth stirred. "Mmm." Eyes still closed, he twined a lock of her hair between his fingers. He smiled wanly. "Have you considered my offer?"

She'd forgotten all about such a thing. "To buy me from the Circle, you mean?"

Kiereth teased his fingers along her face, which he had always seemed to find intriguing. "You are no slave to be bought and sold, my Angel Serris."

"So you say. I doubt my master will part with me."

"A miser," Kiereth said. "But enough gold persuades all men, even the Lord of Tears."

Serris had often whispered to Kiereth of her relationship with Regel—of Squire and Master—and she thought he understood. Every time she and Kiereth shared a bed, the nobleman repeated his intention to take Serris away from the Circle as soon as her duty to Regel was at an end. Not as a consort, but as a... companion, for revelry in public and private. For her part, Serris thought she would find life as the kept woman of Tar Vangr's most powerful councilor pleasurable, but ultimately impossible.

"Keep your gold." Serris caught his hand before he could touch her scar. "You are noble, but I know this bothers you. Would you not rather buy an unbroken tool?"

"Damaged, not broken. Mysterious." He pulled free of her grasp and traced the scar with his fingers, which made Serris tense. "Every time we meet, I ask after the story, and every time you refuse to speak. Do you not know that you are beautiful in spite of it?"

In spite of it. There, in just four words, Kiereth answered his own question, and reminded Serris she could not accept his offer. She had never considered her face any more than passable, and the scar made it distinctive. Every time she looked in the mirror, she remembered her drive to push the damned Ravalis from Tar Vangr into the Ruin they so richly deserved. Not that Kiereth would understand.

"You'll not tell me," he said at length. "Will my lady tell me why she is sad, at least?"

"A lady must keep some secrets," she said. "A whore, even more."

"Even more." He repeated the rhyme, seeming to savor it on his tongue. Then he rolled atop her and held her wrists down. "I can persuade you to part with these secrets. I am insatiable, and I think you are softening."

"Again, m'lord?" His earnestness made her smile despite her mood. "Again, you would dishonor yourself with failure?"

"A sweet, sweet failure." He kissed her.

They made love again, and this time Kiereth lasted longer. Serris was not fully satisfied, but she enjoyed it. Ultimately, she pushed him off her and went to work with her mouth and tongue as he knelt, moaning. The sex was useful: he tended to ramble on while she worked on his little blade, kissing and caressing. She used his ardor to ply him for secrets, but learned little of any real interest.

For the Council's part, there was no news. The attack on the Burned Man had not gone unnoticed, particularly since Ravalis soldiers had died there. None could prove without a doubt that King Demetrus had sent the slayers, but the Tears had enough influence with the Council to press for an investigation. The Ravalis had so far closed their gates and denied all. Since the attack, the Burned Man had seen only more patrons, and silver and gold poured in for the repairs from generous donors.

Serris could not rid herself of the sense that the Ravalis were simply awaiting a proper time to strike. Their antipathy toward the Circle of Tears was well known, though Serris was one of the few who knew its source. She had, after all, seen Regel kill Paeter Ravalis, the heir to the throne. If the ruling blood had any concrete proof Regel had been the assassin, the Burned Man would cease to exist and the Circle of Tears would be slaughtered. Did they know, and they were simply waiting for the Circle to make a mistake and show their hand? And how did the Nar-burned *Bloodbreaker* fit into all this?

It was a dangerous game they played, but then, revenge required one to take risks.

"There is a rumor," Kiereth said as Serris worked, "that the Ravalis have lost their spymaster."

"Mmm." She came up for air and met his eyes. "Indeed?"

Kiereth smiled, pleased to have pricked her interest. "No word as to who the Shroud was, though. It's hard to know a man is missing if his existence was only speculation."

"Mmm."

Kiereth seemed to interpret that as encouragement, shuddered, and groaned as he spent himself for a second time. When he was done and Serris had cleaned him, he kissed her, then fell to the bed beside her and shivered with delight. Serris traced her fingers along the edge of his ear as she considered.

If the Shroud was dead or gone, that would certainly explain why the Ravalis had seemed paralyzed with inaction. A wild fantasy occurred: perhaps the Bloodbreaker had slain the Shroud personally, and that was why the Ravalis had chased her. If so, it gave Serris new respect for the woman, or at least lessened her hatred.

Serris was just wondering if Kiereth had drifted off to sleep when she heard a commotion from somewhere below them in the keep. She might have thought little of it, but she recognized one of the voices, and it made her body tense up like a drawn bowstring.

Lan Ravalis.

Serris disentangled herself from Kiereth and hurried to her clothes, which lay strewn across his chair by the window. The Heir of Ravalis had come here? She could not have foreseen this. She pushed aside her frilly tunic and found the only weapon she would need: the dagger Regel had given her the night they'd first met.

"What is—?" Kiereth asked sleepily. He watched Serris strapping on her ridiculous attire with some disappointment.

"I have to go," she said, sliding on her leggings.

"I was hoping you'd stay all night," Kiereth said. "I've sent for a fine bottle of Echvaari Gold, from three years before the fall. You can taste the spring rain—"

"I'm sure it's wonderful." Serris slipped into her undertunic.

Kiereth put his hands on her shoulders and kissed the spot where her neck met her shoulder. Damn the man, he knew she could hardly resist that.

"I know you are not satisfied," he said, as though it were a great revelation. "Perhaps you could call that beautiful bodyguard of yours—Erim, was it? I'm sure between the two of us we can fix that."

"Tempting, Sweet Yaela, but no," Serris said. "I have to—"

Knuckles rapped on the door, which swung open a crack. Serris could hear Lan in the hall, arguing with Kiereth's steward, Norat, and knew she had only an instant. She bundled up her silken gown and dagger in her arms and climbed into Kiereth's standing wardrobe. She wedged herself between the hanging coats, folding her legs so that the door could just about shut, then watched through the seam.

"I'll see the lord when I please," Lan shoved his way past a flustered steward.

He was beautiful, Serris gave him that, with the majesty of a towering bear in the instant before it pounces like an avalanche. Danger lurked in the hard lines of his jaw and strong chin, and his eyes gleamed like fire. Serris prided herself on fearing few men, but he was one such—rumors called him a sadist, on the battlefield or in the bedchamber. How he and Kiereth Yaela had maintained their odd friendship for so long, Serris could not guess.

"Thank you, Norat." Kiereth had managed to pull on a robe, and he regarded Lan with one of his winning smiles. "Welcome, your Highness. Will you take wine? I've an Echvaari Gold, one of the last bottles from before the fall. You can taste the spring rain in the glass."

"That will do." With the door closed, Lan had stopped shouting, but his calm had not returned. "Old gods, Kiereth—it smells like whore in here."

"I assure you," he said, "we are quite alone."

"You had a woman in here earlier." Lan sniffed at the air and scowled. "The stench of her cunt is everywhere. Tell me, did she please you? I hope you beat her soundly for her trouble."

The words were merely words, but the unbridled contempt in Lan's voice made Serris's skin tighten over her bones. She'd never got the chance to avenge herself against Paeter, but she would very much like to kill his brother if the opportunity arose. Her heart pounded in her throat. Watching him, listening to him, it was all she could do not to burst from hiding and attack Lan on the spot.

"Your Highness knows where my heart truly lies. You can tell me anything." Kiereth's smile widened. "*Anything.*"

Lan gave him a cool look, then turned to the wine. He opened it without grace, grunting as he strained at the cork, which broke as it came free. What a clumsy beast of a man.

"Your council is driving me insane," Lan said. "You sit and you talk and you argue and nothing ever gets done. And my father nods and smiles while your damned edicts tie our hands. The blades are sharpened, the soldiers mustered, the damn engines are almost ready. And still you hamper us."

"The ill-advised push into fallen Echvar, you mean?" Kiereth took a goblet of wine. "Best you content yourself with some of their wine. That place is long lost."

Serris nodded. Kiereth had told her the Ravalis sought to conquer some of the fertile lands of the east, looking to the overgrown Echvaari forests to replace Tar Vangr's dwindling timber supply. The fall to Ruin had turned Echvar's trees into spindly, brittle things, but poor wood was better than no wood.

"Echvar? Hardly." Lan chuckled dryly and he drained his goblet. "What use a rotting grove of trees, when the true prize lies south across the Dusk Sea?"

"I do not understand, Highness. What prize?"

"War, Kiereth," Lan said. "Luether, and war."

War. Serris stiffened at the word. The Ravalis had made noises about going to war to reclaim their ancestral home for years, but none had ever taken the suggestion as anything more than a fond wish. Now she had it from Lan's own mouth, completely in earnest. Serris could not help but think Regel's departure for the southern city spurred the timing. Was the drive to war a cover for killing her master?

But no, it sounded as though the Ravalis had been drumming for this war for years. Lan spoke of troops and arms at the ready, and skyships waiting to be launched. And Kiereth looked not a whit surprised by Lan's pronouncements. Why hadn't he mentioned the war effort to her?

Kiereth cast an inquiring glance back at the wardrobe, and Serris considered what—if any—signal to give him. She wanted to know more, but Kiereth was in danger enough as it was. Serris knew he and the prince were friends, but there was something strong between them that unnerved her.

"Speak to me, Lan." Kiereth assumed a smooth tone. "Your words I will hold in confidence."

The Heir of Blood Yaela stepped behind Lan Ravalis and grasped his shoulders. At first, the Prince tensed, but after glancing around to make sure they were unobserved, he relaxed.

"Stupid," Lan said. "The council, the king, this whole city—all so stupid. And now they're blind, as well, with our spymaster fled."

"So the rumors are true," Kiereth said. "And the Shroud is gone."

"It's all the Nar-burned Bloodbreaker," he said. "We should have killed the whore the night she slew the Winter King for us, but no—'she might be useful,' my father said, so we stayed our hand. And now look at this disaster. All falls to Ruin."

He looked vulnerable, but Serris could tell anger was churning inside him, ready to erupt. Serris realized what Kiereth intended—he had seduced her in a similar way many times before—and shook her head violently. Oblivious, the lord knelt before Lan as he sat on the bed.

"Pass well." Kiereth touched Lan's thigh. "All passes well."

It was too much. Lan shook himself as though to wake from a dream, and his face turned bright red. "You dare?" He slapped the hand away and leaped to his feet. "You *dare* touch me."

Kiereth looked surprised. "Your Highness, I—"

Lan seized him by the throat and wrenched his words to nothing. As much as the Ravalis hated women, they hated men who loved other men more.

"You filthy northerners and your perverse ways. We should have burned this damned city to the ground five years ago. Then, we could start anew without your simpering filth." Lan sneered at Kiereth. "I was wrong, wasn't I? It wasn't some girl you had in here but a boy, wasn't it? You sicken me."

He tossed Kiereth onto the bed and stormed away, trailing curses in his wake. Norat stepped in his path, but Lan shoved him against the wall and walked on, heedless.

Serris slipped from the wardrobe toward the stricken Heir of Yaela. "Kiereth."

"Such a fool." Kiereth's face was pale, and his lip trembled. "I crossed the line with him, so that I could find out more for you. For you." He looked at her with resentful anticipation.

Serris knew she was supposed to thank him, to play the helpless damsel and kiss her hero in gratitude, but she had never been that woman. Kiereth had lied to her, or at least failed to mention that Lan was pushing for war with Luether. "I didn't ask you to seduce him," she said. "If you offended the prince, the fault is yours."

Kiereth eyes widened, then his face grew dark. There was no sweet flirtation about his tone now. "Get out, *whore*."

"With gladness, *lord*." She made her word for him sting just as much.

༽

When Serris found Erim in the waiting chambers of Castle Yaela, only then did it occur to her that she'd been terribly selfish. She'd been well hidden from Lan in Kiereth's chambers, but poor Erim must have faced a much trickier situation when the prince burst in unannounced with Old-Gods-knew how many guardsmen. She hadn't even considered Erim at all, content to rely upon his practical mind to save him from danger. He awaited her, as dependable and unchanging as always.

"We're going." Serris wrapped her scarf tight around her neck against the waiting cold. "And I don't think we'll be back."

"Not to the Blood of Yaela?" Erim asked. "Pity. You speak well of the Heir."

"No longer." Serris gave him a hard look. "And stop hiding your smile. You could at least pretend to be upset we've lost an important fulcrum to leverage the council."

The youth wore a neutral expression but his eyes were delighted. "Yes, Syr."

"Kiereth will have none of me again," she said. "I'll have to see about getting Nacacia into his bed, or perhaps a boy. Meron, perhaps. Or you. He mentioned inviting you for next time."

That wiped away Erim's mirth, and he returned a sober nod.

Serris sighed. It was no secret Erim would be pleased she had broken with Kiereth. Whenever she kept these assignations, he insisted on escorting her, and every time after he gave her a longing look. Serris knew he thought of her as more than a mistress and occasional bedmate, but she didn't have the time to lay all her knives on the table with him. She had too much to do. The Ravalis spymaster gone? A brewing war? The Summer King was weaker than she had dreamed and distracted, too.

"Let's away," she said. "I wish our lord would return. He'd know what move to make."

Outside, Serris looked up into the night sky of high-city, which swirled with dark snow. Doom was brewing in this place, as a city braced for war. She offered a prayer to the Old Gods to protect her master.

"Be safe, Lord of Tears," she prayed, touching the dagger he'd given her. "Return to me."

SIX

The Dusk Sea

Two nights after the duel, it came to pass much as Regel had expected. That first night on the *Dart*, he'd seen Ovelia and the captain share a glance he had not understood. The following day, during the duel, Fersi had given Ovelia such a look as to have broken her concentration in battle. It had taken two more days to determine the significance of their connection.

By the Narfire, the woman could be subtle.

They had spent that afternoon floating toward a dark hulk that rose out of the sea, visible for miles. The waters darkened as they approached, filled with oily sludge that would strangle any monstrosity that tried to breathe it. Fersi and Ovelia stood on the forecastle, and Regel could hear a familiar ease in their voices. He joined them unobtrusively, but of course Ovelia noticed his approach.

"Surely you cannot mean to make berth at Atropis," Regel said to the captain.

Ovelia looked irked at his abrupt tone. They'd not spoken and hardly seen each other since the duel, but she looked to be recovering well. She had not even needed a sling. "Atropis?" she asked without guile, perpetuating the disguise of the Lady Aniset and her servant.

The captain scented a story to be told, and his natural charm took over. "Once, these waters were called the Compass Sea, pointing from the capital Atropis to the four points of the Empire: Angarak, Tar Vangr, Echvar, and Luether." He gestured in each of the four directions, starting west, then north, east, and south. "When Ruin befell the Empire of Calatan, the sea darkened and sailors would wander its waters almost blind. Hence, the Dusk Sea. Behold, Atropis—once City of Light, now City of Shadows. The dead heart of Old Calatan."

Fersi swept his hand out to indicate the ruined island they approached. Its high black cliffs of jagged stone had drawn perceptibly closer, like a spector of doom that awaited them. Buildings were just discernable from this distance, without exception shattered as though by great blows. Even devastated, it towered above them up into the dark gray clouds. Lightning flashed in the clouds, making them glow with deep green and blue light.

Fersi continued. "Two centuries ago, the City of Light stood upon a tremendous diamond, balanced on the point of a needle, burning with its Narfire flowing up from below the sea. Fantastic, no?"

Ovelia was staring up at Atropis, looking suitably awed while Fersi told his story. Regel did not like the almost possessive way the captain laid his hand on Ovelia's arm, but she seemed not to mind—or, worse, enjoy—the touch. "But all things that rise must fall," Regel said.

"Just so," Fersi said. "The dark magic that broke Calatan fell hard upon her capital, and pulled Atropis from its high perch. Now it is but a rubble strewn ruin, home to nothing living."

"Nothing?" Ovelia asked, pointing.

Regel looked up a hundred paces to what at first seemed merely a withered gray banner rustling against a hulk of weathered stone. As he watched, though, he realized that it could be a person watching them, tattered cloak caught in the wind at that height. The White Dart floated on, and rocks obscured the watcher, if such it was.

"No one," Fersi said. A sly grin crossed his features. "It is said shadows peel themselves from the very walls to stalk any foolish enough to enter its forbidden halls." He smiled wider at Ovelia's shocked look. Regel merely frowned. "But do not trouble yourself, my lady. We are quite safe. The *Dart* will not make berth there."

"Why even go near such a horrible place?" Ovelia feigned terror.

"Pirates." When his simple explanation fell on deaf ears, Fersi smiled wider. "For the last day, we have sailed in waters claimed by Shard and his marauders."

"Shard?" Ovelia asked.

"A pirate king known for festooning his skyships with the skins of his mutilated victims or—more famously—loading his cannons with their shattered bones. The *Dart* always takes this route, as no flyer would dare pursue us into that mad bastard's territory."

"And these pirates are allowed to thrive unchallenged?" Regel asked.

"It is a question of resources, m'lady," Fersi said to Ovelia, rather than addressing him directly. "Those who want to destroy Shard and his pirates, such as the Ravalis, lack the strength to do it. Those powers who *do* have the strength—like the Children who rule Luether—do not care."

"And you pay tribute to these pirates?" Regel asked.

Fersi looked irritated to be questioned by a mere servant, but it was clear to him that neither Regel nor Ovelia were folk to be ignored. He shrugged. "Not usually," he said. "What transpires on the water is far beneath them. They dock their skyships somewhere nearby—some believe a part of Atropis above the clouds, where no one would dare approach them. I always carry coffers of coin to appease Shard should his men notice us. Never fear." His eyes caught Ovelia's, and she trembled.

"You are wise, my Lord Captain." Ovelia took care not to touch him, but Regel could tell much in the way her hips opened to him. "I believe there is nothing else, Norlest. You may go."

Regel nodded. "My Lady. Captain."

Fersi dismissed him with a mock salute. Regel was aware of Ovelia watching him as he went below to the common area where his hammock was strung and waiting. The crew no longer offered him the slightest offense, but instead strung their hammocks as far from him as possible.

He would not sleep, though. He had business this night.

The engine broke down that night, setting the *Dart* adrift on the sea. Regel had lain awake in his hammock perhaps an hour before the engine groaned and whirred to a halt, stranding the *Dart* beneath the shadow of Atropis. Crewmen cursed and made signs to the Old Gods.

In the distraction, Regel slipped away and secreted himself up on the deck behind the main mast. The stars hid behind a thick cloak of black cloud. The silhouette of Atropis towered over the *Dart*, like a protective and forbidding statue. Regel found himself searching the jagged cliffs even at this distance, hoping to catch a glimpse of the figure he'd seen before, but he found no success. Perhaps he had merely imagined it anyway.

While the ship's mage swore and battered the engine back into function, Regel crouched and waited. He held his carving in one hand and focused upon it, letting his senses extend. Great plumes of greasy smoke wafted from the loudly cranking mage-engine, giving the air a sickly taste. The crew of the ship snored fitfully in their hammocks. All lay still.

Through the smoke, Regel sensed Ovelia emerge from the guest chambers in the forecastle and make her way to the captain's quarters. She moved with considerable grace, and he might not have seen her if not for his expanded senses.

Whittling in hand, he crept toward the main cabin. His own footfalls, nearly silent in the tense darkness, seemed thunderous to his attuned ears. Other sounds drifted on the breeze—words only he could hear, thanks to a lifetime spent honing his senses. Ovelia's demure voice. Fersi's rougher tones, absent the politeness he had feigned before. A meaty slap of fist upon flesh. He had struck her.

Filled with sudden, hot fury, Regel shed all attempt at stealth and marched forward. The blood raging in his veins would not allow subtlety. How had this woman—this murderess he hated with all his heart and soul—done this to him?

As he heard her pleas, he ceased to care. He kicked in Fersi's door as loudly as he could.

Inside, Ovelia gasped and Fersi pulled away from where they lay together on the bed, cursing and fumbling with his breeches. Ovelia's wrists were tied to the bed-posts. Regel's mind flashed back to five years ago, and he hesitated.

In the heartbeat that bought him, the captain lunged across the room for his sword, but Regel stepped in the way and claimed the curved blade himself.

Deprived of his steel, Fersi caught himself and affected an air of nonchalance. He spread his hands in the face of his own sword pointed at him. "What offends, Syr Norlest?"

Regel considered killing Fersi, but then the crew would rise against them. And even if he and Ovelia proved triumphant, killing every last crewman, it would strand them in the middle of the sea. Either way, that would bring their quest to a close. And besides, he and Ovelia were not lovers.

Not this time.

Regel stepped toward Ovelia, blade raised. Her eyes widened and she recoiled when his blade sliced down, but it only parted the bonds securing her to the bed. "Regel, what are you—?" She cut off, having let slip his name.

Regel held Fersi's sword at the ready. It was inferior to a Vangryur blade, but sufficient to shed blood if it came to that. "We're going, my lady," he said over his shoulder.

Bodies clustered outside the door, and the sound of half a dozen casters clicking filled the chamber. The crew had arrived more quickly than Regel had expected.

"Coin or no, you are guests upon my ship," Fersi said. "Would you insult your host so?"

Regel could slash out Fersi's throat before they could shoot him down, and from their trembling hands, the crew knew it too. Perhaps he was fast enough to kill several of them.

Ovelia, who had laced up her bodice and pulled a blanket around herself, was staring at him just as intently as the crew. He held her life in his hands as surely as he held his own.

"If you would stop me," Regel said, "then stop me."

A shiver passed through the crew, and they looked to Fersi for direction. "Take her," the captain said, with a dismissive wave. "But do not think I will forget this night. There will be a reckoning."

Not gently, Regel took Ovelia's hand and pulled her out into the cold night.

❧

They returned to the passenger cabin in tense silence, heedless of the crewmen gathered around. Shoulder aching, mind roiling, Ovelia walked barefoot through the night's chill. She barely felt the cold, but she was glad of Fersi's blanket, which shielded her from the crew's speculative looks. She walked proudly with her shoulders back, eyes for no one but Regel. She dared him to look back and dreaded it, both at once.

If he looked at her with those judging eyes, she would scream.

Two crewmen lingered near their chamber, faces startled, but Regel slammed the door on them. Then, quicker than a lunging snake, Regel snapped a knife into his hand, reversed to throw. Ovelia gasped, sure it would be lodged in her throat in a heartbeat, but instead Regel flicked it toward the door. It stabbed into the soft wood jamb, sealing the portal with steel. When Ovelia looked back, he had sat on the bed, staring down at his hands.

"You had no right, Regel." Ovelia straightened her shoulders. "You had no right to interfere—" He looked up at her, eyes filled with pain and betrayal, and she trailed off.

Old Gods, she felt the way she had five years ago, when... *Gods!*

Ovelia heard a moan of frustrated gears from the other end of the ship. The engine had started anew, and the *White Dart* lurched into motion. The inevitability of their quest loomed once more, and Ovelia realized that she couldn't say what she desperately wanted to say, because then Regel would not help her, and she would fail. It would all be for nothing.

"I've coin of my own," Regel said. "Whatever bargain you made for passage, he can take my gold for the difference and be glad of it."

He thought... Old Gods, he thought she had whored herself. She wanted to scream in fury at the insult and laugh for joy at her good fortune. If only she had been *whoring* herself, rather than having gone willingly into the bed of a man who would love and abuse her. If she told him the truth—tried to describe the rare thing she had recognized in the captain, and that it had made her want him without wanting to—he would only hate her more. Regel could not understand the hollow inside her—the curse that made her unlike other women. Let him think what he would—it was none of her concern.

Ovelia looked down at her hands. "As you wish."

Regel still wouldn't look at her. "If you needed it, you could have asked."

"And you would have given it?" Ovelia would play his game. What was one more deception? "You would not have, Regel. I know what stands between us. Lies and hate and too much pain."

Regel offered no words. Instead, he drew his carving knife and the hunk of wood he'd been working since Tar Vangr.

"Whittling," Ovelia said. "You'd rather do that than talk to me."

The knife scraped away a sliver of wood and flicked it onto the floor.

"You judge me," she said after a moment.

"No," Regel replied.

"You do. You sit there and you judge me." Ovelia felt more exposed than ever, and pulled the blanket tight over her shoulders. "How dare you—you, who use whores for the secrets they can steal from sleepy patrons—you, who scavenge the lust and wrath of men. You judge me, for doing what I will?"

Regel shrugged. "My students are what they are," he said. "But this is not what *you* are."

But he was wrong. She was not a whore—that he had said truly. But she was so much more than he thought. And less.

"And what's so different about *me*, Regel?" Ovelia challenged, the hairs on her neck and arms rising. "Am I supposed to be pure and beautiful like *she* was— like Lenalin?"

Regel paused in his woodwork, and Ovelia thought he might meet her eye. Ultimately, however, he resumed scraping the knife against the stone.

"Only in your mind, Regel," Ovelia said. "Only in your *mind* was Lenalin sweet and clean. Only there could you have lived with her, both of you innocent and—"

"I killed a man in my seventh year of life," said Regel. "Don't speak to me of innocence."

"You thought *she* was innocent."

"More so than either of us, Bloodbreaker."

The name burned, and she ground her teeth. "Always Lenalin!" she said, choking on the name. "Always her—your perfect, spotless princess. If you had the slightest clue—"

"Do not." Regel's carving knife scraped against the wood. "Do not speak ill of her."

Ovelia wanted to. She wanted to smear Lenalin's name all over the cabin, to strike Regel with her sins and iniquities—all those terrible secrets that she and Ovelia had shared as girls—but it was useless. Fifteen years ago, death had made Lenalin perfect to Regel, and so she would remain.

"I am sorry," Ovelia said, "that I am the one who lived, and not the one you loved."

The vast abyss between them grew, and their voices could not span its width. Ovelia hated this silence—hated that it rushed between them so easily.

"Very well," he said finally. "I thought he was forcing you."

"He wasn't," Ovelia replied.

"I see that now." He jabbed his knife into the wood, gouging two small furrows.

"My—" Ovelia bit her lip. She almost told him the truth, if only to draw his attention, but realized it would be a fool's errand. "All my resources must go to this, and my body is just one more."

"That isn't true," Regel said without looking at her.

"You don't understand how much I *need* this, Regel. The only thing that matters to me is justice for Semana. Let my body be polluted with dishonor. Let war come and the world pass to Ruin. I do not care, so long as justice is done."

"Justice," Regel mused. "Was it justice that slew Orbrin?"

"Please." Ovelia fought the tears welling in her eyes. "Do not ask me that."

Regel looked up at her, astonished. "Why do you weep when I say his name? Why not bask in your infamy like the monster you are?"

"Whatever you may think," Ovelia said. "I did love and honor Orbrin. More than you will ever know or understand."

"Why not me?" he asked, so suddenly that Ovelia jumped. "Why Fersi, and not me?"

"What?" Ovelia sniffed and wiped her nose.

"Why not seduce *me*?"

Because he was not Fersi. Because he was not Paeter. He did not see her as they had.

"I *tried*," Ovelia said. "Or do you not remember seeing through me so easily that night in the tavern?"

"I mean, why not do it *now*?" Regel said. "Trick me. Charm me into believing you an ally. I will aid you on your quest, and rather than slay you afterward, I will spare you. Why would you not do this?"

Because that would not be justice, she thought but did not say.

"Regel, I—" Ovelia laid her hands against his cheeks. How warm his skin felt—how hard from wind and age. "You and I... Regel, I never stopped. How I felt about you. You know that."

"No."

"No?" Ovelia asked. "What do you mean?"

"You never loved me." Regel rose from the bed and shook his head. "You loved *her*—the woman I saw in you."

"That's not true, Regel."

"Then what of Paeter?" Regel asked. "I killed him, you know."

Ovelia stiffened. All her memories and doubts and self-loathing fell away. She could hardly credit what she had heard. "You *what*?"

"The prince died at my hand," Regel said. "It was no less than he deserved, after what he did to Lenalin and to you. Unless you went to his bed willingly, in which case I apologize—"

Ovelia slapped him hard.

Regel slowly touched the blood at his lip. "I deserved that."

"You—" Ovelia trembled. "You *fool*! Paeter was the named heir. He—" Her cheeks felt hot and her hands shook. "How many died over the succession? How many lives could have... *Semana*." She raised her trembling hand to her mouth. "Old Gods, he was Semana's *father*, Regel. He would have protected her!"

Regel laughed aloud. "I doubt that very much."

Ovelia lunged and knocked him to the bed, fingers scrabbling for his eyes. But he was fast and strong, as he had ever been. He caught her wrists, pitting his strength against hers once more. She scrabbled and thrust her knees at him, but he rolled atop her and straddled her to pin her down.

"Stop," he said.

Ovelia glared up at him murderously. She writhed but he held her firmly.

"Stop," he repeated, softer.

"Old Gods, Regel, *why*?" Ovelia looked up through tear-wet eyes. "Why would you kill Paeter? I know you hated him—" She shut her eyes. "You'd not do it for *me*—would you?"

"No." Regel released her and rolled away. They lay panting, side-by-side. "Not for you."

Ovelia rose and stood trembling in the candlelit darkness. They two had sealed the princess's fate by striking on the same night. Fate was a cruel thing indeed, not only in what it took but in what it left behind.

"You should not have done that," she said. "Paeter was a beast but he was Lenalin's husband, and the only hope the Blood of Winter had." She laughed mirthlessly. "All this time, I thought mine was the blade that doomed Tar Vangr, but you shoulder as much blame as I."

"You think I do not know this? You think I do not think about this every day?" Regel looked so old. Ovelia thought he aged a decade in the span of a moment.

"Regel," Ovelia said. "I did not mean—"

Regel shrugged, and the moment passed. "We should stay in here for a time, lest we cross the crew wrongly. You should try to rest. And—" His eyes left hers. "Let me fix you some tea."

"Yes." Her stomach roiled. "Well."

She was tired—tired of this ship, tired of the calmed winds, tired of wanting a man who would kill her in perhaps a quarter-moon's time or less. Even now, with Regel in the room, when she closed her eyes, sleep loomed quickly.

And with it came the realization that only once had she seen Regel so angry as when he had kicked in the cabin door—and only that once had she wanted him so badly.

ACT TWO: SHIELDS

Five Years Previous—Palace of Tar Vangr—
Ruin's Night, 976 Sorcerus Annis

H<small>EAT.</small>
There was heat and shame.

Cloaked in rumpled sheets, Ovelia Dracaris lay on her side, gazing across the chamber into the silvered glass that stood beside the crackling hearth. The pale woman staring back at her—eyes hooded in a haggard face wreathed in hair like fire—seemed like a stranger. She was an old woman almost, aged far beyond this, her thirty-fourth winter. Her hazel eyes seemed almost a dull red in the bloody candlelight.

Movement in the mirror drew her eye to the man donning his clothes behind her in the chamber. Meaty hands slid dark leathers over his once iron-hard frame, now well padded with age. Those same rough hands had been the ones touching her moments before, and she still ached in those places they had been rough upon her. She ached from the urgency of his need and her own loathsome desire.

"Do I have another moon, then?" she asked.

Paeter Ravalis paused. "Eight years, and that is still why you do this? Not for pleasure, or the honor of my seed? Or perhaps to seduce the man who shall be your king?" He made a snuffling sound a little like a laugh. "Certain you're not a little in love with me?"

Ovelia blinked slowly—her reflection did the same. The lionskins strewn about the floor looked up at her with dead, glassy eyes. "Do I have it?"

"You amaze me." Paeter scoffed. "You suffer the bed of a man you hate for eight years, simply for the right to see a child not even your own. Why?"

Ovelia pitied him. With his confident smile and his words of boundless arrogance, he might have seemed a conquering king in his youth. But age had weakened the cords of his flesh and stolen his vehemence. He looked almost comical now, with his pronounced gut and too much ungainly hair. She knew older men much more beautiful than he. And yet...

"Assuage my curiosity, woman," Paeter said. "Why is my Nar-burned daughter so dear to you that you'd whore yourself to my bed simply for the right to see her?"

Ovelia blinked slowly, hoping the world would change when next she opened her eyes. It did not. "Have I another moon with her?" she asked for the third time. "Or must you have more?"

Paeter strode across the chamber and grasped her by the red hair, hauling her face up to his. "Perhaps it is the abasement that you love? Do you long for the

75

awful things I do to you?"

She couldn't deny that, but to agree would empower him. She hung limply in his grasp.

"Astonishing, that you care nothing for this body you sacrifice to me every thirty days." He squeezed one of her breasts—the sweet pain both thrilled and repulsed her. "Are you not the last Dracaris, heir of the Blood of Dragonfire? How far the proud she-dragon has fallen!"

"Do I have the time, or not?" she asked.

"You disgust me." He ran his fingers along her brow. "They should name you Whore's Get, not Dragon's. Unworthy of her blood—unworthy of the Winter King."

She should not have responded but his words struck a deep chord in her. Her spirit could stand any indignity, and though torture might scar her, her body would not break. But to question her loyalty was too much.

"And what would they name you, fallen prince?" She looked over his fat arms and chest. "Would they call you a speared whale? Would they bow to a walking corpse of a man?"

Surprise flickered in his eyes—and unexpected pleasure. For he loved to suffer as she did, and she had cut open his deepest wounds: the Ravalis were ever creatures of pride.

"Fie." Sneering, Paeter turned up his nose. "I'll have no more of you."

"You're having me now, or does your memory pass so quickly?" she asked. "*You* are the one who insists on this... arrangement between us."

At that, Paeter's face lost its humor and became cruel. "Burn you, Shield-Whore." He shoved her down onto the bed hard enough to knock her dizzy. "You've grown too cold for me."

"Too old, you mean," she whispered before she could stop herself.

Paeter sneered and cracked his knuckles. "Speak louder, slut—I didn't hear you."

Ovelia contemplated the unexpected anger on her face in the looking-glass. In her blurred vision, her hazel irises surrounded twin embers deep at the heart of her eyes: tiny flames that told her to rise up and throttle this beast of a man who mocked her. But Ovelia was a woman of honor and duty, and so she stifled those twin sparks of vengeance.

"Very well." Paeter buttoned up his jerkin and crossed to the door. There, he stopped and turned back. His hand went to his belt pouch and came up with two silver pieces. "You should have some coin, whore—to remind you what you are."

He tossed the coins at her, then slammed the door behind him.

One coin struck Ovelia's cheek and fell to the bed. The other clinked to the stone floor between the lionskins. Ovelia watched it roll in a diminishing, forlorn circle. Silver light danced in a wandering ring, which gleamed off something bright in the corner. She heard Paeter curse as he shuffled his way down the corridor beyond. Finally, the coin settled.

She had won the battle, but she dreaded the payment Paeter would exact for her victory. She could bear anything for Semana, but would Paeter even give her a chance after tonight?

And was that truly why she had done this for so long?

Another five breaths passed before Ovelia realized what she had seen in the mirror: the glint of steel. Her heart began to hammer like that of a rabbit that has spied a wolf, only too late.

"Gods of the Nar." She sat and pulled the sheets to her chest. "How long have you been there?"

"Long enough." The man in the darkness moved for the first time, letting her see him. He controlled how much she could see, and to be so completely in his power terrified and thrilled her.

"Regel," she said. "This—this is not as it seems."

"As it seems?" He stood, immobile and unreadable. She saw he wore his re-curved sword of blue steel: the scythe-sword called Frostburn. She felt colder simply *seeing* it.

He would not understand unless she told him all, and that she could not do. Some oaths went deeper than what she and Regel shared. "What—" Ovelia swallowed. "What will you do now?"

Regel walked silently toward her. Ovelia thought she could feel his sword sucking at her warmth.

"Will you kill me, Regel?" she asked. "I would not begrudge you. None would."

His eyes betrayed nothing. He stood before her, his body taut and ready.

"You loved me once." Ovelia closed her eyes and sighed. "Do not make me suffer."

His lungs sucked and pushed out air with a shallowness that whispered of barely controlled wrath. His heart raced loud enough for her to hear in the silent room—or perhaps that was only her own heart. Once their hearts had beat together. Would his go forth alone from this day?

She felt it then, quick as lightning and soft as a lover's caress. Frostburn's cold steel kissed her throat and warm life flowed from her skin, leaving her empty.

"No." Regel drew the ancient falcat away and sheathed it.

"No, you'll not kill me?" Ovelia whispered.

Regel shook his head. "No, I never loved you."

A cold fist closed around her heart. "But—but we—"

"Never *you*," Regel said. "When I could pretend you were Lenalin—only then."

"Please, Regel," she said, tears rolling down her cheeks. "You don't understand—"

"And now." Regel laid his gloved fingers against her cheek. "Now you are both dead."

With that, he pulled away and was gone.

He left her world in ruins.

SEVEN

AT FIRST, OVELIA THOUGHT the orange and gray haze on the southern horizon was a storm. As she stretched out her sore shoulder—remarkably healed but still stiff—she realized the truth. The understanding put a hollow ache in the pit of her stomach, confirmed only too soon as the crow-nest watcher cried: "Land!"

Luether, once City of flame, now City of Pyres. Even from this distance, it was obvious to Ovelia how the city had earned its name: smoke rose high into the sky, covering the Dusk Sea in a sickly, burning haze. She thought she could see flames rising from the high cliffs in the far distance, and they filled her with unease.

She wished Regel was there beside her, and hated how weak such a desire made her feel.

Ovelia had rarely felt so alone, though she had hardly known a moment of privacy in days. Since that night with Fersi two days before, Regel had hardly left her side, but he'd been distant and unavailable. He'd spoken perhaps a dozen words to her, but he was always there, watching. What exactly hid behind those eyes, she could not say, and he *would* not.

As though her thoughts had called out to him, Regel appeared at Ovelia's side. They watched the burning city draw nearer. "It is fate, I think," Regel said, "that we must face evil at its heart."

"Perhaps." Ovelia straightened her spine. "But I have known evil, and I am not afraid."

Regel said nothing, but she thought she saw a hint of an unexpected smile on his face. She had all but given up hope that he saw her as anything but a blade in his hand. She wondered.

They drew closer, and Ovelia could see the truth: Luether was on fire. Something had broken open the stone near the surface of the water, and the Narfire rose to wreathe the walls in white and red flame. She remembered watching in horror twenty years ago as the Narfire burst free of its bonds and ravaged the city beneath the fleeing skyship *Heiress*. That destruction was still visible, but it seemed the surviving Blood houses of Luether or perhaps the Children themselves had at least partly sealed away the fire in the city proper. The flames seemed to be only partly under control, however: Ovelia could see them chipping away at the cliffs and releasing more burning doom into the air.

"Madness," Ovelia whispered. "At any moment, the Narfire could boil over and kill them all. Do the Children *want* to die?" She stopped herself. Perhaps she'd answered her own question.

Regel spoke without meeting her eye. "You should garb yourself elsewise," he said. "Luether is a poor place for a noblewoman like Aniset."

"I suppose," Ovelia said. "Though my mother *was* a scullery maid."

Regel's eyes lingered on the horizon and he did not reply.

He was looking into Ruin, Ovelia thought—into the death of a world.

~

Regel whittled outside the guest cabin while Ovelia dressed within. The carving in his hands took shape as he let his mind lie silent and reached beyond.

Footsteps sounded on the deck behind him. He knew who it was without looking—his years of training saw to that—but Regel glanced over his shoulder anyway. "Hail," he said.

"Hail, Syr Norlest," Captain Fersi said. "If it does not offend, you should wear this."

The captain handed Regel a ragged cloak of stained linen, similar to those the crew of the *Dart* wore. Regel looked at him speculatively.

"The *White Dart* is known in this place, but you are not," Fersi said. "The sentries on the walls must not mark you for an outsider, or they will cast on the instant."

Regel nodded and donned the cloak. "You are aiding me for your own interest."

"Just so," Fersi said. "There exists no malice between us, my friend. Only coin."

Regel nodded, though he kept his blade close to hand. That, he trusted better.

The City of Luether stood in the protected heart of an archipelago, with towering cliffs that forbade any attempting to storm the gates. The *White Dart* floated toward twin walls of fire split by a thin crevasse of dark water. They'd had to approach at high tide, else the ship would dash itself to death upon the hulks of galleys that lay just beneath them. Great plumes of steam rose around them where the waves washed up over the vents of the Narfire's flame. The water around the *White Dart* bubbled and sizzled with the heat, promising a searing death to any unfortunate who fell over the side.

The ship passed between two great guard towers studded with long unused cannon and warded by men in mail of ring and leather, armed with farcasters. Regel saw the dead eyes lodged in their grizzled, ugly faces and knew them for bastard Children of Ruin. The cannon—sculpted to resemble snarling monsters of myth—pointed at the *Dart*. The secret of explosive powder was long gone, but the Children might have found a stockpile or found a way to fire the cannon through magic.

As if in answer to his thoughts, one of the cannon emitted a thunderous clang, and he ducked by reflex. The wall shattered opposite and fifty paces above the ship, sending shards of stone cascading down into the murky water. The crew of the *White Dart* scrambled to steer them clear, and super-heated water splashed up and over the sides. Regel lunged forward to snatch back a crewman, who suffered only a scalding spray to his arm, rather than his body. The ship trudged on, swaying in the disturbed water, while the barbarian who had fired at them cackled madly.

A heartbeat later, a casterbolt sizzled across from the other tower and exploded into the stone near the cannon. The watcher roared in outrage, and a dozen other guards took up hoots of laughter. This was what passed for humor among the Children—the proximity of death.

"Madmen," Regel murmured.

Captain Fersi nodded.

Past the watchtowers, the *Dart* navigated a narrow channel, among stone edifices and the bulks of ships left to rot in the shallows. Before, Regel had seen thousands of murder holes and watch posts, but here, he saw none. It was an eerie feeling, being so alone. "No more watchers?" he asked Fersi.

"These are the Hellfire Straits, my friend. When loosed, the Narfire gushes from pipes laced through the stone, filling these waters with doom. Any guards caught in that blast would simply be more ash, and the fires would spread through the rest of the posts." The captain offered him a gallows-grin and held up a hand. "Ah, but have no fear—the Children have lost that particular secret of Luether's defenses. What you saw at the front towers is the result of their effort to unlock the Narfire, but they could not control it. They could not stop it even if they wanted to. Beautiful, no?"

Regel felt ill, actually, to think of the world's fiery lifeblood and soul gushing into the open air. There was something perverse and ugly about the thought. Fersi was wrong—it was not the Children who had loosed the Narfire, but the old king of the Ravalis, father to he that ruled Tar Vangr. The mage-city of Luether was an oozing, festering wound, and he feared it would never close. He had to remind himself that he and Ovelia had not come to save the world. They'd come for vengeance and nothing else.

"Besides," the captain went on, "even if the Children could wield the fire, they'd be protecting a graveyard." Fersi gestured to a floating hulk of broken wood rocking idly in the water. A figurehead of a lithe woman, now scarred with age and blackened with flame, marked its ship's wreckage. "Few navigate these waters—only the mad or the skilled."

"Which are you?" Regel asked.

The captain grinned.

They floated into the largely empty Luether harbor, which proved a relative respite from the harrowing journey through the straits. Many of the docked ships were burned out and barely seaworthy. Some of them looked familiar, and Regel wondered how many had fought in the Children's conquest only to sit for twenty years rotting in their mooring.

As the *White Dart* approached the dock to tie up, gears creaked and whined as a rusty steel arm from the dock reached for their halting ship. Regel tensed, expecting an attack, but instead the crane closed its pincers around one of the moldering crates on the main deck. Regel eased his taut legs and resolved to accustom himself once again to the mechanical wonders of the southland.

The dock warden stood at the foot of a gangplank to the *Dart* and exchanged words with Captain Fersi, and then they spat in their hands and shook on the accord. The metal arm shuddered into operation and carried the crate back to the dock. The crew and the men on the dock began unloading the *Dart*'s cargo, the nature of which Regel did not care to know. His task had nothing to do with coin, after all.

"Norlest," said a voice at his elbow.

Ovelia wore breeches and a man's tunic. With her dyed hair pulled back under a lumpy cap, her womanly body buried in bulky clothes, and even a dusting of false stubble over her lip, she became someone not herself. "Well?" she asked.

"Passable," Regel said, with his usual aplomb.

"Such a flatterer," she said. Even her *voice* was convincing. "Does he have his coin?"

"Waiting in his cabin."

Fersi traded words with the dock warden, and both sneaked glances at them. Ovelia touched the handle of Draca, which she'd wrapped in cloth. Shadows began to leak from its hilt, and Regel became acutely aware of the dozen or so dockhands eyeing them with ambiguous intent. Now that the coin was paid and the deal complete, one word from the captain and they would turn on their former passengers.

"We should go," Ovelia said. "Now."

"Agreed." Regel looked around for a distraction. "Perhaps—"

Before they could move, a great racket filled the dock. The loading machine whirred crazily and its talons closed too hard on a crate, splintering out its half-rotted sides. The claw shot back toward the ship, flinging the remains of the crate—as well as broken glass and showering foodstuffs—out into the harbor. Two men rushed toward the control box, but the arm swept them aside like ants.

As Fersi shouted orders and the deckhands looked for a way through the arm's arc, Regel and Ovelia slipped away from the dock and up the street. After ten paces, no one cared about the accident at the dock. Regel would not easily forget it, however—particularly how it had occurred precisely when they had needed it. He did not trust coincidence or fate.

He stepped closer to Ovelia and kept close watch on their trail.

~

The first thing she noticed about Luether was the heat: within a breath, sweat coated the inside of Ovelia's clothes. Ruin's sun above was oppressive, and the Narfire burned below to heat the pavement as in Tar Vangr. She wondered if she could even stand the heat during the actual summer season.

Ovelia remembered Luether's heat from her youth, but it had seemed gentler. She recalled a city tinged by the haze of wine, swelling music, and the cacophonous bouquet of hundreds of flowers. She couldn't stop sneezing, but she had been happy, because Lenalin had been happy.

That passionate innocence was gone in these latter years, however. Smoke billowed from foundry stacks above them, while inside engines rumbled hard enough to shake the very street beneath Ovelia's boots. The air tasted not of flowers but of burnt flesh and corroded metal. Below, the forges of the Narfire churned out increasingly powerful casters, great siege engines, mechanized war machines, and other monstrosities. It had been thus before the coming of the Children of Ruin, and even after that fateful day, the barbarians maintained the forges, twisting their constructs to match their own dark whims.

Even fallen into madness, Luether remained a city of metal and of fire.

But even under the oppressive rule of the Children, Luether was still a living city that did trade with Tar Vangr, its supposed enemy. The self-styled King Pervast seemed unlike other Children in that he lived for something other than murder and destruction: coin. Even if hatred pushed men apart, greed always seemed to pull them back together.

In the market, they lost themselves in a crowd of folk: Luethaar, Vangryur, Free Islander, all clammoring for position and shouting orders or greetings to one another. All the while, coin changed hands. Horseless carriages rattled up the crude streets, and soot dripped on them from clanking ornithopters high overhead. Ovelia was impressed and a bit unnerved to see the Children so fully in command of Luether's mechanical wonders. She wanted to think of the barbarians as little more than animals, but to see what they had accomplished in twenty years made her nervous.

Across the way, four chained men worked to scrub white-wash markings from a nearby, burned-out building. They had only just begun the work, so most of the message remained: *Summer Da*— and the ghost of one more letter that might have been a U or a Y. Supervising the work was a big man with bits of blade thrust through his cheeks. Such self-mutilation marked him as a Child of Ruin. He stared across at them and actually growled like an animal.

They took shelter beneath an awning of an open-air shop that peddled broken gears and machinery. The smell of rotting fish mingled with the ever-present stench of burning and the smell of something that had died here not too long ago. Ash hung thick in the air and trash littered the grimy cobblestones. "What was that?" Ovelia asked. "That message?"

"The liberators," Regel said. "Loyalists to the Ravalis, who resist Vultara and the Children at every turn. Rumor says a lesser cousin of the Ravalis leads them. One Garin by name."

"Garin Ravalis, the Fox of Luether." Ovelia pursed her lips in thought. "I've met the man, and did not think him as bad as his cousins. Though that was decades ago, and folk change."

"Indeed." Regel gestured again to the marking. "They paint the words 'Summer Day' where they have done their lord's work." He gestured to a burned out building across the street, where at least two bodies sat propped against the bricks. "They still fight, even after more than twenty years of occupation."

Ovelia nodded. "Hope never dies."

The shop's proprietor glared at them in suspicion, and Regel made placating gestures to show him they meant no harm. Ovelia contemplated the marking. For all she had known, Garin Ravalis and his band of insurgents were long dead, but if they still worked to undermine the Children's control...

"What?" Regel had returned from bargaining with the machinist who owned the shop. He had bought nothing, of course, but it seemed they could stand here unmolested. "What are you thinking?"

"Perhaps Luether is not as lost as it seems," Ovelia said.

Regel looked unconvinced. "Tell that to Blood Vultara. Hope is their curse."

"Vultara," Ovelia said. The name was a curse in Tar Vangr: the Blood traitors who betrayed the Ravalis twenty years ago and opened the gates to the Children. "You cannot mean they still live."

"A few of them," Regel said. "When Pervast crowned himself, he rewarded the loyalty of Blood Vultara by giving their patriarchs to the Narfire. To this day he chooses a few among the heirs for his bed and disposes of the others—gives them to his lieutenants or flings them from high-city."

"All this in punishment for failing to capture Lenalin and Paeter before they fled the city?" Ovelia shivered. "How do you know this?"

"I was there. I saw the bodies flying from the rocks."

Ovelia remembered that awful day—her second and final visit to Luether. She'd lost her father that day, and almost Lenalin too. On that day, she'd sworn never to allow weakness to stay her hand. She was thankful she'd not seen the Children's reprisals.

"Hope is a torment for the Vultara," Regel said. "Every day, the few of the Blood that live hold out hope to one day overcome the Children, but every night, they sleep in the same prison. If they had no hope, at least they would not feel that pain."

Ovelia might have replied, but shadows whispered around the hilt of Draca, and she focused on that. She could not very well draw the sword to examine its warning, so she had to heighten her awareness and find the danger herself. The proprietor was looking at her very directly, and the single other patron picked his teeth as he stared at her. His was an ugly face, obscured by a web of scarred and melted flesh from his forehead to his left cheek, and his eyes twinkled with lustful malevolence that made her skin tickle. Her heart picked up its pace.

"Ovelia." Regel had detected something amiss. "What—"

"We have to go." The street seemed deserted of a sudden. "We have to—"

It was then she heard the monster roar as it loomed over her. She thought it a dragon of legend, its threshing claws rending through the street for any foolish enough to cross its path. It whirred and clanked, billowing steam and smoke in equal measure. One appendage, spinning with blades, reached toward her, and Ovelia managed to throw herself back to keep from being torn to pieces.

She reached for her sword, but Regel took her by the arm and dragged her out of its path. As Ovelia watched, the horrific machine rolled past them, its bladed hands plucking up corpses and other detritus. They panted in the alley.

83

"Old Gods, what was that?" Ovelia asked.

"A street thresher," Regel said. "The Ravalis used them to sweep the streets clean. When the Children took Luether, they added the blades. I suppose they still fulfill their purpose." He touched her forehead. "Are you all right? What happened?"

"Nothing," she said. "I—"

How could she explain her sudden outburst? That she had feared the ugly man's attack, or that she feared what she would do given another moment of such scrutiny?

The scene in the street had drawn attention to them. Many of the men and women around them bore the marks of the Children of Ruin: vicious scars, artless tattoos drawn with as much blood as ink, and shards of metal thrust through their cheeks, lips, and brow. Each of these told its own story: each tattoo was a felled foe, and each piercing came from broken bits of an enemy's arms or armor.

One man in particular seemed to be watching them since the mechanical dragon had passed. He wore two dagger shards stretching his lips into a rectangular distortion, and his yellowed and filed teeth turned his mouth into a pit studded with spikes. This Child wore a rusty war gauntlet, the blades of which clicked. He chuckled in time. Ovelia thought he looked familiar, and she realized she had glimpsed him at the dock as well. It unnerved her.

"We should get off the road," Regel said.

Ovelia nodded and tried not to look at their gape-mouthed pursuer.

Regel bought passage in one of the mechanized carriages the city was known for, and they rode in its cramped, hot interior along the burned out streets. At least there was privacy here in the carriage.

Just north of the market they rode past a massive crane, which shuddered to life as they watched. Such contraptions lifted and lowered folk between the two levels of a mage-city. This one bore only a minor load: half a dozen folk and a small carriage. Looking up, Ovelia didn't see many folk walking up on the pink glass streets of high-city anyway.

As they rode, Ovelia realized that what was beginning to decay in Tar Vangr was already destroyed in Luether. Gone were the palaces, dazzling parks, and cobbled streets—gone were the theaters and vast marketplaces and halls of worship. These buildings had been stripped bare and converted into foundries and smithies that bruised the sky with their smoke. Gutted holdfasts and towers lurched precariously, ready to crash down any moment.

"Why would they burn the buildings?" Ovelia murmured. "Is that not dangerous to all?"

"The masters of Luether punish at whim," he said, "whether justified or no."

The carriage rolled to a halt, its metal wheels crunching over what sounded like glass.

"Why would we stop?" Ovelia asked.

"Hold," Regel said, but she climbed out anyway.

The carriage driver was long gone. Ovelia saw him hurrying back in the opposite direction. She reached for her sword, ready for an attack, but Regel appeared at her side and held her wrist.

A trumpeting groan surrounded them, momentarily cutting off speech. Ovelia looked around for the source of the awful sound. Nearby, a broken-down building slumped like a gutted giant while desperate folk picked its bones for usable metal or wood. Long shards of cracked pink glass studded the cobbles stones like a rosy forest.

"Broken glass." Regel looked up toward high-city. "Get back in the carriage."

"What do you mean?" Ovelia sensed danger, but she couldn't say from what. The shadows around Draca were huge and flat, like a shield or a plateau. And—

From high above, there came a great groan and screech of metal. Far overhead, a great wedge of splintering crystal, twenty paces wide and twice as long, quaked on its supports. That was the firmament upon which Luether's high-city stood. A piece of the city was quite literally collapsing before her eyes.

"Old Gods of our fathers." Ovelia's eyes widened. "Regel, we have to help."

"And do what?"

Up on the glass plate, she saw figures of men—seeming like ants at this distance—scurrying away from the broken wedge as it shivered and dipped. Then with one last, mournful cry of torn steel, the plate wrenched free of the last of its supports and fell.

There was a moment of weightless terror.

Then the plate crashed into the city below not a hundred paces ahead of them, with a thunderous roar of shattering stone. Regel stepped in front of Ovelia, shielding her as a wave of fetid air and smoke blew past them, sending their cloaks billowing backward. His arms encircled her, and she inclined her face to his, away from the destruction.

The explosion stole sound from the world and replaced it with ringing silence.

When Regel and Ovelia unveiled their faces, they saw the chaos that lay ahead of them in the street. Cries of pain and terror rose to the sky, and Regel saw bodies moving amongst the rubble—frantically clawing to free themselves, or twitching as death claimed them.

"Dust and shadow," Regel said. "None of us are more or less." He held out his hand. "Come. We'll go around."

"We have to *do* something," she insisted. "Regel!"

"We will," he said. "We'll kill Mask."

"But they need us," Ovelia said. "Mask can wait. We can help."

"Killing Mask requires that we live." He gestured to the destroyed swath of low-city, crushed by a shattered swath of high-city. "If we enter that chaos, we might make a difference, but the Children will find us—that, or another collapse will kill us. One way or another, we die."

Ovelia pulled. "We can't just turn away."

"This city belongs to Ruin." Regel grasped her hand. "We will do as we must."

Ovelia relented. Much as she hated to admit it, he was right.

"I—" Pain stabbed her belly, and Ovelia groaned. What had she eaten? "We should press on. I took rooms—"

Then her senses lit up. Draca spoke to her, and she knew the danger that would befall before it did. She swallowed the pain in her gut and looked behind them, to where shadowed men emerged from the alleys.

An ambush.

EIGHT

WHEN OVELIA TOUCHED HER belly and looked uncomfortable, Regel cursed silently. Since the docks, he'd had no chance to give her any of the antidote. It would have to be soon, clearly, or this whole errand would prove vain. They would have to find refuge, for if they fell under attack while she was weakened...

Too late.

A change swept over Ovelia's face that Regel instantly recognized. She drew her sword halfway from its scabbard and looked at the flames leaking from its blade. "You expected this," she said.

"It seemed inevitable." He'd hoped to delay it, though. Fight on ground of his choosing.

Regel turned to see six men with warcasters fanning out behind them. One even had a repeating caster that whined mechanically and leaked a thin trail of thamaturgical smoke. A discreet cough from behind the ranks called their attention to Captain Fersi himself. He was fingering a large coin purse at his belt—the one Regel had left in his cabin on the ship.

"Tell me," the captain said. "Did you sabotage the loader arm yourself, or have her do it? It might even have worked, had I not had this one follow you. Goodman Nashar—or perhaps it is *Ruinman*, no?"

"Gnasher." The Child of Ruin with the pit-like mouth they had seen earlier emerged, war gauntlet at the ready. Though he could not show a smile, the man's eyes danced with bloody mirth. He clacked his filed teeth and spoke in a broken, guttural voice. "I's *Gnasher*."

"I misspeak," Fersi said. "Apologies."

The other attackers were Fersi's crew, and for that Regel was grateful. Involving even one Child of Ruin would make talking his way free of this difficult.

"You have your coin," Regel said. "Would you dishonor our agreement?"

"Certainly not." The captain offered his customary solicitous smile and spread his hands. "But we are through, you and I, and now I make a new bargain. This with the Ruin King. Or did you not know you are proscribed in Luether, Regel the Oathbreaker?"

The words elicited a few nervous murmurs, but they faded away when the Ruinman Gnasher stepped forward and spoke in his rasping voice. "I's honored to spill the blood of the hero Frostburn." He gave Regel a mocking bow. "I wear your steel over my heart when it done."

"Wish I had your reputation," Ovelia murmured, her words dry.

"It's a blessing every day," Regel replied in kind.

Gnasher's beady eyes flicked to Ovelia. "Is your boy, Frostburn—or is woman? Either way, I take it, I do." His split tongue waggled between his yellowed teeth. Ovelia bristled.

Regel put his hands to the hilts of his swords. "Walk away," he said. "All of you."

"You men saw us on the deck," Ovelia added, her temper hot in the clipped words. "If you remain, your blood is on your own hands."

Again, they hesitated, but Gnasher's fearsome presence meant they could not back down.

"Kill the Ruinman," Regel said, "and they'll break."

"Or we'll die," Ovelia said.

"Not yet," Regel said. "Not until Mask."

"Bring them." Captain Fersi turned away. "Undamaged, if possible."

Casters took aim, Gnasher loosed a cry of challenge, and swords sang free of their scabbards. Ovelia furrowed her brow, then clasped her hands to her ears and tackled Regel aside. The move startled him so that he almost struck back in retaliation. Why would she betray him now?

Then something small flew into the midst and burst in blinding light, like a star suddenly given life. The violent flash dazzled Regel, and he heard only wet murmurs in place of screams from their attackers, along with a loud, high-pitched keen that cut through his head like a burning casterbolt. All around him, sailors writhed and held their heads in panicked agony. He realized what had happened: an alchemical grenade, one that had affected him only in passing but struck them fully.

Regel did not know who had thrown the device, but he and Ovelia would certainly die if they didn't take advantage. He drew his swords as the dazzled soldiers began firing their casters in a hot cacophony. Regel parried a bolt aside, and the others missed by at least a hand's breadth. At his side, Ovelia had stepped out of the path of fire. She didn't seem to have been affected by the blast, having sensed it coming and prepared herself.

He felt more than saw Ovelia charge into the thick of their attackers and followed suit, closing the distance before the sailors could recover and train their casters again. The poor, mind-scattered bastards had no close combat weapons other than their spent casters. Regel cut forward: one sword rang off a caster while the other found flesh, drawing a hiss of pain. He felt Ovelia at his back, hard and sleek, and they fought in tandem.

"Dancing Deer," she shouted, and Regel grunted his agreement. He followed along as she feinted twice, then struck twice and dropped an unseen opponent to the grimy cobblestones.

They surged together in the filthy alley, cutting and guarding and killing. His blades found throats and gaps in boiled leather and soft spots where they could draw lifeblood. But more importantly, Regel and Ovelia fought well *together*, even after so many years. The fight on the ship had reminded his mind of her steps, but his body still knew them with perfection. They slaughtered their opponents like butchers who had plied their trade for decades.

A big shadow descended and Gnasher roared in his face, driving Regel back. The barbarian's war gauntlet raked in from the side and tore the air where Regel had been standing. A Child of Ruin would make no easy prey, as the hapless sailors had.

He pressed his back against Ovelia's reassuring frame. "Raking Tiger," he said, or perhaps shouted. Hearing was returning gradually, but it was still hard to understand himself.

Ovelia took a step backward as Regel danced forward and slashed twice. His sword bit deep into tough flesh, and Gnasher cried out in pain. Then they spun, and Ovelia dealt Gnasher's hasty defense a withering blow with *Draca* that made his war gauntlet groan in protest. Regel and Ovelia stayed in balance—stayed together.

And before Regel knew otherwise, it was over.

The world stopped shivering, the whine died away, and Regel's senses stabilized. Four of the sailors were down: two of them unmoving and the other two coughing their way into death. Casterbolts protruded out of two of these unfortunates, placed with accuracy that said the shooters hadn't been blinded in the least by the grenade. Gnasher lay unmoving in a pool of blood, with two bolts protruding from his back and a gaping sword wound in his side. The two remaining sailors knelt, hands up, weapons tossed to the dust.

Captain Fersi had fallen to one knee, a casterbolt through his thigh. "It was only about the coin," he said, his tone perplexed.

"I understand." A cloaked man with a viciously hooked warpick stood over Fersi. Regel couldn't see what the cowl hid except for two bright emerald eyes that caught the fading light. "Get up."

"Aye, Fox of Luether." Fersi rose, wincing. "What passes now?"

"Kill him," said another of the cloaked figures—a young man with a high-pitched voice who held a dagger at the throat of a kneeling soldier. "Death to the foes of Summer."

"Hold, Alcarin." The cloaked man held up a hand to stay him. He turned partially toward them, and his fine teeth glittered. Such fine teeth—and a smile to match—marked no mere bandit but a noble.

The young man—Alcarin—looked to Regel and Ovelia. He was a beautiful youth with dark, long-lashed eyes and full lips, but there was nothing soft about his dangerous expression. There was challenge in his stance, and Regel tensed. Perhaps the battle was not ended after all.

The leader of the cloaked warriors addressed Captain Fersi once more. "You've done your last bargain in my city." He brought down his warpick and the captain fell back with a cry. When he looked up, however, he bore only a tiny cut on his cheek.

"Was that necessary?" The captain touched at the blood. "I detest bleeding."

The cloaked man gestured to the oily edge of his pick. Then, as Fersi's eyes widened, he smiled halfway. "No fear, pirate," he said. "This toxin takes time to do its work... but when it does, forever after the Narfire-touched air of this city will become death to your lungs." He looked up at the sun to estimate the time.

"I suggest you flee this place, before such an unfortunate event occurs."

"How very rude." Fersi flinched from the man's warpick. "Rude, but fair."

"Wait." The cloaked man indicated Fersi's coin pouch and looked to Regel. "Yours?"

Regel nodded.

He drew it away from the captain's belt, cut it free, and tossed it to land at Regel's feet.

"Take your ship and go," he said to Fersi. "Return to Luether when you are ready to swear allegiance to the Blood of Summer once again, and perhaps I'll offer you an antidote."

Fersi's lips spread in a cruel smile. "Best fortune upon you, my lord."

The captain hobbled away, grasping the casterbolt in his leg. The captain's remaining sailors followed. The leader of the cloaked men watched, his warpick held casually at his side. He smiled, and deep dimples spread around his lips. "Regel, is it?" he asked. "I think you are the Lord of Tears himself. A pleasure."

"Yes." Sword raised, Regel stepped in front of Ovelia. "And now?"

Ovelia stood easy behind him, but he had no sword to warn him of peril. There were five of them, including the leader with the warpick, and they looked far deadlier than Fersi and his thugss.

"Garin!" Alcarin gestured out toward the main street, where the remainder of Fersi's crew had gone. The commotion would certainly bring curious onlookers, and possibly more Children of Ruin. "Master, we cannot be seen here."

The leader hung his warpick on his belt. "Take care, Lord of Tears. Who can say how many Fersi told of your identity, or how long you might remain hidden? This city is not forgiving of heroes."

As Regel and Ovelia breathed deep of the smoky air, the rebels slunk away as quickly as they had come. Regel listened for sounds of reinforcements, but there were none. Ovelia seemed to be staring after where their leader had vanished, a look of contemplation on her face.

"Garin Ravalis?" Regel asked.

"That—" Ovelia blinked and shook herself. "Yes. That was him."

"The prince in rebellion." Regel nodded slowly. "I thought he'd be dead by now."

"Apparently not." Ovelia grimaced.

"Your shoulder?" Regel asked.

"Nausea. From the journey, no doubt." Ovelia clutched her stomach. "I'll never be a sailor."

Regel nodded. He had asked the question, but he knew the truth. He needed to get her that antidote.

People were starting to gather at the end of the alley, drawn by curiosity. Battle in Luether was common, and equally predictable was the flock of vultures that descended to collect what they could from the dead. Wheezing emerged from the fallen Gnasher, who was starting to move.

"Frostburn," he said, voice bubbling. "Frost—"

"Regel." Ovelia nodded toward the Child of Ruin, pity on her face. "Shouldn't we—?"

"We go." Regel bent to reclaim his purse and turned away, leaving Gnasher bleeding and choking.

He pushed his way through the crowd. Ovelia lingered to look at the dying barbarian, but she hurried to catch him up within two breaths.

～

"Frostburn..."

Bleeding out onto the chipped cobblestones, the mouth-scarred Child of Ruin lunged at the crowd of slack-jawed onlookers that bore witness to his impending death. Mostly, they were the beaten down masses of Luether, but here and there stood a fellow Child, marked by a scarred face and a wicked smile at Gnasher's distress. One stood laughing low to herself through filed teeth, heedless of the thin ribbon of drool hung down her chin. None approached the deformed man, however; they seemed content to wait until he breathed his last. Gnasher's body was dying, but he remained fearsome even so.

That, Davargorn could respect, even if he found the sight a bit pitiful.

A small creature emerged out of the alley, one that paid no heed to the customs of Luether: a fox. Life on the ruinous streets of a dying city had rotted chunks of fur away from its mangy body, and a thousand alley fights had scarred it badly, including one dead eye. And yet it struggled on, heedless of any of the Children of Ruin who eyed it hungrily, and made its way to Gnasher's boot, which it promptly began to chew. The Child kicked at it, but the fox simply retreated to let him miss, then attacked again.

Davargorn admired such courage. In his eyes, it placed the fox on a higher level than the dying barbarian. He activated his boots, surrounding him with swirls of black smoke as he rose into the air.

The fox's example spurred the other onlookers forward, and they took shaky steps toward Gnasher. The slavering barbarian woman came first, filed teeth clicking in anticipation of a fine meal.

Davargorn alighted between her and Gnasher, perched on his toes like a hunting cat. His cloak swirled around him, its edge glinting like polished steel. The woman hesitated.

He gave her no warning. She would heed none, and he would only look weak if he tried.

Davargorn whirled, snapping his cloak between them. The daughter of Ruin staggered back, clutching at the blood pouring from her throat. She gagged and burbled, her filed teeth clicking and biting at her tongue. Davargorn lunged through the air and kicked her down, then balanced upon her chest as she squirmed and died. He put his hand on the hilt of the sword at his belt.

"Another?" he asked the crowd.

His cracked voice crashed against the assembled Luethaar like a tidal wave breaking on the rocks—and the rocks crumbled. One man gasped as though he'd been struck a physical blow, and his nearest companions glared at his display of weakness. The crowd dispersed in a chorus of mutters and accusing stares. Davargorn smiled, though of course his bone mask hid his expression.

"An odd pairing," he said. "A broken woman and the angel of death."

Regel, who had once killed at the behest of the Winter King, was the finest slayer the Calatan Empire or its heirs had ever seen. And that was precisely what drove Davargorn: his need to strike down Regel and be the best. He shivered just thinking about it.

He stepped off the barbarian he had killed and crossed to where Gnasher lay. The man was still alive, if barely: his chest rose and fell shallowly, even as the fox chewed at his midsection. The fox regarded Davargorn warily, its snout smeared with blood.

"I've no desire to steal your prize," Davargorn said. "Not when you're the only one strong enough to take it."

The fox went back to its meal, but not before a black gloved hand that was not Davargorn's touched its neck. The fox jerked taut, startled, but the newcomer merely caressed it from ears to tail.

"Speak, Squire," the figure said.

"They have arrived, Master." Davargorn dropped to one knee. "And they seem determined to find death at every turn. I sabotaged a loader at the dock to cover their escape, and still they managed to wander into an ambush. I wonder if we should—"

His master coughed—a low, hacking sound that made Davargorn reach forward, concerned. Two bright, determined eyes warded him off.

"They will die," his master said. "But not yet. Follow them."

Davargorn nodded. Already, he'd wasted too much time with the fox and the Child. He gestured to the wheezing Gnasher and touched his sword. "Shall I?"

The eyes bore into his masked face, and he looked away.

Power flared—dark, cursed magic from an even darker age. Sickly green energy connected one silver gauntleted hand to Gnasher's heaving chest, and Davargorn could see energy drawing away from the dying man and up the trail of magic. The barbarian moaned one last time, then rattled his way into death.

When Davargorn looked back, his master was gone. Time to focus on the task at hand.

He'd lost sight of his quarry. He felt confident, however, that he could find them once more—particularly with the thick black boots that sheathed his feet and ankles. And if he failed, well, he had set a failsafe in motion with Regel's squire in Tar Vangr. Try as he might, the man who had once been the Frostburn would not elude the trap closing around him.

Not, of course, that Davargorn would fail.

He breathed a word of command, and smoke began to leak from the boots: the stirrings of corruptive magic. "Soon, Lord of Tears." Davargorn smiled. "Soon."

Power coalesced around his boots and he soared into the air.

NINE

JOVIAL AND WARM, THE Crimson Bath had not changed much even in the twenty years since Ovelia had been here last. After the battle and the horror of the falling glass, it relieved her to see folk actually smiling and jesting. True, the humor was crude and the folk worse, but it reminded her that not all of Luether had fallen to Ruin.

Dutiful servants scurried between the tables, dodging speculative glances and eluding groping hands. Many were young women, which rankled her a bit. Service was considered beneath a man's dignity in Luether, Ovelia recalled, though she saw little about the Summerlands men that made them better than the women. Quite the opposite, in fact: the men of Luether seemed, by and large, uncautious, boistrous, and uncouth. She'd seen more fights break out between braggart men in her few hours here in Luether than in half a year back in civilized Tar Vangr. Defending one's manhood with fists appeared to be the style of the day. The women, on the other hand, were quiet, unassuming, and could get things done. She respected them far more for their discretion than the men's bravado.

She let her mind drift back to her first visit to Luether, when she and Princess Lenalin had been mere girls of ten or so, come to meet the Prince Paeter, who would be Lenalin's husband when she reached the age of majority. Such a thing would never happen to Ovelia, of course—"marriage" was the exclusive province of nobles forging alliances and even then, it was all but unknown in Tar Vangr— but she had been excited to support Lenalin. Ovelia was her lady in waiting and sworn shield, even if she was not yet strong enough for real armor or weapons.

"You'll ward her, yes?" Syr Norlest had asked. *"Against all enemies?"*

To that, Ovelia had nodded vigorously.

At one point, Lenalin and Paeter had sneaked out of the palace to this very tavern, and of course Ovelia had followed her princess. Here, she'd beaten a grown man senseless for the way he looked at Lenalin. She remembered Lenalin had laughed, as had Paeter's crude brother, Lan, who made it a point to remind Ovelia of the incident for the remainder of the trip. Paeter had been the only Ravalis who'd not laughed—instead, he'd fixed Ovelia with a discerning stare that made her blush. Had she known then, as a child, that when they came of age, his pretty princess would not please him? That he would lust instead after her red-haired knight who longed to be abused?

Ovelia shook the unpleasant memory away and signaled the owner of the Crimson Bath, a grizzled former sailor by the swagger and smell, her face lined and worn with hard years. Predetermined signals flashed, coin changed hands, no names were given, and the woman led them down a set of stairs through a hidden trapdoor to a secret room off the cellar.

The mostly natural chamber was cavernous, saturated with the earthy smell of hewn stone and blood-soaked soil. Cracks were sealed tight with pitch so sounds of clandestine meetings and illicit trysts would not reach the floor above. Secret murders could befall in this place with no one the wiser, though the earthen floor had, over the years, acquired a distinctly red tinge. She and Regel could spar all they wanted, and no one would interfere.

There was only one bed, but that was a matter for later.

Ovelia nodded and put two silver coins in the owner's hand. After biting them and nodding, the woman climbed back up the stairs and shut the trapdoor. Doing so stole the light from the room but for thin rays that filtered down through the occasional crack whose pitch had worn away. One of these rays fell on a tiny shelf cut out of the wall at the head of the bed.

"A godshelf," Regel murmured. "Remarkable, to find such a thing in Luether."

The shelf boasted a scattered collection of clay figures and carvings—trinkets left to honor one or another of the nameless Old Gods, or an ancestor the carver considered a paragon of nobility or honor. They had coalesced over the years into an entire pantheon to watch over a sleeper. How many prayers had been uttered in such a place, begging for providence on a quest such as theirs?

Ovelia bent a knee and inclined her head out of respect for the divine.

"We need to eat," Regel said. Ever the practical one.

The last thing Ovelia wanted for her roiling stomach was food, and the last thing her uneasy heart craved was time with Regel, but she nodded anyway. The figurines on the godshelf looked like tiny corpses in the semi-darkness.

A fifty count later, Ovelia sat alone upstairs in the common room, feeling nauseated and uneasy. The journey through the streets had shaken her, and she felt exposed waiting for Regel to return from the kitchen. Still disguised, her features attracted no great notice.

At length, Regel appeared with two trenchers of unappealing stew and two mugs of steaming tea. Ovelia passed over the food for now, but the tea settled her stomach somewhat.

They sat in silence. Ovelia felt strangely unsettled: unmoored and alone, almost as though Regel had become not her companion any longer but a stranger. She found herself staring out the tavern's window, searching for a way to distract herself. Seeing the violent world slipping into Ruin was better than watching Regel do the same.

"You're angry with me," Regel said at last.

Ovelia sighed. "That man back there. What you did to him."

"He was a Child of Ruin."

"He was a man all the same," Ovelia said. "You could have had the mercy to kill him."

"I do have it," Regel said. "But the Children rule in Luether, and here mercy is a challenge to their power." He looked at her sidelong. "I thought you would do what must be done. For Semana."

Anger rose in Ovelia that he would question her loyalty, but she stayed her tongue. Perhaps she was being unfair. He had seen what she was willing to sacrifice, and he seemed able to accept it. Could she not do the same for him, now that she saw what this quest would make him? Not that the realization mollified her—she still felt a dull, radiating anger at his actions. There must have been another way.

Uneasy with how unsafe she felt with or without Regel, she looked instead out the window. Though it was midday, she could not see the sun through the smoky haze that gripped the city. The smoke caught the light and heated the city to a sweltering extreme. Wrapped in the smog, Luether occupied a greasy prison of its own making. What choices did they really have in such a place?

"You should eat." Regel indicated her stew. "It's clean. I checked."

"One cannot take too much care in a fallen city."

The bland stew looked far from appetizing, but she had only sipped a little of her tea before the ache in her stomach turned to ravenous hunger. The stew was over-salted and spicy enough to make her eyes water while the trencher was tougher than stone, but she ate greedily.

"So, what is it?" Regel asked over his stew.

"You always seem to know when I am bothered," Ovelia said. "Is it a gift or a curse?"

"Both," he replied. "So what is it?"

She couldn't tell him her true concerns. She had no right to do that, and it would not avail them. Perhaps she could speak of it indirectly. "It is this place," she said. "This city is so different from the Luether I remember. When I was last here, the taverns were full day and night, stuffed with folk drinking wine and jesting to all hours. But now..." She gestured around the common room, which was empty of all but a few hunched patrons who avoided her eye. "I watched the Ravalis flee from the city—saw the Children conquer Luether. Why did they allow the city to live, rather than tearing down every stone? Why let it endure like this? It is as though they torture it."

"Sometimes Ruin takes years, particularly when there is profit to be had." Regel pushed aside his half-eaten stew and took out the piece of wood he'd been carving. It had taken shape, but Regel cradled it in his hand such that Ovelia couldn't tell what it was. "The Children pillage Luether's corpse and squeeze out all the life they can devour. Only when all hope is gone and all coin exhausted, only then will the barbarians raze Luether and move on to a new victim. Like Echvar."

"Did the barbarians do this to that city as well?" Ovelia asked. "I thought you stopped them."

"We did." Regel looked down at his carving. "We killed everyone."

Ovelia shivered. "Perhaps... perhaps that was a mercy. The Children are horrific enough, but the Luethaar—nothing remains in their eyes. They are empty husks—little more than dogs, gnawing at one another's bellies. Why such misery? How can any man or woman live like this?"

Regel stared at her with piercing intensity. He had paused in his carving.

Ovelia fidgeted. "What passes?"

Regel set the carving on the table. "What do you think of the rebels? Garin Ravalis and the proscribed freedom fighters of Summer."

"What does this matter?" Suspicion rose in Ovelia. Regel was not one to speak idly, and she could not see why he would ask.

"Answer my question," Regel said. "Do you understand what they fight for?"

"They want their city returned," she said. "The Children spit and piss upon everything they hold dear. Of course they want it back."

"And they desire vengeance," he said.

"That as well," she said. "How many heirs of Ravalis died that night? If Orbrin—" She narrowed her eyes. "Why are you asking about this?"

Did he suspect her? Did he see through her game? She had to be cautious.

"What of the Children?" Regel asked. "Are they so much better than the Ravalis? Do they not have as much right to rule?"

"If you mean to ask me a question, Regel, ask it," Ovelia said. "None of these feints and gambits. What is your meaning?"

Regel stared down at the carving in his hand. He seemed far away and barely conscious of Ovelia's presence. When he looked up finally, he stared through her as though she were but a ghost—less than an illusion. In that moment, she knew exactly what he was thinking, for it echoed her own thoughts: that the years had left her but a shadow of the woman she had been.

When finally she could bear no more of Regel's indifference, Ovelia reached across the table and seized his face between her hands. "Regel, speak to me. What is it?"

Regel's eyes shot to her, and there was anger there. "You act as though you are so different," he said. "But in truth, you are no better than the worst of the Children."

Ovelia stared. "What?"

"It happens again and again." His jaw tightened. "A bright flame stands against the darkness, illuming the path of the world's destiny. But darkness festers at its heart, and vermin breed inside the walls of civilized men. A traitor strikes, and chaos befalls. Angarak, fifty years ago. Luether, twenty years ago. Echvar, fifteen years ago. And Tar Vangr, of course, five years ago."

Ovelia understood with a start what he meant. "But Tar Vangr yet stands against Ruin."

"Does it?" Regel's eyes narrowed. "It is as in Luether, when Blood Vultara threw open the gates to the barbarian hordes. Blood Dracaris—you—betrayed the rightful king of Tar Vangr to his death. And now the barbarians of summer rule our homeland. I see no difference." His voice grew cold as wintersteel. "Cities die slowly when mortally wounded."

Ovelia's heart beat faster. "Regel, that isn't what happened."

"No? You slew the last great light in Tar Vangr, and the Ravalis were the only ones who stood to gain." His eyes were glittering icicles. "I wonder if you were ever loyal to the Blood of Winter, or if you belonged to the Ravalis from the beginning."

"You cannot think that. You know how I loved Lenalin. You know how I loved Semana. She—"

"I do not believe you meant to slay Semana, no," Regel said. "But draw my sword for a breath: knowing what I know, seeing what I see, how can I not suspect that you are a servant of the Ravalis? I am simply to believe you were their prisoner for five years, and not that you are working with them to some greater evil?"

Ovelia could scarce contain her anxiety. He knew. Somehow, he knew, and he'd chosen this moment to confront her. "Regel, I—" She clenched her fists. "You don't understand. I have no love for the Ravalis. I—"

"You left me for one of them," Regel said, looking down at his hands.

Ovelia sat for a moment in startled silence. Then all her tension exploded in a cacophony of relieved laughter. She cut herself off an instant later, hand over her mouth.

He wasn't suspicious. He was *jealous.*

Also, he was angry, no doubt partly because of the laughter. He looked as though he might break his carving if he squeezed any tighter. "This... *amuses* you?"

Shame tinged her mirth, and she looked down at her stew. "I am sorry," she said.

"How long, Ovelia?" Regel asked. "Were you rutting him while we were together?"

"You... but..." Ovelia willed her quick boiling temper to a slow simmer. "You wish to discuss this here? In a public place?"

Still, he did not look upon her. "No."

The contempt in the word stole her breath. The silence stretched between them. Then, at length, he spoke again. "How did it feel?"

"Paeter and I—Regel, you were there. You must know that I—"

"Tsch." Regel made a dismissive sound, sucking on his teeth. "I care nothing for Paeter—I mean Orbrin." His blank eyes met hers. "The man we both loved—the man *you* killed."

"Do not—" Ovelia felt her heart thudding in her ears.

"How did it feel, to know every year of his life was draining away through your fingers—all of it cut away, on your blade?"

"Please." Anger rose in Ovelia, and her world shrank around her. She stared at Regel, her teeth on edge, her hands trembling. Draca smoked under her hand. "Do not ask me—"

"A man who trusted you," Regel said. "A man who entrusted his child to you."

"Regel." She saw again Orbrin's face, as she plunged the sword home. "Don't do this."

"A man you were supposed to love," he said. "A man who loved y——"

"Stop!" Ovelia shrieked, clutching her hands to her forehead. "Just *stop!*"

The Crimson Bath went silent and all eyes turned to their table. Ovelia was dimly aware of them, and every one was a spear pointed toward her. And the one who would kill her sat across the table, spear raised and ready to drive home.

"So he made you feel it," said Regel. "That's something for him, at least."

He picked up his spoon again and fell to his stew with a new interest.

"Burn you," Ovelia said.

Her chair scraped as she rose and strode to the mercyhall at the back of the tavern. She thrust the door shut and stood panting in the empty wasteroom, fighting the urge to scream. Her heart raced and her lungs couldn't seem to fill with air. She pressed her back to the oak door and covered her mouth, sure that if she did not, she would cry out and all would hear.

Finally, when her world expanded again beyond her own head, she looked around at her surroundings. Flaking paint on the walls of the mercyhall depicted lewd images of men and women at play. Along one wall ran half a dozen drainage bowls connected by a long pipe. This marvel unnerved Ovelia almost as much as the street sweeping machine from earlier: why could they not use proper chamberpots, as in Tar Vangr? The little bit of irked contempt made her feel better. Each stall was parted from the others by a thin green curtain that could be closed around it for privacy. Two of them were shut, but she saw no feet beneath the screens, so at least she was alone.

Across from the bowls, a series of taps stuck out of the wall over a long basin—a communal sink for washing hands. Some of these were rusted or twisted beyond repair, and some leaked grayish water. A thin pool of red and brown liquid rested at the bottom of the tub. Above the sink, a mirror hung on the wall, one end of it shattered by a blow. There were flecks of old blood upon the glass.

In this cracked mirror, Ovelia saw a split image of herself. She thought she looked very old—and angry. "I should be," she said. "It is not fair—not *just.*"

Orbrin had once told her—in this very city, no less, almost thirty years gone when she had railed against a false judgment by a Ravalis magistrate—that justice was a lie told by men to separate themselves from other men. He'd put his hand on her shoulder and said she must make her own justice. Ovelia had argued at the time, but in the past five years, she'd come to understand.

She turned the spigots and splashed water on her face. It felt oily, but at least it was cool. It melted her makeup, and she rubbed vigorously to rid herself of the rest of the stuff. She tore out her carefully arranged hair so that it hung haphazard around her face. Within five breaths, she had shed her disguise and looked like herself again, albeit haggard and half-mad. When she looked up at the mirror, she willed herself to ignore her red, cracked eyes. Her white-blonde hair was growing long now, revealing more of the red-brown roots near her scalp. Time marched relentlessly, and now her true colors were replacing the ones that made her another woman—the woman both she and Regel had once wanted her to be.

She wondered how to find silver dye in Luether, then smiled at her own folly. Would she live beyond the next few days—or even past tonight?

She admired her false smile in the mirror—it would hide anything a woman could think or feel. Lenalin had taught her that.

"He doesn't know," she told her reflection through her teeth, demanding mirth from her face. She forced herself to laugh. "He was just jealous—he doesn't know."

"A likely tale," she heard her own voice say.

Ovelia looked up, into her falsely smiling reflection. Had it spoken?

"Why would he be jealous?" she asked herself, watching her lips move. "He loved Lenalin, not her maid—her little red-haired *whore*."

The smile in the mirror looked positively hateful. It was not her. It was Lenalin, smirking at her.

"Sister," Ovelia hissed—at the mirror and at herself. "*Sister!*"

She struck the mirror with her gloved fist. Glass splintered and the whole mirror rocked back and forth on spindly wires. Ovelia backed away, startled, as the left-most hanging gave way and the mirror swung down at her like a sword. She dodged and it struck the long basin, shattering half the glass into the murky liquid. The remaining mirror swung madly from the wire on the right end.

Ovelia looked at her dozen images in the mirror as it rocked back and forth, distorting the room with every pass. Which of them was she? Which—?

"You loved every word he said to you," the images accused. "You *want* him to hurt you, you whore. Nothing more than you deserve—"

"It's not true," Ovelia argued. "It's not—"

A figure moved behind her, and she had just enough time to whirl before a hand clapped over her mouth. "Syr Dracaris," said a voice in her ear. "Mask awaits."

Cold steel kissed her throat.

~

After a thirty-count, Regel looked up from his stew once again. It had long ago lost its warmth and now tasted of nothing so much as sodden paper, but it had done the job. It had provided a distraction while he needed it.

It let him watch the man following them.

Regel had seen him back near the docks, and again after the roving machine almost struck Ovelia. The same man had been waiting in the common room of the Crimson Bath when they'd come up from the cellar. Ever since, he'd been watching them from a table across the way, in front of a plate of food that he barely touched.

The man's loyalties were a question, so Regel had given him plenty of talk to listen to, hoping to provoke a reaction. All the while, he'd used his focus to watch the man without watching, paying little attention to Ovelia. The plan had gone well until he'd found himself asking about Paeter Ravalis and she had laughed. That reaction—her *laughter*—at the reminder of her treachery had caused Regel to forget all about the man following them. He'd found himself speaking without thought, words falling from his lips meant to wound. He'd been cruel, and cruelty was not in his nature. He'd thrown her bloodbreaking in her face just to hurt her, and it had worked. She had stormed off, furious and newly set against him.

Worse, the man who'd followed them was gone. No doubt, he'd gone to report them to whoever was coming to kill them now. Regel would have to get Ovelia out of here, but first, he'd have to apologize. Arguing with her had no purpose, when they were united in a single cause.

And so he found himself opening the door to the mercyhall, Ovelia's name on his lips.

He stopped, and his mind came to a sudden, violent halt. Ovelia was standing near the south wall, held about the neck by the man who'd followed them, with a knife at her throat. He had a southern tinge to his skin and the reddish-blond hair one might expect of a summerblood.

"Syr Dracaris," the slayer said. "Mask awaits. I have found—"

Regel darted across the room and ripped the man away. His voice cut off and Ovelia collapsed, coughing, to the floor. The knife skittered away under the washbasin and the slayer reached up to where Regel's strangle-wire tightened around his throat. The man slammed him back against the wall hard enough to make his teeth ring, but Regel held on anyway. They spun and the man dashed Regel into the stand of waste bowls in a hail of splintering wood. Regel held on, sweaty red hair plastered to his cheek.

He was strong, Regel gave him that.

Face red, the slayer slammed his elbow back into Regel's side, crunching ribs. This time, Regel faltered, and he got a hand under the wire. No use for it now. Regel disengaged and rolled free to crouch beside the kneeling slayer, who coughed and sputtered.

"Regel?" Ovelia murmured, her voice cracked. "Regel—wait..."

The slayer went for another blade, but Regel followed through with a knee to the stomach that doubled the man over. He went for his own steel but the slayer shoved forward, driving them away from the wall and into the water basin. Hard ceramic snapped off behind Regel's backside, and the sharp edges cut into his legs. His head crashed back into the wall, destroying his balance. Dimly, vision shaking, he saw his attacker grab him by the shirt and wind back a fist.

By instinct, Regel flinched aside and his attacker cried out as he punched the remaining shards of the broken mirror. The shock startled him, and Regel saw shards of glass among the spy's knuckles. Regel got his arms around the man and shoved. His cloak caught on the broken basin and jerked them both sprawling to the floor.

Both men went down in a heap, punching and kicking and ripping. Blood from the slayer's wounded hand smeared across Regel's face as fingers scrabbled for his mouth and his eyes. Regel elbowed him in the ear, stunning him, and rolled over on top. He drew back his hand, palm open, ready to shatter the man's nose and crush his head into the floorboards.

"Wait!" Ovelia pleaded. "Stop!"

Regel looked, and his muscles froze in hesitation. With the light shining in her white-gold hair and her hands clasped before her, pleading, he almost thought it was Lenalin kneeling there.

But it was only Ovelia, he realized, and he had hesitated too long.

His opponent punched him hard in the center of the chest. Regel jerked, fire lancing through him, and fell to the floor with a groan. The slayer pulled a knife from his boot and jabbed it down, but Regel caught his wrist and held him back.

"For the Ravalis," the man hissed.

Regel pushed, but the spy was younger—stronger.

"Stop, Syr Damos!" Ovelia said. "I command you!"

The slayer shivered, caught with indecision, and Regel reversed his thrust. The man wheezed as the blade sank between two of his ribs. Blood welled around the hilt. He blinked, mouth working.

"Syr," he murmured, looking at Ovelia. "Silver F—ahh!" His cry of agony split the room, until Regel choked it off with a warding hand.

"Look at me." Regel crouched over him, hands grasping his face. "Look at *me*, not at her." He locked eyes with the slayer. "Where? Where is Mask?"

Ovelia spoke cautiously. "Regel—"

Regel shot her a dangerous look. "You shut your burning mouth!"

"It hurts." The man coughed blood onto Regel's face. "By the Fire, it hurts!"

"I'll end it," Regel said. "Tell me where Mask is, and I'll end it."

The man—barely more than a boy, Regel realized—met his eyes. "In... in Aertem's temple," he said. "Seek... the rose stone... Please!" Blood flowed out his mouth. "Please!"

"Burn you, Regel!" Ovelia cried.

Regel punched his hand into the butt of the dagger, driving it so deep the hilt slapped against flesh. The slayer's eyes rolled up and, slowly, he toppled back to the floor. Regel could just see the blade tenting the back of the man's leathers— which grew quickly sodden with heart blood. There was pain on the man's face, but it eased. He closed the slayer's eyes.

Slowly, Regel rose and turned to Ovelia, who was staring at the scene. "Syr." Regel wiped the blood from his face, smearing it with the blood on his hand. "He called you *Syr*."

Ovelia didn't seem at all like Lenalin anymore. Her eyes were dangerous and she had her hand on her blade. They stood together, two warriors breathing in the familiar scent of death—letting it arouse their senses and remind them of violent, glorious days. Days spent *together*.

Ovelia backed a step away.

"You knew him," Regel said. "You knew his name."

"Regel." Ovelia put her hand to the hilt of her sword and backed toward the door.

He crossed the room, seized her by the shoulders, and shoved her against the door jam. "Speak," he demanded. "And no lies. How did you know that man? Who was he?"

"Syr Damos, Knight of Summer," Ovelia said. "He was one of mine."

"One of *yours*?" Regel grasped her tighter. "What do you mean?"

"He——" Ovelia looked at the man's corpse. "He volunteered for this, for a chance to meet you. You, the legendary Frostburn. You were his hero."

"Make this make sense!" Regel shook her. "How did you know him? Whom does he——?"

"The Ravalis," she said. "Old Gods, Regel—think! I live because of the *Ravalis*."

"You serve them." He narrowed his eyes. "You *serve* them."

"*Served*," Ovelia corrected. "After Orbrin, they made me their spymaster. Yes—I was the Shroud, all this time." She gave him a warning look. "I knew all about you. I knew all about your Circle of Tears."

"And you never moved against me, why?" Regel said, daring her to lie. "Out of sentiment?"

"No," she said. "I haven't moved against you because I've been waiting—waiting for a chance at Mask. I knew I would need you—that without you, I would fail. For five years, I have waited, and he has finally resurfaced. Now I've played everyone against each other so that I could gather the resources—people—I needed, and get free to exact justice. Nothing matters more than that. *Nothing*."

"I don't understand." Regel grasped her arms tighter and pressed her into the wall. He nodded over his shoulder at the dead man. "If he was yours, why did he have a blade at your throat? Why?"

"Because I *betrayed* them, Regel," she said. "I manipulated them as I needed, found you, and fled. I had set Damos to find Mask in Luether, and when we arrived together, he—he didn't know what to think, and I couldn't stop you from killing him." She reached up as though to touch his cheek, but Regel caught her hand roughly. Any tenderness she might have held at that moment fled, and when she looked into his eyes she spoke without emotion. "You're hurting me."

"I'll hurt you more if you don't answer," Regel said. "The castermen in the Burned Man, the Dusters at the safehouse... they were yours as well? You planned all of this. Why?"

"I needed it to seem real," Ovelia said. "I told them we were attacking you, that this was all to get a clear shot at you. I lied to them, Regel, just like I lied to you, because I needed you to believe the Ravalis were after me, so that you'd help me. I know the sort of man you are, Regel."

The skin of Regel's arms and neck prickled at the realization of how she had manipulated him, but he stuffed down the anger. "You have done nothing but lie to me," he said. "Why should I trust you now? Why should I believe that you are no longer in league with the Ravalis?"

"You can see the truth on my face." Ovelia turned her head, showing him the mark on her cheek where the slayer had narrowly missed her head with a casterbolt.

"As soon as they shot to kill in the Burned Man, I knew. They'd seen through my betrayal, and they were there to kill me. I'm alone now. Alone but for you."

"No." Regel slammed her back into the wall, wrenching a breathless gasp from her lips. "You're still alone." In a heartbeat, he drew a dagger and pressed it to her throat. "Stop lying to me!"

Tears welled in Ovelia's eyes. "I'm not—"

There came a knock at the door behind Ovelia. The sound froze them both in place.

"Syr?" It was the owner of the Crimson Bath. She could not open the door with Ovelia pressed against it. "Syr? Pass well?"

Regel opened his mouth, but Ovelia shook her head and mouthed a single word. "Me."

Of course. Ovelia had rented the cellar, and she had been the one who went loudly into the mercyhall. She was the one who had to respond, or the whole game ended. Regel realized, abruptly, that even though he was the one with the knife at her throat, she still had just as much power to end him. And if he did not let her speak, he lost anyway.

Through the door, a caster was being wound. He had to decide quickly.

It was like another moment, in far away Tar Vangr, when the patrol had come upon them in theSquare of the Fallen, and she had pressed him against the wall like a lover, hiding them both in the open. He'd kissed her then as well, with lips rather than steel. Ovelia's eyes were unreadable, looking to him as though considering or for guidance. Was she remembering the same moment?

At length, Regel nodded and eased the knife away.

Ovelia cleared her throat. "Well," as she looked into Regel's eyes. "Well?"

Regel held her tight as the woman left. His fingers clenched tight around the handle of his knife. She'd given him all the power again, sacrificed her chance to escape. She trusted him.

"Regel, please." Ovelia's voice trembled. "I'm telling you the truth."

"Are you?" He nodded to the corpse on the floor, which was going pale as its blood leaked into a spreading pool. "This is all a game to you. My life, the lives of my Circle, of Serris..."

"No." Ovelia shook her head, tears streaming down her cheeks. "I wanted none of your folk hurt. I only wanted you to come with me. I didn't lie about Mask, Regel. I give you my word." Her hot breath tickled his face. "You have to believe me."

"Why?" His heart hammered in his chest. The knife trembled in his hand.

"You want to believe me," Ovelia said. "Do you not?"

"That's not enough." He pressed himself against her, felt her body melt into his like fire-softened wax, stinging and thrilling. "Why shouldn't I kill you right now?"

"Because—" He could feel Ovelia's heart fluttering. "Because—Regel, I—"

The knife clattered to the floor, falling from Regel's opening hand.

He caught her face between his palms.

Then he was kissing her—and she was kissing him back.

TEN

Tar Vangr

REGEL HAD BEEN GONE for six days when the doors of the Burned Man burst open, admitting a swirl of snow. A haggard man staggered in, his legs trembling at the effort required to hold him up. Meron was his name—an elder of the Circle of Tears and given a very important task. The common room fell silent and all eyes turned toward him.

He did not need to speak. His ashen face said all that needed to be told.

In her private booth, Serris heard the sudden hush and drew aside the curtain to look. "You should eat something," Erim was saying, but she held up a hand to silence him. She'd allowed him to rub her shoulders tonight—Old Gods, she was tense—and perhaps it would have turned into something more. After all, the beautiful boy had never proved entirely useless in her bed. She did not love him the way he wanted, but she enjoyed his company.

As soon as Meron appeared, though, she ignored Erim's ministrations completely and went to meet her agent. He gave her a weary salute—a finger held beneath his eye—which she returned, then held him under the shoulder while Erim took his other side. The Tear agent was obviously exhausted and needed help to hobble to the back rooms. There, he tried to speak, but Serris shushed him and tore open his cloak to look for wounds. His middle was a mess of blood and sweat.

"Erim!" Serris said. "Fetch Vidia."

The boy ran off, leaving Serris alone with her wounded agent. Meron was one of the best Tears: a former specialist in the army of Winter, discharged after the Ravalis came to power. He knew the value of completing a mission, regardless of the sacrifices required. She helped him to an open bedchamber and shooed away the two men using it. Meron groaned as he lay back on the soft sheets, spattering them with blood. "It's not all mine," he said.

"Speak to me," Serris said, shoving her hands on top of the wound.

"Krystir is dead," he said.

Serris had feared that. When the agent they'd placed in Lan Ravalis's bed had not reported back after the attack on the Burned Man, she'd feared the worst and sent Meron to learn what had happened to her. Clearly, he had. "They follow you? We can hide you."

"No—no need." He shook his head. "Three men came after me. I killed them all, but I didn't get out clean. Sorry, Syr. There's more—"

"Save it," Serris said. "It can wait."

"No." Meron reached up and caught her collar with one shaking hand. His breath tasted like blood and bile. "There's more. I—you need to hear this."

"What is it?" Serris asked.

"The *Avenger*," Meron said with effort. "She's leaving high-city tonight, bound for Luether."

Serris's heart picked up a quick pace. "What?"

The door banged open behind them, and Erim and Vidia pushed in. The healer had brought her kit. "Serris, move," she said.

Serris scowled and looked Meron in the eye. "When?"

"Within the hour," he said. "I only just—*nhh*—heard word of it. I—" His words dissolved into choking, and Vidia shoved Serris aside so she could get to work.

Serris drew away and ran her crimson-drenched hands through her hair, smoothing it back, and laced her fingers at the back of her neck. "Old Gods," she said. "They're going after him."

"Are we sure this is a problem?" Erim asked. As ever, his logic tempered Serris's reaction. "It might just be a quiet trade mission, or some Blood Heir out for a jaunt."

Serris considered. Even if he was a Child of Ruin and a sworn enemy of the Ravalis whose throne he had usurped, King Pervast did trade with nobles of Tar Vangr who could stomach him. Twenty years after the fall of the Burning City, a sort of peace existed between the mage-cities, and those with coin could travel between them. Many wanted to see the fabled city on the edge of Ruin for themselves. Rumors abounded that elements within the Vangryur nobility often met with Luethaar nobles to plot against the Ravalis, so most trips were made under the watchful eye of Ravalis Dust Knights.

But no one could overlook the symbolism of sending the *Avenger*, which was no mere noble pleasure craft. After the Ravalis had come to power, they had stripped the flagship of Tar Vangr of its armaments, but it remained a military ship: fast, heavily armored, and ready at short notice to be deployed to carry hundreds of troops. It could reach Luether within a day, two at most, and a clandestine launch meant they were hiding their movements. It made Serris feel cold and afraid: whatever the Ravalis intended, this launch was not a good thing.

"How many troops on the *Avenger*?" she asked.

Meron gritted his teeth against Vidia's ministrations. "I don't know. Only that if we're going to catch the launch, we have to move now."

Serris nodded. "Make ready."

"Serris, wait." Erim said. "Think. What if this is a trap?"

Serris shook his hand away. "We move," she said. "Fetch Nacacia and Daren. Bring steel, casters, and whatever mortars we can drum up. Wear masks."

"I'll be up in a breath, Syr," Meron said.

He tried to rise, but Vidia pushed him down onto the bed. "No you won't," she said. "This isn't a mortal wound, but it's deep enough. You're not leaving this bed."

Meron looked at Serris. "I can do it," he said. "Nacacia and Daren aren't enough. You need me."

Serris weighed the risks, then nodded. "Patch him up. We move within the hour."

Vidia scowled to indicate her diapproval, but she nodded and started her work all the same. She shoved Serris toward the door. "Out!"

Serris led Erim into the corridor. Several of the Tears were already there, including Nacacia and Daren, come to investigate Meron's dramatic arrival. Serris gave them swift instructions, and they hurried off to obey while she leaned against the wall, seething. Erim stood waiting and looking at her with a familiar, doting look she found at times appealing and at others—like now—infuriating.

"Are you sure about Meron?" Erim asked. "He's one of the best we have, but he's no Lord of Tears. If he's too hurt—"

"This is unacceptable, Erim." Serris pushed herself up off the wall. "Say you understand."

Whatever he'd been expecting her to say, that caught him by surprise. "I just thought—"

"I don't care what you thought," Serris said. "I'm in command in my master's absence. You don't question me, particularly in front of the other Tears. Say you understand."

"I understand." Erim hung his head. "I just thought it might be dangerous."

Serris made a dismissive sound. "Well, good thing you'll be there, too."

❧

As the five rode the clanking, shuddering lift toward high-city, Serris's body shook with anxiety and excitement. For days, the Ravalis had done nothing, but she'd waited in constant readiness for their move. She'd slept only an hour or two each night, and had to force herself to eat what little she had. The constant vigilance was beginning to take its toll on her.

And until that night, it had seemed for naught. Mostly, the ruling Blood had gone about their usual business, but the patrols had notably increased in the streets, ostensibly to combat "unrest." But that could be because the Council was making noises about questioning their decisions, particularly the massive build-up in weapons that the Summer Princes seemed to have initiated. Strengthening patrols was a natural response, which would slacken off as politics died down.

The Ravalis refused to acknowledge the incident at the Burned Man in any way, and of course they wouldn't. It would make them look weak at best, or in direct conflict with the Council's edicts at worst. The Ravalis seemed to have let it go, but they had to know their agents had failed. Was sending the *Avenger* their counterstroke? Dispatch a small army to retrieve Regel and the Bloodbreaker, alive or dead? The very thought made Serris want to scream or kill someone. Preferably the latter.

Serris kept her gaze fixed on the skyport, high above. She could make out the

Avenger, which was being prepped for launch. Beneath its hull, Serris could see its mage-engine spooling up for the journey as its three great golden rings stirred. They had little time. If they were to use the mortars on Daren's belt to disable the skyship, it would have to be soon, before she launched and soared out of range. So Serris had two reasons to want to be out of the snow quickly and done with this business.

Nacacia coughed and fidgeted with her mask. "Pass well?" Serris asked.

"Can hardly breathe," Nacacia said, her voice muffled by leather and the porous breath filter. Daren extended his cloak over her head while she adjusted her mask. "Hardly see, either."

Serris's own experience agreed. The snow grew thick as they ascended out of low-city, even as the air grew cleaner away from the slums. If they were caught outside in a blizzard in low-city, their lives would be short and painful. Fortunately, the constant heat of the Narfire beneath the streets turned most caustic snow to acidic rain, which was bad but tolerable. The snow in high-city was mostly an annoyance rather than a risk, but Serris did not relish fighting in the stinging haze.

"What about you?" Serris asked Meron, who shivered at her side. "You with me?"

"Ready for a fight, Syr." He coughed and adjusted his stance.

He'd seemed recovered after the Burned Man, but his newfound vigor seemed to crumble beneath the blizzard's onslaught. Vidia had cleared him for service, but she'd made it clear it was against her better judgment. Serris was short on choices, however, with the Tears spread over the city and Regel a thousand leagues away. She prayed she hadn't jeopardized Meron's recovery by bringing him.

"Shouldn't have brought *any* of them," she said beneath her voice. "Should have just come alone. That what you would have done, Master?"

But of course Regel was not there, and could not answer.

Erim touched her wrist and nodded toward the liftmaster: a summerblood by his coloration, though he'd pulled his cowl low over his face.

"What of him?" Serris asked. "He look at you wrong?"

"That's the problem," Erim said. "He hasn't looked at any of us this whole time. Not when I gave him the coin, not when I tried to address him. He's anxious."

Serris felt cold, and it had nothing to do with the snow. They wore thick weathercloaks and leather masks, but if the Ravalis were waiting for them, then disguises would not matter. Had they already been identified? She reached for her dagger—the same one Regel had given her five years ago, when he had named her. With her other hand, she smoothly drew her caster. The others noticed and tensed.

The Ravalis ambush awaited them as soon as the lift shuddered to a halt and the gate swung wide: seven Dusters, all of them bearing swords charged with smoking thaumaturgy.

Seven, Serris thought. Even *one* would be bad.

This was a trap, and she had led her companions straight into its jaws.

She looked at her fellow Tears, who were starting to fade away in the growing blizzard. Their faces were determined beneath frost-rimmed masks, and their hands lingered on their steel. They would follow her into the Narfire itself if she led them there.

The leader of the Dust Knights she recognized: an aspiring knight by the name of Rieten, not an heir of the Ravalis but a "married" relative. Serris had nothing but contempt for the concept, which the summermen had introduced to Tar Vangr when she was a child. Based on what she had seen, "marriage" was like the alliance of two noble Bloods, sealed with a half-moon of passionate sex and other intimacies, followed by a lifetime spent in a single bed. To her, a "marriage" seemed mostly an excuse for a weak man to exercise power over a woman far his superior, little more than another Ravalis invention: slavery. How anyone could justify such cowardice she could not guess.

Even if he was related to the Blood Ravalis only through such a blasphemous union, Rieten certainly hated women as much as they did, and more than once Serris had seen Tears patched up after an encounter with him. Serris herself had shared his bed once, and it was not an encounter she meant to repeat. Rieten wore fine armor and carried a duelist's sword in a scabbard inlaid with gold—powered with lightning thaumaturgy, no doubt, as was the wont of a Summerland bravo. Rieten was not a warrior, that much was clear, but Serris knew that he had not a scrap of pity in him.

Rieten stepped forward with a satisfied grin. "Unknown slayers, down arms and submit—"

Serris shot him in the face with her caster.

She hadn't scored a direct hit—she'd had to fire on a quick draw—but blood bloomed. Rieten staggered and fell so hard on the glass floor of the dock that it cracked under his weight.

The night erupted in a flurry of casterbolts and flashing blades. The Tears took them by surprise, which they needed. Otherwise, Serris knew they wouldn't have survived the first moment of battle.

Duster blades lit up with borrowed magic, and the Tears scattered to make themselves difficult, separate targets. Serris had to trust them, as it took all of her focus to dodge aside just before one of the Dusters fired a bolt of lightning through the spot where she had been standing. The intense current made her skin shudder and her teeth vibrate in her mouth, but it missed. She rolled along the edge of the lift and balanced precariously over a vast dropoff. The liftmaster raised a caster, but Serris kicked out at his wrist and sent the weapon sailing off into the bleary night. He blocked her follow-up punch and knocked her staggering back toward the edge. Even over that short distance, he vanished back into the swirling storm.

The snow whipped into a blizzard around her, making steam rise from her weathercloak. Serris clasped the cloak tight about her body, and breathed raggedly through her mask. The flurry had to pass soon, or they would choke and die out here. The dirty snow cut her sense of the rest of the fight to nothing, except for occasional cries of pain and flashes of light as a Duster's blade exploded with magic.

Sighting on one of these, Serris set a bolt in her caster, but before she could recharge it for another shot, a single hazy shadow loomed over her. By luck, a chopping blade hit the caster rather than her hand, and the weapon fell crackling to the glass floor. The tip of the sword tore her sleeve open to the snow, but her flesh was unbroken.

As Serris fell back, her hand ringing with pain, the liftmaster raised his weapon for another strike. It was a short and heavy thing, more like a butcher's cleaver than a sword. A poor man's blade.

"Little bitch," he said. "Rut you with this blade, I will. Make you scream for more."

Serris held her dagger pressed against her arm in an overhanded grip. She did not know what had driven the Ravalis and their loyal servants to hate women so much, but at least it meant the man might underestimate her, which would prove his undoing. Not that she could afford to underestimate *him*: he was heavier, stronger, and better armed. She backed up cautiously, and her feet edged over empty air. The lift railing had broken off in this spot long ago. The liftmaster could shove her over the edge without much difficulty—not that he would have to, with his superior reach. She had to lure him in close.

"Want to rut me?" she said. "Come claim me."

He reached forward with his empty hand, and Serris waited until he had almost closed it on her arm. Then she brought the razor-sharp dagger around and cut his hand open with a quick slash.

The liftmaster withdrew, surprised, and looked at the bright blood oozing through his cut glove. "You're a prickly one. I like that," he said, as though it were a compliment.

He reached forward more forcefully, as though that would make a difference, and Serris stepped past and opened him three times: hand, wrist, and arm. He scrambled for her, and she cut him in the armpit. He lacked the Dusters' steel armor, and his leathers parted easily beneath her sharp wintersteel.

She expected the liftmaster would retreat, having suffered five wounds in quick succession, but instead he bulled foward. The man ignored her cuts like the stings of angry but merely annoying bees. The look on his face was one she'd seen before: a big man who simply does not understand how a much smaller woman could be thwarting him.

Serris slashed the liftmaster and dodged his clumsy strikes again and again, bleeding him cut by cut. When he switched to the sword to hack at her, he lacked the strength to lift it. He struck lazily, and when she slashed the inside of his elbow, the liftmaster dropped the sword with something like relief. When he finally staggered back, he bled from over a dozen slashes. Only three ragged breaths had passed between them.

The liftmaster looked at her confusedly, and Serris shrugged. She did not need to explain his stupidity, only exploit it. He lurched toward her with one final grab, but she side-stepped and let him stumble over the edge. He flailed weakly for balance, fingers scrabbling at her, but Serris only wrenched her weathercloak away. The man fell silently into the snowy night.

Snow swirled to reveal the shadows of Tears and Dusters struggling to find one another in the flurry. Serris thanked the Old Gods for the snow that had saved their lives thus far: the stinging, clinging muck distracted the Dusters and threw off their aim. Several of them flailed blindly in the blizzard, hacking at every flicker of movement. A clatter of steel drew attention, and one of the Dust Knights sent a blast of flame in that direction, causing a second knight to curse as the dust magic shattered on his shield.

One of the Dusters looked more confident in the snow—perhaps this one was native to Tar Vangr and thus accustomed to fighting in the weather, like Serris herself. She had pinned down Nacacia and was hammering at her sword like a woodsman splitting a stump.

Serris kept low as she scuttled toward one of the confused Dusters and leaped onto his back. She took advantage of his surprise to seize hold of his swordarm and wrap her other arm around his neck. Against his strength, she pointed his sword, which burned with imbued thaumaturgy, at the Duster who had almost broken Nacacia's defense. When she had the aim right, Serris tore her dagger across under her captive's helmet. Blood gushed, and the dying man loosed his sword's fire. The intense heat scalded Serris through her cut sleeve, but she held on. The struck Duster shrieked as her armor melted onto her body, and Nacacia ducked aside to let her leap off the lift.

Serris swore inwardly. She hated killing women, and the Ravalis—with their hereditary contempt for anything female—usually obliged her by setting men in her path. The Duster she'd just killed must have fought hard for a position in the king's elite guard. She'd been winterborn, too, which made her death an insult to the Circle of Tears and Tar Vangr. Shame.

Serris wiped lifeblood from her face and surveyed the situation. Four Dusters were down, along with the captain, and the liftmaster was long gone. Erim and Nacacia were dispatching a fifth Duster, who fended off their blades desperately. A sixth, increasingly weary Duster traded blows with Daren. Against all odds, the Tears were winning. And yet, the ground trembled under Serris's feet.

Then a horn rumbled like resonant thunder, so loud it forced Serris and the other Tears to their knees. A fire lit in the darkness behind the swirling snow, like the burning eye of a great beast.

"Ironclad!" Nacacia cried.

The two women threw themselves aside as a bolt of flame burned the air between them, searing the mage-glass black and crackling where they had stood. A Lancer charged onto the lift station, its mighty axe screeching against the glass at its side. Daren shot at it with his caster, but the bolt skipped off its armored shoulder. The Lancer turned and dispelled the snowy mist with its cannon, catching one of the staggering Dusters with the blast. The man burned away in a white hot beam wherein his body became a blackened skeleton. Dazzled by the thamurgical explosion, Serris could not see if Daren had survived.

Across the way, Meron hurled a grenade at the Lancer, but the alchemical blast hardly bruised its thick armor. It turned its cannon on him, and he ducked behind the wall crenellation just in time—Serris hoped. The mechanical beast headed that direction, ponderous and wary. Its axe hacked at Meron's cover while its cannon recharged, ready to blast him to dust if he reappeared.

Serris leveled the stolen Duster's sword at the Lancer's back, but its dust magic managed only a sputtering flame that did little more than draw its attention. The burning eye settled on her, and she could see the smirking face of a Ravalis soldier inside. The Lancer's scoping axe haft extended and the blade shot at Serris like a hurled spear. She rolled aside, even as the blade cracked the glass where she had stood, and rolled to her feet. As she ran, she hurled the useless Duster sword into the blizzard.

She had to get to Daren and the mortars. Nothing else they carried could take out a Ravalis ironclad: their blades would bend and their casterbolts skip off its armor to no effect. They could keep drawing its attention, but sooner or later the soldier inside the Lancer would start ignoring their attacks and simply kill them one by one. Serris wasn't sure she could fire a mortar accurately enough to hit the Lancer, and the thing stood directly between her and where she'd last seen Daren and his pack anyway. She risked a glance, and across the way she saw Darren struggling to push himself up—the blast must have winged him. A wonder it hadn't cut him in half.

"Keep moving!" Serris shouted to the Tears.

She ran, trying to circle around the ironclad, but a massive axe crashed down into the glass right in front of her, and she fell back, startled. Cracks spread in all directions. The cannon took aim at her, but she kicked off the axe and scrambled the other way, and the fiery beam did little more than make her ears ring. If she couldn't get to Daren, she had to keep the Lancer occupied so it did not turn on him. She had to give him a chance to fire at its back.

"Hey, small-blade!" Serris cried at the Lancer. "Can't hit your target? Small wonder women laugh at you." She made an obscene gesture.

The pilot of the Lancer probably couldn't hear her, but the hand signal seemed to have worked. The cannon adjusted its aim, though it could not keep up with her. Its axe, on the other hand, kept smashing into the glass not a pace from her, or slashed over her head as she ducked and rolled.

A shadow appeared out of the gloom, bent over and waiting for her. She realized it was Meron, retching out his guts onto the mage-glass at their feet. Blood soaked his chest, and Serris realized his wound had come open again. He must have lost his mask because when he looked up at her, his face was white as death. "Syr," he panted. "I—"

The butt of the Lancer's axe caught her on the backswing with enough force to rattle her bones and send her sprawling toward the sheer drop-off. She rolled to a stop, half on, half off, and lay flat on her back, staring at the roaring blizzard, ears ringing and her senses scattered in all directions.

How beautiful the snowflakes were, swirling above her head, swept cautiously around one another in what could be a duel or a dance of passion. Her leather mask had come loose, and a flake of snow landed on her skin. It burned.

The searing pain woke her with a start, and she rubbed at her scarred cheek. She bolted up, remembering only afterward that the Lancer was still there. By chance, the backswing of the axe had knocked her behind a solid stone wall half the height of a man, erected to keep anyone from wandering off the edge of high-city. She knelt only a pace away from snowy oblivion—indeed, one of her legs had been hanging off the edge. With a shiver, Serris got her bearings and peered over the low wall.

She could only have been stunned for a few breaths, but in that time the Lancer had pinned the Tears down. Nacacia crouched behind the wall on the opposite side, winding one after the other of her heavy casters, charging each for a shot. Even as she did, the Lancer methodically advanced on her, the mage-glass groaning under its heavy tread, its axe hacking away at the wall over her head. Erim and Meron were nowhere to be seen, if they even still lived. Serris could just make out Daren lying where she had left him, but she couldn't tell if he was dead or simply feigning death to keep from being a target. Either way, he could not ready a mortar without the Lancer shifting focus and blasting him to ash.

A wild thought occurred to her. It was tantamount to self-slaughter, but so was doing nothing.

"Cass!" Serris signaled to Nacacia, who nodded and tossed a heavy caster in Serris's direction. Serris rolled into the open, plucked the weapon from the air, and leveled it at the Lancer. The casterbolt flew straight and true and blasted into the Lancer's central hatch. The metal groaned and a crack ran through its bright orange eye.

That got the Lancer's attention. It turned and leveled its cannon at her. Serris could see fire roiling inside the weapon, like screaming, burning death.

Behind the Lancer, Daren rolled over, two mortars in his hands. They fired off, trailing smoke, and flew right past the Lancer, then up into the night. And like that, all was lost.

"Get back!" Nacacia shouted.

At first, Serris could hardly think, let alone understand. Even the Lancer looked up, registering the attack but seeming to laugh at its ineffectiveness. The burning eye fixed upon Serris once more and the cannon took aim.

Then she heard a loud whine, turned, and ran.

The mortars shot back down and detonated on either side of the Lancer, throwing off its aim. The ironclad staggered as the glass around it cracked, splintered, and finally gave way. The mage-glass collapsed beneath its feet, and the Lancer tumbled down into the blizzard amidst a cascade of glass, stone, and flame. The war machine scrambled at the edges like a drowning man, then was gone.

Cracks shot through the glass beneath Serris's feet. She leaped, and Nacacia reached down to catch her. Her weight almost pulled Nacacia into the abyss after her, but the woman's tightly-corded muscles strained and she kept Serris aloft with a groan. Serris slapped at the broken edges of the glass, cutting open her gloves and fingers, but she couldn't get a grip. She was going to fall.

Then Erim leaned over the edge and grabbed her wrist in both hands. Meron appeared, choking against the blizzard, and put his hands over Nacacia's to help the already strained woman Together, they pulled Serris up, then lay together heaving in the swirling blizzard. Nacacia panted and heaved air into her already burned lungs while Meron sat against the half-wall, panting and smiling. Erim helped Serris rise shakily. He looked terrified and weary and beautiful. She had never been more grateful to see him, and she wanted nothing more than to throw her arms around him. Then his eyes went wide as he saw something over her shoulder.

"Serris!" Erim cried in warning, his blond hair tangled in his masked face.

Too late, she saw the final two Dusters lurking by the edge of the lift: Rieten and one of his last knights. The commander had survived her casterbolt, but he bled profusely from a vicious gash in his forehead. Like the coward he was, Rieten had secreted himself behind the controls, along with his last Duster, who pointed a sword dripping venomous green magic straight at her.

"Kill her, Squire!" he shouted. "Kill the scarred whore!"

The last Duster—he must be a mere boy if Rieten called him squire—held the sword pointing at her, his hands trembling only a little. "Whore." He hid behind the word like a shield. "Whore."

Serris saw indignation in Rieten's brown eyes, and knew its source. It enraged him to see a *woman* who was the equal of not one of his companions, but three or more, and an ironclad besides. Rieten was defeated and he knew it, but his squire could strike one final blow.

Serris locked the young Duster's eyes with her own. She raised her master's dagger to throw just as the magic blazed forth in a sizzling torrent. There was no way she could dodge.

"Serris!" A shadow interposed itself in front of her. It turned its back, raised its cloak, and intercepted the eruption. Magic exploded over her protector's back, spattering around the edges of his cloak. Serris saw his bone-white face—it was Meron—and watched his expression go from shock to agony to acceptance. Finally, it was over, and he collapsed forward, smoke rising from his back. She caught him in her arms and staggered under his weight.

Serris stared past Meron in shock at the Duster squire, who looked right back at her. His gaze dropped to the wound he had inflicted, and Serris saw him stand up straight in shock.

When Meron pressed his shoulder into her chest, Serris could not help but look down his back. The magic had burned right through his weathercloak and armor, leaving scraps fused to his flesh. The skin and most of his musclature was gone, and dissolving ribs arched out of a corpse left to rot in Ruin's rain. He pressed his sweaty cheek against her neck and shuddered.

"Meron, all passes well." Serris eased Meron to the glass below them. "You saved me."

The sounds of mage-engines roared to life farther up the dock. The *Avenger* slid off into the night. It slipped toward the ground a few paces before the engines flared and the ship rose into the sky. The engine's three gold rings began their slow orbits around the ship, cloaking it in buoyant magic. The Tears were too late, but that no longer mattered.

"Hold, Meron," Serris said. "Just—"

Instead of speaking, Meron coughed traces of acid onto her face. Bloody foam leaked from the edge of his lips. He should have died instantly, but instead he leaned against her and shuddered. Great rending sobs ran through him, and a horrible screeching sound wrenched itself from his throat. He drooled blood and bile and convulsed, his body fighting to stay alive. Meron pawed at Serris, tearing at her clothes and twisting his fingers in her hair.

"Help!" Serris said. "Someone help him!"

Nacacia and Daren stalked toward the last two foes. Reiten shouted orders at his squire, who merely stared at what he had done to Meron. Finally, as the Tears approached, the unknown boy noticed them and realized he had to defend himself or flee. He took the third option: with a sob, he leaped from the skydock into the fragmented abyss. Rieten stared after him, then his shoulders slumped in defeat.

"Someone help!" Serris cried.

Meron burbled something nonsensical. His eyes pleaded with Serris, and his hands clawed at her.

"Serris," Erim said. "You have to end it."

He was right, of course. Meron was already dead, even if his body had not accepted it. Serris wrapped her arm around Meron's head. "Pass well," she said. "It ends."

Then she drove her dagger up between his ribs and pierced his heart. His spasms ended, and he gave one last, relieved sigh. Then he was dead.

Serris wiped Meron's lifeblood from her face and surveyed their choices. With the *Avenger* launched, they had no more business in high-city, and to stay would only invite more Ravalis guards after them. The blizzard cleared somewhat to reveal a horror of blood and shattered glass. The elements would wipe the blood away, but such devastation would not go unnoticed. At least if there were no Ravalis survivors, no one would know who was to blame. Efficiently, the other Tears were hauling the bodies to the edge and hurling them over. Only one Duster had survived: Reiten, who was even now chuckling at her where Nacacia held him at swordpoint.

"You ugly whore." He touched at his torn face. "Look what you did!"

Serris stalked toward him. Her face burned in the snow and afterheat of battle, but she made no move to secure her mask. Let the scar shine like a beacon for the monster who had killed her friend.

"What's on the *Avenger*?" she demanded of him.

Reiten sneered. "Dead whores."

Serris hadn't expected an answer. "You came to stop us. You knew we were coming. How?"

Reiten nodded. "We've known about the Burned Man for years," he said. "It was all a matter of smoking you out. The *Avenger* did that. And now you've been caught, whore."

Serris listened, but there were no sounds of horns.

"Perhaps," she said. "But if you knew we were coming, why didn't you bring more Dusters? And no mages? What about the reinforcements I don't hear coming? Either you underestimated us, or you're stupid." She shook her head. "We happened across you. Just Nar-burned luck. And not yours."

Reiten's face flushed. "You're going to die, whore," he said. "I will see it personally. I will stick my blade in you until you scream and—"

"But you can't prove it," Serris said.

He looked startled. "What?"

"You can't prove anyone at the Burned Man stands against the Ravalis." She kept her emotions under control. "If you could, you would have struck long ago, by law of the Council. You still can't."

"Burn the Council. You will slip up. And when you do, I'll kill you personally."

Serris turned and headed back to the lift, signaling the Tears to follow her.

"I'll find your man, whore," Reiten called. "Your Nar-burned *daughter*."

Serris stopped and stood there, breathing heavily.

Reiten's face brightened. "Oh I know," he said. "I've rutted enough of your whores to hear. Your daughter. I'll bash her head open on the wall. I'll make you watch when I—"

Serris turned, strode to him, and slashed her dagger across his throat. Blood sprayed and Reiten fell back, choking. His eyes were wide and surprised, as though he'd expected his words to harm her, rather than enrage her. Then she kicked his dying body through the hole in the mage-glass, and watched the debris break its bones and cut open its flesh as it fell.

"We go," Serris said.

As they rode the lift down, Serris thought of Regel in far-away Luether. Even if she caught a mage-caravel tonight, she would get to the City of Pyres days after the *Avenger* arrived, with whatever forces the Ravalis had sent. Regel was on his own against an unknown threat, and she had no way to warn him. She could only trust that he would return safely, and be quit of that damned Bloodbreaker.

If the Old Gods smiled, he had killed her already.

ELEVEN

Lyether

REGEL SAT NAKED AGAINST the cool earthen wall beneath the Crimson Bath tavern. Overhead, feet stomped and muffled voices bickered. Firelight filtered through cracks in the wood, cutting through the dusty mist. Regel let these things soothe him as he sat, muscles relaxed, gazing at the dragon that perched before him.

The beast of crimson was a thing of beauty, with its glittering gold eyes and graceful form. Its contours were soft and smooth, and he could almost taste the sweat that set it to shimmering. Deep scars ran across its body, but it floated unbowed and unbroken. When he stretched out his hand and touched one of its wings, the dragon shivered and straightened. It radiated heat. He traced the wing to the spine, then down its back to its tail, before he finally let his hand rest at his side. Freed of his touch, the dragon relaxed again, bending away from him with a sigh.

"We should talk," Regel said.

"We do not have to."

"Yes." Regel closed his hand into a fist. "Yes, we do."

Ovelia sat on the edge of the bed, knees pressed to her chest, chin in her hands. Even as her pose stretched her dragon tattoo proudly, it also spoke of vulnerability and deep weariness. Fire roiled just inside her skin, however. Regel could see it and feel it.

"I just made love to the Shroud. Surely that entitles me to a few words."

"Did you?" Ovelia gave a humorless sniff. The sound was loud in the empty basement. "I think it was *her*, not me."

"What?"

"Lenalin." Ovelia looked over her shoulder at him. "Tell truth. Was it me, or was it her?"

"It was you."

"You need not lie, Regel." Ovelia turned away. "We *have* used each other before."

"And if I told you it was her, what then?" Regel asked. "Does it matter?"

"Of course it matters."

"Then yes," Regel said, feeling cold inside. "It was her, and not you."

Ovelia sighed and said nothing.

"And when you were rutting me," said Regel. "Who were you?"

"Her." Ovelia shrugged, setting her dragon tattoo writhing. "The way you looked at me, like you were looking at *her*. I did it..." She touched her bleached hair, letting her words fade.

116

"Because you still love her," Regel murmured.

"Yes." Ovelia lowered her hand from her hair. "Always."

Regel touched her bare shoulder. "Lenalin is dead, Ovelia."

"Oh yes." Ovelia pulled away and wrapped her arms around her knees. "Death has made her eternal and untouchable. She will never age for you as I have. She will never fade." Her voice trembled. "How long must I stand second to a corpse in the ground?"

Regel wanted to assure her that she was wrong, but he kept his silence. Ovelia *had* changed, but she had not faded. She had more scars than five years ago, and he wanted to know the story of every one. She was older, of course, but he desired her no less. If he said that to her, would it comfort or pain her?

"You were right," he said. "We don't have to talk."

He put out his arms, and she slid between them. They lay together for a silent breath. Ovelia traced her fingers along his chest, and he could feel her warm breath teasing the sparse hairs that lined his muscles.

At length, Ovelia turned and pushed herself atop Regel. She pressed her body into him and lifted her face level with his. "Why did you love her so much?"

"I thought we weren't going to talk."

"Lenalin." Ovelia lay across Regel. "Why did you love her more than me?"

"Ovelia—"

"Was it her eyes?" She winked at him flirtatiously. "Or her lips?" She leaned down to kiss him. "Or could it have been these?" Ovelia brought her hands to her chest.

"None of those," said Regel.

Ovelia rolled her eyes and sighed. "You are *certain* that these meant nothing to you?" She squeezed her breasts, which sparkled with light sweat in the candlelight.

"Yours were always far more impressive," Regel said.

"Bigger and more impressive are not the same. But you *are* a man."

"So I am." Regel put his hands on her chest. Her nipples hardened under his callused palms. Ovelia made a sound deep in her throat that was half-sigh, half-moan.

"Say it again." Ovelia reached down to where Regel had grown hard and moved him into her.

Chills passed through Regel as she sidled atop him. "Ovelia," he said.

"Not *Ovelia*." She ran her fingers through her white-blonde dyed hair. "Say it again—please."

Her eyes pleaded as her fingers traced electric lines along his skin. He could not deny her.

"Lenalin," Regel whispered. "My princess—"

Ovelia shut her eyes and moaned.

~

Sometime later, they lay pressed tight into one another. Regel breathed softly, drifting, while Ovelia curled a lock of his black hair in her fingers. He liked the sensation, and also the feel of her strong frame against his chest. One hand he trailed across her strong backside, while in the other he held the carving he had been crafting over the last days. He had fallen mostly asleep thinking about it, and the implications of what he meant to do with it.

"What oath have you broken?" she asked in a whisper.

Regel stirred back to wakefulness, led by her voice. He clutched the carving tighter.

"In Tar Vangr," Ovelia's fingers traced his jaw. "When Serris was about to kill me, she named me Oathbreaker, and you suggested we were alike in that. What did you mean?"

"Ovelia—"

"I'll not be swayed." She put his hand on her cheek, matching her own hand on his. "Why are you an oathbreaker, when you have ever been loyal to the Blood of Winter?"

Regel looked away, fixing his eyes on the candles at the side of the bed. "When first we met," he said. "When we were children, did I not vow to defend Lenalin with my last breath?"

"You did," Ovelia said. "And so did I."

"That is the oath I broke," he said. "I swore to protect her, but I could only avenge her."

"Avenge her?" Ovelia looked puzzled. "But it was an accident. Lenalin fell."

He saw again the fear and doubt in her face as she spoke, and it drew him back fifteen years to that awful night it had all come to pass. Lenalin bloody and screaming as Orbrin's chiurgeons tried to save her. Everyone had insisted it was an accident. She'd had a free-standing mirror in her chambers, and she'd tripped. All of them believed that—all but Regel, who knew better.

"Paeter Ravalis," Regel said. "It was his hand that killed Lenalin."

Ovelia's fingers froze where they had been reaching toward his neck, and she drew her hands to her chest. She seemed to age several years in that moment—her face knitting in lines of pain. "No," she said, mostly to convince herself. She must always have suspected. "No. Orbrin said—"

"Ovelia, you know the truth," Regel said. "Orbrin could not move against the Ravalis—he was already too weak. They murdered the heir of Winter and he didn't even chasten them."

"Why?" Ovelia's face was white. "Paeter—why would he do it?"

"You know the Ravalis—how they *own* their women," Regel said. "From the moment they are born, a father owns his daughters until he sells them to another man. How Orbrin gave Lenalin willingly to one such."

"Yes." Ovelia's voice was distant. "But how did that—"

"He beat her," Regel whispered. "He did it often. Almost daily, near the end."

"Old Gods, I..." Ovelia said. "I saw bruises, but she... She never told me."

Regel leaned up to kiss her cheek. "Do not blame yourself," he said. "Lenalin kept it a close secret. She must have wanted you to know nothing—or Paeter told her to stay silent."

"But she told *you*."

"She had no need—I saw the marks," he said. "Lenalin commanded me— *begged* me—to do nothing. So did the king, even after Paeter beat her to death."

"Why didn't you tell me, Regel? Have we not shared enough?"

"She..." Regel sighed. "When we were young, she took an oath of me that I would always follow her commands, and she held me to it. I saw the bruises after her first night and confronted her, but she bade me breathe a word to no one— not even the king. On my oath, she bade me do nothing."

"And you kept your silence." Ovelia shivered. "Old Gods. Regel, I didn't know."

"How could you know?" Regel shut his eyes. "We both thought Paeter would stop when Darak was born: a son to steal his attention. And for a time, the prince cared more for his heir than his woman. To him, she had vanished. She was lonely... but at least she was safe." He trailed off.

"And then Semana was born." Ovelia looked back over her shoulder.

"Yes," Regel said. "Just before we left for the war with the barbarians in the east, Lenalin grew great with child. Paeter became angry. He accused her of treason against the crown. Of adultery."

"How could they?" Ovelia said. "And even if Lenalin had a lover—and she would have told me—Semana was blooded and bred of the heir of Winter. No one could deny she was of the Blood."

"But not *Ravalis* Blood, they said. She had hazel eyes, yes—like the summerborn—but nothing else. Her face and hair were those of Lenalin, her speech and mannerisms those of Winter. And you know the Luethaar cannot stand a woman defeating a man, even in the battle of blood."

Ovelia cast her eyes down and said nothing.

"Paeter grew worse," Regel said. "One night, on the eve of the Semana's fourth year—when I came back from the war in Echvar. You remember?"

She nodded.

"Lenalin covered it well, but her skin was a wasteland of bruises." His fists clenched. "She begged me to stay my hand again. I conceded. That was the last I saw of her—the last time *alive*."

"Ruin's Night." Ovelia's hand strayed to his, and he held it.

"Ruin's Night. " Regel looked away. "That morn. Do you remember?"

"Yes. I remember your eyes." Ovelia lowered her gaze, and Regel thought he could see tears in her eyes. "They told me in the night. They said it was an accident, but... Lenalin was always so *graceful*."

Regel's chest felt hollow. "Darak was there. It must have been his sixth winter, and you were holding Semana in your arms." He held up his hands as though to cradle an invisible child.

Ovelia nodded. "I didn't want to believe it was an accident, but I did. It was easier."

"Orbrin knew," Regel said. "He *knew*, and he forbade me to take vengeance. He could not punish the Ravalis without breaking the Blood alliance. To accuse the prince or even to speak of it in court would mean civil war in Tar Vangr, and

Blood Denerre was weak. Even if I killed Paeter by stealth, that would be just as damning. Orbrin had no choice but to accept it."

"We were fools—all of us." Ovelia's body tightened as though Regel's words had stabbed her in the belly, and she rolled over to slump at his side. "Old Gods, here I was, furious at you, when I would have done far worse. I would have killed not just him, but his whole boiling Blood."

He lay beside her, staring up at the ceiling. He believed her.

"Did Paeter do that to you as well?" Regel asked at length. "Try to own you?"

Ovelia clenched her jaw. "Their rule over women is not strength but weakness."

It was not an answer, but Regel understood. He ran his thumb along her cheek. The determination on her face elevated her features beyond themselves, and he could not look away. The carving bit into his hand, as though reminding him of its presence. "Ovelia," he said.

"So why didn't you? Kill Paeter, I mean—that same day." Ovelia sat up and the dragon on her back sparkled, seemingly enraged. "If you knew, why didn't you?"

"You were there when Orbrin commanded me not to," Regel said."

"That isn't why. You would have killed Orbrin *and* me if we stood in your way. And yet you did not kill Paeter that day. Why? " Ovelia touched him lightly. "Because *Lenalin* asked you not to."

Regel exhaled. "I swore to defend her from all foes, to punish any who harmed her—but also to obey her."

"You had to choose." Ovelia hugged herself tightly. "And you could not refuse her, even after she had breathed her last. You kept one oath, and broke the other."

"Just so," he said. "And so I took the name Oathbreaker. We are the same."

Ovelia looked away. "Yes," she said. "I suppose we are."

The candles flickered and dust sprinkled down from the ceiling. The sounds of riotous laughter and merriment filtered from above in stark contrast to the solemn silence below. Regel considered the carving he hid in his hand. With that, he could hear every word that was said up there, and that would be easier than these words they two shared. There was heat there—life and passion—as there was between Regel and Ovelia. But down here, in the hidden cellar, it had cooled here to an angry simmer.

"But you *did* kill him, eventually," Ovelia said. "Paeter. You killed him, five years ago. There must have been some victory in that."

"Yes." Regel frowned. "Though that night, the king..." He let the words trail off into the cellar air, which seemed to grow colder in an instant.

Ovelia's reassuring smile faded. She eased a little farther away. "Why have you never asked?"

Regel reached for her. "Asked what?"

"Why I killed my king, to whom I had sworn my life and my sword. The king who was a *father* to me. To both of us." Ovelia clenched her fists. "Why have you never asked why I destroyed our lives?"

"You would lie."

"You will not know until you ask," Ovelia said. "Shall I tell you?"

He reached out and twisted his fingers gently around a curl of her dyed hair. It was red half a thumb out from the scalp. Everyday, she seemed less Lenalin and more herself.

"Does it matter?" he asked. "The Blood of Winter is spilled and gone. Orbrin, Lenalin, and Semana are dead, Darak exiled for treason. The Ravalis rule Tar Vangr. So does it matter, truly?"

"Yes," she whispered. "Yes. It matters."

"Ovelia." He unfolded his hand and held out the carving to her. He'd shaped it into a dragon to match her tattoo, and strung it on a thong of leather. "I want you to have this."

She stared at the offering. "You... but..." She looked into his face. "No, Regel. I know what this means. You can't give this to me."

"Ovelia, listen to me." He closed her hands around the carving and met her gaze. "We broken servants are all that remains of the Blood of Denerre. We are the shadows left of the Winter King—his last blades left unsheathed." He caressed her cheek with his thumb. "Perhaps—"

"No." Ovelia set the wooden dragon medallion on the bedside table and rose. She stood naked in the cellar, her hands worked into fists. "We aren't children anymore. We both loved the Winter King, but only one of us *slew* him, Regel. And what has been done cannot be undone."

"Ovelia—"

"This changes nothing." She struck herself—slammed her fist into one taut thigh hard enough to leave a red mark. "I slew King Denerre. I brought the world to Ruin. And you must kill me. You *must*."

Words slid around Regel like cool water, and he shook his head. "If you hate yourself so much," he said. "Why do you yet live? Why not cut your own throat?"

"Justice," she said, the word whispering in the corners of the hot cellar. "You had Lenalin to avenge—let me have Semana. Please, Regel. Let me have this."

"Revenge will not soothe you," Regel rose and stood beside her. "When I slew Paeter, it gave me no pleasure—not even the release I sought."

"I do not care," she said. "I will have vengeance and I will die and that will be the end. Justice."

"Ovelia." Regel put his arms around her shoulders, and despite her anger, Ovelia relaxed into his embrace. "Think on what I am saying."

"No," she said, but her voice was losing its strength. She seemed to melt into him.

"Vengeance is an empty thing," he whispered in the Bloodbreaker's ear. "Better to live."

Ovelia came alive and wrenched herself out of his grasp. She turned on him, face wrought of anger and pain, tears in her eyes. "But *you* are here," she said. "Why did you come, if not for vengeance?"

The candles had been burning long hours, and several chose that moment to gutter and wink out in a puff of smoke. The cellar grew darker, casting long shadows across Ovelia's heaving shoulders and her furious face. It was a dire omen.

"Very well." Regel left her and sat back on the bed. "We'll be about your vengeance on the morrow. I hope you will take comfort in it."

"And you will plunge the knife into my heart then? I want it to be you."

She was marching to her death—eyes open, angry and determined. Regel nodded.

"Promise me that mercy." She climbed atop him and kissed him on the lips. "Promise me, Regel."

"As you ask," Regel said. "I will be there. I will look into your fading eyes as you die."

"Good."

Ovelia enfolded Regel in her arms and they breathed together in the sweaty darkness. The revelers above had quieted, and no more dust filtered down from the creaking floorboards. The young had left the Crimson Bath, perhaps in search of a rowdier tavern, and only the old remained—them, and the two worn-out knights sharing the stillness below.

After a moment, Ovelia spoke. "Should I stay?" she asked.

"As you will." Regel closed his eyes.

Ovelia breathing slowed beside him, lulling him to peace. He shifted in Ovelia's embrace, pressing his face into her neck. Her scent was familiar, and the world drifted.

"Before," he murmured. "When I said it was her... that I loved her, and not you?"

"Yes?" she asked.

"I lied."

"Do not tell me that." Ovelia stared at him, her eyes soft and pained. "You are asleep."

"Yes." Regel picked up the carved dragon she had refused and clumsily set it on the godshelf at the head of the bed. "For when we are dead," he said. "So that someone might find it, and remember us."

He slept.

TWELVE

THE SUN ROSE HIGH and late the next day for Dark Solstice—the darkest day of the year, and the day when they would finally face their enemy and all this would end. Greasy clouds smeared the sky, but Regel could see well enough the two bodies merging far above. On this day, the cracked moon would block out Ruin's hazy sun for a full hour, sparing the world the worst of the heat. Here in Luether, they called the solstice eclipse the Hour of the Mask.

How appropriate, Regel thought.

Far above, in the wilting high-city, a skyship was docking: the *Avenger*. Regel recognized the massive ship from years ago, and for a brief moment, he wondered if it brought an invading force to the city as it had then. His heart beat faster at the thought that perhaps the Ravalis had come for them after all, and their time grew short indeed. He saw activity up on the height, but nothing like a battle: only a few debarking passengers, exchanging bribes and meeting contacts. He saw no massive army of Ravalis soldiers hunting for him and Ovelia, and even if such a force waited inside the ship, it would have to move slowly and quietly or risk open conflict. Either way, Regel had time before they could be deployed. He relaxed, confident that Serris was protecting their journey from a distance.

His quest was safe, at least for a little longer, which was all he'd need.

Regel studied the façade of the abandoned temple, with its faded carvings of the rising sun and crippled statues of nymphs and phoenixes—and scratched his fresh-shaved chin. Once, Luether had venerated the patron goddess Aertem, but the Ravalis had long eschewed the ways of the Old Gods. Denerre had been the last great Blood to hold to the divine—cleaving to the winter god Amanul—but now few remained to keep the old ways and pray for their return. Regel's own goddess, Lenalin Denerre, had perished fifteen years ago, and would not come again.

Regel stood before the old temple and listened. If Ovelia's spy had spoken truly, Mask should be waiting inside. He wished he had a carven focus to make his task easier, but he'd given Ovelia the dragon. It could not function as it had before, because he had given it away. He would do this like any other man.

Surely Mask expected this attack. If Fersi could take them by surprise and the Ravalis could follow them even this far, then surely the greatest slayer in the World of Ruin saw their attack coming. Lacking surprise, the best Regel could do was stack the odds in his own favor. He had faced Mask five years ago, and he had failed, but this time he was prepared. Regel touched the dragon hilt of Draca at his belt. The Bloodsword could foil an ambush and devour slaying magic, making it the only weapon a sorcerer need fear.

He thought of Ovelia for a heartbeat, but pushed her from his mind.

123

The great doors were shut, but Regel made his way to a loose window shutter he'd found an hour previous. The air was cooler inside the temple—ironic, for a place sacred to a summer goddess. Thin rays of sunlight trickled through the boarded over windows, making the place a prison of shadow. Dust thicker than the soles of Regel's boots cloaked the floorboards, and a trail of distinctive footprints led deeper into the temple. The right foot stepped normally, but the left foot dragged slightly.

Perhaps only one person lay in wait, but then, many folk treading in the same steps like knives scratching in the same groove would look the same. Regel could not guess how many might lie in wait. He was walking into an ambush, and he had to trust to his sword and plan to see him through. He drew Draca, from whose hilt wisps of shadow curled away to no effect, and held the heavy blade in both hands. He could not be certain, as the magic did not sing to his blood as to Ovelia's, but he thought that if death lay in wait for him, the sword would prove much more urgent in its warnings.

Had he made a misstep, one that would cost him everything? It was too late to turn back.

Regel climbed the central dais through the circle of dusty benches with withered cushions laid out haphazardly before them. A single shaft of light fell across the altar, illuming dust that swirled up from its matted surface. He set Draca on the altar within easy reach and drew one of his falcata—the whisper of steel on leather was blasphemously loud in the stillness. The caked dust fell away like paper, revealing rose-pink stone beneath. This stone picked up the light from high windows and cast it around the chamber.

For the first time, Regel saw the flowers that grew inside the temple: stretch upon stretch of bright blossoms on coiling vines, illuminated by the radiant altar. Reds and blues winked up at him from the once dark corners, and the temple seemed a veritable garden. A rare sight indeed, especially in one of the mage-cities where the very air hung tainted with the corruption of magic. Somehow, life lingered in this, Aertem's abandoned temple. Perhaps the Old Gods had not left the World of Ruin entirely.

On the altar, Draca bled uneasy shadows. A warning.

"Beautiful, eh?"

Regel turned. There, twenty paces away, stood a man in a gray-black cloak, right hand at his belt, his left hand hidden. His right eye gleamed deep blue, while the left seemed milky and dead. His face hid behind a mask of interlaced bones.

"It is," Regel said. "Life among the dust."

"Ah, but wait," the man said. "The true beauty arrives in a moment."

The red altar gleamed in the weak light—light that, even as he watched, faded. The moon was passing between Ruin and its cruel sun—the Hour of the Mask. The altar glowed even after the light from above faded to a mere trickle. In the dark, it illumined the chamber like a torch.

"Marvelous, no?" asked the man. "Dawnstone, imported from the Sunlands before the fall of Calatan. Once, the faithful journeyed thousands of miles by land or sea just to see it."

Regel shook the falcat free of dust and sheathed it. He laid his trailing hand on the hilt of Draca, ready to reclaim it at any instant. He could feel its warning shadows burning stronger, starting to coalesce.

"I am told—" The man took two steps forward—the first strong, with his right foot, and the second an awkward hobble on his left. "The stone drives evil from all who touch it. Does it do the like for you, Lord of Tears? Cleanse *your* heart of its darkness?" His voice hissed slightly, like that of a snake. "I do so hope it does not."

"You," Regel said, stepping down from the altar, Draca in both hands, "are not Mask."

"Indeed." The man affected a bow, but Regel saw his left hand did not leave his cloak. The hem of his cloak gleamed with the hint of metal. "I am Davargorn. Mask is my master."

"I have not heard Mask had a squire," said Regel. "Nor have I heard of you."

"I shall take that as praise," he said. "I am not a man who likes his name known. Not *yet*, that is."

"Indeed?"

Davargorn bowed. "I am not worthy of a name that men know—not yet. But when I have killed the legendary Frostburn, ah—then."

"That man is long dead."

"I think he stands before me. I hope he does—for your sake."

There was no way to avoid a duel here. At best, Regel could find an advantageous position.

Davargorn circled Regel like a wolf. Regel followed suit, stepping the other direction. The light dimmed as the moon obscured the sun, and Regel realized Davargorn had planned this confrontation for this particular effect. Regel would keep him talking as long as possible to let his eyes grow accustomed to the gathering dark.

"Where is your master?" he asked.

"Where is your *mistress*?" Davargorn nodded to Ovelia's sword. "Or did you kill the Bloodbreaker, I wonder?"

"Yes."

Davargorn's cloak swayed as he walked but never revealed his heavily-guarded left hand. Regel wondered what sort of weapon he held. "Do you expect me to believe you?"

Regel shrugged without moving his hand from Draca's hilt.

"Just so." The bone mask seemed to grin in macabre fashion.

Regel felt the sword's magic flare. He had always experienced it the same way: tingling warmth when danger drew near, and a sudden flush of heat running up his arm when a blow was coming. Instinct told him how to move, and without seeing the attack, he cut across.

A loud *crack* filled the tranquil sanctum and Regel spun under the impact of a casterbolt that shattered off Draca. The useless bolt toppled off toward the far wall and Regel darted forward, Draca high. Davargorn tossed the caster aside, drew his own curved dust-sword, and caught the overhand strike. Sparks flew as magic clashed and warped, Regel's genuine, Davargorn's thamaturgical.

"The famous speed," Davargorn said. "I am honored, Winter's Shadow."

"You are dead," Regel replied.

"I thought you a slayer, not a jester."

Regel dodged back and Davargorn bore after him, steel weaving. The masked man moved in an awkward sway, his slower left leg betraying weakness on that side. Regel sidestepped and struck at the opening, testing Davargorn's defenses, and Ovelia's sword screamed off a raised steel gauntlet. Regel barely dodged an underhand counter by leaping back and around. Davargorn sneered and turned to put his right foot forward once more.

Old Gods, but Davargorn was good. Part of it was age—the youth had to be twenty years younger or more—but rarely had Regel faced such a tight and efficient swordsman. Moreover, Davargorn fought in an unexpected style, weaving back and forth on his crippled foot. Regel wondered if he would live long enough to find the flaws in the man's style.

In the darkness of the Hour of the Mask, their duel traced curving pathways in the dust. Regel eluded more than he parried and kept moving. The younger slayer varied time, swaying slowly at first only to spring suddenly and thrust fast and hard. Regel barely ducked, and Davargorn's thaumaturgy-enhanced sword carved a deep gouge in the nearest pillar of the temple. The dust magic discharged with a thunderous roar, making the edifice tremble, and Regel heard stone grumbling above. Distracted, he missed his chance as Davargorn pulled his sword from the carved stone, the last of its magic expended.

"Afraid of a little dust, Lord of Tears?" Davargorn grinned. "Very well. I'll not have the bards call me a coward. Mortal steel it is."

Regel batted aside a sudden lunge, curled around Davargorn's arm, and grabbed for the man's throat. The younger slayer was too fast, however, and dodged away before Regel could touch him. He might have struck freely, but he only laughed and fell back.

The lining of Davargorn's cloak glittered. "I've waited long for this, old man," he said.

"Disappointed?" Regel asked.

"Very."

Davargorn twisted his blade when he struck, eluding simple parries, and Regel suspected it was as much for show as for deception. The man enjoyed his artful style, which meant his arrogance could be exploited. Regel tried a straightforward strike, only to meet a vicious parry and a sudden counter that pierced the leather over his shoulder. Davargorn smirked as Regel felt at the hole. No blood.

"Close." Davagorn let the word hiss to silence.

The man seemed familiar somehow—the eyes, the crippled foot—but he could not place him. "I know you," Regel said.

Davargorn only smiled.

They fought in circles, blades dancing high and wide. Davargorn kept to a high guard but relied on distance for defense. He held Regel at bay with his warding blade, seeming always on the defensive until Regel missed a step. At the tiniest opening, Davargorn darted in like a lunging viper to slash or stab. At such moments, Regel had to ply all of his tricks just to hold the man at bay.

Regel missed a step, and Davargorn danced forward, struck, parried the counterthrust, and whirled to strike again. Regel dodged and parried, then countered with a deceptive double-slash that cut clean through a nearby pillar. His mundane falcat would have reflected off the stone hard enough to numb his arm, but Draca cut right through, making the pillar crumble. Regel and Davargorn split apart as shards of stone crashed to the floor between them.

"Heh." Davargorn patted his belly, which had come within a hand of sharp steel. Regel heard the thump of flesh on metal. "For an old man, you're a *quick* burner, I'll give you that."

"For a young man, you're a terrible sport," Regel said. "Toying with me thus."

"Enjoying myself."

The ceiling gave a mighty groan, and dust filtered down onto the flowerbeds.

"You realize if the temple collapses, you die with me," Regel said.

"Best finish our duel quickly, then." Smoke flowed from Davargorn's boots. Magic. No thaumaturgy this, but true, genuine magic from a long-past age.

Propelled by the boots, the masked slayer flew at Regel like an arrow shot from a bow. Regel parried, but the unexpected force of Davargorn's charge drove his blade wide and slashed across just over his wrist. Itching pain shot up his arm. The younger man's muscles bulged as the sword snapped like a whip. Regel took a high guard, warding Davargorn back.

Then instinct brought Draca down in a hasty defense. Davargorn whirled, slashing the glittering hem of his cloak into Regel. Steel screeched against steel, and Regel staggered back and looked down at his leather vambraces, where the razored edge had cut a jagged line.

"Do not despair," Davargorn said. "You're hardly the first man to miss that."

"Am I the first to *be* missed as well?" Regel raised his arms. There was no blood—Davargorn had slashed only leather.

With a snarl, the slayer lunged at him again. Regel parried low and their swords locked against the dawnstone altar. A jagged knife appeared in Davargorn's free hand, but Regel dropped one hand from Draca to catch his wrist. He strained to keep the point away from his throat.

"Somehow," Davargorn said. "I expected more from the master slayer of Tar Vangr."

The knife drove slowly downward, gradually overcoming Regel's strength. Davargorn twisted Draca out of his other hand, and it clattered to the floor.

"I have more to offer," Regel assured him.

"Oh? And what—?"

"Villain!" came a cry from behind them, and Davargorn's eyes darted to the side.

Regel twisted to let the knife drive past him. The jagged steel screeched against the dawnstone, trailing sparks of red that fell like embers to the floor. Davargorn cursed, and with all the strength left him, Regel shoved him away, right into Ovelia's attack.

The slayer turned into a rushing shield. He tried to block with the dagger, but the shield blew through his defense and struck him full in the chest. He sailed back, borne aloft on his boots' magic, to smash into a pillar. Dust rained around him as he fell to the floor awkwardly, though he quickly collected himself into a spider-like crouch. "There she is."

Ovelia, who had bashed him away with her shield, took the moment to recover Draca from where it lay on the floor beside the dawnstone altar. Its magic sang to her, and Regel saw shadows flow up around her wrist. She assumed a low guard, sword and shield gleaming in the fading sunlight. "Tell us where your master hides, and you shall be spared."

"The Bloodbreaker herself." Davargorn chuckled. "I knew you wouldn't throw away something so pretty, Lord of Tears."

The slayer rose into his flamboyant dueling stance, sword high and pointing down, body tense like a fox ready to pounce. His limbs seemed inhumanly contorted, as though he took part in a farce, not a battle. He looked nothing if not confident.

"Ware his lunge," Regel said to Ovelia. "His boots—"

Davargorn leaped at her, sword slashing, but rather than retreat, Ovelia stepped forward. The shadows had told her exactly how to move, and she tore through his lunge without effort. She caught his sword with Draca and smashed her buckler into his face with a wet crunch. In his arrogance, Davargorn had not expected such an aggressive defense, and could not dodge. He fell back, shrieking and clutching at his broken mask.

Ovelia stepped to Regel's side, set Draca on the altar, and pulled him up by the arm. "See?" She raised her shield so Regel could see the blood from Davargorn's nose. "Shields are useful after all."

Regel coughed in agreement, then looked to Davargorn. Inhuman mewls burbling from his lips, the man scrabbled vainly at his shattered bone mask, which had bent into his face. Blood dripped from its edge. "That isn't Mask," Regel said.

"So I gathered." Ovelia felt at Regel's wounds. "I've bought us a moment. Are you well?"

Regel gritted his teeth. "You were to wait for Mask before you attacked. That was the plan."

"Burn the plan." Ovelia gestured toward Davargorn. The slayer reached back and unfastened the clasps of his mask. He was trying to pull it off, but every tiny tug wrenched a yelp of pain from his lips. "He would have killed you."

"But he did not," said Regel.

"No," said another voice—this one cold and rasping. "He did not."

~

Ovelia's heart froze at the the voice, and from the recognition in Regel's eyes, she knew who—*what*—had appeared. She turned, and saw the sorcerer emerging from the shadows.

Mask's leather-wrapped arms and legs looked more like black bones than the limbs of a living being. It wore heavy battle gauntlets, one light and one dark, and they made its hands look grotesquely large. Its face hid behind stitched leather with only small slits for eyes and a mouth. Ovelia might have thought Mask a lifeless manikin, but for the way its fingers clicked together in a mocking sort of applause. Even at this distance, the sorcerer reeked of blood, as though its leather armor bound not living flesh but rotting meat.

"Your arrogance unmakes you, Davargorn." Like a withered puppet on invisible strings, Mask turned to its student, who was still clawing at his faceplate. Mask's silvery left gauntlet rippled as though distorted by massive heat. "And there are consequences for failure."

Mask gestured, and Davargorn cried out in pain and fell to his knees. On his face, the broken bone mask seemed to twist of its own accord. Then Mask tightened its gloved fingers into a fist.

Blood streaming, Davargorn wailed, and Ovelia heard flesh rip. The broken bone mask dislodged from the man's face and shot to Mask's open right hand. Davargorn gasped and retched on the floor. His face had become a mess of hair, gore, and spit. With his right hand, he feebly pushed a flap of skin and flesh closed over his cheek, while he tried to rub blood from his eyes with his left.

"Invisible hand," Regel murmured.

The sorcerer waved away the inky smoke that trailed from its left-hand gauntlet—the cast-off detritus of channeled magic. The glove itself was silver and steel, and might have come from a much finer suit of armor. It was a relic of another age, which meant the unseen force sprang from the gauntlet, rather than from Mask's body. What other relics did the slayer bear?

"You have failed, broken squire," Mask said in its icy voice. Steam rose from the cracked mask in the sorcerer's hand. "You have served me ill, and I'll have no more of you. Begone."

Even without the blood, Davargorn's face was a horror. Much of his cheek and nose were scarred and twisted as though by fire, the lip curled in a perpetual grimace. One eye was larger than the other, dead white in color where the other was a soft blue.

She thought dimly that his face seemed somehow familiar. But where had she seen him before?

"One day, whore of Dracaris," he hissed, drizzling blood. "One day."

Mask's left hand gestured toward Davargorn, and his body went taut. He choked off a cry and flipped backward to sprawl on the ground. "Begone," Mask repeated.

As Davargorn half-ran, half-hobbled away, the sorcerer looked down at the bone-mask in its right hand. The mask began to glow and crackle with heat. Greasy smoke rose from Mask's black gauntlet—the same magical leavings that scorched the skies—and the reek of burning leather filled the temple.

Fire magic as well, then.

Ovelia felt Regel's reassuring fingers on her spine and her muscles relaxed. Whatever came to pass, he was with her. Ovelia set her teeth and raised Draca.

Finally, Davargorn's bone-mask gave a hissing whine like that of a wounded animal. Mask's concentration wavered, and the remains of the mask quieted to a dull gray. The sorcerer tossed it aside and it crumbled to dust before it touched the floor.

"Now"—Mask's silver-wrapped left hand rose—"to settle accounts."

Ovelia heard a high-pitched keening in the air, and fiery warnings danced from Draca. She drew a circle around Regel and herself with the bloodsword, its edge gleaming with furious red light, just before Mask's power struck like thunder and the world exploded in a brilliant flash of white. Dust stormed into the air, and the bricks of the floor splintered in all directions. The dawnstone altar broke into pieces, sending shards of red stone cascading.

Coughing in the gray smoke, Ovelia rose from where she had crouched and raised the sword anew. Outside the red shield she had drawn, the dais was blackened and blistered. Greasy smoke rose from it into the temple air. Mask stood a few paces away, hand still raised and ready. Ovelia could not see the sorcerer's face, but she took some satisfaction in imagining a shocked expression there.

"Yield." Ovelia raised the glowing blade to point at Mask.

In response, Mask leveled its right hand at her. Upon this hand, the sorcerer wore a fire-blasted war-gauntlet, the fingers of which ended in twisted metal talons. A bolt of flame danced toward Ovelia, only to melt into the devouring sword of Draca. The warding shadows boiled madly.

"You've a fine blade, Bloodbreaker." The sorcerer thrust its left hand to the side, the movement mechanical and independent of its shoulder. The hand shimmered and smoke rose from the fingertips. "I've waited long, and 'twould not please me if you died easily."

Ovelia took a step, then staggered as Regel tackled her from behind. They went down in a tumble as half the dawnstone altar flew at her from the floor. It sheared over them, and Regel grunted as it clipped his shoulder and back. He sprawled away from her, blood flying.

"Regel!" Ovelia cried, reaching for him.

"Worry for yourself, Bloodbreaker." Now, the sorcerer's mask itself glowed with magic.

A bolt of sickly green light streaked toward Ovelia, and she barely parried with her sword. Her arms screeched in agony and her belly roiled. She knew little enough of the arts of sorcerers, but Ovelia recognized flesh-rending magic when she saw it—*felt* it—nearly strike her.

In the wake of its thwarted magic, Mask backed away from Ovelia, hands raised.

"Again—yield." Ovelia stalked forward to interpose herself between Mask and the fallen Regel. "I shall give you the mercy of a quick death, should you yield."

Mask coughed violently, then slashed its left hand at her again. A blow like that of a hammer struck Draca with a whine. Ovelia staggered back, her sword high, and the invisible force clashed into her defense again with numbing force. The sword drank it in, but Ovelia's arms tingled with numbness.

"You are a mockery, Bloodbreaker," Mask said. "With your blonde hair, like that of Semana—the child you betrayed. You proved no more loyal than those she thought her friends. Less."

The invisible sword struck with such force it knocked Ovelia to one knee. Draca vibrated cruelly in her hands, numbing her arms and shoulders.

"Would it pain you to hear how she died?" Mask asked. "I will tell, but only if it will *hurt* you."

Images of Semana danced before Ovelia's eyes, and she fought back tears. Draca's shadows confirmed what she already knew: this was the moment. Now— when her arms ached and her body nearly failed—now she had to strike.

"She never pleaded for her life, even as I bathed in the blood of those around her." The chapped lips sneered through the slit in the leather mask. "Would you do the same?"

"Last chance!" Sword raised, Ovelia stepped toward the sorcerer. "Yield!"

Mask moved its smoking hands in a vicious downward chop, and the invisible sword struck harder than ever. Ovelia deflected it but fell to her belly. Her cheek smashed into the dusty stones, and she felt wetness creeping down the side of her face and over her chin. Draca's red glow was fading. Even as she looked at the bloodsword, it shook free of her numb fingers and clattered to the floor before her.

She had come all this way only to fail.

"You disappoint me, Bloodbreaker." Mask's spindly fingers waved. "If you had followed through with your plan—waited to strike until I appeared—you might have won the day. But now—" The sorcerer raised its trembling hands. "Now you will die."

Ovelia knelt, helpless but defiant. She would meet death with open eyes.

Then, even as the leather-wrapped hands came forward, a shadow blurred across Ovelia's vision: Regel. With both hands, he swung his falcat at Mask's head, and the steel screeched against a shimmering coat of azure energy that flared up around the sorcerer. The wintersteel shattered in Regel's hand and did not bite into the leather beneath, much less the flesh, but the force snapped Mask's head back. The magic around its hands evaporated.

Regel discarded his destroyed sword and punched Mask in the belly, then in the face as it doubled over. It must have felt like punching solid brick, but Regel struck anyway, and the shield shimmered and weakened with each blow. Finally, the thin creature fell to the floor like a puppet without strings and lay unmoving. Wisps of smoke rose from the armor's midsection, where the shielding magic must reside.

Regel drew his second blade, but abruptly Mask's hand rose, fingers twisted into claws, and green energy shot between them. The falcat tumbled from Regel's limp fingers and he curled tightly, face contorted and body retching. Ovelia saw smoke distort Mask's monstrous visage and realized this magic came from the sorcerer's mask itself. Ovelia saw Regel's vitality draining away.

"You are fortunate, Dracaris," said Mask, its voice low. "That was meant for you."

The world was falling apart. The temple ceiling shook, its broken pillars wavering, then started to collapse toward them. Mask raised the silver gauntlet and a dome of force appeared over them to catch the toppling bricks like drops of burning rain. The sorcerer exercised the peak of its powers, letting smoky exhaust bloom from its mask and gauntlet. The air grew thin as the magic corrupted the crumbling sanctity of Aertem's temple.

At first, Ovelia wondered why Mask had shielded them from the collapsing ceiling: the three of them occupied an invisible globe of force that kept the stone out. Then she realized that she and Regel were close enough the sorcerer had to protect them as well as itself. If that magic stopped, all three of them would die.

Ovelia took a step forward, but Mask's face shot to her. "Do not move, Bloodbreaker," the sorcerer rasped. "Touch me, and the ward collapses. And—" Mask clutched its fist tighter, making Regel groan and paw at his chest. "Even if you are too noble to care for your own filthy life, your man will die. Is that what you want?"

Ovelia raised the sword. "Yield, and I will show you mercy."

"Mercy?" Mask's red eyes seemed almost bemused. "Mercy as you showed the king?"

Ovelia took another step, closing the distance between them to just over the sword's reach.

"I warn you, Bloodbreaker!" Mask said, voice breaking. "You are killing him—and yourself."

Blood trickled from Regel's mouth and nose, but his expression showed fearful purpose. "For Lenalin," he gasped. "And Semana."

Ovelia nodded and turned toward Mask. Her fingers tightened on the hilt of her sword.

A ray of light cut through the collapsing temple, setting the swirling dust to dancing. The Solstice eclipse was passing. The light touched the sorcerer's black mask, setting the reddish eyes alight. The sorcerer looked stunned—even fearful—as Ovelia stepped forward, blade raised.

"You are mad." Mask coughed and fell to one knee. The effort of sustaining the protective magic was making its whole body shiver.

The temple was collapsing in earnest now, as great hunks of brick fell around them like rain into the dusty stones. Mask's protective ward flared as it deflected brick after brick. Sheltered under the same protection, Ovelia stood untouched, holding her sword high. Draca drank at Mask's magic, and the stones fell closer as the shield shrank around them. It had become a trap from which none of them would escape.

"Wait," Mask said. The black and green magic waned. "Listen—you have to—"

"For Lenalin and for Semana." Ovelia raised the blade high.

"Semana lives!" Mask rasped. "The Blood of Denerre *lives!*"

The temple rained down around them.

THIRTEEN

THE ANCIENT TEMPLE COLLAPSED in a geyser of dust and peal of thunder, drawing eyes all across Luether. The place of worship had stood in place for centuries beyond reckoning, and while the Old Gods had abandoned Ruin long ago, most Luethaar considered the temple a keystone of the city's former glory. Some in the city raised their fists and voices in celebration of Ruin's final triumph over one of the last shards of Luether's broken legacy, but more hunched their shoulders a little lower and struggled on, cursing the day. Aertem's Fall stole just a little bit more of their resolve.

Heart in his throat, Davargorn felt a mixture of elation and fear. His master had betrayed him and sent him away, so if he had his vengeance that way, so be it. At the same time, though, it was his *master*.

His whole face burning and screaming, Davargorn sheltered against the far wall as a massive wave of dust swept through the street. Stone blocks the size of his whole body tumbled past and cracked the cobblestones. A pillar crunched into the wall over his head, making the entire building shudder. Any one of those would have slain him. It seemed impossible anyone could have survived inside.

But he had to know for certain.

As the dust began to clear, Davargorn saw shapes moving in the street. Scavengers, no doubt—looking for corpses to loot or defile. Despite the circumstances, seeing them filled Davargorn with such rage he instinctually groped for his sword, only to find his scabbard empty. He must have lost the blade in the temple, when he fought the Oathbreaker and that damned whore Bloodbreaker. He saw her in his mind, casually swatting him aside and turning her back like he was nothing. His anger redoubled.

Davargorn swept over the nearest silhouette: a frail man with a pronounced lower jaw into which he had thrust blades like crude tusks. The man was pawing through rubble after something or other and not paying attention. Davargorn wrapped one muscular arm around his neck and twisted sharply. Bone cracked, and the man's body jerked against Davargorn, hands flopping madly. He had a caster hanging at his belt, which Davargorn took as he let the body fall. Then he bounded on.

The bulky man ahead of him seemed more like a warrior, being at least twice as wide as Davargorn himself. A bandolier of knives stood out on his otherwise bare chest, and a barbed chain enwrapped one of his hands. Worse, he saw the attack coming as Davargorn ran through the cloud. The warrior's eyes were shockingly big and green, and Davargorn realized that someone had removed his eyelids to produce just that effect.

Had he been another man, Davargorn might have been distracted by the deformity, but his mind mattered less than his body in that moment. He exerted his will toward the flying boots he'd borrowed from Mask, and a sudden burst of magic sent him sailing at the massive barbarian like a fired arrow. The warrior managed to lash out with the end of the chain, but he was too slow. Davargorn landed on the man's chest, plucked two daggers from his bandolier, and planted them back into his neck. The brute toppled, blood spurting, and Davargorn rolled off him.

He willed the boots to activate again, but they were nearing their limit and would need time to rebuild their magic. Burn them, then: he had two feet of his own, even if one was weaker. He locked onto another dark shape and ran that way, blades up, blood spattered and roaring wordlessly.

Then he hesitated, heart roaring in his throat.

It was a woman, half her face a gory mess of blood and bone. She held her right arm, which twisted oddly at her side, held on by only a length of sinew and some flesh. She was screaming, but not in challenge—instead, her cries were terrified. This woman was no Child of Ruin, but an innocent Luethaar wandering past the temple when the fateful battle took place.

Davargorn backed away at the unexpected vision of horror. "You—I—"

His words drew her attention. Her big blue eyes fixed on Davargorn and horror filled her ruined face. It was as though even to this woman, with her skull crushed and half her face gone, Davargorn was the ugliest thing she had ever seen. She lunged for him, crying out incoherently and raising her good arm. In her madness, she must have forgotten to let go of her other arm, because she ripped it the rest of the way off and batted at him with it. Without effort, Davargorn eluded the clumsy attack and stumbled past her over a flow of bricks. He saw a route up through the broken stone and started that way, but the screaming held his attention. With her savior or enemy gone—Davargorn couldn't say which he was—the woman collapsed to one knee and tried stupidly to fit her arm back into place.

"Burn me." Davargorn reversed one of the knives, aimed, and threw. The blade took the woman in her good eye, and she fell to the ground.

He raised the other knife, ready for an attack, but none was forthcoming. It seemed most other folk had kept away, if they could. Shaken, Davargorn scrambled into the crumbled entrance. Since he would need both hands, he adjusted the caster slung over his shoulder, set the bloody knife between his teeth, and leaped onto the shattered wall to climb.

The boots chose that moment to fail, their magic exhausted, and he started to fall halfway through the jump. He slammed into the stone chest first, and the air blew from his lungs in a rush. He spit out the knife rather than cut off his tongue, and it went tinking off down the shattered stone hill. He flexed his arms and pulled himself up, sputtering and cursing, then lay for a moment on the outcropping of stone. His hands trembled and breath seemed hard to find, even without the dust that scorched his lungs. His fingers found something soft and yielding, and he realized it was one of the flowers, which had miraculously survived the devastation. As he watched, it wilted in his hand, deprived of the magic that sustained it.

Heart in his throat, he scrambled up to what had once been the top of the wall over what had been the great hall. He wiped blood from his face and peered down into what had been the main hall.

What he saw froze him in place.

The daylight burned down after the eclipse, reflecting vividly from the remains of the dawnstone altar. The shards gleamed like rubies amid the shattered floor stones and the settled dust. In the center of the room, Ovelia stood with her thrice-burned sword pointing down at something on the floor. Davargorn saw her first, and his first instinct was to put a bolt in her face. Even as he was reaching for his borrowed caster, however, he saw Regel not too far away, a throwing knife in his hand. Both looked miraculously unbroken.

"Do not," the man was saying. "Ovelia, wait. We need him."

Davargorn furrowed his brow. Then he saw Mask laid prostrate at Ovelia's feet. Draca was at the sorcerer's throat, and the tiniest flick of Ovelia's wrist would plunge the blade home. It was why Regel had not thrown yet, Davargorn realized. Also, if Davargorn himself shot her with the caster, Ovelia would almost certainly kill Mask in her death throes.

Davargorn, who had come here with only death on his mind, suddenly froze, terrified at what he had almost done. He stared at them, sweat dripping down his distorted face. Hatred and fear warred in him, and ultimately he hesitated. What had Mask told them? What was happening?

"No," Ovelia said. "No, I won't believe it. Semana is dead. She— I— This creature can't give her back to us. It's a lie!"

Davargorn was ugly, but he was not stupid. He knew exactly what Mask was doing, and he realized what Mask had already done. All of this had been a trap, and he was part of Mask's game, as he had always been. "Burn you, Master," he said.

He took aim at Mask's leather-wrapped face and squeezed the caster's trigger. Sweat trickled down his gnarled face, even as a voice inside him demanded he cast. Kill Mask. End the torment.

But he could not.

Of course he could not. Mask had owned him for so many years, and he could no more break his vow than he could stop breathing. Instead, he turned the caster on Ovelia. It was her fault. If not for her, none of this would have happened. She deserved to die. And if Mask died as well, then Davargorn would be free. He aligned the bolt with her face and squeezed the trigger.

Click.

No loud *crack*, and no streaking death. The caster had misfired.

Davargorn screamed inwardly. The caster was useless, and now he had only a tattered trick cloak and no real weapon to take his vengeance. Mask's boots had

136

precious little of their magic left, and he wasn't sure how long it would take them to build their charge back up.

He had faced worse odds, he remembered.

"We are not done, *Master*," he murmured, then climbed away.

～

The throwing knife trembled in Regel's hand. In the wake of Mask's pronouncement—the revelation that Semana lived—he could hardly make himself think. He had never—could never have expected such a thing. But he knew, true or not, that he had to follow even the slightest of hopes.

Ovelia, on the other hand, seemingly had no such need. "It's not possible," she said, as much to herself as to either of them. Did she even realize Regel had drawn steel on her?

"Indeed, Lady Bloodbreaker?" Mask coughed where it lay at Ovelia's feet. The sorcerer was their prisoner, yes, but by its relaxed tone, it might as well have held all the knives. "I think it at least *possible*, as you have spared me this long to speak of it."

"That can change." Ovelia turned Draca where it hung across Mask's throat. In contact with the magic-devouring blade, the sorcerer could not fight back.

"Ovelia," Regel said.

She looked up at him sharply, face livid with rage and doubt.

Regel and Ovelia had eyes only for one another, each poised to strike. The world faded around them. It felt like madness, to threaten his only companion in Luether—the woman who had shared his bed just yestereve—in order to protect one of his greatest enemies. And for what? A thin sliver of hope that his greatest mistake could be undone?

"Will you kill me, Regel?" Ovelia asked. "To protect that monster?"

"If it saves Semana," Regel said. "You would do the same."

Ovelia held the sword in trembling hands. Warning shadows spread across the red-tinged blade.

Then Mask began to laugh, the sound maniacal and resonant in the dusty hall. The wiry body shook with the rippling sounds. The wretch lay under Ovelia's knife, and it *laughed*.

"Spare me those threats you'll not act upon," the sorcerer said. "If you were going to slay me, you'd have done it. You want what I promise—the princess you both love—and you cannot have her if I am dead. Aye, Bloodbreaker?"

Ovelia's face reddened and her features drew together in rage. Regel had never seen anger breach her iron composure so completely as now, in Mask's presence. He still held the knife ready to throw.

"This was a scheme," Regel said. "Manipulating our confidence, bringing us here."

"And here you are." Mask's unflagging confidence chilled him.

"You are bluffing," Ovelia said. "No one could do what you claim to have done."

"No one, Bloodbreaker?" Mask gestured to Ovelia. "Have you not spun such a web yourself, to force the Lord of Tears to do as you wished? Have you not laid plans within plans—feints within feints—oh Spymaster of Ravalis? I think we all know you have." Mask looked to Regel. "I wonder what the Bloodbreaker promised to bring you here, Lord of Tears. Coin? Her body? I see you've already had that."

"Watch your tongue," Ovelia said. "I'm the one with the sword at your throat."

But not the one with the power, Regel thought.

"Half a summerblood with a temper to match." Mask indicated its spindly body splayed out on the floorstones. "Move. This is uncomfortable."

Ovelia narrowed her eyes but said nothing. Finally she drew the sword away and let Mask rise. Regel lowered his throwing knife, but kept it pressed against his forearm.

"Good girl," Mask said. "Now put the sword down."

Regel expected to have to add his voice to the command, but Ovelia slammed Draca down on the broken remains of the dawnstone altar without argument. "You could not have done this alone," she said.

"I had my erstwhile squire watching you." Mask sat up and stretched its arms, making loud popping noises. "Davargorn had his uses."

"*Tithian* Davargorn, you mean." Regel had begun to suspect the man's identity during the fight, but when Mask had named him, he'd known it for certain.

"Tithian—" Ovelia opened her eyes wide, only now understanding. "Old Gods have mercy," she said. "Semana's pageboy?"

"The same." Mask uttered a huffing sound that might have been mocking laughter. "He was quick to betray his mistress in her hour of need. He failed her, and now he has failed me. I suppose I should not be surprised." It stretched its arms and loosed a sigh of relief. It moved not unlike a marionette given life by some hidden puppeteer.

Regel remembered taking the young page of Semana aside and giving him a dagger in exchange for his vow to protect the princess. How poorly he'd placed his trust that day.

Ovelia's face had turned white as that of a corpse left to rot for days. She put her free hand to her forehead. "Why?" she asked. "Why bring us here?"

"I can answer that." Regel looked to Mask. "It's because you need us."

"Just so." Mask turned its head slightly, its reddish eyes flicking to Regel. "I have need of the great Frostburn and the Bloodbreaker as well, and I'll pay with your princess."

Regel saw it, as surely as he had seen it when Ovelia had approached him at the Burned Man tavern. His path was laid before him, and if he left it, what then? Ruin.

Ovelia sat up straighter. "Prove it," she said. "Prove Semana lives."

"Reasonable. I expected you would not believe me." Mask reached down, and Regel tensed. "Stand easy, Lord of Tears. I merely seek to do as your woman asks."

"She's not my woman," Regel said.

"As you say." Mask reached down with its left-hand gauntlet—a glove made of linking silver hoops—and unbuckled one of the clasps at its chest. From beneath the flap, it withdrew a small leather parcel and held it out to Ovelia. "Careful. It's dear to at least one of us."

Warily, Ovelia approached, took the parcel, and unwrapped it. Her face paled.

"I imagine you believe me now," Mask said.

Ovelia let her hand slip, and Regel could see the contents of the parcel: a silver ring—Semana's signet—which encircled a pale finger. Semana's finger.

Ovelia's hands trembled. "How dare you," she said. "How *dare* you!"

"Oh yes, Bloodbreaker," Mask said. "Pretend to grieve. It suits you."

Before Regel could stop her, Ovelia leaped upon Mask, fingers curled into claws. Ovelia was bigger and stronger, and she bore the sorcerer to the floor. Mask kept barking ragged laughter until Ovelia finally slammed its head on the stone. As the thing made choking sounds, Ovelia reached for its throat.

"Enough!" Regel grasped her shoulder.

Ovelia drove her elbow into the center of Regel's chest, blowing the air from his lungs. Regel managed to dodge her follow-up strike in part: her knee ended up in his midsection instead of his groin. He staggered back and raised his throwing knife, even as she reached out and snatched up Draca.

"Yes—" The sorcerer lay on the floor, coughing and wheezing. "Yes—fight each other."

Ovelia rounded on Mask, sword raised. "How dare you." She pronounced each word like a dagger thrust. "You—"

"I dare much," Mask said. "Accept my bargain or kill me now. The Lord of Tears has already chosen, and now it is your turn. Decide quickly, for time passes."

Regel's arm trembled with tension. He would not waver in his aim.

"Do it, Whore of Dracaris," Mask said. "See if you can strike before he cuts you down."

Regel lacked Mask's confidence as to his own speed. Perhaps he should throw now, while Ovelia was distracted. She might not see Draca's warning shadows... Then Ovelia moved. Startled, Regel pumped his arm and threw. Too late. Draca slashed around, batted the dagger from the air, and ended up at Mask's throat.

"I will not kill you—not until you give us Semana," Ovelia said to Mask. "But do not think I could spend five years as the Shroud without learning about pain."

"I believe you." Mask huffed a laugh. "Good choice, Bloodbreaker."

Ovelia looked to Regel, and he saw that she was in control of herself. At the same time, though, she would not forget he had tried to kill her. "What must we do?" she asked Mask.

"One life for another. Help me kill a man, and I'll return Semana to you."

"What man?" Ovelia asked.

"Does it truly matter?" Mask's voice was near a whisper, and the creature crept close enough to kiss him—or bite him. "Are there limits to your love for yon princess? Did I manipulate the wrong former knights of the Winter King? Do you know of any others I should try?"

"And if we decide to kill you instead?" Ovelia asked. "You cannot harm Semana then."

"Not I, no," Mask said. "Remember though, Bloodbreaker: all this has come to pass as I intended. Perhaps I left instructions for my men to cut the girl's throat if I do not return—that, and worse. Both before and after." Its chapped lips smiled inside the slit of the mask. "*Explicit* instructions."

That stilled Ovelia. They were beaten, Regel knew, and Ovelia was realizing it.

"Fear not, once-Shield-and-Shadow of Winter, it's not a death you'll mind overmuch." The sorcerer stretched, making its joints pop loudly. "In fact, I suspect you crave this man's death nearly as much as you want mine."

"Enough riddles." Regel said. "We will walk what path we must. Name this man we must kill."

Mask looked at him for a long time, considering. "He is Summer King Demetrus Ravalis, Lord of Tar Vangr, Usurper of Winter's Crown." Something like bemusement touched Mask's voice. "A regicide isn't too much to ask, is it?"

Neither Regel nor Ovelia laughed.

"Why us?" Regel asked. "Surely you can kill any man, no matter how powerful. Even a king."

"I should think that obvious." Three trails of smoke rose from Mask's fingers to disperse into the air. "First, because you, Lord of Tears, are the greatest slayer among Calatan's heirs—as you proved by defeating my student and myself. Second, because of that fabulous magic-drinking sword you bear. And third"— Mask nodded at Ovelia—"because *she* has done it before."

Ovelia whirled upon Mask. "Foul creature! You—"

"It is simple truth." The sorcerer spread its hands. "You are the Bloodbreaker, are you not? I watched you do the deed."

Ovelia grasped her forehead as though in pain. "Enough."

"Do you not see the agony in her, Lord of Tears?" Mask asked. "She, who has hunted me for five years? She, who has used all the resources of the hated Usurper to find me? Who knows how she has compromised herself—how she has sullied her honor and betrayed her Blood and..."

"Enough!" Ovelia grasped Mask by the collar and pulled the sorcerer into the air. It dangled like a straw doll in her hands. "Enough of this!"

"Ovelia," Regel said, drawing her attention. "Stand down."

She looked at him beseechingly, anger clear on her features. He could well imagine the indecision within her—the war between hope and wrath. She did not understand. But she would.

"Do not blame the Bloodbreaker, Lord of Tears," Mask said. "Her enmity is well founded. She is a slave to her feelings and her judgment is tainted."

Finally, Ovelia set Mask back on the floor and turned away. "We will do this thing," she said. "But speak another word to me, sorcerer, and it will be your last breath."

"So like a woman, to speak with her heart. I would hear the one who speaks with his head. " Mask looked to Regel. "What say you, Lord of Tears?" Stone skittered underfoot outside the destroyed temple. Finally, someone was coming to inspect the devastation—coming in force. "Your vow, please."

Regel looked down to the rubble on the floor. He selected a piece of rosy stone about half the size of his hand. The stone was soft, almost as easy to work as wood and perfect for carving. He saw something in it—something that the stone should be. In Regel's hand, the hunk of dawnstone aligned with Mask's body at a distance. Regel beckoned the sorcerer forward.

Mask approached, until they stood only a pace apart. This far from Draca, the ensorcelled parts of Mask's armor crackled back into life and power whirred. Ovelia gave Regel a questioning look and reached for the sword. Regel stared down at the piece of dawnstone and let his senses take in the scene around him: the settling dust, Ovelia's sweat and quickening pulse, the stench of rotting flesh that wafted from Mask. And most of all, the cold, sharp edge of the throwing knife flat against his palm.

"What say you?" the sorcerer asked.

ACT THREE: SLAYERS

Five Years Previous—The Dusk Sea—Ruin's Night, 976 Sorcerus Annis

THE *HEIRESS* CUT THROUGH the night sky on its northbound journey toward Tar Vangr, which lay shrouded in darkness at this distance. Dark clouds drifted across the crimson moon, rolling like smoke trapped inside the black dome of Ruin's sky. Far to the east, over the Burning Lands where the sun stirred from its slumber, silver traced the edge of night to herald the coming dawn.

Tithian leaned against the gilded rail of the skyship, peering down at the Dusk Sea as it lay like an edgeless sheet of dusky glass a thousand paces below. Every few seconds, one of the mage-engine rings would scythe past in front of him on its slow spin around the ship, sweeping magic in its wake. The breeze at this altitude pricked at his cheeks—the one fresh and smooth, the other scarred and numb.

He didn't want to be here at the prow of the ship, where a boy his age shouldn't be. Tomorrow would mark the end of his thirteenth winter, and he was far from a man grown. The blackness frightened him more and more with each increasingly rapid breath. The knife at his belt—a gift from the Frostburn himself—had seemed impressive before they'd left Tar Vangr, but the endless gloom rendered it insignificant. He clutched the hilt for reassurance, even if he had no idea how to use the blade.

He would never admit his fear, of course—particularly not to she who had asked him to wait for her. He shouldn't be here. He *wouldn't* be here, if it weren't for the princess. Syr Sargaunt hadn't wanted him along, but she had insisted. She was going to be the death of him one day.

A white-gloved hand slid over his, and a warm body pressed itself against his back. A voice whispered in his ear: "What do you see, Tith?"

He yelped and whirled away into what he meant to be a defensive stance. Instead, his club foot caught under him, and he landed on his backside on the deck. His attacker's hazel eyes filled with laughter. "Your—Your Highness!" Tithian said, and haltingly dropped to one knee.

Princess Semana Denerre nô Ravalis raised her chin and peered down at him like the noblewoman she was destined to become. Wind rippled her white-blonde hair—the mark of the Blood of Winter—and she wore a magewrought cloak to match. The fabric seemed to flow into the night, less like a garment than mist, tinged by the red silk scarf she wore around her neck. As Semana stood there heedless of the night, the breeze revealed a hint of red and pink petticoats below her silk gown. Tithian was probably not supposed to be staring at these so intently, so he looked to the deck beneath her feet.

"What, did I scare you?" She crossed her arms. They were of an age, he and the princess—three years short of majority—but when she looked at him that way, she seemed much older. The scrutiny of her vivid, topaz eyes made him uneasy. "What sort of warder is so scared of a girl in a cloak?"

"Just startled, Highness." Tithian rose shakily. He released his white-knuckled hold on the dagger. "I didn't see you."

"Thank you." The seriousness of the moment fell away as the princess beamed. The dimples at either end of her mouth made her seem much younger.

Tithian kept his eyes carefully on the deck. Her well-sculpted face always reminded him of his own ugliness—how the skin hung limp and dead on the left side of his face. His left eye had grown too big and had never seen anything in light but could see in darkness, like a thing out of a two-bit bard's song. Semana, on the other hand, was a princess of Winter—a perfect creature carved from snow and ice.

"Tithian," she said. "Look at me."

Could she hear his thoughts? Tithian felt warm and sick at once. "But Highness, I—"

"Must we play this game every time?" Semana's soft fingers touched his chin like cold steel, setting his skin to tingling. "Look at me. I command it."

Tithian sucked in a breath, then raised his head—haltingly—to meet her gaze. When he caught her eyes, all his fears flew from him in the wake of her smile. He had the body of a beast, but just then, he felt like the handsomest man ever born in the World of Ruin.

She leaned in close to whisper in his ear. "I'm glad you're here."

For a heartbeat, he thought she might kiss him. Tithian nodded dutifully, trying to hide his suddenly very hot cheeks. "Of course, Highness," he said. "Your will commands me."

Semana pulled away, her expression fallen a little. "Oh, must you? Tith, I bring you with me for your honesty. Don't become another of those weak-lipped morons, bowing and sniveling and providing *absolutely* no fun."

"No, Highness," he said. "Certainly not."

"Good." Seemingly oblivious to his deepening blush, Semana put her hands on the gilded rail and gazed off into the darkness. "So. Will you answer my question?"

"Pardon, Highness?" He didn't remember her asking a question, much less what it was.

With a bemused smile, Semana gestured ahead into the night. "What do you see?"

Hesitantly, Tithian crept back toward the rail. He made sure to stand to her left, so as to present his best face to her. He squinted to no avail. "It is too dark, Highness," he said.

"No, no!" She pulled him to the rail and pressed him into place beside her. "Look harder!" Then she gave him a daring look. "Or are you *scared*?"

Balling his fists for courage, Tithian stared into the void again, then shook his head. "I still see nothing, Highness. Only darkness."

She looked at him fully now, and he saw again the mischievous girl who had sneaked up on him and whispered in his ear. "Exactly," she said.

"What?"

"Something my mother used to say." Semana leaned against the rail and let her hair trail over the side into the night. She looked sidelong at him. "The darkness—is it not beautiful?"

Tithian tried to respond, but he couldn't think clearly with Semana pressed against into his side. Her touch did funny things to his mind and especially his body. He hoped she wouldn't notice, or he would get a whipping from Syr Sargaunt for sure.

"The night, just like this." The princess looked over the rail. "I love it. I can stand here and look and there is only me. No wastrel father, no honored mother ten years dead. No kingdom of Winter—no war with Luether—no Ruin." She closed her eyes and sighed. "Just me and the darkness. Free."

Fear gripped at Tithian's bowels, but at her side, he could banish its haunting caress. Indeed, unusual courage rose in him in that moment, and his hand crept toward hers. He watched his hand move and knew he should stop himself, but chose not to do so.

"You feel it?" she said, making him hesitate. "Alone, out here in the vast... I can almost forget."

Tithian was about to touch her. "Princess—?"

At that instant, something pinched him hard on his backside, and he yelped and fell away from the rail to the deck, fumbling for the dagger at his belt. The princess covered her mouth in a half-hearted attempt to stifle laughter. "Ah ha!" she said. "I *knew* you were afraid."

Tithian's face burned. "Am not!" he cried as he climbed to his feet.

Semana peered down her nose. "Am not, *Highness?*"

He bent his knee halfway and spread his hands. "Am not, *Semana.*"

"Insolent boy!" she said, trying not to laugh. "I shall have to berate you for that."

Light glimmered in the distance, and Tar Vangr appeared before them. The watch-fires atop the battlements broke from the gloom first, then the forges kept eternally alight in the never-ending silver flame of the Nar. As they drew closer, Tithian could see a glow within the great glass window of the palace throne room.

"There," he said. "I feel much better now that we can see the lights."

Semana wore a pensive expression as she considered the city's muddy radiance. "We fear the darkness," she said. "And that which we fear becomes our master."

"Did... did you mother say that as well?" Tithian asked.

Semana made no sign of having heard the question. She seemed far away.

Whatever courage had filled Tithian a moment before fled in the face of those words. He was not and would never be a brave soul—not like the undefeatable

King's Shield or the legendary Winter King's Shadow. Nor even, he realized, like Semana. As the princess stood unflinching in the face of darkness, all her ugly pageboy wanted to do was hide below. At the same moment, however, he would not leave the rail unless Semana went with him. He found that he simply could not do so.

As they drew closer to the city, the gloom receded around the crescent-shaped harbor, and Tithian could see the dull lights of low-city as well. Thick smoke hid them, caustic haze clinging to the underside of the great support decks that held aloft the shining buildings of the high-city.

"Wow," Tithian said. "I grew up in low-city but I've never seen it from above. It looks so..."

"Miserable?" Semana suggested.

Tithian nodded gravely, then his cheeks went white. "Princess, I did not mean—"

"No—no it is true. It is my greatfather's fault." She gestured toward the low-city. "Years ago, the cities were closer—nigh-touching." Her jaw clenched. "In those days, a man's worth lay in his honor and the strength of his arm, not the name of his Blood or the coin in his pouch. But since the Blood War and the coming of the Ravalis..." She scowled. "The Blood of Summer would doom the old ways."

Tithian thought she might be jesting for a moment, but when she turned her baleful eyes on him, his chuckle died in his throat. "Highness, you must not speak so of the Ravalis Blood. Your father—"

"Old Gods burn Paeter Ravalis," she said. "I am my *mother's* daughter. Mine is the Blood of Winter, not of Summer. It is not fevered and self-indulgent, but strong and determined. Unyielding." She shook her head free of the cowl, loosing her white-blonde curls to tumble around her shoulders. It exposed her red scarf, which made him think of blood—and heat.

Tithian winced at her words. "I am sorry, Highness. That was thoughtless of me."

Semana smiled wanly at him. "You do me no harm to remind me of my mother on the eve of her death-day. She has been gone these ten years, but I'll not forget her."

"Then," Tithian said. "Perhaps I should stay, that I might bungle my words and remind you?"

He took refuge behind the gentle jest, as he often did. "Humor is the ugly man's shield," his gutterborn mother had told him, when the other boys mocked him. He had just seen his fifth Ruin's Night, and her words stuck in his mind as one of his first, clearest memories.

Semana pursed her lips, considering his offer. "Promise?"

"You've my sworn vow, Highness." He offered a little courtly bow that made her laugh, and he swore it was the most beautiful sound he had ever heard.

"Tithian, I—" She edged closer to him, and her eyes scanned his face. When she spoke, her voice sounded nervous, which surprised him. He'd never known her to be afraid. "I liked it when you called me Semana. You should—you should do that all the time. Call me that." Her cheeks brightened. "That is, surely we know each other well enough, right?"

There was jesting in her tone, but Tithian could tell her request was deathly serious. He had not realized until just then how much he had longed for this moment.

"If..." He could not resist the draw of her eyes like whirlpools. "If you will it so."

"I do. I—" Then she cried out. "Ah!"

Her cry startled him out of the madness that would have taken his lips to hers. The wind caught Semana's crimson scarf and wrenched it from her throat. Tithian made a lunge for it, but the scarf slipped his grasp and danced toward the sea below like a leaf on the wind.

"Curse you, Old Gods of the Nar!" he cried to the night, half serious, half jesting. He shook his fist at the moon.

Semana laughed. When Tithian looked to her, startled, she only laughed harder. The musical sound was infectious, and he started laughing too.

"What is this?" called a gruff voice from behind them, near the stairs to the forecabins. Tithian looked, and there stood the great whitebearded Syr Sargaunt, a patch over his scarred eye and a farcaster in his hands. He marched toward them, limping stiffly on his bad left leg.

"Naught, Armsmaster," said Semana. "Merely a jest."

Tithian held his tongue. One wrong word and he would be beaten for sure.

Sargaunt loomed over them both, glaring down with his one good eye. The sickly-sweet odor of sweat and old blood in leather wafted from the big veteran soldier. Vangryur soldiers wore their war-scars proudly, unlike the perfumed Summer folk. Once, Tithian had dreamed of being a warrior, but with his club foot he could hardly walk straight, much less learn the graceful dance of swordplay.

"A jest, eh?" Sargaunt looked at Tithian the way he always did: with disapproval. "This one's got a bit of wit to him, eh, Your Highness?"

"Indeed." Semana glanced sideways at Tithian. "Perhaps only half of one, though."

Sargaunt snorted. "Methinks half of the half, but well, as your ladyship wishes. Is Your Highness finished with the boy? We'll be in dock soon, and he has duties."

Tithian winced and gave Semana a pleading look. She returned him a doleful expression. She understood as well as he did how unpleasant his duties could be. "I'll return him after a hundred-count," she said finally. "Tithian was telling me a tale and I wish to hear the end of it."

"A tale—" Tithian furrowed his brow, then realized Semana was lying for him. He nodded vigorously. "About the Red Sorceress. Not, uh, one of the ones I'm not supposed to know, though."

"Indeed." Sargaunt grunted. "Count hundred, boy, and attend me then."

"Aye Syr." Tithian began a mental count. It wouldn't do to disappoint the armsmaster.

Sargaunt marched away, grumbling below his voice about the idle follies of young folk—"telling tales" among them—and Tithian breathed a sigh. "Thank—" he said, but Semana pulled him to the rail.

"See?" she said, pointing downward. "It's just there—quickly now, if you want to see!"

The scarf was caught on one of the orbiting gold rings of the mage-engine. They watched the scarf circle up and around until a gust of wind blew the scarf free over the ocean. They both leaned on the rail to watch it float down. Tithian breathed out a sigh and closed his eyes, content in this moment.

"What do you suppose that is, Tith?" asked Semana.

He opened his eyes once more. "Where?"

"There, just over the water," said the princess. "Can you see it?"

With the sun just peeking over the eastern horizon, touching the world with gray, he could see it—if just barely. Far below, a black shape sped along the surface of the water, heading from Tar Vangr toward the skyship *Heiress*. Toward *them*. The Dusk Sea parted in its wake like unto a fast-moving warship, but it was far too small for a ship.

"A bird, perhaps?" He suggested, though he felt in the pit of his stomach that he was wrong. A shudder passed through the princess at his side.

As they watched, the flying shape twisted from side to side, tracing zigzagging patterns in the black waters. Then—heart doubling its pace as he watched—Tithian saw it pull up, swoop up, and hover in place about half a hundred feet away, alongside the *Heiress*. He thought it was staring directly at him.

High, cruel, mocking laughter rolled all around him. His skin crawled across his bones.

"Arm-Armsmaster—" he stammered.

Then he saw fire crackle around one of the creature's hands, and he wrenched Semana back just as a bolt of flame erupted through the forward rail where they had been standing. They rolled across the deck and huddled behind a ballista as something exploded in the night and the *Heiress* shuddered.

Tithian looked into Semana's wide eyes, which shifted from shock to genuine fear. He had never seen her afraid before. Despite his own racing heart, he nodded to reassure her, then peeked from cover.

The entire front of the skyship had become a smoking ruin. Frightened shouts rose from below as the *Heiress* lurched and began to tilt to the side. The pilot must have fumbled the controls—that, or the blast had killed him. Semana slipped from Tithian's grasp, but he lunged and caught her in his arms. She grabbed the base of the ballista, and they steadied each other as the ship trembled.

Men were rushing up onto the deck, including Armsmaster Sargaunt. He saw Tithian holding Semana and gave the boy a tight nod, which Tithian returned.

The appearance of the soldiers also stirred Semana back to her senses, and she pulled at Tithian's arm. "Come," she said. "We have to get below. Tithian!"

"Ready!" Sargaunt shouted. The one-eyed veteran pointed a farcaster down over the rail and bellowed a command. The dozen soldiers took aim.

"Cover your ears!" Semana ordered, and they both pressed their hands to the sides of their heads.

A series of cracks split the night as the Winter soldiers fired. Their target wove and turned circles around bolts that left trails of smoke. More casters cracked, but those bolts flew false as well. Tithian thought its laughter grew louder.

"Get her below!" Sargaunt shouted at Tithian, pointing at Semana. He turned back to the battle. "Fire the main!"

Tithian heard a violent clack-clack-*clack* from belowdecks—the main cannon being prepared. The orbiting gold rings lined up around the *Heiress*, which hummed with building force. On instinct, Tithian wrapped his arms around Semana's head just as thunder split the air. The noise was deafening and he reeled, dazed. Air burned around him. The *Heiress* shuddered under the force of its own blast, and Tithian watched a great bolt of crackling lightning flash toward the flying creature.

The black thing in the air waited for it, hands raised. Tithian thought he heard chanting.

The lightning struck full force and split into a storm of screaming, dancing sparks that would have reduced a score of men to cinders in an instant. The sound swallowed up the cruel laughter. Tithian had to look away lest the discharge burn out his eyes. He cradled Semana so tight he could feel her lungs shuddering and her heart racing, and she embraced him just as tightly.

In heartbeats, the screeching lightning cloud shuddered and died, leaving a great bank of greasy gray smoke wafting lazily upward. The men breathed out in relief.

Then the laughter renewed, and Tithian gasped. The black form flew out of the smoke, sickly green light dancing around its head, and streaked toward them. It was a person, Tithian realized in the illumination—some sort of horrible flying man dressed all in black. It thrust its hands forward.

A blast of green-black magic tore through the side of the ship, catching half a dozen Winter soldiers in its wake. Before Tithian's eyes, their skin peeled and flecked away, leaving gray-and-red flesh beneath. Then their bodies rotted in heartbeats, turning first to skeletons, then to dust. Where the magic touched the ship, the metal corroded, rotted, and dispersed in the night air.

Something thick and heavy slammed into Tithian's face, knocking him to the deck. Dimly, he realized it was Armsmaster Sargaunt's hand, still gripping a cocked caster. Then—

❧

Tithian only realized the world had vanished when the ship shuddered and he awoke with a start. Steel groaned beneath him and heat raged inside his body.

His eyes opened just in time to see the aftcastle explode. A mage-engine wheel sliced like a barbed disk along the deck and missed him by a hand's breadth. Its maniac path left a deep gouge in the iron and wood of the *Heiress*. It took Tithian a full five breaths before he stopped starring at the flaming wreckage, unable to think, let alone move. He half sat, half lay, and choked in the smoke and the smell of dissolving flesh.

Then he heard a familiar voice, raised in terror. Heart in his throat, Tithian looked around.

There, in the middle of the deck, stood a skeletally thin creature wrapped from the tip of its toes to the crown of its brow in black leather. A cloak fell in tatters from its shoulders and whispered around heavy, iron-shod boots. These, Tithian saw, did not touch the deck—instead, the air blurred beneath them as though distorted by heat, which somehow kept the creature floating just aloft. *Magic.* The thing's face hid behind a thick black mask with thin slits that exposed lips cracked like bark and eyes that smoldered like coals. And dangling from the horror's hand, flailing to break free of its grasp on her collar, hung Princess Semana.

Tithian cried out, but a thunderous explosion tore the sound away. Good thing, too, as he realized the scream might have alerted the creature. A strange calm descended upon Tithian when he realized how close he stood to death, with Semana's own life hanging in the balance. He would not fail her.

Tithian's fingers twitched along his belt to his knife. He closed his grip around the leather-wrapped handle—felt the cold wood engraved with the sigil of the Winter Blood. He remembered the promise the Frostburn had elicited, when he'd handed Tithian the knife:

"Ward her," the Shadow of the Winter King had said. "Kill whoever and whatever you must. Only protect her."

Tithian hadn't known then if he could do such a thing. Now, he knew.

He drew the tiny fang quietly, praying to whatever dead gods were listening that the masked horror would not turn and blow him into a rotting corpse. Tithian rose, supporting himself as best he could on the broken rail, and took one trembling step forward.

The leather-wrapped creature cackled. "You are such a pretty girl." Its voice—a thin, dry rasp as of splintered bones scraping across a dry riverbed—sent pangs through Tithian's arms and down his neck. It traced barbed fingers over her soft face. "I wonder if I might keep you."

Semana's gaze slid to the side—to where Tithian had crept within half a dozen steps—and her captor began to turn. Then the princess looked back up to him. "I'm not afraid of you."

"You are a fool, then," the creature said. "A worthy one, but a fool."

Certain the thing would hear his heart thundering in his chest, Tithian stalked forward. He set down each step hesitantly, like a cat on a crumbling roof. Another day, he might have found it amazing he could move so quietly, but instead he became aware of every tiny sound he made. Each scuff or panting breath might mean death, not just for himself but for Semana as well.

When he got within two paces, he realized if he came any closer, the creature would hear him. Semana must have realized it too, for she struggled to draw its attention. "I will kill you for this," she said. "You, nameless thing, will be punish—nggh!"

Suddenly her body went taut and she coughed greenish foam. Tithian saw green magic flowing from the creature's mask to Semana's chest. He knew nothing of magic, but that looked like killing magic if he had ever dreamed of it.

"How brave!" The creature laughed. "But now it's time to—"

At that instant, Tithian drove the dagger into the masked creature's back with all the strength he could manage. Bright light flared from the sorcerer's coat, pushing back against his thrust. He poured all of himself into the blow, and the deflecting magic began to falter. Suddenly, the dagger punched through the leather and into softer flesh beneath. Tithian bit his tongue at the shock.

The life-draining spell fell apart, and the masked creature looked around at him with red eyes. Its narrow chest pushed out, then in. For a horrible moment, Tithian thought the blade had done nothing.

Then blood—hot and red—welled around his hand. The sorcerer staggered and released Semana's collar, fumbling instead at the dagger hilt. The princess fell to the deck, and Tithian threw his arms around her. Her face was haggard, her eyes half-closed listelessly.

"Are you well?" he demanded. "Are you *well*?"

She shook her head, then looked past him. "Ware..."

The creature's arm bent sharply like an artist's model, grasped the knife low in its back, and pulled the blade free with a grunt. Tithian could see blood spilling from the wound, and puckered brown flesh through the slit in the armor. The blood vanished against the dark leather.

Black hides blood, he realized. He would remember that for the rest of his life.

Backing away, Tithian cradled Semana and did his best to look ferocious when all he felt was fearful. At his feet lay Armaster Sargaunt's severed hand, clutching the still-charged farcaster he'd meant to fire at the masked beast. The red eyes flickered balefully in the firelight. The sorcerer's mouth opened.

"Well struck, Tithian," said the leather-wrapped thing. "Well struck indeed."

"How do you know my name?" he demanded. "Get... get away!"

"It seems—" The creature turned the dagger over in its hand. "You know me not, or else you would flee." It tossed the blood-stained blade over the rail and spread its hands. Its boots began to glow with red light, trailing smoke, and it rose into the air effortlessly. From on high, it spoke to them. "I am Mask, and I am the greatest slayer that bards' tales will ever know."

"Well, burn you and get back!" he shouted. "Leave us be!"

"Tithian, Tithian." Mask floated back to the deck and smiled. "Do you not know me?"

And with that, it reached up and pulled off its mask. Tithian sucked in a breath, and could not blow it out again. He knew that face. He had seen it in his dreams every night that he could remember.

"You've become such a fine boy," said the gnarled and smoldering face, the voice rasping, the teeth shining brilliant white amongst the corrupted lips. "I knew you would."

A scream was growing in the depths of Tithian's throat and he fought hard to keep it down. The world swam and gray spots drifted over his eyes.

When trembling fingers touched his back, he remembered Semana was there. He seized hold once more of his body and faced the slayer who had come for them. He would not fall—not with the princess he loved depending on him.

"Has your life found purpose, Tithian?" Mask was no longer facing him, but had looked away across the dark waters toward Tar Vangr. "Have you found your cause?"

There was a chance—now, while Mask's gaze was turned. Tithian squeezed Semana's hand, then laid his other hand on the caster in Sargaunt's limp fingers. The dead hand still clutched it hard, so he released Semana's hand and set both hands to prying the caster loose. As he worked, sweat ran down his face and he prayed that Mask wouldn't turn.

"Sometimes," Mask said. "Sometimes, one must look into the abyss to see what is in one's heart." The sorcerer rose and started to turn. "Is this not so... Semana, my child?"

The princess made a mewling sound, and Tithian gritted his teeth. Just— there. He had it.

Now, as the mage-slayer turned back to him, Tithian held the caster low— threatening. Mask's red eyes gleamed in the flames rising from the skyship. With a face ravaged by both fire and plague, the sorcerer looked like a creature from the worlds beyond—a burned god, or the darkest and cruelest Deathless One in the tales of a mad bard.

"I see," Mask said, indicating the caster with one long black finger.

"Just," Tithian said. "Just leave us. Fly away, or what you will. I'll cast."

"I have no doubt of that. Though I see that you doubt yourself, Tithian Davargorn."

His aim wavered. "Wh-why do you call me that?"

"If a slayer you would be, then *slayer* shall be your name. I name you Davargorn—the son of the one who kills. For your father is a monster, and you—you are as deathless as he."

"Deathless?" Tithian's hand was shaking. He put both hands on the caster to make it stop. "I am not some fey creature from the tales, but a mortal man. The man who will kill you!"

Mask smiled. "It is only fitting that you should slay me, you who are born of such violent blood and cold. But you've no idea, have you? As to your father and your mother?"

Tithian's heart leaped. Behind him, Semana breathed harder and faster. She was afraid.

"We shall make a bargain, Tithian Davargorn." Slowly, Mask's skeletal hands drew the black leather mask back over the burned and mangled face. "You require a master, and I lack a squire. Swear yourself to me and I will tell you all you would know: your Blood, your heritage, your destiny."

Sweat trickled down his brow. Semana was staring at him, terrified.

"Would you deny me for *her* sake?" Mask indicated Semana with a nod. "You are such an ugly thing, Tithian Davargorn. Do you truly believe she can ever love something like you—like *us*?"

"She doesn't see my face as it is." Tithian's voice broke into a sob.

"As you say," said Mask. "If you will be a fool led around by your little blade, consider this: should you refuse me—should you slay me—you both die. I can fly her to safety." The black fingers flicked threateningly at Semana, but Mask had eyes only for Tithian. "Can you do the same, boy? Do you have such magic at your command?"

Steel groaned and the deck shuddered under them. Shrieks of metal grinding on metal rose from within the *Heiress*, and the deck began to buckle and tilt. Tithian saw that the rear of the skyship was tilting the other direction, raising a hillock in the middle, over the failing mage-engine. The ship would tear itself apart, and there would be no escape from that.

"What is your answer?" Mask asked. "Will you serve me, or will you let her die?"

Tithian looked to Semana. Tears leaked down her face, but she held her chin high. She would be strong, even to the end. Even without him.

"Tithian," she said. "Tithian, wait—"

He turned to Mask, who stood waiting, green smoke floating up from skeletal fingers. He lowered his caster. "I've an answer," Tithian said. "*Master.*"

FOURTEEN

THE MIDDAY SUN HEATED the rusted iron sides of the ancient ships in Luether's sky-dock nearly to scalding. Light reflected from the corroded metal and flickered across the old stone and mage-glass of the nearby buildings, there to be caught and focused into hot rays that the darker things of the world took care to avoid.

One of those dark things lurked across the way in the window of the Mewling Mink—a tavern of considerably ill repute. Sweat dripped down his hooded face, and thick breath made his shoulders heave. His face ached with a simmering fire to match the one in his heart. Partly hidden behind a curtain, the man gazed across the thoroughfare to the skyship being loaded and readied for launch.

To be betrayed and cast out, after all he had sacrificed... No. Not Tithian Davargorn. He would have his vengeance.

From his post at the window table, he watched as lines of tattooed men and women in white breeches boarded the massive skyship *Avenger* across the high street. Such pleasure ships passing between the mage-cities were an uncommon but not unknown occurence: Luether and Tar Vangr had uneasy diplomatic relations at best, but it had been long enough since open war that the two cities had settled into a truce based on mutual survival. Even if they had the official blessing of the Ruin King, the ship's crew took great care around the many Children. As many carried swords and shortcasters as carried trunks and valises. They escorted merchants who traded the most delicate of goods or else nobles who had the coin and idleness to travel between the mage-cities at whim on pleasure ships filled with drink, music, and rutting. How wrong it seemed, that in a world of poverty, folk wasted so much coin on debauchery.

The *Avenger*—once the flagship of Denerre, now the favored pleasure ship of the Ravalis—passed between the two cities rarely in these latter days, as the Ravalis were proscribed in Luether. At first, Davargorn had seen its arrival and assumed Prince Lan had grown impatient and sent an army after the Lord of Tears and the Bloodbreaker, but no Ravalis troops had emerged. Perhaps the *Avenger's* arrival indicated new negotiations between the mage-cities, but having met the Blood Prince of the Ravalis, Davargorn found that extremely unlikely. What other reason could the skyship have had to come to this awful city? Davargorn wondered if his former master had arranged all this. How long had all this been planned, and he had known nothing of it?

His face still ached where Mask had ripped it apart, and his hands trembled.

He would have his vengeance. Of that, he had no doubt.

Whatever its mission, the *Avenger* had been in Luether only one day before it loaded up to make the trip back north. The folk milling about the high dock were of two sorts: frail men and women, relieved to shed their heavy furs in favor of immodest silks and short skirts, as well as a few dour-faced nobles trading coin in the shadows. The ship disgorged a small horde of indolent nobles and merchants brave enough to do trade with the Children of Ruin. Not a single threat among them.

Two of the passengers, however, were neither merchants nor nobles but certainly dangerous. The attendants handed up a black-wigged nobleblood and an older gentleman one might take to be her personal warder or perhaps an unnamed lover. It was a deception with a touch of truth. Behind them, two bare-chested, white-girded attendants carried a heavy leather trunk locked with a bronze clasp. Davargorn wondered whether the "lady" actually carried the key to that chest, or if her "warder" did. Would the Lord of Tears trust his pet so much?

He did not see his former master.

Perhaps Mask's treacherous plan failed after all. Perhaps the two aging knights had proved impossible to manipulate and thus they had refused whatever task the sorcerer had planned for them. Perhaps Ovelia—how Davargorn *hated* her—had slain Mask with her magic-devouring sword. Or perhaps Mask had succeeded and the three of them were following the sorcerer's deadly course.

Regardless, Davargorn would follow.

Fingers traced along his shoulder. "What do you seek, Syrah?" a woman asked.

Davargorn turned.

One of the brothel's celebrants sat beside him: a doe-faced woman with pushed up breasts and heavy make-up. When Davargorn turned to her, the woman saw his ugliness and the thin color evaporated from her powdered cheeks. She did not flinch, however: the squeamish of stomach did not last in a place like this. Her quivering hands betrayed her anxiety.

"Take ease," Davargorn said. "I reserve my desire for one creature, and it is not you."

Relief flooded her face. Before she could leave, however, he caught her wrist. "Wait."

He saw revulsion in her eyes, and it awoke a fire in Davargorn's belly: a deep, abiding resentment he recognized only too well. He traced a finger down the inside of her forearm, causing the hairs to rise.

"You." He pulled his lips back from his teeth and grinned. "How much for you?"

She chewed her lower lip in a way that aroused him. Such false innocence. "Ten silver swords for the hour, to do as most men wish." She met his eyes, and her face grew cool. "Should you desire longer or anything *unusual*, 'tis more."

Expensive, but she was worth it, not the least because she could master her fear. She must be made of cold steel, and he liked such women. They reminded him of his lost princess.

"Very well." He guided her to sit beside him. "I wish something... unusual."

The woman did as he bid, though warily.

He unbuttoned and drew up his sleeve. The skin beneath was smooth as fresh cream, crossed with hairs and thin scars like faded bruises.

"You... you've sweet skin," she managed. Reaching.

"Stop your flattering prattle. I know I am ugly." From his sleeve, Davargorn drew a throwing knife—small but very sharp. He turned the blade over, letting the edge gleam in the dawn's rays through the window. "This will do."

Her eyes followed the dancing light. "If you touch me with that, it'll cost a great deal more than ten silvers."

"No fear, you hard whore. It's not for you." He pressed the knife's hilt into her hand. "Cut me."

"What?"

"I'll guide you." He clasped her hand harder. "Cut me."

Her fingers trembled in his grasp. "But Syr—"

He pressed his face to her ear. "Cut me now, or I'll slice up your face so you're uglier than I am."

The woman trembled, but she did as he bid. When she brought the knife down to his flesh, she loosed a gasp just louder than a whisper. "Good," he said. "More."

Together, they drew the blade along his arm, slitting the flesh open as neatly as sun-softened butter. Red spread along the path of the knife, and blood welled. The pain was sweet indeed.

The woman panted faster and faster as they cut. Her face turned red and her eyes unfocused. A horrified moan escaped her throat. Davargorn smiled. And concentrated.

His skin rippled. The blood ceased flowing from his arm. The flesh drew together as though pulled by invisible stitches. In a matter of two breaths, the cut became a pink crease. It left nothing of the wound but a niggling pain, which left him breathing hard and aroused.

Alas, there was no time. He had a skyship to stow away upon.

The woman was still staring at his arm. "What magic is this?"

"The magic in my blood," he said, his voice shaking.

"I... I am honored," she stammered. "To speak with one of the Blood."

"No need to be honored—mine is not a named Blood." He slid his sleeve over the healed wound, rose, and strode away. "Not yet."

~

The high sun of midday began to sink as the *Avenger* got underway.

A handsome skyship attendant led Regel and Ovelia aboard and lit mage-lamps inside their two guest chambers, making the room fill with the sickly smoke of the world being burned. The appointments were lavish by the standards of Ruin: a wide, soft bed, an ever-flowing basin, and personal heating stones for cooking. A sideboard waited for them, replete with drinks of all sorts, including a decanted Echvar wine and a small beaker of Angarak brandy. The mage-city of the west had fallen to Ruin nearly a century ago, and the fruit of its orchards was quite rare indeed. Traveling on a pleasure ship in the guise of wealthy patrons had its benefits, and also its risks.

After what had happened in Aertem's temple, Regel suspected they would not enjoy this journey.

Two more attendants made to carry in a heavy trunk, but Ovelia raised her hand imperiously. "Hold," she said, not meeting their gaze. "Leave that for a moment."

The attendants eyed her dubiously—in particular the linen-wrapped sword at her belt. Only barbarian women bore steel in Luether, but most Vangryur did, regardless of sex. The noble scions on the *Avenger* wrapped their blades in cloth to signify their purpose: fashion, not fighting. This blade, however, was clearly functional.

"My man will care for it." Ovelia nodded to Regel, who took the cue to pass two silver coins to the attendants. The metal silenced any protests. They set down the trunk with a loud thump, like a coffin set upon stone, then left.

Regel looked at her quizzically, and Ovelia gave him a look that said to follow her into the chamber immediately. He did so and shut the door behind them, leaving the trunk in the corridor. As the door closed, he saw a spindly young man chasing a chubby young woman down the hall, both of them laughing and roaringly drunk. The *Avenger* was, after all, a pleasure ship in these latter days, and that meant this would be a long journey.

"You wanted a moment alone. What—?" Regel's words died when he saw the veins bulging in Ovelia's forehead, her face turning bright red. "Pass well?"

She tore the black wig from her head, exposing a wild mass of mostly silver curls with crimson roots. She hurled the wig at the bed, where it fell limply to the floor. Ovelia clawed at her cheeks, trying desperately to rid herself of her disguise, or possibly scratch her own face off.

"Ovelia," he said again, and caught her arms. "Stop it."

She shook her head, raising her hand to her mouth. "Regel, I—" she said. "I can't—" She kept trying to begin, but the words tumbled from her lips without coherence or control.

He put out his arms, and she gladly pushed herself into them. He held her tightly.

"Mask—is he telling the truth?" Ovelia spoke in a whisper. "Are we doing the right thing?"

Regel pressed his nose into her hair. Beneath the perfume that was part of her disguise, Ovelia smelled like sweat and steel—like *her*. "We do what we must," he said. "The rest is dust and shadow."

"Dust and shadow," Ovelia echoed, her voice breaking. "You cannot know how hard this is. Five years, Regel—*five years!* How can she have been alive all this time?"

"This is our path, Tall-Sister."

Calling her by this, her oldest name, had a definite effect on Ovelia. No one else used this name—no one but they two and Lenalin.

She pulled away. "I abandoned Semana," she said. "I *abandoned* her, Regel."

He understood. It was easier for Ovelia to believe Semana murdered and try to avenge her, than to believe she had let the girl languish in the captivity of a horrid monster. "You—" he began.

There came a groan of steel from below and the ship rocked. Startled, Ovelia caught herself on Regel's arm. After a moment, the shuddering passed. They both looked at her hand on his arm. Though they had embraced only a moment ago, now it felt like an intrusion. Whatever wall had crumbled between them, this day had rebuilt it. Silently, Ovelia drew her hand away.

"What—?" she asked, hugging herself. "What was that?"

"Mage-engines that barely work," he said. "The *Avenger* was built for the Blood War, forty years past. Age defeats all in the end, even the craft of titans."

Ovelia looked unconvinced. That wasn't what she had meant.

As if in response, the skyship vibrated and whined. Regel could almost feel the frustration as the sorcerers belowdecks strained their powers to batter the engines into alignment. He drew open his belt pouch and perused its contents: a rose-hued chunk of Dawnstone, his carving knife, Semana's signet ring, and one last object, which he withdrew and held in his palm. He considered it—it, and its implications.

Ovelia's eyes lingered on the key in Regel's hand as upon a drawn knife. "We cannot." She was going white. "I know what you would say, and I want it so badly, but we cannot—*Regel!*"

He turned from her and opened the door, but she slammed it shut with one strong arm. "You do this," she said, "and there is no going back. You know that."

Regel nodded. "We do what we must," he said again.

That struck her. Bowing her head, Ovelia released the door, then crossed the room to place her hands on the footboard of the bed. There she leaned, looking far older than he had ever seen her.

The trunk waited out in the hall where the attendants had left it. Awkwardly, Regel drew it into the cabin. He grunted with the weight, and the tainted air of the cabin made him wheeze. A foolish old man should not have to walk such a path, but he had taken the first step, and now he would see it through. He set the trunk down in the middle of the room, then closed the door to the corridor. He held the key flat in the palm of his hand.

"We cannot run from this, Ovelia," he said.

She was looking at him through her trailing silver hair. "I will follow you, Lord of Tears," she said. "But it will not please me."

That tugged at his heart. "I understand," he said.

She straightened. A single flick of her wrist tore away the silk wrappings from her sword—cleverly tied to resemble a peace-bond without truly securing the blade—and she drew it smoothly. Shadows swirled around Draca's hilt. "Ready," she said.

Regel crossed to the chest, knelt, and slid the key into the lock with a soft hiss of metal on metal. Ovelia watched as the lock clicked open and Regel pulled back the lid.

Mask lay within. With one leg splayed out and its arm swaying listlessly over one knee, it seemed more a carelessly flung manikin than a living creature.

"Regel." Mask's reddish eyes gleamed up at him.

"I think," Regel said. "I think it's time you outlined this task you mean for us."

Mask made a reedy sound that might have been a chuckle. "Gladly."

FIFTEEN

A N HOUR LATER, THEY sat in their cabin as Mask finished outlining the plan for assassinating the Summer King Demetrus Ravalis. Regel found himself nodding. "A worthy plan."

"It's doomed," Ovelia said from where she sat at the table, spinning Draca against the floor.

"Oh?" Mask said. "And you see a flaw, do you?"

Ovelia stared hard at Mask. "It assumes that we trust you."

"Ah." Mask glanced at the bloodsword in Ovelia's hands. "That little detail."

Mask sat on the bed, still as a corpse, and seemed hardly to notice Ovelia's sword. One knee rose into the air and one arm crossed its chest, fingers dangling. The other hand flicked idly at the crank that wound the bed tight. The sorcerer seemed totally at ease.

"Reconsidering our arrangement, Bloodbreaker?" Mask said. "It was easy to agree in the heat of the moment, but now that I have explained my tactics, you grow leery, no?"

Regel considered. The plan was both deceptively simple and audacious. Their attack would unfold on Ruin's Night, in conjunction with the masquerade the Ravalis held every year. They would walk into the palace and murder the king in his own bed.

"I thought you two would appreciate the symmetry," Mask said. "Luether fell on a Ruin's Night, as did each of the would-be rulers of the Blood of Winter. Revel as they might, death will come to Tar Vangr this year, as it did fifteen years ago, ten years ago, and five. Let us honor Death, the only true god of Ruin, on that night of all nights."

The sorcerer raised its silver gauntlet, and Ovelia readied her sword. "Have no fear, Bloodbreaker. This broken wretch merely thirsts."

Mask indicated the sideboard set with numerous beakers of wine, water, and mead. Magic steamed around the silver gauntlet and a beaker of water rose up from the table and floated toward the sorcerer. Droplets trailed down the sides of the glass and dripped onto the floor in a damp path. Mask drew a pouch from its belt and sprinkled some tea leaves into the water. Of a sudden, Regel remembered making tea for Ovelia this morn, so that she would not perish of a rotted belly. He had not intended their task to take as long as it had, and he would have to watch her carefully in the days ahead.

A doubt passed through him as to this course, but Ovelia had made herself clear. By killing her, was he not simply honoring her wishes? He was not certain.

"So tell me." Mask placed the beaker atop its right palm, as though demonstrating a newfound wonder. The talons of the gauntlet wavered with heat, and water sizzled around the base of the beaker. "Now that I have spoken too much and told you of my plan, do you have any questions?"

As Regel watched, bubbles rose and the water shook in the beaker as it began to boil. He gazed upon them, keenly aware of the shard of dawnstone in his pocket.

"Why do you want him dead?" Regel asked. "King Demetrus."

"Why..." Mask paused, as though the question had caught it by surprise. "As to that, I keep my own council. It will suffice that I want him dead, just as much as the Bloodbreaker wants *me* dead, and just as much as you want *her* dead." Mask nodded to Ovelia. "I don't trust you, and I don't expect you to trust me, but Semana's life depends on my victory." Mask looked keenly at Regel. "She's very beautiful, you know. Like her mother was."

Regel nodded. "As long as you keep your word and deliver what you have promised, we will walk this path of yours."

"Outstanding." Mask put the beaker to its chapped lips and sipped the foul-smelling tea. Its gaze slid to the side. "And what of you, Lady? Do you harbor doubts?"

"She and I stand together in this," Regel said before Ovelia could speak. He did not like that doubt in her eye.

"I'll hear it from her, as it please." Mask's broken voice dripped with confidence. "Speak, Bloodbreaker: you, who would rather rip out my throat than look upon me."

"No."

Regel looked at Ovelia, perplexed. "Ovelia, we cannot—"

"I know what we can and cannot do." Her Bloodsword gleamed as though streaked with blood. Shadows leaked from it, suggesting a battle to come.

"Ovelia," Regel said more forcefully.

"You had best listen, Bloodbreaker," Mask said. "Listen to your lord and *master*."

"I have no master." Ovelia spoke with winter's chill. "No longer."

"Of course not," Mask said. "You killed him."

Beneath their notice, Regel reached for a blade.

"Get out," Ovelia said.

"Many apologies, my dear seducer," Mask said, "but that's not an option. Unless you want the crew to see me and spoil our game before it truly begins."

"Not you." Ovelia looked to Regel. "*You.*"

"Ovelia," Regel said. "Think about this."

"This must pass," she said. "Mask and I have words we must share, and we can only do so in private. Have no fear: on my word, your pet sorcerer will be well when you return."

"But will *you* be, Bloodbreaker?" Mask asked, showing sharp white teeth.

"Go," Ovelia said to Regel, "or I swear by all the Old Gods that I will cut out this monster's throat right now."

Regel saw there was no reasoning with her. She was determined, and one thing he found impossible—and admirable—about Ovelia was her pride. "You are in earnest."

"If you don't trust me"—Ovelia extended him Draca, hilt first—"then take my weapon."

Mask watched the entire exchange, its face unreadable behind that damnable leather faceplate. By contrast, Regel felt naked under the scrutiny. What was the creature thinking? Its red eyes traced the fault lines of doubt and anger that ran through them both like black veins.

Regel withdrew his hand from the proffered hilt, leaving Draca in Ovelia's hands. "Keep it," he said. "Draca does not lie."

"No," Ovelia said, looking him in the face. "It does not."

Regel crossed the room and stepped out into the over-perfumed corridor, which was filled with laughter and music from the communal hall down the way. When he closed the door behind him, he wondered if he would see either of them alive the next time he opened it.

~

"So." Mask stretched its legs at an impressive angle and it leaned forward. "As the powdered gentleman said to the painted whore—what now?"

Ovelia considered. Regel's instincts to the contrary, she felt certain this was a trap. What reason had she to believe Mask was not in league with the Ravalis? And even if regicide was Mask's true aim, surely the sorcerer could see that Regel and Ovelia were the two souls in the World of Ruin with the most reason to *despise* it. Killing them would be a matter of self preservation. She had no reason to trust Mask.

No more than Regel had to trust you, she thought.

"Can your magic ward this room so that none will hear us?" Ovelia asked.

"Yes." Magic wavered around Mask's left gauntlet, and the sorcerer drew a rippling curtain of force across the entrance to the chamber. Abruptly, the rugged sounds of a skyship vanished, as though they were suddenly enclosed in an orb of glass. Ovelia had seen such magic before: it would block movement and sound, both concealing and trapping them inside the cabin.

At length, Ovelia set Draca on the floor at her feet. Then she undid the first button of her coat.

"Hmm," Mask said. "Interesting."

Ovelia loosened her traveling coat, slipped it free of her muscular shoulders one arm at a time, and tossed it on the bed. Next, she unlaced her gown and let it fall to the floor around her feet. She felt lighter, stripped to her undershirt and breeches. Purified.

"You certainly have my attention," Mask said. "By all means, continue."

Ovelia knelt and whispered a prayer over her sword, reclaimed the weapon, then stood and backed away slowly. When she had put six or so paces between herself and Mask, she stopped.

"You're sure this is wise, Bloodbreaker?" Mask's voice was cautious. "So far away, how will you bind my power?"

"I won't." Ovelia fell into a dueling stance.

"Oh, so it is to be war after all. Lovely." Mask raised its hands, both of which pulsed with magic. Reeking smoke rose to stain the ancient wood ceiling.

"A test," she said. "I stand here with no secrets. No tricks. Pit your power against mine."

"And what would that prove?" Mask asked. "Did you not triumph in Aertem's temple, in the City of Pyres? Were you not sated then?"

"You planned that duel from the first blow. You meant for us to come against you, you meant for us to defeat you. Else, how would you have known to prepare that grisly proof of Semana's life? No." Ovelia raised Draca to the level of her eyes. "I would defeat you myself, or see that I can't."

Mask's dry chuckle told her which the sorcerer thought more likely. "Why should I fight you? I don't suffer the same self-doubt you do."

"Then kill me," Ovelia said. "Tell Regel I attacked you and you had no choice. The two of you can accomplish your task without me."

"You would sacrifice your chance to see your princess?" Mask considered. "You do not believe me that she lives. Despite the proof I offered."

"Should I?" Ovelia breathed heavily. "Which is more likely: that you have hidden Semana for five years, and in all that time, despite all my spies—and all of Regel's—there has been no word of her, not a single sighting, or that you took her signet ring on the *Heiress* and put it on some poor girl's finger to fool us?"

After a beat, Mask made a rasping sound that might have been a chuckle. "You are angry. Searching for a way to deny your failure. I am glad to have aroused such hate in you."

"Accept my challenge or do not, but you will not mock me."

It was a gamble. If Mask won, then Ovelia was dead. If the sorcerer lost, then it revealed the limits of its power. Surely Mask would refuse such a gambit. Surely...

Shadows bled from the Bloodsword, warning of an attack to come. Ovelia saw herself, crouching to one knee, fighting to stand. The near future.

"Very well," Mask said. "I will match you, Bloodbreaker."

Power surged around Mask's hands: humming distortion around the silver glove, and crimson flame around the blackened talons of the war gauntlet. The sorcerer raised its left hand.

Magic hit Ovelia with a force that, if she hadn't known what to expect after their battle in Aertem's temple, would have knocked her dead of shock. Soundless power crushed down upon her like a hammer. Somehow, she remained standing, holding Draca like a shield between herself and Mask. Flames roared around her sword, burning away the magic.

"This is the power of the Unseen Hand, and it was this magic that brought mighty Atropis plunging into the sea." Mask's voice was casual despite the fearsome attack. "I did not do the deed myself, understand. I may not be young, but that was two centuries gone."

Ovelia focused around the pain. She trusted the sword as her father had, and his father before him. The blood of dragons surged within her, and magic sang in the blade. Mask's power roared into Draca, the sword sucking at it like a thirsty man forced to drink a waterfall.

Then slowly the force began to ease. Mask's body trembled, and the sorcerer gave a frustrated grunt. Draca could endure this punishment, and so could Ovelia.

The sword drank more and more, until finally Mask lowered its hand. The power flickered away into a muted crackle around the silver gauntlet. The sorcerer made a last dismissive gesture, and the magic vanished entirely. "And what does this prove to you, Bloodbreaker? Is this not what passed between us in the temple of Aertem? Would you have that dance once more?"

Ovelia stepped forward. "Now invoke the fire." She put both hands on her sword to steady it. "Show me Luether's bane."

"As you wish."

Mask raised its right hand and obliged. Hungry red flames descended, and Ovelia held Draca before her like a talisman. As the intense heat built around her, Ovelia felt every small hair on her arms awaken and every bit of exposed skin light with searing life. Her teeth vibrated in her mouth. But the sword absorbed this magic, too, leaving Ovelia untouched. Draca glowed like the sun in her hands.

Mask slouched over, coughing. The sorcerer's own attack seemed to have harmed it more than Ovelia. "Are you well?" she asked.

"Fear for yourself," Mask said. "Your relic is greater than mine—one of them, anyway."

Ovelia had not realized until this moment how many riches Mask was carrying. Two gauntlets, the mask, and probably the armor itself . . . How many relics of the Old World did the sorcerer possess?

Sword raised, Ovelia stepped forward. "All of it," she said. "This test means nothing unless you use all of it. Or don't you have the strength?"

"Oh." Green-black lightning crackled around Mask's leather helm. "Oh, I've a strength to me you've never *imagined*."

The world sizzled as a green-laced cloud of inky darkness swelled from Mask and shrouded Ovelia. Her lungs filled with agony as she breathed in the fumes. Where her flesh touched the corrosive haze, all feeling bled away and left itching numbness. "This—" Ovelia said. "The magic you used in the temple... against Regel..."

"This is *Plaguefire*, Bloodbreaker." The black mist wreathed Mask's head and shoulders like a corona. It sprang from the oldest and most powerful of the sorcerer's relics: the mask. "The bane of Echvar, City of Rain, and—if the legends are true—the killing stroke that fell upon the Old World. This"—Mask raised its arms wide—"is Ruin itself."

Ovelia held her breath as she fought against the magic. Her sword's light dampened in the darkness as a war raged between its consuming fire and the killing cloud.

Father, Ovelia prayed. *Father, aid me.*

163

Mask's power began to wane, and for the first time, the sorcerer looked unsettled. "No," it said. "I will not be thwarted by a *toy*."

Mask brought both its gauntlets up—one blazing, one pulsing with invisible force—and sent all the power in all three relics against Ovelia's one. Magic poured from the sorcerer's head and arms, filling the air with its noxious smoke. The force knocked her to one knee, but she held on.

Draca drank it all—everything Mask could hurl at it. Ovelia pushed herself up until she stood tall amongst a storm of flames. She stepped forward and placed her sword tip against Mask's helm.

At that, the sorcerer let the power die away and stood panting. Its narrow chest heaved and its hands curled. Ovelia could see that the sorcerer was in agony.

"Does all pass well?" She reached toward Mask's face.

"Away!" Mask slapped at her extended hand and held up its still-burning talon.

Shadows poured from Draca in sudden warning. Ovelia managed to bring the blade around, but she couldn't parry the packing trunk with her sword. It dashed her to the floor with breathless force.

"Did you think my magic meant only for attack?" Mask asked.

Ovelia lay stunned as the trunk rose of its own accord, then slammed down into her a second time. Draca clattered across the floorboards. The fires of its magic dimmed as it lay, untouched.

"I appear to have won, Bloodbreaker." Mask leaned down. "Yield."

Ovelia struggled vainly against the traveler's chest pressing her down. She fought and thrashed like an animal caught in a trap. She could scream, but no one would hear through Mask's warding over the door. She was alone.

"Bloodbreaker, really," Mask said. "This is no way to behave with dignity."

Ovelia cried out and pushed herself halfway loose. The chest scraped along her battered body, awakening new hurts. She felt a deep pain in the pit of her stomach, as though someone had driven a spike through her. She thrashed and struggled against Mask's power.

She had to get up. She had to keep fighting. Semana needed her.

Semana...

"Bloodbreaker," Mask said, warning in its voice. "Yield now."

Ovelia opened her mouth to speak, but all that issued forth was a moan so piteous that even Mask stopped, taken aback by the cry. At once, all the fight left Ovelia, and she slumped back onto the floor. "Kill me, then," she said. "Kill me and have done with it."

"Why?" Mask asked.

"What does it matter?" Tears pooled against Ovelia's nose and fell across her cheeks. "I *abandoned* Semana. I left her, when I should have believed in her."

Mask stared at Ovelia without comprehension.

"I gave everything for her from the moment of her birth—my duty, my honor, my body—and when she died, I kept giving for her. And now... *now* you tell me she lives?" Ovelia uttered a tiny cry of pain. "You cannot say something worse to me."

"I—" Mask seemed momentarily unsettled. Then the sorcerer set its jaw. "I did not know you for a hateful woman, Bloodbreaker. To hate so many, so much... it is neither godly nor noble of you."

"I hate no one so much as you."

"Except yourself?" Mask asked. "I see it now. You hide your face—shroud your name in any of a hundred masks. King's Shield, Bloodbreaker, Shroud... Why do you hate yourself so much?"

"Don't—" Ovelia coughed and shook her head to clear it. She thought of Regel making love to her and calling her by another's name. "Don't pretend you understand. Don't you dare."

"I certainly know what is is to hate yourself," Mask said. "You remind me of me."

"Old Gods, I was wrong," Ovelia said. "There *is* something worse you could say to me."

Mask knelt, knees popping, and brushed a lock of hair out of Ovelia's tear-streaked face. "You and I are creatures of retribution. We have suffered great wrongs, and they must be avenged."

"My only vengeance lies in your death," Ovelia said. "So kill me now, for I will never stand beside you."

The sorcerer considered her a moment. Then it rose and made a dismissive gesture with its silver gauntlet. The magic faltered, and the tremendous weight lifted from the trunk pinning Ovelia down. Suddenly, sounds rushed into the cabin—clanking, scraping, and the whir of mage-engines. Mask's ward had vanished from the doors to the corridor.

Ovelia shifted the trunk off herself. She felt intact, though the trunk would leave substantial bruises across her middle. Draca gleamed on the floor just a pace away. Slowly, not daring to look back at Mask, she reclaimed the blade.

Let there be an end to it. Let Mask's lies come to nothing, and let Semana be avenged.

When she turned, however, the sorcerer stood apart from her, reaching back to unbuckle the burned iron clasps of its mask. Ovelia smelled sweat and ash, mingled with the scent of blood. Battle—that was what Mask smelled like. Battle and death.

"What are you doing?" Ovelia asked.

"I will show you the hate upon my face," Mask said. "Perhaps then, you will understand why I must do this thing—and why you must help me."

Ovelia tightened her grasp on Draca.

The leather creaked as Mask loosened the belt clasp then drew the back wide. Spider-like fingers trailed up along the rim of the mask and curled beneath the edge. Then Mask pulled the leather away with a sucking sound.

Ovelia's eyes widened and her mouth fell open. There were words, but she could not speak them—could hardly *think* them.

"Now," the face beneath the mask whispered. "Let us talk plainly, Ovelia Dracaris."

～

Regel stood on the raised aft deck of the *Avenger*, carving while he watched the narcissistic nobles taking their ease on the middle deck. It pained him to see the mighty skyship turned from the most fearsome weapon in Tar Vangr's fleet to a glorified orgy barge, but he supposed all folk had to cope with the madness of a broken world in their own way.

He could not deny the utility of the skyship, in particular the marvelous difference between travel by air and sea. It would take only a single night to fly to Tar Vangr—a journey that had taken more than a quarter-moon by ship. If they kept hidden for that long, they could reach their destination unmolested.

He suspected few on the Avenger would pause in attending their own pleasures to consider three passengers who did not partake. On the main deck below him, men and women coupled with abandon in the great pool of water or reclined on benches, trying vainly to catch the last rays of the setting sun. This far south, folk lost their inhibitions, blaming their indiscretions on the proximity of Luether. Perhaps the laws of morality and order waned as one moved south, and chaos crept into the minds and bodies of those who came to the Summerland. That was their great excuse, at least—it was imminently fashionable to "give into Ruin" without ever actually experiencing the misery of a city where it held sway.

Had the same sort of madness driven Regel into Ovelia's bed? He could not say. His mind became no clearer as they journeyed north, however.

As night fell, the nobles retired to rut in their privy chambers or communal halls, replaced by crew who went to work cleaning the main deck, maintaining the ship, and securing cargo. Men grunted and heaved, strapping crates in place and lowering them into the hold. The great gold rings revolving around the ship hummed disconsolately in the mystic grip of the *Avenger*'s sorcerer pilot.

Ovelia joined Regel at the rail looking out over the main deck.

"You just left Mask alone?" Regel carved a fleck of stone from the dawnstone chunk and tossed it over the side. The stone was soft, almost as easy to work as wood.

Ovelia hesitated before she replied, and when she did, her voice was somber. "Would you feel better if I said I chopped its head off?"

"Perhaps," Regel allowed.

"Well, in that case..." Ovelia waved her hand. She left the jest unfinished.

The night lengthened as the skyship shuddered its way through the clouds.

"Thirty years past," Regel finally said, drawing Ovelia's sidelong gaze. He made two quick cuts in the stone. "Thirty years past, this ship carried five thousand soldiers to war. I rode it myself, when first I carried steel for the Winter King." Regel swept his hand across, indicating the crew and passengers milling about the main deck. "Now, it can barely manage a few hundred passengers."

"All things fade with age," Ovelia said. "As you and I have."

"Fitting." Regel looked away, down into the surf crashing on flame-shrouded rocks far below. The water hissed into steam as it rose, and white curled up toward them.

"A fitting name, as well." Ovelia nodded toward the bow, where perched a figurehead statue: spear-wielding Arys, the angel of vengeance. "*Avenger.*"

"Vengeance upon the Usurper," Regel said.

Ovelia nodded soberly.

The vibration in the deck was less now that the journey was underway. The sorcerers of the *Avenger* had wrestled the mage-engines into quiescence. It flew toward Tar Vangr as smoothly as a river flowing inevitably toward the sea.

"We have to do it," Ovelia said. "We have to help Mask."

Regel nodded. "He leaves us little choice."

"It—*he* doesn't." Ovelia looked away and closed her eyes. "If we kill Demetrus, it will lead to war. You know that it will."

"Yes." Regel turned the dawnstone in his hands, exploring its facets. No clear image had occurred to him as yet, but now he began to see what he would carve.

"This will be the spark that lights the flame of the Last War," Ovelia said. "Many, many more will die from this—perhaps the last of Calatan's heirs." She shivered. "We will bring Ruin."

"Yes." Regel put his hand on her arm. "Do you trust me, Tall-Sister?"

"I do."

He drew her into his arms and kissed her. Ovelia reached her hand up around his neck and returned the kiss. He might have lost himself in her embrace, but he sensed hesitation in her.

Mask had done something to her, Regel thought, and now she was unnerved.

"What is it?" Ovelia pulled away.

"Naught." Regel squeezed her hand. "You should rest."

"You mean... I should share a chamber with Mask?" Ovelia looked further unsettled.

"Let Mask sleep in the trunk," Regel said. "Just because we walk where he guides us does not mean we have to spend time with him."

Ovelia accepted this with a nod, though Regel felt again that hint of hesitation in her bearing. What was she hiding?

"And where will *you* sleep... *Lord of Tears?*" She made the last words a rasping imitation of Mask's broken voice, such that Regel chuckled.

"*Bloodbreaker,*" he mimed back, though he confessed her imitation was better than his own. Ovelia had ever had a gift for mimicry. "I suspect I'd find little sleep in a cabin with you."

"Bestain my virtue!" Ovelia smirked, seeming for a moment like young Lenalin, who had honed innocent flirtation to such a point as could pierce steel.

"I shall simply have to accompany you, Lady Dracaris," he said. "I suspect you won't close your eyes without me."

"Certain of my bed, eh?" Ovelia pressed her lips to Regel's cheek. "It is that sort of confidence I admire in you."

She left him then, standing as he did watching the waves far below. His mind turned to the poison yet working in her—he had been taking care to delay it with judicious servings of food and tea laced with sweetsoul powder. He considered telling her, but he wanted to know why she was playing him first. If he revealed his treachery now, she would never trust him.

Also, it was too late to save her. What would be the purpose of it?

He gazed out into the encroaching dark.

SIXTEEN

IN HIS DREAM, SHE stood before him, a radiant angel with silver-blonde hair down to her waist. Her white gown swirled around her as she turned to him, laughing.

"Come, Regel," said her voice. "Dance with me."

He opened his mouth, but the words refused to emerge. What could he say?

"Do you not love me, Regel?" she asked, her eyes pleading. "Won't you love me?"

But he shook his head, light trailing in arcs from his eyes. "I swore an oath."

She disappeared then, her perfect, willowy form dissolving into the folds of her white gown. The fabric flowed around him like mist, then vanished entirely. For a moment, he was all alone in the candlelit room, breathing shallowly in the thickness of her lingering scent.

"Lenalin," he murmured. "Princess—"

Then she lay in his arms, blood pouring from her mouth and trickling from her eyes. Her body was a wasteland of flapping cuts and deep gouges. She gasped and choked and tried to say his name. His hands soaked up her blood like sponges as he tried to cover her wounds, but there were too many.

Her eyes opened and met his. "My child," she said, her voice burbling. "Where is my—?"

Regel awoke, still and unmoving in an unfamiliar bed in an unfamiliar place. A woman lay beside him, her left thigh cushioning his head. She was not Lenalin, even if both of them wished her to be.

He wanted to scream and scratch his skin to ribbons to get rid of the blood he still felt on his hands. But he had dreamed this dream a thousand times before—twice that—and he knew the terror that gripped him when he awoke. Knew it and could master it.

He sat up and let his breathing slow. He clenched and unclenched his fingers. He let his mind remember that he was not Regel Frostburn, Shadow of the Winter King, but Regel Oathbreaker, the Lord of Tears, an old man with a new purpose.

Beside him, Ovelia stirred. He felt her naked body tense as she came awake all at once.

"What is it?" she asked in a cool voice below a whisper. Hers was the voice of a warrior, ever prepared to reach for steel at a heartbeat's warning.

"Naught." He laid a hand on her hip. Her skin was warm, her muscles powerful. He leaned down to kiss her shoulder. "We are safe as yet. Sleep."

She did as he asked, though her eyes closed slowly. She rolled onto her stomach and pressed her face against his thigh. With one hand, Regel explored the gentle curve of her back, the crimson dragon inked in her flesh, the soft swell of her breast pressed against the sheets. She shivered when he traced her spine with his fingers, then sighed in release when he drew his hand away. Ovelia was a different woman, yes—fuller, stronger, harder—but still he could not help seeing Lenalin when he looked upon her.

"*We have used each other before,*" she had said.

At length, Ovelia's breathing turned to the gentle rhythms of sleep. He sat for a time, naked in the chamber beside her slumbering form, and contemplated his hands. Finally, he scraped them together to remove the sweat. Despite his dream, it was not blood.

Regel pulled away.

~

Out on the deck of the *Avenger*, the night became increasingly cold as Tar Vangr grew close. No wonder the nightmare had returned. After the stifling warmth of the bedchamber, the air fell upon Regel's face like a chill rain. His neck and chin prickled with two days of gray-black stubble. He sniffed and rubbed his nose, then climbed the stairs to the upper deck, where the cold had chased away even the most dedicated hedonists.

It was as he climbed the fifth step that he heard it—a soft crooning hum, like a siren's song on the night's breezes. He froze on the stairs and listened. He knew the tune: the gentle caress of notes almost like a lullaby. A vision came to him of a beautiful, silver-haired lady clad in a flowing white nightgown, who stood at the window over a wide winter-garden and sang. Was he still dreaming?

Fingers shaking as he gripped the rail, Regel climbed quickly and silently, eyes constantly moving for a sign of danger. He had not worn a weapon up onto the deck, but for *her*, though, he could tear men apart with his naked fingers—he could shatter stone with his fists.

He gained the upper deck and looked around wildly for a heartbeat before his eyes fell on a figure at the rail. Its black cloak blended into the night beyond the *Avenger*'s rail, and Regel saw it with such suddenness it startled him: Mask.

It was *Mask* who was singing.

Somehow, its cracked vocal cords produced a melody so haunting in its beauty that he could hardly think. The sorcerer sang into the darkness, its voice neither low nor high but somewhere between. Coming from that creature, it must be a song of mourning, and not of love. Regel stood and listened. The familiar song bore him away to another, softer time. Finally, he could take no more.

"Do you not think it dangerous," Regel said. "To stand in the open and sing?"

Mask turned so suddenly Regel realized he'd come upon the sorcerer by surprise. Its red eyes opened wide for a heartbeat, but composure quickly returned. "Danger is the point, Lord of Tears," Mask said. "The question is: did you like it?"

Regel shrugged. "Your voice is fair."

"A compliment," said the sorcerer. "And from you, Lord of Tears. I am flattered."

Regel shrugged and leaned against the rail. He tried hard to keep his voice level. "Where did you learn that melody?"

"Here and there," Mask said. "That is not such an uncommon song. Surely your mother sang it over you when you were a babe. Did it awaken your memory, perhaps?"

It had, but not a memory of his mother. Had Mask caused his dream?

The sorcerer always seemed to sense his distress with unnerving skill. "Does this song carry a bad memory, Lord of Tears? What manner of monster would I be to disturb your rest needlessly? I will stop."

"If you wish to sing on, do not let me stop you," Regel said.

"Very well. Pretend not to care." The sorcerer made a snuffling noise. "I sing only when I am alone. Pardon me if I do not wish to expose my flaws to you."

"Of course."

They looked into the empty night for a time, and Regel listened to Mask's ragged breathing. It no longer pained him to hear the rasping sound.

"A woman I once knew," he said at length. "She loved that song."

"Oh?" Mask asked. "And what happened to her, I wonder?"

In his memory, Regel heard Lenalin's beautiful voice contorted in cries of agony. He heard the bells announcing death in the house of Winter.

"Troubled sleep, Lord of Tears?" Mask asked. "Is yon strumpet not to your liking? She seems lovely and willing enough."

"A curious sentiment for a creature without lusts."

"I never claimed I had no lusts," Mask said. "To desire and not to act is merely restraint. I might desire your woman as well, Lord of Tears, were I yet a man." The red eyes slid to him. "Does it reassure you or unsettle you, to think of me desiring another creature?"

"Why would I care?" Regel asked.

"If I am merely a monster, you know me in one way, and can easily face your fear," Mask said. "If I am rather a man, ah, then that is different."

Regel had expected Mask to be vile, treacherous, and horrid to behold, but he had never expected wisdom. "Perhaps," he said. "But man or no, I imagine you are beyond such things."

"How true. I am no longer the man I once was." Mask stretched, bending his arm backward to an almost impossible angle. "You are kind to hide it, but I see you cringe when you look upon me," he said. "Tell me, how many men have you left ruined as I am? Have you looked into any of their eyes?"

"No." Regel looked down at his hands. He could still feel Lenalin's blood upon them. He would not think of her eyes—her beautiful, diamond-like eyes. "I look away."

"You should not," Mask said. "You might be surprised what you find in the eyes of the dying."

Regel looked hard at Mask, his mind alight. Of a sudden, he was possessed of a burning urge to see what lay beneath the black leather mask. The sorcerer wielded several ensorcelled relics, but no power of its own, at least as far as he knew. Since anyone could use those devices, given time and training, that mask could hide anyone's face.

"You are wondering why you find me familiar," Mask said.

Was he so easy to read? Regel shook himself. "What do you mean?"

"It is like looking into a mirror, perhaps? To see your darkness outside. Unmasked." Mask drew deeply of the night air. "We are not like the Dracaris woman. Warrior she may be, but she is only flesh and sinew, breath and bone."

"I am made of such things." Regel tamped his pipe. "You are not?"

"This business," Mask said. "It is why folk such as you and I are born. We are blades forged of flesh. Thin skin stretched tight over sharp steel. You, me—we are weapons."

"Weapons," Regel said.

"Our bodies are ephemeral, like egg shells that nurture the serpent within. Until one day, we break free of our shells and understand the world." One gloved hand indicated the stairs, ostensibly pointing toward Ovelia's adjoining chamber. "The Bloodbreaker's shell is just beginning to crack. She will find her darkness soon—or she will die."

"What makes you think she has darkness?"

Mask regarded him sidelong. "We all have darkness, Lord of Tears," it said. "Only some of us choose to wear it like skin. For some of us—" Mask's fingers slid over the black leather wrapping its face. "For some of us, it *is* our skin."

Regel paused. "Is there no skin beneath that mask?"

"Perhaps." Mask's teeth flashed. "Care to see?"

Regel felt the half-carved shape of the dawnstone sculpture in his pocket. Its touch emboldened him. "Did Ovelia react any better to this speech?" he asked. "It seemed a bit rushed to me."

Mask considered him a moment, then uttered a guttural laugh. "Was that a jest, Lord of Tears? That, I did not expect." It turned back to the rail.

Neither spoke for a time. Rather, they stood together staring into the abyss. The air was far clearer over the Dusk Sea than near one of the mage-cities, and they could see hints of stars twinkling far above.

"Why do you want him dead?" Regel asked. "To prove that you can, or for vengeance?"

Mask gazed off into the night.

"Do you look, Lord of Tears?" the sorcerer asked. "Into the darkness, I mean."

"No," he said.

"Pity." Mask looked at him. "You remind me of him, you know—my old squire."

"The one you dismissed from your service with a shredded face for his pains?"

"Indeed. Davargorn is his name. *Davar* means 'the one who kills' in the tongue of Old Calatan."

"I know it." Regel knew also that *gorn* was the word for "son," though if Davargorn was the son, Regel did not wish to meet the father. Perhaps Mask itself bore that dubious honor.

"He is gone, and now I have no slayer to destroy my foes for me."

"What a shame that is." He turned to go.

"I wonder—will *you* slay for me, Regel?" The red eyes bored into his and the lips spread in a thin, cruel smile. Its voice was husky. "Can you?"

Regel paused on the stairs, remembering similar words from long ago.

Will you slay for me, Regel? Lenalin had asked him. *Can you?*

"That woman you knew, who sang that song," the sorcerer said. "I'm sure she forgives you."

Wordless, Regel descended to his cabin, lay down beside Ovelia, and slept.

~

Again, Regel dreamed the same dream.

Lenalin appeared again, one breath beautiful, the next beaten and ruined beyond repair.

But now, instead of dying as her blood poured over him like an endless flood, she rose up, smiled cruelly, and donned a black leather mask.

SEVENTEEN

THE *AVENGER* ARRIVED IN Tar Vangr's high dock as the sun set the next day, shuddering beneath her feet. Through the rail under her hands, Ovelia could feel the mechanical claws engage like the grip of an executioner. Behind them, the horizon lit with pink and purple clouds, the legacy of ancient mage-wars.

"Such beauty out of Ruin," Regel murmured at her side. "Eh, Tall-Sister?"

"Hmm." Ovelia had been watching the distant glow, her mind far away. "Oh. Yes."

She had other, darker matters to consider. What she had seen beneath that mask, for one.

If Regel read anything into her distraction, he did not show it. He'd taken up his carving again, gouging tiny grooves in the fragment of dawnstone. Ovelia wondered what form the carving would take but knew that, regardless, he would make it beautiful. He always did.

Such beauty, she thought, *out of Ruin*.

"We should move," Regel said.

Ovelia nodded.

As they entered the cabin, Ovelia averted her eyes from where Mask lay inside the open packing trunk. The sorcerer watched mutely as Regel shut the lid. Ovelia traced the battered leather surface lightly, her fingers spread apart and caressing ever so gently. She almost thought it would break at her touch, like withered paper.

Softly, Regel reached across and touched her wrist with two fingers. Instantly, her hand twisted over and caught his. Her eyes like polished topaz darted up to meet his gaze.

"Are you with me?" Regel asked in a whisper.

"Of course," Ovelia said. In truth, however, she wasn't certain.

There came a knock at the door. "Enter," Ovelia called. She moved away from her "servant" for the sake of appearances, but not quickly enough the staff would not catch them. Deception was about telling a story, and it had to be told in every moment: in every little glance or gesture. Ovelia took refuge in the guise of the noblewoman and her lover, because it let her not think about Mask, or what the sorcerer had asked of her: a request she was powerless to resist. Ah, the game of lies.

Two men in the white uniforms of the *Avenger* crew entered. "The chest, lady?"

Ovelia waved dismissively. "Yes, take it, Syrs."

They took Mask's transport away, and Ovelia heard Regel exhale softly in relief. Not so with her, however. Indeed, seeing Mask depart filled her with more anxiety, rather than let it dissipate. She finished the tea Regel had brewed for her, which settled her stomach. Her innards had grown temperamental during the flight, and she hoped solid land would help.

"Ready?" she asked finally. "Regel?"

He looked up, but she had caught him glancing warily at her stomach, as though he could feel her unease. Did he hold the same suspicions she did? Most men were clueless about such things, but he had always had sharp senses. And she and Regel *had* shared a bed often of late. Could it be possible?

"Let's make an end of this," Regel said, and gestured her out into the hall.

Her insides ached.

~

Davargorn watched from atop the aft deck as great steel talons ground into place through gaps in the *Avenger's* hull. The clamps locked, holding the ship aloft by aged steel girders. The mage-engine groaned as it powered down, and the great gold rings slowed and came to a rest, aligned with one another beneath the skyship.

The passengers of the *Avenger* debarked with alacrity, including first Regel with a heavy trunk, then—after a few moments—the black-wigged Ovelia escorted by two attendants. He suspected they'd purposefully made their exits separately, not only to maintain their fiction on the ship as illicit lovers, but also to discourage any Ravalis agents who might be watching for a man and a woman. Clever.

Davargorn, however, had been cleverer still, taking the place of a skyship attendant who wouldn't be missed for a few days. It had let him spy upon them with impunity, as the brainless nobles of the pleasure barge hardly looked twice at the liveried waitstaff. Even if they had, the uniform included a full helm, which disguised his telltale features. So long as he kept his crippled left hand hidden in his sleeve, he became another anonymous servant until the moment came to strike.

Crewmen put the trunk on a magewrought disk of steel, which floated obediently a dagger's length off the ground. Regel thanked the white-breeches with gruff nod and a silver coin. Davargorn waited while he steered the trunk across the gangplank and through the dock. Without her protector, Ovelia would be vulnerable, and Davargorn suspected his moment drew nigh.

In his guise, Davargorn dutifully escorted the half-drunken, exhausted passengers off the *Avenger*. When Ovelia reached the deck, Davargorn palmed a knife in his left sleeve and offered his right hand to guide her. He said nothing, as his voice might give him away. He gave Ovelia no reason to avoid his hand—indeed, her guise as a noblewoman demanded she accept his help. And then he would...

"Pardon." A red-haired man stepped past Davargorn and took Ovelia's hand. "If I may, Lady?"

Davargorn turned away before either of them could see his face.

"Certainly," Ovelia said in a voice so far from her own that Davargorn could have applauded. She blushed on command. "Your assistance is welcome, Syr."

The man bowed and escorted her down the final steps. She stumbled, though

Davargorn saw it was feigned. Her guise worked well on this red-haired dandy. A pretty man following the noble—his valet, perhaps, or lover—gave Davargorn a stern look and dismissed him with a wave.

Davargorn murmured a curse under his breath. He'd have liked to stick his blade a few times in both the Bloodbreaker and the interloper, but now he felt vulnerable with so many eyes watching. This was not the place to move. His vengeance could wait, and perhaps that was for the best. A new plan stirred in his mind, one that he'd set in motion as contingency, and one that could catch all three in the same trap: Ovelia, Regel, and especially Mask.

When the passengers were clear of the skyship, he vanished into the streets of Tar Vangr's high-city, shedding his borrowed uniform in a muddy alley.

He knew exactly where to go.

~

"My thanks, Syr," said Ovelia as the man led her down the plank from the *Avenger*.

"Of course," he said, his voice rich and his manner gallant.

He wore the plain but well-appointed clothes of a traveling merchant, lacking any blood insignia or colors other than simple black. He had deeply tanned skin and bright red hair, and his features were those of Luether—bold, lively, and noble. Also she knew him: Garin Ravalis, who had come to their rescue in the streets of the City of Pyres. The timely question, however, was whether he knew *her*.

"I am surprised to find such a beautiful woman unescorted." He pointed back to where she had purposefully stumbled. "Who would have guided you over yon treacherous step?"

"That one seemed eager enough." Ovelia nodded to a crewman who was limping away.

"And why would he not?" Garin gave her a grin that nearly touched his emerald-green eyes. The man had dangerous dimples. "But it appears the good fortune is mine, no? I am Garin."

He had not given her his Blood name. Interesting. "Aniset of Dolvrath. Quite charmed."

"A lady of a potent Blood." Garin bowed. "The charm is yours, the pleasure mine."

He did not recognize her then, or if he did, he hid it well. Despite what he had said, the Blood of Dolvrath was thin, and that told Ovelia that Garin meant to flatter her. To Garin, she was just a lovely Tar Vangryur returned from business in the southern city. His smile was infectious, and his eyes bright and sharp as they roved her face. Ovelia resolved to be careful of his obvious charm, as to compromise her true identity now would be as good as death.

"Alcarin," he said to the man following them. "Mind the lady's luggage, if you would?"

The youth returned a long-suffering scowl and looked about for Ovelia's non-existent suitcases.

"No need," Ovelia said. "I have a manservant of my own, who has gone on ahead."

"Ah, of course, of course." Garin gave the youth an intimate look of acknowledgment that told Ovelia the man was no mere manservant, nor a bodyguard. She understood, then, the looks that had passed between Garin and Alcarin on the streets of Luether, and knew how deep a secret it must be. How scandalous it would be for one of the scions of the brusque Ravalis to have a kept boy to warm his bed.

She remembered Alcarin from Luether, though she had glanced at him only for a brief moment. She had worn a disguise that day and he did not seem to recognize her any more than Garin had, but she hid her visage just the same. She brushed air over her face with the sort of black-and-white paper fan often carried by merchant ladies such as she appeared to be. It served a second purpose in hiding her face.

They descended to the main dock, amongst the men sweating and shouting orders over the crates that came down the ropes. Men operated pulleys and levers, and Ovelia saw several sorcerers lingering about. Skyship workers or waiting mage-slayers? She could not say.

"Something troubles, Lady?" Garin eyed her keenly. "You are plying that fan like a swordsman."

"No, no trouble," she said. "It is unseasonably hot for a Vangr winter, don't you think? I had expected relief after the heat of the southlands, but the winds blow as they will."

"Ah, but I am a child of the south—the Blood of Summer beats in my veins." He caught a strand of her fake black hair between his fingers. "Unlike the winter's daughter you seem to be."

"Oh?" Ovelia suppressed the urge to pick at her wig. "Finally escaped the barbarians?"

"Perhaps." His eyes flashed. "Though I fear my stay in the city will be brief. I've come to pass Ruin's Night with my Blood and entertain a business offer."

"A business offer?" Ovelia asked, though she should not have. Curiosity often aroused the like in others, and it would not do to have Garin Ravalis seeking to find out more about her. She played off the question. "You must be an important man if you flew all the way to Tar Vangr."

"Would it surprise you if the *Avenger* flew all the way to Luether, just for me?"

He was teasing her, she knew, but she knew that hadn't been a lie. It explained the *Avenger's* presence in Luether, but why would they go to so much trouble to bring one of their own back into the fold? And moreover, Garin was the Ravalis scion who never played the political games of the rest of the Blood. After all, he'd stayed in Luether despite its fall to Ruin, swearing vendetta against King Pervast and seeking at every turn to overthrow the barbarians that ruled the city. And now he returned to Tar Vangr, but he did not claim the Ravalis Blood or name. Was his visit a secret one? To what end?

"Perhaps this offer is significant to a woman of business," Ovelia said. "Perhaps you might offer me a hint?"

"Over a fine meal and finer libations, Daughter of Dolvrath?"

"I doubt I am the sort you wish to woo, Syr." Ovelia cast a meaningful glance back over her shoulder. Hinting at his secret was a gamble, and she stood to win little, but information was power. "Do you not know that Dolvrath is the Blood of Chastity?"

"Pure body, pure mind, indeed." Garin smiled, deflecting her hint as neatly as a swordmaster's parry. "It matters little, fair one, for I shall inevitably decline, and then I'll away to the southland once more. I suspect on the morrow, in fact." He tossed up his hands. "Oh that it should be even so long! I cannot abide the chill of you northerners—though I make exception for beauteous queens of ice." He gave her a meaningful smile.

It was a fine game, this flirtation. But even had she not seen how he looked at Alcarin, she would have guessed he was trying just a bit too hard. He bore a heavy burden, trapped in a body that wanted what his Blood frowned upon. She knew more than a little of such a thing.

"I am sorry Tar Vangr is too cold for you, and that your city was too hot for me," Ovelia said.

"We are a poor pair, are we not?" He squeezed her hand. "Unless there is some way we might reach a happy middle. Your blood might cool mine and mine warm yours."

"How shocking!" Ovelia held the fan closer over her face, as though to hide a blush. "You southern men are all one—do you think of nothing but rutting?"

"I pray every day that I never shall," he said, and bent to kiss her fingers.

Strange thing to hear him invoke faith, Ovelia thought. The folk of summer notoriously paid little heed to the Old Gods, and yet Garin spoke of prayer a certain honest ardor that almost convinced her. His hand lingered in hers, clutching her fingers tightly, and some part of Ovelia murmured a warning. He'd so adeptly deflected her question about his purpose. Luethaar were notorious flirts, and Garin could easily be their king—if she had not recognized the way he looked at Alcarin, she might have been taken in. He used flattery like armor, keeping anyone and everyone at bay so none could learn his true intentions.

"Pray, good Lady Aniset." Garin had lingered by her side and was smiling. "If I find my stay in your homeland a lonely one, might I call upon you for company? I may know little of your city, but I have stories for pleasing you and coin for drinks."

Ovelia smiled despite herself. She thought she should get away from this man as soon as possible, but rudeness would foil her disguise. Besides, she liked him.

"Perhaps, good Syr. Though how might you be so certain your stories would please me?"

"I should love to make the attempt. My tongue is quite deft." He kissed her hand again. "Would you not let me call upon you, Lady Aniset? I would hear your stories as well."

The flattery was in earnest, but beneath it ran an undercurrent of genuine curiosity. She felt scrutinized like a puzzle only partly assembled. Ruin's Night drew close, though, and she had little time to explore this particular riddle. "I think not, my Lord of Summer," she said. "No doubt my husband would not approve."

That gave him pause. If anything was sacred to the Blood Ravalis, it was a vow of matrimony. The Luether of ages past had been a city of obsessive love, where folk pledged themselves to one another by exchanging vows of constancy and devotion. By contrast, marriage was rare in Tar Vangr, and mostly practiced among nobles building alliances between their Bloods. By and large, smallfolk did not partake at all, as they had only tiny legacies to secure. The Ravalis were ostensibly a noble Blood, though Ovelia knew better. Paeter's vows had been a thin shield to hide his whoring, and by all accounts Lan Ravalis was even worse. She wondered how Garin would act.

"Ah, what a pity." Garin took her hand, then gave her an inquisitive look. "My Lady, you seem familiar. Have we met?"

Ovelia suppressed her automatic shock through icy discipline. "I am certain I would remember." She pulled her hand from his grasp and walked on without him.

"Have I offended you, Lady?" Garin reached out and cupped her hand on the rail. "I can—"

Ovelia stepped closer to him, forcing him to let go of her. "I am quite capable, thank you," she said, harsher than she meant. "You summerborn think us women weak and fragile things, do you not? You have much to learn of my people."

He bowed his head, but his smile remained. "My honor, were you to teach me."

Ovelia stormed off, glancing over her shoulder when she thought she could manage it without being caught. Garin watched from the dock, still smiling. When Ovelia reached a certain alley where she and Regel had decided to meet, she looked over her shoulder, but Garin hadn't followed.

She wasn't sure what had come over her in Garin's presence. The Ravalis had taken everything from her, and yet she liked this one. He'd seemed, with his crimson hair and his gold skin and his swagger, much like Paeter Ravalis, and the comparison was hardly flattering. Paeter had always smirked at her as weaker because of her sex, no matter how strong she had proved herself. By contrast, Garin hadn't said anything of the sort, but she had reacted just the same.

Garin Ravalis, the Fox of Luether. He'd been a legend during her time as the Shroud: a man with nothing to lose and everything to gain. A dangerous man. And if a fraction of the stories about him held any truth, she had come within a single careless word of death. But she'd learned his secret—the reason why he never came to Tar Vangr.

Ovelia passed a lift they had intended to take down to low-city, but it was little more than a smoking ruin of fractured glass and warped metal. It reminded her unsettlingly of the destruction she'd witnessed in Luether, and she hurried on, lost in thought.

She wondered what had changed that the Ravalis had gone to such lengths to bring their outcast cousin back into the fold. Their need must be great to dispatch a skyship to fetch him. Did they wish to know more of Luether, in preparation for a move against the southland? Did it have to do with her, perhaps, to ply his excellent mind to the task of finding her?

Then it occurred to her in a lightning stroke: Garin had spoken of an offer, which could only be one thing. The Ravalis meant to make him the new Shroud.

And knowing what she did of him, Ovelia found that unsettling indeed.

Tar Vangr's high-city was smaller than its low-city, and the streets led straight from the dock to the palace. Ovelia felt the sudden and mad impulse to draw Draca, march straight into the throne room of Tar Vangr, and put an end to all this madness. That path, however, could have no end but in her death, and her odds of success were long. Had she not spent the last five years perfecting the arts of subtlety—learning how to wait for the right moment? Ovelia wondered. She had thrived for five years as the Shroud, but she had tossed all of it away at the revelation of Mask's survival. She had even run to Regel, the man who most hated her, begging for help. She could not deny that impulse had ruled her that day.

And what now? Now that she had seen the face lurking beneath the sorcerer's mask...

"Ovelia." Regel fell into step beside her. "Problems?"

She thought of Garin, but the man hadn't seemed to recognize her. Also, she thought of Mask—of the sorcerer's secret.

She shook her head. "Let's away."

EIGHTEEN

THEY ARRIVED AT THE Burned Man tavern as the sun climbed high over Tar Vangr. Here in low-city, the Narfire forges beneath the streets raised the already hot late-winter day to a sweltering roast. Since the Ravalis had taken the throne, it seemed they had done all in their power to make the city as hot as their ancestral home. The great ice floes that isolated and protected Tar Vangr from barbarians had even begun to thin, and cracks could be seen from the city walls. Many voices on the Council—particularly the Blood of Yaela—spoke regularly about the twin threats of stoking the Narfire and using too much dust magic, but the Ravalis had thus far dismissed such concerns as alarmist nonsense. Tar Vangr had abided in its icy fastness for over a thousand years, they said, and one unusually warm season was no cause for concern.

Regel stepped under the Burned Man's darkened eaves, and paused to gaze up at the pale silver ivy that hung over the door and windows, dripping with bloated snowmelt. The tenacious vine grew regardless of the season, however heavy the snow might fall, and could harm unwary travelers with its sharp thorns even while hidden. It was dangerous even while disguised.

"What is it?" Ovelia asked softly.

Regel looked at their travel trunk and shivered. "Naught," he said.

The door flew open, and Regel had his hand on the hilt of his falcat before Serris threw herself into his arms and pressed her lips to his. Over Serris's shoulder, Regel saw Ovelia withdraw deeper beneath the vines and turn her face away. When Serris released the kiss, her expression was relieved. "Almost thought you weren't to return, Master," she whispered.

"You were almost wrong then, Squire," Regel said.

Serris beamed and kissed him again. "Doubt, but do not disbelieve," she said sagely.

Regel smiled.

"What of the *Avenger*?" Serris asked. "Erim told me it was back, and I feared the worst."

"Erim? What of Meron? I thought he watched the docks."

Serris's expression grew dark. "We had word that the skyship was leaving high-city two nights ago. Assumed the Ravalis had sent a force after you and went to stop it, but Dusters were waiting for us. Meron... he fell." She chewed her lip, and Regel knew the fire in her eyes was a vengeful one. "At least you have returned safely. You slay all the honorless Ravalis on that wretched ship?"

Regel closed his eyes. "No," he said. "There were no soldiers on the *Avenger* when it docked in Luether. Your attack was needless." Serris's face went pale, and Regel instantly regretted those words. Meron's death had hit her hard, and now to learn that it was for nothing? "I did not mean—"

181

"You said *we.*" Serris went pale when she saw Ovelia lurking behind Regel. "Why is *she* here?"

"I have no quarrel with you," Ovelia said. "You need to hear all—"

"Forgot to kill your little traitor, Master." Serris pulled aside her skirt to reveal her favorite dagger strapped to her thigh. "Let me do you this honor."

Regel seized Serris by the arm. "Inside."

They moved through the Burned Man, followed by Ovelia with the hovering crate. Filtered among the two dozen or so patrons, the other Tears watched them with general incredulity. The patrons seemed oblivious, but Regel could tell the Tears had taken the cue from Serris's reaction and braced for battle. Nacacia and Daren stood nearest, and Regel saw the blades they palmed. One might have felt a slight chill, but otherwise the Tears were such perfect actors that only patrons who knew what to look for would note the change in the atmosphere in the Burned Man.

There was no time for this. Regel slashed his hand through the air, and the Tears stood down. "Daren," he said, and nodded toward the trunk. Then, ignoring Serris's questioning look, he drew Ovelia across the common room past a curtain into the cramped darkness of the back corridor. Heat from the kitchens just down the hall filtered their way and glazed Regel's forehead with sweat.

"That could have gone better," Ovelia said.

"Stay a moment before you judge." Regel put a finger to her lips and shook his head.

The curtain thrust aside and Serris's pale eyes blazed at them, saying clearly that the matter was not settled. She stepped into the corridor and let the curtain fall, stealing light and vision again. She pulled a stick of wax from a pocket inside her vest and murmured a word of Old Calatan. Her candle—magewrought and worth every coin—flared with a heatless azure light, casting them in blue half-light. "This isn't going to please me, is it?" she said.

"I shall explain in time," Regel said. "For now, we need a room for our guests."

"Guests? Only see the one."

"Serris, please," Regel said. "Hear me, Squire."

"Always you use that against me. Well, then." Serris scowled at Ovelia. "Climb the stairs, second door on the left side." She turned to Regel. "Master, I must speak with you."

"In a moment." Regel squeezed Ovelia's hand to reassure her. "It will be well."

"As you say." Her voice was calm, but her eyes told Regel to be wary. She climbed the stairs, watching Serris carefully all the while.

The instant Ovelia was out of sight, Serris stepped close to Regel. "When you said you trusted her before, I thought it was foolish," she said. "Now you bring her back here? You will kill us all."

"I need her."

"You said you'd kill her," Serris said. "I was earnest in my offer to do it for you, if sentiment or lust stays your hand. Nay, don't deny it. I see the way you look at each other."

"She is my guest, and she will not be touched," Regel said. "If, of course, this is still my tavern."

"Yes." Serris sighed, and the tension slipped from between them. "Yes, this is still your Burned Man, and we are still your Tears."

"Good," Regel said. "If you knew who else I brought as guest—"

"Don't care." Serris pressed her cheek into his chest and hugged him tightly. "Glad to see you," she said. "I have to tell you something very import—" Her eyes widened as she looked behind Regel.

"A tender reunion," came the sorcerer's rasping voice. Mask leaned against the wall watching them. "You must be the Angel Serris."

Two Tears pushed through the curtain and pointed their blades at Mask. Regel held up a hand to stop them. "Stand down," he said.

"Jumped right out of the chest, m'Lord," said Daren. It was unsettling to hear the burly tough from the northern ward sound ill at ease. His grey-blue eyes coldly appraised Mask and his thick fingers tightened on the hilt of his blade. "Frightened Erim near to death."

"Not so." Erim was a beautiful boy with shoulder-length blond hair and sparkling blue eyes. By his coloration, the Blood of Winter was strong in him, and more than one foe had underestimated him because of his fine features. "Surprised me is all. Is this thing a friend or a foe, Lord?"

"An ally," Regel said. "You may go."

Daren obeyed immediately, but Erim hesitated. The pale-haired lad looked past Regel to Serris. A question passed between them, and Serris gave him the slightest of nods. They were close, if Regel recalled. Serris had always kept herself aloof from emotional entanglements, but it pleased Regel to see that perhaps she made an exception of the lad. A blade untempered becomes brittle.

"Go," Regel said, letting his fingers trace Erim's shoulder.

The boy looked up at his touch and smiled, reassured. He went away.

"What handsome creatures you keep." Mask nodded to Serris. "Lovely scar. Reminds me of me."

Serris touched her cheek. "Master, is that who—*what* I think it is?"

"And she's heard of me." Mask hissed a laugh. "Delicious.

Serris stepped forward, knife drawn, but Regel knocked her arm wide. "Peace."

"Have you gone entirely mad?" Serris tried again to get past him, but Regel caught her arm and took the blade from her hand. "That's *Mask*, by the Old Gods! The Mage-Slayer! You can't —"

Serris arched back like a hunting cat about to pounce. Regel had no doubt but that she would strike again, blade or no blade. Then she saw something that made her face take on the hue of the bones beneath. Her lip trembled.

Regel looked around at a small child, perhaps two winters of age, who watched them wide-eyed through a door left a little ajar. The girl had inky black curls that fell to her shoulders and eyes seemingly as big and green as spring apples. She was staring straight at Regel.

"Child," Serris whispered. "Don't—"

Mask moved first, stepping past Regel toward the nameless child. The black-wrapped creature bent and fell to one knee—the movement surprised Regel in its smoothness—and extended one thin hand. Serris sucked in a startled breath, but no magic swelled forth. Instead, Mask's hand beckoned and the sorcerer uttered a soft, almost hypnotic hum. The child's bright green eyes turned to Mask, and her mouth fell open. Slowly, she raised her own hand to match Mask's and stepped forward.

"*No!*" Serris snapped.

The girl gave a little cry and clasped her arms behind her back. She looked for a moment as though she might cry, then disappeared into the room behind her.

Regel opened his mouth, but it was Mask that spoke in a voice that was surprisingly gentle. "What a lovely child." The sorcerer bowed to Serris. "Blessings to the mother."

Then the sorcerer climbed the stairs, coughing, and was gone.

Serris and Regel looked at one another. His student's face remained cool, but behind her eyes Regel could see a maelstrom of unspoken words. "Speak," he said.

"No," she said. "You first. First the Bloodbreaker, and now—?" She gestured after Mask.

"I hardly understand it all myself." He put a hand on her shoulder. "Trust me."

Her bright green eyes met his. "You see a prize worth the risk?"

"Yes." He nodded.

"What?" She shook her head. "What could *possibly* make you ally with those monsters?"

Regel thought of Lenalin and of Semana—of his duty to the fallen king, and of his broken honor. He thought of Ovelia, and his head started to ache. He thought of Serris. At times, she seemed the only reliable constant in a life turned to constant surprises. He was glad to have her.

"Someday," he said. "Someday, I'll tell you all."

Serris laid her fingers on his cheek. "Someday soon?"

Regel nodded. "When this comes to an end."

She smiled, but he could see pain in her eyes. She leaned in close as though to give him another kiss, but he pulled away. "What's wrong?" she asked. "Won't you let me please you?"

"Serris—" Regel trailed off, unsure what to say.

"Old Gods." Her eyes went wide. "Old Gods! You're in love."

"No," he said.

She crossed her arms. "Burn you, Regel," she said. "Who'd have thought it? The Lord of Tears has a heart after all." She pulled him toward her chambers. "Now I want you all the more."

"Serris, we cannot." He shook his head sadly.

Serris recoiled. The scar on her cheek burned hot.

Silence lay between them, but for the first time since they had met the night

Regel killed Paeter Ravalis, it seemed impenetrable. His words had split a deep crevasse between them.

"That was what you had to tell me," Regel said finally. "Your child."

Her eyes shot to his. "What?"

"That you have a child." Regel nodded to Serris's door, where the child had gone. "Too young for a name, I think, but clearly yours. Blessings."

"Oh." Serris hugged her arms around herself. "Yes, I—you were away since before she was born. I meant to tell you the day you returned, but then that letter about the mark on the Bloodbreaker came, and you then were off to Luether. There was no time."

"I am sorry," Regel said. "The world does not always allow us the moments it should."

Serris nodded wordlessly, her eyes on the toes of her boots.

"Who is the father?" Regel asked. "Erim? Another? Will you tell me?"

"Someday." A dark cloud crossed Serris's face. "The right day."

"The right day." Regel's fingers felt old indeed against the well-worn banister.

"Just—just tell me this," Serris said. "It's the Bloodbreaker, aye? Not that other creature."

Regel furrowed his brow. "What?"

But Serris was moving off in the direction of her chambers.

Hoping he had misheard her, Regel tried to ignore a rising memory of his dream: of the face that lay behind the mask.

Serris almost stumbled as she hurried to her room, she was shaking so hard. Her face stung as though lit aflame. She felt humiliated, cast aside, and ignored. She'd meant it in jest, about Regel falling in love, but as soon as she'd spoken the words, her heart had begun to ache. She'd waited too long, acted too late, and now she could not have what she wanted.

Finally, she made it to the safety of her chambers. She closed herself inside and slumped backward against the door. Her eyes tightened, her lip trembled, and she raised one shaking hand to her brow. She sniffled—her only concession to the sobs that threatened to rise. She was stronger than this, but why did it *hurt* so?

"Child," she said weakly. "Child, can you—"

She looked up and saw something that slew the words in her mouth.

The little girl sat cross-legged, staring with wonder at playing cards laid out before her. No child of that age could play such a game, of course, but the girl could identify each of the images and she loved to watch the combinations. Usually, it would be Vidia laying out the cards for her to watch, but the baker was nowhere to be seen. Instead, Serris saw the slayer who had attacked her the night Regel left Tar Vangr. His mask was gone, but she knew his mismatched eyes and distorted body. His face looked even worse than she had imagined.

He didn't seem to have seen her, and if the Old Gods were watching, perhaps he hadn't heard her. Heart in her throat, Serris rose, drew her knife, and stepped forward. Unfortunately, her daughter looked up and her face lit with joy at seeing her mother. She was, after all, a child.

"Angel Serris," he said without looking. "I apologize for my rudeness before, when I failed to introduce myself. I am Tithian Davargorn, and as you can see, I go where I please."

The girl beamed up at Serris, oblivious to the threat the slayer posed.

Serris heaved for breath that would hardly come. "This is my home," she said. "What do you think you are doing here?"

"Playing a game," Davargorn said. "I believe you're familiar with the rules."

Serris fought against the lump rising in her throat. "Child, be calm. Watch the cards."

The child looked back to the cards and Serris glared at Davargorn. "This is my place," she hissed at him. "*Mine*, understand? You have no right—"

"I have what rights I take." Davargorn smiled at her. "Listen well, and I shall not need to take more than I already have."

"Doesn't matter what you say to him," Serris said. "Doesn't matter if it's his child or not. There's nothing to destroy between us."

"You misunderstand the threat, I take it." Davargorn looked pointedly at the girl and touched the hilt of a blade that lay on the bed. "This was never about him and you. This is about you and her."

"You'd harm a *child?*" Serris reached for her steel. "Even a creature like you cannot be so vile."

"Can I not?" Davargorn made a face and the girl giggled. "You'd be amazed how much hate one can brew in five years' time."

Purposefully, Serris drew her hand away from her weapon and closed it so tightly her fingers turned white. "I know what you asked of me. I won't do it. I won't betray him."

"You've a choice?" Davargorn reached back idly and brushed a lock of black hair out of the girl's eyes. The child didn't seem to notice, so intent was she on the cards.

"Touch my child again, and it'll be the last thing you ever touch. I swear by my death and yours."

The child looked up at the vehement death curse, and Serris did her best to reassure her daughter silently. She spoke with her eyes and her heart, hoping the child would understand.

"I believe you, Angel Serris. Truly, I do." Davargorn shook his head. "Amazing, the depth of loyalty you have for a man who has spurned you in every way. He left you for years to fend for yourself, and no sooner does he return to the city than he leaves again, in the presence of the great Bloodbreaker, whose word he trusts better than your own."

"The Lord of Tears is his own man," Serris said. "His choices are not my concern."

"Is it also not your concern when he takes the Bloodbreaker to his bed?"

Davargorn grinned. "Oh, how he ruts her, over and over, until she weeps for pleasure. I have seen. I have listened."

Serris's neck prickled, but she waved it away. "His choice where he sheathes his blade," she said. "You won't goad me with jealousy."

"I pity you, loyal squire," Davargorn said. "I was like you once: loyal to the death, at least until my master betrayed me."

"It sounds like we are not alike then." Serris drew up to her full height. "My loyalty will not waver, whatever you say."

That stole his mirth, and he glared at her dangerously. They stared at one another for a long time, fighting without drawn blades.

Finally, Davargorn smiled again. "A time is coming, Scarred One, when your loyalty will be tested," he said. "The Ravalis plan to slay your master, and he will walk willingly into their blades. His honor demands no less. Will you shield him then, I wonder?"

"Get out."

"As my beautiful lady bids," he said. "An invitation is coming soon, one you must accept. Watch for the smiling face that hides a monster. You will know your course then."

"I won't say it again."

Davargorn rose from the bed, leaving the card game unfinished. The girl made a cry of displeasure, and Davargorn leaned down to kiss her on the brow. "I have an appointment to keep, child." He glanced at Serris. "Your mother will finish the game."

Before he left the room, Davargorn put a hand up to her face. Serris flinched away.

"Ever a pleasure," he said.

He brushed past her out the door.

~

Far up in high-city, the necromancer of Blood Ravalis gazed out over the snowy city through the frost-streaked window of his personal chambers. A faint smile played about his lips, as though he could almost taste the bloodletting to come.

Vhaerynn should have been worried. The agents he'd sent after the Dracaris woman hadn't returned, and now that fool Garin Ravalis testified Regel was back in the city but he could find no trace of the Bloodbreaker. The Ruin's Night to come rested on a fragile fate.

Things were not proceeding as he had planned, but Vhaerynn had not lost a moment's peace. He sat unconcerned in his privy chambers, passing his ornate gold dagger from hand to hand, remembering a particularly fine meal he'd once had. As the years passed, his mind often drifted to those fine experiences: the terror, the useless pleading, the sweet consumation as he ripped another life into himself.

A knock at the outer door of his sitting chamber disturbed the Court Necromancer. The taste of blood turned to bitter gall in his mouth as one of his better stolen memories collapsed, leaving him abruptly sitting alone and cold in his chamber. Not alone, he realized. He had not known true solitude in many years, since he had first wielded the blade of Aza the Red King. When he touched the dagger, he suddenly had a thousand companions—a thousand times a thousand—all of them wailing for mercy, release, or simple oblivion. It had become the greatest pleasure of his life to deny them those things.

There was another in the room, of course, who probably thought himself hidden.

"How amusing." Vhaerynn sent out a silent call, speaking from blood to blood. There was power in the blood, and it was the necromancer's to command. "My old friend has betrayed you."

Summoned by the singing blood in his veins, Davargorn emerged from where Vhaerynn had felt him lurking. "How did you know?"

The necromancer smiled. He'd tasted the ugly boy's blood only a moon ago, and he would never forget that particular coppery tang—anger fueled of regret—tinged with just a hint of rotten self-loathing.

"I see you've no mask any longer," Vhaerynn said. "Has your master cast you out?"

Davargorn said nothing. There was a blade in his hand but Vhaerynn paid it no mind.

"No matter. Dealing with Mask has ever been fraught with peril, and it is good to see that you have survived." The necromancer arranged his robe and rose, his old joints cracking. He'd not fed in some time. The blade of the Aza hungered, and it was the same hunger he felt in the pit of his black soul. "And yet you return. Perhaps you have an offer to make me?"

The boy set his visage into stony indifference, but Vhaerynn could hear the blood singing angrily in his veins. "What if I could deliver up the Lord of Tears and the Bloodbreaker?"

Vhaerynn inhaled deeply of the boy's rage. The smell was sweet. "Vengeance, is it?"

"That is not your business." Davargorn drew his sword. "Answer my question."

"That will not avail you over much." Vhaerynn raised a hand, and the boy's sword froze where he held it. The boy strained, but his arm wouldn't move—at least, not of his will. The magic of the Red King could not be denied.

"I... don't..." Davargorn struggled vainly, but the sword laid itself across his throat.

"Slaying you in this moment would be simplicity itself, but your offer intrigues me," Vhaerynn said. "Only know that if this is a trick, I will take great pleasure in feeding on you."

Vhaerynn crossed to the young man and drew the golden sacrificial knife from the folds of his robes. What a wonderful relic this was: not only might it steal a life's energy, but it could store it. Like a larder filled with screams and pain. When he had first touched the blade, he had sensed countless terrified lives inside, all with their own memories and experiences, all waiting to feed him. The stronger the life, the greater the nourishment. Davargorn's life would prove a thin, bitter morsel, but Vhaerynn *had* been feeling peckish.

He slashed the knife across Davargorn's cheek and blood welled. Vhaerynn turned away, admiring the blood on the blade, watching it awaken the dagger's magic. With casual ease, he flicked it down at his feet, where it spattered the floorboards.

"Is that—" Davargorn's words trailed off into a grunt of pain. His flesh withered away from the wound, turning to gray flecks. The golden blade of the Aza did its work, and Vhaerynn could feel the slayer's life flowing into him like a river of hopes, fears, and memories.

Then the river diminished to a trickle, then cut off entirely. Vhaerynn watched, intrigued, as Davargorn's cheek drew itself back together. The gray flesh pulsed and flaked off, leaving smooth pink skin beneath. It was as he had suspected. Magic that would have reduced another man to dust within heartbeats had left little more than a crease on Davargorn's face. Delicious.

"Is that—is that meant to scare me?" The slayer felt at his cheek. "I have magic of my own."

"Oh, I know."

The blood on the floor moved of its own accord, pooling and congealing into a spongy black mass. This mass redoubled, growing and swelling until it took the vague shape of an arm, whose fingers curled in agonized pleading. The hand clutched at Davargorn's ankle.

"Now, now, there's naught to fear," Vhaerynn said. "Watch."

Before their eyes, the arm found purchase on the floorboards and wrenched a bloody body out into the room. The vague human shape rose up, then fell writhing to the floor, and the blood congealed into bone, flesh, and skin. Within breaths, a woman lay before them, moaning and crying in obvious pain: the Tear agent from low-city he had previously given to the blade.

"Burn me," Davargorn cursed. "What have you—?"

Vhaerynn knelt by the woman and ran his fingers down her cheek. She looked up at him, begging with eyes long devoid of anything like sanity.

Then he rammed his dagger through her heart. She jerked around the blade, sobbing soundlessly, and collapsed to the floor.

"Passable trick," Davargorn said. "What does that prove?"

"Nothing." Vhaerynn set down the bloody dagger. "This, however—"

He passed his hand over the dead woman, and her body dissolved into crimson radiance that flowed up into his hand. As it touched his skin, he felt the pain of old joints ease—felt new life flow through him. When he looked back up at Davargorn, it was with eyes alight with life.

"I have not taken regular food or drink for some years," Vhaerynn said. "I am limited, alas, in the number of prisoners in the palace dungeons or low-city rabble who can go missing at any given time. You, however—" He touched the tip of the knife to Davargorn's restored face. "With your magic, I could feed from you for some time. And now that my knife knows your blood"—he raised the blade up for Davargorn to see the smeared edge—"you will find no place in the World of Ruin you can hide from me."

To his credit, Davargorn did not show fear. "Do we have a bargain," he said, "or not?"

Vhaerynn almost liked the lad. "Yes," he said. "Yes, we do."

He sent out another call, blood-to-blood. This other man was close by—coming this way, in fact. Perfect. An inner door of his chambers opened, revealing a powerfully built man with blazing crimson hair and deep tanned skin. He wore the red and black of the ruling house, and he looked tired of the long wait. Crown Prince Lan Ravalis was not a man accustomed to waiting.

"Well, necromancer?" Lan asked. "You said Dracaris was returning today. Where do I find the treacherous whore?"

"This one does, in fact." Vhaerynn gestured to Davargorn. "No doubt you two have much to discuss."

The necromancer smiled. This would be a fine Ruin's Night after all.

NINETEEN

Three hours after Regel and the others arrived, Serris watched the sun set. It was the night before the eve of the New Year, Ruin's Night. As the light began to fade, an iron-clad heavy ornithopter set down in the street outside the Burned Man and Ravalis troops poured out in force. Prince Lan had come himself, and brought twelve Dustblades in their distinctive gray cloaks, and fully a score of castermen in steel hauberks and helms. The Crown Prince of Summer had come prepared for war.

"And here I thought they'd never come," Erim murmured, checking his steel.

At Serris's side, Regel nodded. "Doubt, but do not disbelieve. Eh, Squire?"

Serris didn't feel like jesting with either of them. In truth, she had expected the Ravalis earlier, shortly after she saw Davargorn again. They hadn't come, and she'd spent the last hour shaking with anxiety. The visit had set her on edge, and she didn't feel safe even surrounded by her fellow Tears. She wore her dagger openly, and she longed to draw it. She preferred solving problems with steel flashing in her hand, rather than worries roiling over in her mind.

Lan strode up to Regel and glared at him, like a bear staring down a wolf. Lan wore a calm face, but there was an anxious excitement about his powerful build and the way his hands kept moving. He was looking forward to this. "By order of my father, King Demetrus Ravalis, we've come to search for traitors to the crown of Tar Vangr."

"You'll find none such here, search as you might," Regel said.

Serris appreciated the irony of a son of the usurper searching for "traitors" to Tar Vangr in this place where loyalty to lost King Denerre steered their course. All agents of the Circle of Tears were patriots to the Winter King, which made them traitors to the Summer King.

For her part, Serris wanted to cut Lan's smarmy smile from his face, but she followed Regel's lead. "Speak if you desire anything, Highness." She forced a sultry smile. "*Anything.*"

The familiar words—the very phrase Kiereth had offered him that awkward night at the keep of Blood Yaela—set Lan off balance. The prince looked at her warily, his anxiety turned in a new direction. Serris almost couldn't contain her delight: if she could unseat the man from his comfortable saddle, then she considered that a victory.

"Out of my way, whore," he said finally, and shoved past her into the Burned Man.

"What passed there?" Regel looked suspicious.

"No idea," Serris said. "Contemplating my scar, perhaps."

While the soldiers scoured the rooms, rooting through wardrobes and storage lockers, arguing with Tears and patrons alike, Serris sat with Regel and Erim at the center table. The lad veritably shook with the tension, but at a smooth word from Regel, he relaxed. The Lord of Tears himself looked very much at ease: he took out a piece of rose-colored stone and started carving with a small, sharp knife. Serris found his calm irritating.

"What is the meaning of this?" Kiereth Yaela marched over to Lan, his face bright red.

Unfairly, Serris thought his reaction had less to do with genuine outrage than escaping the company of a pair of the Burned Man's most handsome lads at a nearby table. The Heir of Yaela was usually free with his favors and desires, but Serris understood Kiereth's discretion after his disastrous seduction attempt on the Ravalis Prince.

Lan's eyes narrowed on Kiereth. "Leave, Lord Yaela."

"Your Highness," Kiereth said. "Surely—"

"Leave." Lan put his hand on the hilt of his sword.

The Heir of Yaela's face paled, and he stepped cautiously away. "The Council will have a say in this," he said as he headed for the door of the tavern. "There will be consequences."

"Tell yourself what you want." Lan scoffed at him, then turned to survey the dusters swarming around the Burned Man. Dust magic crackled along his gold-inlaid breastplate, and his eyes dared anyone to challenge him. The Tears knew well not to give him a reason to turn the tense confrontation into a battle, though Serris was sorely tempted.

Serris saw Regel staring at her, and she looked away lest he read her face. "What passes?"

She shook her head.

Regel put his hand over hers. "I need you."

Her heart eased a touch. "Since when?"

The banter reassured her. Over the last hours, Regel had told her of his mad scheme to slay the Usurper King, and she had agreed to aid him. If it hadn't been for Davargorn's visit, in all likelihood she would have assured Regel he was insane. It was true, of course, but the slayer's warning about monsters and smiling faces would not stop echoing in her head. She would stay as close to her master as she could, so she would be there to protect him when he needed her.

As the Dusters overthrew tables and peered behind curtains, a second man pushed across the common hall. He had the coloration of the summerborn and bore a faint resemblance to Lan, but no one seemed to recognize him. Murmurs died as he approached and only resumed in his wake. He caught Serris's attention with his green eyes and soft gray stubble peppering his chin and throat. Fine clothes complimented his fit body, and he wore about him a patient assurance that the Crown Prince definitely lacked. Rather than a sword, he wore a warpick at his belt. Serris found his features easy to look upon, and the instant he saw her, he smiled with genuine delight.

"My lady!" He bowed to her, ignoring her master at her side. "How dare we prove such ungracious guests. You host us beneath your roof, and my cousin does you no honor at all."

Serris rose to receive him. "And you are, m'lord?"

"Garin Ravalis, my beauteous Lady of Winter." He took her hand to kiss it. "Lately the Fox of Luether. And you?"

"Serris," she said, "of no great Blood or name."

"Ah, you are named for an angel of old. Your parents must have seen a great destiny for you."

Serris had to smile. "I chose the name myself, m'lord."

"Then you are doubly deserving," he said. "I have heard that the Blood of Winter choose only names they have earned. Is this not so, Lord of Tears?" He bowed deeply to Regel. "I am honored to be in the presence of such a legend."

"Likewise." Regel sounded sincere.

Recognition passed between the men. Serris wondered where they had met—on one of Regel's wanderings, perhaps—and even more so, she wondered why her master would even tolerate a Ravalis, much less consider one worthy of respect? The man was handsome and his tongue prettier still, but long experience taught her such affectations often hid sharp blades indeed.

As though drawn by her thoughts, Lan meandered over to their table and sat with a wary expression that said he was just as curious to see his cousin sitting with Regel. There was nothing subtle or hidden about Lan Ravalis: he was all cruelty, from face to hands to iron-shod boots. "So what will it be, Oathbreaker?" he asked. "When we find your traitorous little whore, will you submit to the king's justice, or will you take your own life in shame? I'm told you winterborn have a fondness for that."

"Your Highness." Regel inclined his head a touch. While he would show respect, he bowed to no one in his tavern. "Will you share bread and mead with us?"

"You think being a good host will save you?" Lan asked.

"The ancient forms should be respected," Garin said.

Regel beckoned one of the Tears forward with a bowl of mead. Lircia stepped forward, and Serris thought her a good choice for this task. Her mixed features of Summer and Winter might appeal to Lan: red hair, copper-burnished skin, and dark eyes. She averted her eyes, seeming every bit the demure serving lass, though from the hard set of her jaw, she disdained the prince's ogling eyes. Serris knew what Lan truly desired, of course, but to suggest it to Regel now would be to spark a battle.

"This is what you offer, Lord of Tears?" Lan slapped the mead aside, caught Lircia's arm, and pulled her to him. The woman shut her eyes as he drew down her gown to expose one milky breast. "Your awful mead, your hard bread, or this mongrel girl?"

"My hospitality includes all three, as you wish," Regel said. "I offer you the protection of the Old Gods. Eat my food, drink my wine, love my servants, and be safe, by the Narfire that warms us all. If, however, you do not..." He let the threat hang.

"I need no superstitious nonsense to ward me." Lan shoved Lircia away. "And neither do I care for the laws of your Council and its sallow fools. You saw how I dispensed with Yaela."

Serris scowled. It was not a surprise the prince rebuked the Council's law: while most of the summerblood politely danced the dance of politics with the Council, Lan remained its most outspoken foe. But to spit in the face of the traditions of Tar Vangr? Under a pretext of adjusting her skirt, she drew her dagger and pressed it against her inner forearm. Just to make ready, she told herself.

"Perhaps you've naught but contempt for the law of hospitality, but such it is," Regel said. "Would you break it, and see the outcome?"

"You think your rabble can match my Dustblades?" Lan reached for his sword. The common room fell deathly quiet. The Circle of Tears tensed.

Regel rose smoothly. "I will not say which of you will die in the first strike, Highness," he said. "But I expect if your hand touches steel, my lined face will be the last you ever see."

"A threat, is it?" Lan raised an open hand. His swordsmen—their faces waffling between nervousness and offense—readied themselves to draw. For his part, Lan looked not at all worried. "Shed my blood. See what happens. I promise death will come for you swiftly, and not from my own men."

"By your leave then, Prince," Regel said.

The silence filled with cold, restrained breath and the creak of leather.

Inwardly, Serris swore that she would be the one to kill Lan if it came to blood. He was distracted looking at Regel, and that gave her an opening. If Serris struck quickly—before he even declared the battle begun—Lan would be dead before his bodyguards could move. She could rise and slash out his throat in a single fluid motion, much as Regel had done to Paeter so many years ago.

Then Serris realized Garin was staring at her, his green eyes sparkling with warning.

"I for one," the Fox of Luether said, "would love some mead."

Garin reached over, took Lan's bowl of mead, and drained it. Also, he bit into the sweet black bread that waited on the table. Relief passed through the common hall and blades eased in their scabbards. Once bread had been broken and drink shared, the customs of Calatan held sway, and those ran deeper than Vangr law—deeper than blood.

Lan slumped in his chair with a disappointed sigh. "Silver Fire burn the young and sensible, eh Oathbreaker?"

Regel inclined his head. "Old Gods bless those who wield reason as well as the blade."

"Fine, then." Lan scowled. "Wine, then." He nodded to Garin. "My cousin is arrived today of Fallen Luether, here to pass Ruin's Night with his kin. He is a stranger to our enmity."

"What a blessing," Regel said. "I have heard of your bravery, Prince Garin. A Ravalis heir who lingers in Luether, despite the proscription of the Children of Ruin, is a prince worthy of my respect."

Garin nodded in return. "My thanks for the kind words, my lord."

"Not really a lord," Lan said. "The Oathbreaker here is simply a castoff from a dead king."

Serris drew in a wary breath. It was an open secret that the Circle of Tears had little love for the Ravalis, but an open accusation of sedition was another matter entirely. These words were dangerous.

Garin, however, smiled. "It seems we have in common a passion for old causes," he said. "For some of us, honoring the old ways is how we live in the world that awaits us. We simply try to live."

Regel nodded. "Well said."

Those words seemed to diffuse the tension, at least for the moment. Lan looked furious.

Serris appraised Garin with new interest. What was the man's game?

"This gathering is a bit dour for me." Garin pushed back from the table. "Perhaps I'll leave you gentles to your threats and find entertainment elsewhere." He drapped his arm around Lircia and headed up the stairs, heedless of the Ravalis soldiers guarding the steps.

Serris felt Regel touch her wrist under the table, and he glanced toward the stairs: a silent command to follow Garin. Any other time, she might have been happy to do so, but just at the moment she couldn't shake her persistent disquiet with her master. She gave Lan one last challenging look, but he focused on his food, ignoring her. Going after Garin suddenly seemed much more appealing than remaining here in the common room.

"My lords." She rose and nodded to them. Lan regarded her with a knowing smirk she would have gladly cut away. Regel did not look at her at all, and that cut deeply.

She took her leave.

～

Upstairs, Serris heard Garin's deep voice and not one but two sets of feminine giggles at his jest. The man worked remarkably fast, to have picked up two of the Tears in the five-count he had before Serris arrived. She sighed.

She followed the laughing voices to the Crimson Destiny room, so named for the silks that hung from the rafters. In this chamber, a celebrant might lead a patron teasingly through, or allow him or her to become lost in the crimson sea, but eventually they would meet at the center bed where the true delights began. No time for that nonsense now: Serris brushed the silks aside and made her way straight for Garin and the two women he'd lured along to attend him. Lircia, Serris had seen him recruit, but somehow he'd drawn along Nacacia as well. The two women were not rutting him, though, but rather lounging with him and laughing at the amusing jests he told. The women pulled away respectfully when Serris appeared.

"Alas, my winterborn beauties!" Garin held aloft an open wine bottle. "Turned cold already?" Then he saw Serris, and his smile only widened. "The mistress of the house, herself."

"Leave us," Serris said. Lircia walked straight out, eyes on her toes, while

195

Nacacia favored Serris with a sly smile. When they were gone, Serris crossed her arms. "Breeches still intact. Those two not to your liking, or do your tastes run elsewhere, Lord of Ravalis?"

"Ah, women are like flowers slipping past in a stream—fine to watch, but passing little to hold," he said. "Yon lovelies can tell quite the jest, though. That Nacacia, she's seen almost as many blades as I have, but it's Lircia who surprises me. The things that come out of that one's mouth, by the Old Gods..."

Serris crossed her arms. "What's your business here?"

"Direct," Garin said. "I should have thought that obvious: while your stodgy Lord of Tears and my terribly repressed cousin compare blades, I was hoping to wine and rut my way into a drunken haze."

"Oh is *that* your intention," Serris said. "I've been standing here, dressed like this, and you haven't once looked lower than my face." She brushed her scarred cheek. "Do you have such contempt for a broken toy like me?"

"No, certainly not, Lady of Winter. Your first guess was correct." Garin raised his wine jug to his lips. "I need the fortification to make it through the investiture tomorrow."

She didn't quite understand, but that caught her attention. "What investiture?"

"My uncle making me the Shroud, of course." Garin offered her the opened bottle. "Wine?"

His casual admission gave Serris pause. The identity of the Ravalis spymaster—if such a person even existed—was a closely guarded secret. She remembered thinking that for Kiereth Yaela to tell her the Shroud was gone was a large step, and she'd been stunned when Regel told her Ovelia had been the spymaster for the last five years. But now Garin had told her that he himself would become the Shroud?

"Why—?" She mentally rebuked herself for sounding like a weakling. "Why tell me this? You barely know me."

"I know your name," Garin said. "And you have a face worthy of trust."

Serris's scar burned. "You're a fool then. I am a liar."

"My assessment stands," he said. "You bear that scar with grace and strength, and it does not weaken you. You have my admiration." He took another pull of wine.

Serris's feelings hardened and she glared at him. "Save your pity."

"You took that for pity. Interesting." He rose, crossed to her, and knelt to kiss her hand. "Tell me: the Lord of Tears calls you his squire. Does he teach you many fine ways to please a man?"

"Some," she said. "Learned a few on my own."

"Mmm." He pressed his lips to her knuckles. "I could teach you a few more."

Garin's smile was infectious, and Serris couldn't help enjoying his flirtation. She had to remind herself this man was dangerous. After all, he had claimed to be the Shroud.

"I am surprised he is only your teacher," Garin was saying, fingers caressing the back of Serris's hand. "A beauty such as yours, and he has not married you?"

"Hardly a beauty." She pulled her hand away. "And that would never happen, Highness."

"Garin," he said as he rose. "And I'm intrigued. Say on."

"In Tar Vangr, Prince," she said, "only nobles bind themselves so, for the furtherance of their blood. My master and I are commonblood, and so will never bond with any man or woman. We take lovers as we desire, man or woman."

"Ah," said Garin. "My pardon, lady. I am not familiar with your customs. I suspect you do not know those of Luether, either."

"Well enough," Serris said. "You bind 'your' women with rings of gold and strings of jewels to keep them as bedslaves to raise broods of men who treat 'their' women the same way."

"You might as well have spoken a simple 'nay, I do not,' my lovely one," Garin said. "And I think you know nothing of me, if you think of me in those terms."

"Own no woman of your own, Garin Ravalis? One you bind to home while you go whoring, then strike her for doing the same?"

"No *woman*," he said.

A moment passed between them, then Serris let out a breath. "Oh."

"Indeed."

Serris reassessed. She had thought him contemptuous, so disgusted with her disfigurement that he did not even think of her as a woman, whatever she wore. But now she saw the truth of the man with whom she dueled, and it filled her with relief. "Why tell me this? Secrets are power."

"This one is a curse," Garin said. "I'd be careful whose ear I whispered it into. We are such assertive men, we Ravalis. I told you of myself so you would understand why I had to bring your fellow Tears up here, even if I had no intention of rutting either of them, or you for that matter."

Serris looked him up and down. "Standing quite close for a man who isn't going to rut me."

"This is not to say I do not appreciate feminine beauty." Garin touched her chin lightly with his fingertips, and she met his eyes. "Yours is a powerful light, one your mark only defines, not mars. I see that you are strong and skilled—a warrior, not born but trained and honed. The Tears respect you and defer to you, and yet—"

"And yet?" She put her hand to his well-muscled chest. Garin kept his body in a fine state, no doubt of that, and Serris found herself thinking it a shame he had no desire for women.

"And yet." He put his arms around her. "I envy you winterborn your freedom to love as you will—without judgment or consequences—and yet I see that it binds you as well. The way you look at the Lord of Tears, it is obvious you love him. You would kill and die for him. And yet he holds you back. He stifles you from becoming something greater."

Serris stiffened. "You know nothing of either of us," she said. "Don't need anyone to save me from myself—least of all a man."

"Better." Garin smiled and put his hands on her hips. "Is your child Regel's?"

A shock ran through Serris. "What?"

"I can feel that you've given birth," Garin said, "and the way you look at the Lord of Tears, coupled with your reaction to my extremely impertinent question tells me..."

Serris drew her dagger and put it to his throat.

"Indeed," Garin said, undaunted. "Also, I just saw a little girl in the hall. I swear, she looks just like the two of you."

"Don't," Serris said.

Garin smiled. "Good. So we understand each other." Slowly, he reached into his tunic and drew forth a scroll sealed with wax that bore the mark of the king's signet. "My uncle wishes all noble-folk of Tar Vangr to attend his revel on Ruin's Night. To commemorate the fifth year of Ravalis rule, and to honor the fallen—winter and summer both. You are not noble, but you are worthier than most who are."

"You came here to invite my master to a revel?" Serris asked.

"Him and whatever guests he chooses to bring," Garin said. He handed her the scroll, and just like that, it hit her. "I hope for the pleasure of your company as well, Lady Serris."

"You can certainly hope for whatever you will, Child of Summer."

"I see you haven't killed me yet," he said. "I take this as a favorable omen."

Serris withdrew the dagger, but Garin made no move to step away. He leaned in as though to kiss her, and whispered in her ear. She barely heard his suggestion, however: she stared at the letter he had given her, and her hands began to tremble.

"Lady Serris?" Garin asked, knocked off balance by her unexpected reaction. "Pass well?"

"I'm going." She turned away. "I'll send up a boy on my way. Erim. You'll like him."

Garin looked uncertain, but ultimately he nodded. "Until tomorrow."

She nodded and managed to keep her balance until she was out of the room. Then she leaned on the wall and tried to slow her racing heart. Davargorn had said she would soon receive an invitation, and she must accept it. Garin had looked at her with legitimate concern, so she thought he did not know. How far did Davargorn's reach extend?

～

An hour after the Ravalis arrived, Regel saw Garin descend the stairs just as Lan was ordering the soldiers to assemble and board the ornithopter after their fruitless search. Serris, who had reappeared sometime before, had sent Erim away and replaced him as cupbearer. She pointedly avoided Regel's eyes and said absolutely nothing, even when Nacacia almost provoked two Dusters into a fight. Something was the matter with his squire, and Regel looked forward to getting her alone so they could talk freely.

"I am grieved I cannot aid you, Highnesses," Regel said when Garin approached. "Unless you wish the services of one of my Tears. As I mentioned to the prince, they are excellent mummers and even better lovers."

"As I daresay His Highness knows"—Nacacia winked—"from previous patronage."

Lan paused in commanding his soldiers at glared at Nacacia, quite as though he'd only just not realized she was there. "You dare a great deal, whore, to slander the Crown Prince to his face."

Never one to lack courage when another Tear was threatened, Serris bristled. "Only in the Summerlands is shared pleasure called insult," she murmured, "and nowhere is truth called slander."

Lan put hand to steel. Nacacia's jest had irked him, but Serris had apparently gone too far. "Still your whore's waggling tongue, Oathbreaker, or I'll still it for her."

Regel expected Serris to retort—she was never one to back down from a threat—but instead she looked away. She almost spilled the mead pouring him a fresh bowl.

"Truly, my prince?" Nacacia licked her lips and slid her hands down her sides to her waist. "You've never before asked *me* to still my tongue when I use it on you."

Lan glared but Garin put a restraining hand on his arm. "The laws, cousin."

Lan spat on the table. "I should raze your tavern to the ground, Oathbreaker—make it the *Burned Man* for true. What of that?"

"Be welcome to try," Regel said, inclining his head once more. "And see how the Narfire treats blasphemers of the old laws, royalty or no."

Lan made a derisive sucking sound with his teeth. "We shall see."

With that, Lan waved to his Dusters and strode away. The soldiers filed out after him. Garin stopped his cousin and they argued quietly.

"You risked his bed?" asked Regel.

Nacacia smirked. "It was not so bad," she said. "Rough, but all his strength disappears into a flush when he spends himself. He thinks himself in control. It's actually quite charming."

"Wonderful." Regel tried not to picture the way Ovelia flushed during lovemaking.

Garin returned, his face apologetic. "I see that you do not call my cousin a friend."

"We tried to kill each other once," Regel said. "As you can see, it went unresolved."

"Indeed." Garin turned to Nacacia. "And my lady, you are very brave indeed."

"A whore often ruts and rarely tells." She bowed. "Highness."

"Of course." Garin returned her bow, and smiled as she swayed away. "Pay Lan no mind. He fears my uncle withers under the Council's laws. It is suggested that the Ravalis will cede the throne any day now. Perhaps on the new year."

Regel found the admission startling, but Serris caught his eye and shook her head. Apparently, she'd had much the same experience with something Garin had said. Wordlessly, she offered him an unsealed scroll. He tried to meet her eye but failed. What was the matter with her?

He unfolded the scroll. "A masquerade," he noted.

Garin nodded. "The better to bring certain personages who wish to go faceless, aye?"

"Why would such folk attend?" Regel asked calmly. "If they existed at all, of course."

Garin smiled. "Let us speak plainly," he said. "One spymaster to another."

Regel schooled his features to hide his surprise. He looked to Serris, who nodded slightly, confirming it. So Garin was the new Shroud. That explained why he had returned: in the wake of Ovelia's treachery, the Ravalis would certainly seek to fill the post she'd left vacant.

"Speak, then," he said. "One spymaster to another."

Garin nodded candidly. "My uncle Demetrus wishes to offer a truce—a general amnesty," he said. "If Ravalis is to win the coming war with King Pervast and the Vultara, then we must set aside our petty jealousies and squabbles and fight side-by-side."

"So there *is* a war," Serris said, but Regel waved her to silence.

"Even foes of the Ravalis are welcome?" Regel asked.

"*Especially* foes." With a pleased smile, Garin bowed to Regel, then turned to go. "And tell the lady to wash out that atrocious silver dye and leave her black wig behind," he said over his shoulder. "Neither suits her."

TWENTY

"TRAP," REGEL SAID AS the curtain to the back corridor swung closed behind them.

"Yes," said Serris. "It may be a trap, but it is a trap you can use to get to the king."

"No."

He turned toward the stairs but she caught his arm. "No?"

Regel shook his head. This played too perfectly into Mask's plan, almost like another manipulation. Regel felt like a tiny skiff tossed about on waves in an ocean he could not see. Also, he did not know Garin's game. If he had recognized Ovelia in Luether, why had he not told the Ravalis? He needed time to puzzle this out—time to find another path.

"No," Regel said finally. "If Ovelia enters that hall, it would be death for all of us."

"What of the ancient customs?" Serris asked.

"You saw Lan's contempt for the old ways," Regel said. "If we did not have so many casters ready, he would have struck regardless of custom." He pulled his arm gently from Serris's grasp. "Better to risk Demetrus's displeasure and change our plans."

"I'll make an assignation with Garin for tonight. I can get more from him—"

"No," Regel said. "Rut him if you will, but no more. We are made and marked. To move against Demetrus now would be to fall upon our own swords. Did you note Lan's confidence when he spoke of spilling his blood? He wanted us to attack."

"Magic in his blood?" Serris asked. "He has a ward of some sort? From their pet necromancer?"

"Perhaps," said Regel. "We have to stay our hands. That is my decision."

"But what of that *creature*?" Serris asked. "She will be displeased, no?"

Regel scoffed. He turned to march up the stairs, then paused and looked back. "She?"

Serris looked up in confusion. "What?"

"I thought you meant Ovelia when you said *she*, but you did not," Regel said. "You were talking about *Mask*."

"Of course," Serris said. "Will she not be offended if—?"

"*She*." He hadn't been certain of Mask's identity, but he'd always assumed the sorcerer was a man. But to hear it from Serris now—that simple declaration of Mask's identity—it unlocked something in his mind. "Mask is a woman," Regel said.

"You—it's not obvious?" Serris said. "All your skill, Lord of Tears, and you can

201

be so blind." She stifled a laugh behind her hand, then frowned at his expression. "Regel, I did not mean to offend..."

Mask was a woman. And beneath those tools of her magic, Mask could be *any* woman.

He remembered his dream: blood dripping through silvery blonde hair, a dying breath at his ear. Then the dead woman drew on black leather and smiled.

Regel clenched his hands tight. "I am finished being a toy," he whispered.

He started up the stairs. Serris made to follow, and he didn't care to stop her.

Regel kicked his door open. He saw in a heartbeat that Ovelia and Mask had climbed out of the hidden passage and were conversing. Ovelia moved to block his view of Mask, who was donning the dark leather cowl. Regel caught a glimpse of stark white hair—or perhaps blonde.

~

From Regel's room, Ovelia listened through the cracked door as Regel and Serris argued about a path forward. She pressed herself against the wall, straining her ears, trying her best to do anything but focus on Mask, who sat completely at ease on the other side of the room.

While the Ravalis had been here, Ovelia and Mask had hidden in the crawlspace between the floors—ironically, no more than two paces above where Lan had thundered and blustered. When the princes had left, she and Mask had crawled out of their hiding place and into Regel's room.

"You're still with me, are you not, Bloodbreaker?" Mask asked.

Ovelia turned and saw the sorcerer's bare face. "What are you doing? What if Regel—?"

"If he approaches, no doubt you—my Shield—will warn me," Mask said. "Now answer the question. Do you harbor doubts? About what needs to be done with the Lord of Tears?"

Ovelia realized the sorcerer had taken off the mask to unsettle her emotions, and Old Gods, it was working. She found it nearly impossible to deny any request from those lips. Ovelia turned away and pressed her face into the smooth wood of the door. "This... this is very hard for me."

"Of course." Mask waved one hand through the steam from the tea. "But we must travel the path fate traces before us."

Ovelia looked around Regel's room for an escape and found none. The room was austere but comfortable, and the bed looked very inviting, as she had slept little in days. Mask lay there, legs crossed without the slightest shame or concern. The gruesome leather mask sat on a nearby table.

Ovelia went away from the door and leaned heavily on Regel's desk. "Is there no other way?"

"King's Shield," Mask said, in a familiar voice that chilled Ovelia to the bone. "You have no choice. He will kill both of us otherwise. You understand that, do you not?"

"We could tell him the truth," Ovelia said. "About who you are. About what you want."

"You think he will understand? Is there any part of you that doubts he will see this as treachery and attack us on the instant? Surely we two could kill him alone, but in his own house, with his army of whores?" Mask shrugged. "Or does he love rutting you that much? Because if he does, then—"

"Please do not ask me to betray him."

"You served the Winter King and slew him," Mask said, the words bitter as a spider's venom. "How does this differ?"

The words stole Ovelia's breath, and she clutched at her stomach. "You do not understand," she said. "What I did... I loved Blood Denerre. More than I can say."

"Ovelia." Mask crossed the room smoothly to stand beside her. One black-wrapped hand touched her cheek gently. "You know there is no choice. We have chosen this path. You must walk beside me."

"You cannot—" Ovelia clenched her fists. "You cannot ask these things of me."

"Remember your princess, Ovelia. Remember she you once swore to serve."

"But you—"

"Do this and she will forgive you. Do it not—" Flames rose from the black-wrapped fingers.

Ovelia's face grew warm as anger filled her. "Would you slay me, then?"

Mask's eyes narrowed. "I have waited many years for this, and I will do what I must."

"Listen to me." Ovelia looked up into Mask's reddish eyes, into her firm grimace. "This is folly. There is naught to be gained by this path."

"Gain?" Mask's mouth spread in a grin and she laughed. Ovelia shivered to hear the cold crackle that went into the sounds of mirth. "What makes you think I wish to *gain* anything? This is not a matter of ambition but vengeance. Nothing else."

Mask started to move away, but Ovelia grasped her arm and held her fast. She stood over the sorcerer, who looked small and frail before her. Vulnerable. "Come with me," she said. "Leave this behind and—"

Warning shadows flowed from the hilt of Draca, just out of reach on the desk. Mask turned toward the door, behind which Ovelia heard footsteps. "*Mask*," the sorcerer hissed.

Heart thudding at the word, Ovelia released Mask. The thin woman staggered to the table and drew up the leathern shroud she'd laid next to her tea. She tucked her pale hair in place and buckled the clasps behind her head. Ovelia turned toward the door, instinctively shielding her ward.

The door burst open and Regel stood before them, murder in his eyes. Behind him in the doorway stood a very pale Serris.

"Regel, what is it?" Trying to seem casual, Ovelia inched closer to the Draca sword, which lay sheathed on the desk just out of her reach. "What has passed?"

The fire in Regel's eyes was the same she had seen in Luether, that day when he had slain the Ravalis spy and looked up at her. It was the fire Regel reserved for one woman only.

"Stand aside," Regel said, his voice cold as that of a corpse. "I have business with *her*."

He knows, Ovelia thought with a shiver.

Mask coughed discreetly, and Ovelia realized she had moved closer to them. "I had wondered when you would reason it out, Lord of Tears."

Ovelia adjusted her position between them, making sure to block Regel's path. "Speak to me," she said. "Please, Regel, we can talk about—"

He put his hands to the hilts of his blades, and she lunged for her sword. She brought Draca up in front of her. "Hold!" she shouted. "Stay back."

"Stand aside." Regel hardly seemed to notice her steel. "I won't ask again."

"It is well, Bloodbreaker," Mask said. "Let him pass."

"Stay," Ovelia said. Warning shadows boiled around her hands. "Just a burned moment!"

"If you stand between us, I will cut you down," Regel said. "Last chance."

"Regel—" Ovelia exclaimed as pain erupted in her hand and her whole arm went numb. Faster than her eye could register, Regel had drawn and struck her with the flat of his sword, sending Draca clattering to the floorboards, then hooked his blade around her throat. She had never seen him move so fast— she had seen his attack in Draca's flames but she had hesitated. And now she would die.

"Stop!" Mask cried, green magic flaring between her fingertips.

Reacting like the warrior he was, Regel slipped a throwing knife from his left sleeve.

"No!" Ovelia clawed at Regel's left hand, heedless of the blade at her neck.

She fully expected death, but the blade remained still. Ovelia thought it mercy—until she saw Serris holding a dagger to Regel's throat.

"Squire," he said, warning in his voice. "Do not defend her."

"I'm not defending her, or anyone," Serris said. "I've never seen you like this, Regel. Please, let's talk—uhh!"

Serris doubled over when Regel kicked her in the belly, making her knife go wide. He spun like an unbound whirlwind, slamming the hilt of his sword into Serris's face even as he wrenched free of Ovelia's grasp. Heedless of the razor-sharp edge, Ovelia grasped his throwing knife with all her strength, but Regel let go of it and her own weight sent her sprawling.

Ovelia recovered in time to see Regel standing not two paces from Mask, his falcat hooked just under her chin. The sorcerer stood on the tips of her toes, straining to keep from his steel.

"How dare you," Regel said. "How dare you use her against me."

"Whom?" Mask asked.

"This is your game, isn't it?" Regel asked. "You make me suspect what face lies beneath that mask, then you do not show me. But you do not know the truth—what she and I shared. So no more lies and no more games." He leaned in close. "Tell me plain: are you she?"

Ovelia's heart froze in her chest. Her fingers trembled as she sought the hilt of her sword on the floor. Serris struggled to her feet.

"She?" Mask's red eyes gleamed at Regel. "You can't even name her, coward? I wonder if you ever loved her at all."

Regel pressed his blade against Masks's neck, and it creaked against the leather. *"Are you she?"*

Ovelia picked up Draca and started forward, but Serris laid a hand on her shoulder. The woman shook her head, and Ovelia understood. To interfere was to court death, for her or for Mask. Even now, Regel was shaking the manikin-thin body like a dog with a fallen toy in its jaws. If she startled him, he might kill her. This was their fight, and Ovelia could not interfere.

"Are you not a man? Take my mask off and see," Mask challenged. "Or are you afraid?"

"No," Regel said.

"I think you are," Mask said. "I think—"

Mask's words became a stunned groan as Regel caught her throat and slammed her backward against the wall. "Tell me!" he demanded.

Ovelia slapped her red-glowing sword against the bedframe and it rang loud, drawing Regel's attention for a breath. "Stop!"

In the distraction, Mask's hand appeared in Regel's face, trailing magic, but he was too fast. He let go of his falcat, caught her arm, and wrenched it up high. Mask screamed and green smoke wafted from the black-wrapped fingers to trace a greasy stain up the wall. Regel let go of her throat and palmed a knife from his sleeve.

"Regel, wait!" Ovelia cried.

He didn't seem to hear her. His hips holding the spindly woman against the wall, Regel held his belt knife to Mask's throat. "Tell me."

"Listen to me, Regel." Ovelia's hands trembled and she bit her lip. "Do not do this."

Mask trembled in Regel's grasp, her free hand clawing the wall like a spider.

"Do not do this," Ovelia said. "You do not have to—"

"Shut up!" Regel snapped. He turned back to Mask. "Tell me that you are she."

"Who?" Deep in the eyeslits, tears of pain and despair glimmered in Mask's eyes. "Who do you want me to be?"

"You know who you are." Regel shook Mask like a doll. "Tell me!"

Gods of the Nar. Ovelia's face went white. "Regel, she isn't—"

"Lenalin!" he roared. "Are you *Lenalin?*"

"No!" Mask shrieked, the word broken like the cry of a child. Then again, softly: "No."

Silence fell in the room, broken only by Mask's gasping, shuddering breaths. Regel held her taut against the wall, and Ovelia held her sword at his back.

Release her, Ovelia meant to say, but the words caught in her throat like bones.

Then the belt-knife fell from Regel's hand and stabbed into the floorboards with a thunk of steel into wood, where it stood quivering. His trembling fingers drifted to the edge of the black mask.

"Do it." Mask's bony limbs shook like quivering wires. "Just do it, if you must."

Then Ovelia's heart skipped as Regel's hand rose to the sorcerer's faceplate. She raised her sword—waiting for Regel's hand to stray around to the clasps. She had to stop him. She—

Regel drew his hand away. "No."

"I don't... understand," said Mask, the first words clear, the third cracked.

Unceremoniously, Regel loosed Mask to slump against the wall. Breathing hard, the sorcerer gazed up at Regel, then over to Ovelia, whose heart raced fit to burst.

"I no longer care," Regel said. "Whoever you may or may not be, whatever lies you mean to tell and whatever manipulations you intend for us, I don't care. We have a task to do, and I mean to do it. I never need to see your Ruin-burned face."

Regel turned to Ovelia then, and looked down at her sword hovering over his heart as though the steel were of no consequence. "You defend her, do you?"

"As I must," Ovelia said, lowering her sword.

"I see." Regel's eyes followed the line of steel to her hand. "Is your hand well?"

In truth, her hand beat with its own inner fire, sparked from the slap of his blade, but she would not show weakness. "Yes. Very well."

"Let me see it." She pulled away, but he caught her hand before she could escape. She might have expected the touch to hurt, but instead his fingers were gentle and warm. Almost soothing.

"Regel," she said. "I—"

A strangled sound that might have been a word broke the moment.

Regel's eyes slipped past her. Ovelia looked over her shoulder at Serris, whom she had forgotten was even there. Regel's squire was staring, hand to the ugly bruise on her cheek where her master had struck her. Then she fled the room.

A loud creak broke the silence as Regel wrenched his blade free of the wall, sheathed it at his belt, and stepped past Ovelia. "This thing is your charge now. I'll have none of her any longer."

He paused at the door and looked to the nearby table.

Ovelia followed his gaze and saw the tea tin they'd carried on the *White Dart.* It caught a beam of the light and gleamed. "What is it?" she asked.

"Naught." He turned to go, then looked back over his shoulder. "I am not some beast like Paeter Ravalis to be lied to and toyed with. It would do you well to remember that."

And with that, he strode from the room. Ovelia felt empty in his wake—empty and cold.

"Fear not, King's Shield," Mask whispered when he was gone. "Our way is open."

Ovelia shivered.

TWENTY-ONE

On Ruin's Night—THE EVE of the new year, the last laugh of the World of Ruin before hope began anew—the skies of Tar Vangr filled with the pops and bangs of mage-crafted pyrotechnics. The Vangryur were not a wealthy folk, but almost every family dipped into the year's coin to purchase fireworks from city alchemists to light the darkness. The children whooped with delight as they fired the rockets, and the grown folk would sit about guzzling winterwine and bragging about exploits that had never happened.

Few could remember exactly why the eve of the year was a time for such displays. The tradition dated back thousands of years—before the founding of ancient Calatan and its Sorcerus Annis calendar, before the Great Return centuries previous, perhaps even back to the Old World—and the records of the greatest sages were incomplete as to why. Thus, the celebration had come to mean something different to all who practiced it. For some, it welcomed the new year in loud, fiery style, while for others it dispelled the cold of a winter past. For grizzled veterans of the wars, it represented Tar Vangr's victory over Echvar or even Luether, and for those who still clung to the Old Gods, it was the great annual battle between the Lady of Summer and the Lord of Winter.

For Regel, Ruin's Night was far from a celebratory occasion. The exploding fires over the city reminded him of watching as Semana's skyship—the *Heiress*—broke up over the bay five years ago. The smoke that rose from the bursting mage-rockets put him in mind of burning wreckage and seared corpses. And then he had watched the Winter King murdered. His master was gone, his path obscured, his future lost. Why had he not taken his life that very night? Why had he fought so hard to live?

"Pass well, my lord?" Walking at his side, Serris squeezed his hand firmly.

Regel adjusted the mask that did little to hide his identity. "Remembering something Lan Ravalis, of all people, asked of me."

"Something important?" Serris's voice was a mere whisper.

Had Regel known somehow that all this would come to pass, that he would walk a dark path for a vain sliver of hope? Or had he merely been a coward, too fearful of death to do what honor demanded?

"It matters not." Regel shook his head. "Focus on the path ahead."

Serris nodded and looked up at the brightly lit palace gates, flanked by ironclads that scanned all those walking past. She relaxed her body, and Regel forced himself to do the same.

Strength suffused the palace of Tar Vangr—a sense of timeless power that could endure the worst of Ruin's storms. A thousand feet above low-city, it stood strong atop and within a towering mountain peak that provided Tar Vangr a spine, while the two city levels became its hollow bones. At the very crown of the palace, the great throne room gazed out into the darkness of the World of Ruin through a half-dome of stained glass. In these latter days, it seemed more a skull than a face, try as the Ravalis might to brighten it with alchemical lights and fanfare. The palace stood eternal: the constructions of man might rot and slide down the mountainside but it would remain, as steadfast as the stone.

At the front gate stood two lancers burnished bright and shining and—Regel noted—fully armed and ready for a fight, as well as half a dozen soldiers armed with thamaturgically enhanced arms and armor. Surprisingly, the dusters didn't even ask them to remove their eye-masks, much less reveal any weapons they carried. Regel and Serris showed their invitation, and aside from a customary bow, the guards hardly glanced at either before waving them right through.

"That was easy," Serris said. "Trap?"

"Definitely a trap," Regel murmured as they passed into the grand foyer.

"Mmm." Serris seemed distracted.

He would have paid hard coin to know what she was thinking. After what had passed between them the previous night, she had left the Burned Man for a time. From the disgust and fear in her eyes in that moment, he knew she'd been perfectly glad of the opportunity to escape his presence. She'd returned a few hours before the masquerade, and they'd shared only a dozen words in preparation for the night's festivities. The silence between them now felt like cold air that steamed their breath, and her hand on his was like ice. But they were both of the Circle of Tears, and both knew how to pretend.

The great ballroom hall of the palace was huge and cavernous, with billowing tapestries and imposing statues of old kings that flanked them on all sides. It had an austere beauty, its every carved wall and withered bust speaking of the ancient history of Tar Vangr, the world's eternal cornerstone. The Ravalis had left their mark on the room, of course: they'd hung massive mage-candle chandeliers and decorating many of the surfaces with gold-plated ornamentation. Many of the queens of Tar Vangr had fallen victim to the refurbishment, and while the statues were still there, the Ravalis had done their best to hide or diminish them with gaudy decoration. Just enough to offend, not enough to provoke. Even Queen Denes, the legendary first ruler of Tar Vangr, had become a painted caricature, almost a woman of negotiable virtue rather than the warrior sorceress who had led her people into this new, harsh world

Fully three hundred folk crowded the hall, representing the bloods of the city, great and thin, as well as a wide assortment of warders and servants. They wore every sort of color, except the blue and green of Vultara and the red and green of Dracaris. Most avoided green altogether: it was a cursed color, hearth wisdom said, and would call the angels down upon a wearer. Regel and Serris, having no noble blood, had chosen subtle tones. Regel wore earthen hues and added a scarlet half-cape as a gesture of respect to the Ravalis's favored crimson. Serris wore black and had opted for a scarf of Ravalis blue, their lesser Blood color.

208

Many attendees wore such tokens of loyalty, though Regel suspected most meant it only as much as he and Serris did.

In the center of the grand hall, dark-skinned, flame-haired summerborn whirled and leaped and clapped in an energetic dance of the southland. The stately Vangryur did not dance this way, and Regel thought it odd to see the Ravalis asserting their distinct culture so keenly. The dancers were few, though they drew a great deal of attention with their daring outfits and alluring movements. Lenalin had hated every aspect of the Ravalis, except their dance. Regel could have watched her on the floor all night.

No attack seemed forthcoming in the hall full of laughter and merriment, so Regel relaxed slightly. "Circle," he instructed Serris. "Hear what you can."

The woman nodded without meeting his eyes and broke away from him casually. She cut through the revelers like a stalking cat, glimpsed only when she wished. He had trained her well.

Regel found an out-of-the-way corner and grasped the mostly finished dawnstone carving in his pocket. He would need a new carving project after this night. How well the symmetry flowed: he had finished a jackal for Paeter Ravalis five years ago, a dragon for Ovelia in Luether, and now he drew close to completing this piece. He only hoped he got the chance to give this as it was meant to be given.

He fell into contemplation of its lines and shape, letting his awareness expand and take in the other revelers. Bloodlord Fars Vargaen, in his red military tunic with many chains and sword-shaped brooches, argued loudly with blue-and-gold draped Captain Vette Saras, Bloodlady of her family of skyship builders. The two were discussing building a whole fleet of ships, which would need crews under Vargaen's command. Regel heard a private talk between a purple-and-crimson clad heir of Blood Rolan and a trader of Blood Yaela. These bloods had made their fortune from trade in all sorts of flesh and steel, and they would surely provide both soldiers and provisions to a war effort.

Serris reappeared. "Nothing to report," she said. "The usual posturing and intrigue. You?"

"There is much talk of this war you mentioned," Regel said. "Can it have come so close?"

Serris shrugged. "Has it ever been far?"

Indeed, since the Children had conquered Luether all those years ago, rumors had circulated of a looming war. Rarely, however, had they become open declarations, but from what Serris had told him of the encounter she'd witnessed between Kiereth Yaela and Prince Lan, Regel felt uneasy. Regel wondered whether King Demetrus's death would spark or avert such a war. It would certainly plunge the city into the chaos of succession for a time, which was bad enough. Would Luether muster an army in the interim?

Regel shook that frightful concept away. "Any sign of the others?"

Serris shook her head. "One of us should have entered with them."

"I offered," Regel murmured. "Better to let them arrive alone, so they are not marked." Through her mask, Serris was looking at him intently. "What passes?" he asked.

"Naught." Her hand rose, seemingly unbidden, to her powdered cheek.

Regel tried to ignore the itch in his fingers, which reminded him of striking her. "Can we talk?"

"No, m'lord. No need."

Regel's stomach turned. "Serris—"

"We should dance," she said. "Folk are staring."

The fire dancers in the center of the room had moved away, clearing the space for the more staid and dignified dancing of the winterborn. Serris turned her face away from Regel and would not meet his eyes. Regel fell into the rhythm of the steps, bowed to the women who greeted him in the circle, and watched for Ovelia and Mask. He wondered if they would even make it through the door without being caught, and for a moment, Regel hoped they *would* be caught. Before the previous night, he had almost come to trust them. He'd even considered telling Ovelia about the venom in her belly, however angry it made her. Now, she'd chosen her ally, and it was not him.

He supposed it mattered little. After tonight, all would be finished—one way or another.

"Hmm." Serris was looking at something over Regel's shoulder.

Regel nodded, and she slipped around him. He gazed after her but couldn't see what she had seen. Instead, he looked around the ballroom from amongst the whirling dancers.

On the dais beside the vacant thrones, he saw that several of the Ravalis had arrived. Prince Lan wore an open tunic to show off the great tattoo of a bear on his chest, and his mask was a furry head Regel imagined had once actually belonged to a living bear. The Bear was his personal crest, while his brother Paeter had been the Jackal, for his mocking laughter. He saw Garin standing beside Lan on the dais, dressed more conservatively in muted crimson with a plain black eye-mask and a warpick at his belt, studying all in attendance. He wore no pelt, but then, that was just like a fox to hide its true skin amongst the hens. The Fox of Luether was a mystery to him, and mysteries were dangerous. Also present were two lesser Ravalis cousins Regel barely knew—Boulis the Hound and Tolus the Falcon, sons of Demetrus's younger brother Toblius—and their fauther Toblius, Demetrus's younger half-brother. He saw too Alcha Ravalis nô Varas, Toblius's wife, as well as Lan's wife, Laegra Ravalis nô Vargaen: a weathered skeleton of a woman who nonetheless bore herself with the grace that only a neglected noble knew. And that was all: five bloodlords and two bloodbond allies. Hardly a horde, but a fitting show of solidarity.

It occurred to Regel that he had not seen the Ravalis gathered in one place for some time, and that their house seemed so small now—almost as diminished as the Blood of Denerre had been in the end.

"Is that not the Lord of Tears? Tar Vangr's *second* greatest slayer, here amongst us."

It was only when he heard the familiar chill whisper that Regel looked up into the masked face of the dancer opposite him in his circle. Bending low in an elegant—if stiff—curtsy, the lady wore a tight, snowy white gown trimmed in silver, its filmy silk covering every trace of her skin. She wore a burst of silver lace at her throat and a silver-banded, broad-brimmed hat, which covered her face as she inclined toward him. When she rose to meet his eye, her face hid behind a porcelain doll's mask painted with a wide, innocuous smile.

Regel's eyes widened but he hid his gape behind a raised hand. "By the Fire."

"I shall take your surprise as flattery," Mask said.

Across the way, Serris also looked startled, her face pale.

Regel raised his hands to join with Mask's—her long, silk-shrouded fingers interlaced his and her palms felt very hot, as though the leather wrapped heated steel rather than flesh. They turned, but Regel saw only Mask's doll face, not the room. Was she smiling as the mask was?

"Grotesque," Regel said.

"Isn't it?" Mask sounded pleased. "I think it suits me."

"Remind me to have a talk with Nacacia," Regel said. "Unless she doesn't know you borrowed her gown?"

"It looks better on me."

Regel shivered. "Where is Lady Dracaris?"

Mask's child-smile mocked him. "You mean *Lord* Dracaris, I think."

She nodded to where Serris danced with a handsome man dressed in faded red and Bloodless browns as well as a dull black leather belt that hardly matched the rest of his attire. He wore his vivid red hair tied back in a tail to the shoulders and a red half-mask hid his face down to his thin lips. His movements, posture, and dress were all what Regel might expect of the son of a minor lord of Tar Vangr, out to court a bride. Except that of course he was no man at all.

"Whose decision was this?" Regel asked.

"I grew tired of playing the man."

Regel wanted to part their hands—to find another partner—but he saw Garin watching from his place on the dais. Creating a disruption in the crowd of dancers would draw unwanted attention for certain. He bit his lip and danced on, hoping to enjoy himself.

It was not so difficult. Seeing the enthralled faces of revelers—lords and ladies turning in circles, laughing and flirting—reminded him of such moments under the Winter King's reign. Too many nights to number, he had watched from a raised balcony or even from within the crowd itself as Lenalin—laughing and smiling to rival the light of the sun—danced the hours away with partner after partner. Silently, he would imagine he was dancing with her. Privately, he would dream that he was the cause of her smile.

Surprisingly, despite her hidden scars and ruined body, Mask showed Regel flashes of that same sort of grace. Her movements seemed awkward or forced at times, but every few heartbeats she would turn perfectly, her hips would sway just right. Mask danced like she was born for it, as Lenalin had.

He realized he had begun to lose himself in the dance when a chance look drew him back to the greater world. Mask saw his hesitation. "What is it?" she asked.

"Garin," Regel said.

Indeed, the Ravalis cousin was even now making his way through the throng—bowing and kissing the hands of noble ladies, shaking men's arms. He angled toward Ovelia and Serris.

"We should stop him," Regel whispered.

"Surely the Bloodbreaker can ward herself." Mask held his hands surprisingly tightly. "I was enjoying our dance."

Heedless, Regel twisted out of her grasp and moved to intercept Garin. "Hail, Highness."

The Shroud looked surprised, as though startled from a particularly complex calculation he'd been pondering. "A safe Ruin's Night, Syr," he said with a nod. "I'd ask you to unveil, but I think such is unnecessary, Lord of Tears."

Regel bowed. "Indeed, Garin, noble son of Luether," he said. "A safe Night to you also."

Garin's smile almost reached his scarlet eyemask. "You are barring my path."

"My apologies," Regel said with a bow. "I meant only to pay my respects."

"Assuredly," he said. "But who is this lady?"

Hands wrapped in white silk encircled Regel's arm. Mask curtsied to Garin but said nothing. Instead, she looked to Regel, her blank doll face smiling as ever.

Garin looked intrigued. "Surely you are not the Angel Serris, risen from the low-city?"

"No, indeed." Regel's mind was empty of names. "My cousin. From beyond Tar Vangr."

"I had not known the Oathbreaker had blood yet living. I am honored."

Garin bowed low and kissed Mask's hand, making Regel wince. He remembered the heat in that hand, and feared Garin would feel it as well.

"Do you not speak, lady?" Garin applied his analytic gaze to Mask.

Regel answered before Mask could. "She is wary in the presence of men," Regel said. "My apologies if she does not speak to you, Highness. I pray you do not take it amiss."

"Ah," he said. "A proper lady, I see."

Garin made to draw away, but Mask's fingers abruptly tightened around his hand. She pulled close and whispered something in Garin's ear, causing the Shroud's eyes to widen. "Yes—a pleasure, indeed." He glanced at Regel uneasily. "Your pardon, Lord of Tears."

He passed them by, heading once again for Ovelia. Regel started after, but Mask held him back. "Naught to fear," she said. "All's well."

"What did you say to him?" Regel whispered.

The doll mask was impenetrable.

Garin made his way across the foyer to Serris and Ovelia and bowed to both. This roused smiles from the surrounding dancers—it pleased them to see a prince of their ruling Blood—but when he extended his hand to "Lord" Dracaris rather than Serris, the gathered dancers gasped.

Regel started forward again, but Mask held him.

"Peace," she said. "Trust in her—and in me."

Regel wasn't so sure about either. "What did you say to him?" he asked again.

"It is of no consequence," she said. "It begins."

Soldiers in scarlet cloaks streamed from the curtain behind the throne, flooding the raised dais like blood from a wound. King Demetrus would emerge at any moment, and to move now would draw attention and spoil their game.

He had to do what Mask said: trust in Ovelia and Mask both that all was not lost.

~

Ovelia saw Garin coming and took a deep breath. This would be the most dangerous moment, she knew, and she would be ready.

"Lady Serris, I think." Garin kissed Serris's hand. "You are radiant as the angel that names you."

Ovelia gave Serris a warning look, but the woman bowed to him. "None named me but me, Syr."

"An angel, as I said." He looked up at Ovelia, who was trying her best not to meet his eye. "And you will introduce me to your lord of this eve? I know this is not the Lord of Tears."

"M'lord relies upon my discretion," Serris said. "Not his wife, after all."

"That I knew, for you told me yestereve no man shall be bound to you."

"Wouldn't say anything of the sort." Serris smiled tightly. "Many have bound me many times, and the reverse. But with ropes, not rings."

They shared a chuckle at that. "But I simply must know your companion, Angel Serris. He is an elegant man, and I cannot help but think of the beauteous face that must lie under that mask."

Serris's mirth turned to steel. "No, m'lord Ravalis, I think I won't. There are many things I might say—about last night, perhaps—that countless listeners here at the revel might wish to hear."

"Indeed." His eyes never left Ovelia's masked face. "How very uncouth of me. Of course, lord—you shall not be named on my account this eve." He drew off his mask and bowed to her. "I am Prince Garin Ravalis, at your service."

Under his piercing gaze, Ovelia grew self-conscious—particularly of her cracked black leather belt, which did not match the rest of her garb. She felt trapped, but she couldn't deny she enjoyed Garin's attention, even if she knew he did not desire her as a woman. Why did he have to be so charming?

"I wondered if I might have the honor of a dance," Garin said.

"Certainly," Serris said. "You are a Prince of the Blood and may ask—"

Smiling broadly, Garin extended his hand not to her, but to Ovelia. The color in Serris's exposed face drained away. Silence fell around them and folk stared.

In Tar Vangr, it was perfectly acceptable and even commonplace for a man to dance with another man or a woman with a woman. Such a romance was called a mirror courtship, and many great Vangryur songs spoke of such dalliances. The Ravalis, however, were summerborn through and through, and in the southern lands, men paired with women strictly. Since their ascension, the nobles of Tar Vangyr had to hide other assignations behind closed doors or risk public ridicule. To see a prince of the Ravalis openly courting a man was shocking. Garin's expression, however, showed full faith in his calculation.

"But your highness!" said Serris. "I must protest—"

"Surely your lord may protest for himself, if he so wishes." Garin winked at Ovelia. "What of it, Syr? There is no fear I might know your voice. I am a stranger to Tar Vangr."

Ovelia opened her mouth but Serris stepped between them. "Highness, m'lord's voice might be known by someone nearby—"

"It is well, Serris," Ovelia said softly. "I will dance with him."

Both Serris and Garin looked stunned. Ovelia spoke in a man's voice, of low tone and rich timbre. It was one of many voices she had crafted over five years as the Shroud, and by the look on Garin's unclad face, those had been years well spent. His certainty wavered, which gave her confidence.

"If it should please you, Prince of the Blood," Ovelia said. "Then I will dance with you. But shall I act the lady or the lord?" From the tamest waltz to a fiery dance of passion, Luetharr high society assigned male and female parts in the ballroom, while Vangryur dances made no such distinction.

The prince looked at her carefully, his eyes unreadable—even to her. He was no longer the aggressor but the defender. "I know both steps. You are more adept at the lord's part, I expect?"

"Of course." Ovelia smiled, keeping her unpainted lips pressed to a thin line. "But if you desire, I can be the lady."

Garin opened his mouth, but then the king's chimes filled the chamber and a short flurry of horns rang out to interrupt the dancing. "Alas, Syr. We are thwarted."

Ovelia inclined her head silently. She had almost been looking forward to the dance, madness that it would have proved. Had she truly almost risked herself so?

"Farewell, Syr." Garin bowed to Ovelia, then to Serris. "And Angel."

"Our honor, Highness," Serris said. She cast a dangerous look her way, but Ovelia ignored her.

Vhaerynn—King Demetrus's seneschal and high sorcerer—stepped forward between the thrones. The necromancer's gaunt body hid within a long, sleek robe of satin so deep red it seemed black, but it flickered like fresh wounds when he moved through the light. His cold gaze swept the chamber, and Ovelia averted her face so that he would not see her.

"On this day of days—on this night of nights." Vhaerynn spread his arms to the high ceiling. "On the eve of a new year, in this, Fallen Calatan's most glorious of cities—"

Garin made his way through the crowd of revelers to the dais. Prince Lan asked him a question, Ovelia saw, but Garin only shook his head. Ovelia breathed easier.

"That was madness." Serris was staring after Garin. "He'll know you. I'm sure—"

"I know what I do." Ovelia saw the way Serris was gazing after Garin and squeezed the woman's hand. "He will not betray us. I know it."

Serris shook her hand from Ovelia's grasp. "Have you gone mad, old woman? You're marked and made. You're out, as of this moment. Flee if you will or be caught, I don't care."

Ovelia cut her off with a sharp grip on her hand. "Silly girl. I *meant* him to see me."

Serris blinked, dumbfounded. "What? Why?"

Ovelia pulled Serris toward a retiring room. Applause told her the king had arrived on the dais. In the swell of welcome, they would go momentarily unnoticed.

Servants nodded to Ovelia's wave and brought around a standing shade to shield them from view. It was not uncommon for men at a Ravalis revel to wish to retire for a few moments alone with female companions. Under Denerre it had been the same, but in those days, women as commonly called for privy time. The partitions gave them some semblance of privacy.

Ovelia took off her belt and handed it to Serris. "Hold this."

The woman's nose prickled, but she took the belt. "What are you about?"

"Now that he's seen me, the Ravalis will believe me to be found amongst the revelers," Ovelia said. "So now I am free to go elsewhere."

"Elsewhere?"

Fingers moving fast, Ovelia unlaced her man's tunic and breeches as soon as the partition was unfolded. Beneath, she wore a woman's underthings as well as a carved pendant on a leather thong around her neck. It looked like a bird of some kind, or...

Serris's eyes widened at the charm. "Is that—?"

"Take off your clothes, and don't make a fuss." Ovelia pulled off the red wig she had worn over her dyed silver hair. "I'll need them."

TWENTY-TWO

DEMETRUS RAVALIS—WARRIOR, KING, USURPER—APPEARED on the dais amidst mighty applause and cheers. Regel remembered the solemn silence that had greeted King Denerre five years ago, like to the attention soldiers pay a beloved general. The Ravalis, by contrast, had no decorum: they had brought customs of loud cheers and clapping that grated on Regel's ears.

"We should go," he murmured, seeing an opportunity in the distraction.

"Nonsense," Mask said. "I would hear this."

The rulers of men strive to seem immortal, and King Demetrus had never proved an exception, with his hard face and strong limbs. None could say for certain how old he was, though Lan, his grown son, was hardly his first child or even his fifth, but in truth, his youngest and last. Demetrus had outlived three wives and more than one child who would have seen at least fifty winters, had Ruin not claimed them one and all. His last wife—a treacherous Vultara Blood called Anthien, Lan's mother but not Paeter's—had perished in the fall of Luether, and only his insistence on not marrying again kept him from having a dozen princelings besides Lan to choose among for a successor.

"So many lost," Regel said. "Has the Blood Ravalis suffered any less than the Blood Denerre?"

"Ravalis lives," Mask said. "Of course they have suffered less."

"Truly?" Regel asked. "Denerre was a small house in the end, and four deaths were enough to break it. Ravalis lost scores of its blood heirs when Luether fell. Have they not suffered more?"

The sorcerer said nothing for a long time, only looked at Regel, considering. "Ruin is a vicious bitch," Mask said at length. "And she will have her due."

Demetrus ascended the dais to give his traditional Ruin's Night address. Despite his age, Demetrus walked with a smooth, strong gait to his throne and stood before it with no trouble. The king's lips parted, revealing a line of fine teeth that sparkled like ivory. They were false, if Regel recalled correctly: the work of mage-craftsmen. There was a reedy waver to his words that hinted at years of smoking summerweed.

"Friends," he said. "Our friends—who have welcomed us in this city—your city—for so long. Be welcome in this place, as you have welcomed us."

He swept his hand to take in the chamber. Voluminous sleeves hid his velvet-gloved hands and his blue and red robe stood up from shoulders girded with thick pads. He held in his hands the rod of rulership and Raeve, the Bloodsword of Ravalis, which he himself had carried from Luether as the barbarians stormed its gates twenty years ago. He was a Ravalis prince head to foot and his eyes surveyed the room imperiously, like those of a lion.

"Brave friends of Tar Vangr and Luether, Blood of Calatan," he said. "This Ruin's Night marks the fifth year we have sat in this seat not ours, worn this crown which fits not our head."

"He speaks true in that, at least," Mask said. "It's a trifle small, no?"

Regel gazed at Demetrus's brow. There, atop his still-red curls, sat the Diadem of Winter: a silver coronet etched with ivy and snowflakes, its high-reaching prongs long as daggers. Legend claimed that the Diadem cured diseases, halted venoms, and healed wounds, making its wearer invincible. But its blessing extended only to a wearer who bore the Blood of Winter, and Demetrus was not such a man. Indeed, Mask was correct, and the crown looked out of place on Demetrus's head. While the heirs of Denerre shared a slight, wiry frame, to a man the Ravalis were built on a heroic scale, and the crown almost looked like a child's costume hat. The colors did not match either: his brown skin and scarlet hair favored gold, not silver. Not once in the five years Demetrus had worn the diadem had it seemed to fit him. He wore it only rarely, at formal events such as this gathering.

The Coronet of Summer, by contrast, was a gold-wrought treasure, embedded with rubies that gleamed like living flame. That crown would have suited Demetrus, but the Ravalis had lost it the night Luether had fallen. He should be wearing that crown instead, Regel thought, rather than the crown of King Orbrin—of Lenalin and Semana.

"Five years, and in truth, far more," Demetrus continued. "We have been your guests twenty years, in which we have drunk wine and supped on bread not of our land. We have loved women not of our own blood—loved them well and poorly."

It was surprising to hear Demetrus utter these words, which prompted a few murmuring laughs and unsettled throat-clearings. Demetrus had refused to remarry after his wife perished in Luether, and high Tar Vangr society had always taken that as a slight. For him to joke of it now... Lan laughed loudly, and the sound chilled Regel. The prince should have been offended by the mere mention of lovemaking, however subtle. He should not have found it amusing. Regel glanced at Laegra, who had paled at her husband's crudity. She looked as trapped as any of them.

The king waited as the chuckling died away. "Some of you may ask, how long are we guests to stay here in your city? How long before we might return to our own southern land? It is a question we ask of ourselves, every day." Demetrus brought his hands together at his belly. "Would that we could lead an army south to crush the usurpers and restore peace... but, of course, your Council will not have it. That is the will of our hosts, and the Ravalis honor their hosts, as the ancient laws dictate."

Those words were bitter. In politics, Demetrus was like his son Lan, if somewhat more patient: very little love lay between him and the Council, which had so far restrained the Ravalis' march to war. Serris had relayed rumors of the Council moving against the crown, and Garin himself had spoken of the Ravalis ceding power. Was this the night it would come to pass? Was this the very moment?

"But let us not digress," Demetrus said. "We gather together this night not only to commemorate the fifth year of our rule and the twentieth of your hospitality, but to remember those brave and beautiful who have fallen that we might stand amongst you. A libation!"

He snapped his fingers. A goblet appeared, borne by a handsome red-haired boy clad in a gold loin-cloth and crimson and blue paint. A serving girl similarly attired—with the addition of a silken chest-wrap—bowed to Demetrus and poured a healthy draught of summerwine into the cup. Servants filtered amongst the revelers, offering small glass goblets of rich red wine. Regel took a glass, but Mask ignored the servant until he went away. The boy shivered a bit, his attire not made for a Tar Vangr night.

"Five years," Demetrus said, raising his goblet high. "Five years since our friend King Orbrin passed from this place, and Princess Semana too, his beloved greatdaughter and my own." He shut his eyes. "May they remain in our hearts, by the Silver Fire."

"By the Fire," echoed many voices in the room. Members of the Council and those loyal to them smiled guardedly.

The king drained his goblet, and the revelers followed suit. Only three did not drink—Regel, Mask, and Lan, who seemed too busy trying to control laughter that threatened to overwhelm him. Up on the dais, Laegra excused herself, looking ill, and Lan hardly seemed to notice. His mirth continued to make Regel uneasy. What jest did he know, that no one else did? This was about to go bad.

Demetrus raised an open hand. "Councilor Kiereth Yaela."

"Majesty?" The Lord from Blood Yaela—a handsome man of perhaps thirty winters, proud of stance and attired in gold and black—put a hand to his chest. His dancing partner—an unknown woman or perhaps a clean-shaven man, knowing Kiereth's flexible tastes—backed away, nodding.

"Please," Demetrus said. "Approach."

"By your leave." Kiereth started toward the dais.

The Heir of Blood Yaela was one of the most powerful men on the Council, and if Regel remembered correctly, he was one of Serris's favored patrons. He looked for her now, and caught a glimpse of her before she vanished behind a privacy partition. What was she doing?

Regel started that direction, meaning to slip away and follow his squire, but Mask held his arm with surprising strength. "Do not miss this," she said.

The councilor looked more than a little confused as he ascended the dais, but he had a smile for all. He bowed gallantly to Prince Lan, then knelt before Demetrus. His bow was courtly but lingered on the edge of respect. In a land as steeped in tradition and etiquette as Tar Vangr, his countrymen would understand the gesture but the Ravalis might not. The summerblood were more casual about such things.

"We have been enemies, do you not agree?" Demetrus asked.

"Perhaps not *enemies*, Your Majesty," Kiereth said. "We do not always see eye to eye, indeed."

This gave rise to muted laughter. The animosity between the two men was well known—in the Council chambers, no voice was louder in denunciation of Blood Ravalis than that of Kiereth Yaela.

"Draw your dagger," the king said.

Kiereth looked startled. "Your Majesty?"

"If you would spill my blood, then let it be by your blade rather than your words." The Summer King drew open his robe, revealing the tusked boar tattooed across his chest. "Fight me for Tar Vangr."

A gasp swept through the chamber, and for good reason. The gathered lords and ladies had never imagined such madness. All knew Councilor Yaela was not a warrior. He wore a knife as part of his dress, but his weapons were rhetoric and wit, exerting political pressure to accomplish what swords could not. But he was still a young man and hard. Why would Demetrus call him out, so very publicly and apparently over Tar Vangr itself? Had age finally caught the king and eroded his wits?

All eyes were on the exchange between Demetrus and Kiereth, but Regel knew to look beyond the obvious. He grasped the carving in his pocket and focused, allowing his senses to expand. Sure enough, more was afoot. On the dais, Garin reached for his warpick, but Lan clapped a hand on his shoulder. A wicked grin flickered across the face of the crown prince. That subtle expression warned Regel of what was to come, and he could do nothing to stop it.

"Your Majesty." Whatever Kiereth had expected, it was not that. He drew back, and his face flushed. "I will not fight you. That is not our way."

"But it *is* mine—the way of the Ravalis and of Luether," Demetrus said. "When you want something, you must fight for it. Kill for it." He looked back at Kiereth. "The wrong blood rules Tar Vangr—the wrong king consumes your wine and his sons defile your women. Are you a man, Lord of Yaela? Will you not defend your homeland? Draw steel and drive out the invaders?"

The king stepped closer and whispered in the councilor's ear, too softly for Regel to hear. He could see the effect in Kiereth's body, however: his face went white and his hand went to the hilt of his dagger. Regel glanced to Mask, who seemed to be watching the exchange raptly.

Finally, Demetrus drew away from Kiereth and spread his hands wide. "As I thought," he declared to the whole of the revel. "You are a nation of cowards. You trust to words and intrigues, and believe those braver than you will stand in the way of your foes. When the Winter King died, you lost your great defender, and five years later, here you stand, unwilling to face your foe with steel drawn. This is why we rule you—because you cannot rule yourselves."

And with that, he turned his back to Kiereth, offering him the greatest dishonor of all.

Regel willed the councilor to do nothing, but it was too late. Whatever Demetrus had whispered to him, Kiereth had abandoned sense. His dagger scraped free of his scabbard with a sound of nails pried from a coffin. He stepped toward Demetrus, faster than any bodyguards could swoop in to stop him.

The Ravalis King was turning when Kiereth struck, and he responded with the reflexes of a trained warrior. He raised an open palm like a shield, and the blade plunged through his hand. With his expanded awareness, Regel could hear the small bones of Demetrus's hand rattle against each other as they parted. Blood welled around the blade.

The king grasped Kiereth's arm before he could pull away, locking them together in a violent embrace. He looked at the wound and shuddered, like a dog shaking itself of water.

Finally, a smile crept onto his face. "I misjudged you, winterborn," he said.

In a heartbeat, the ballroom was in chaos. Bodyguards on all sides drew swords and casters, and a horde of dusters appeared from behind the dais, weapons ready. Shouts of treason and challenge rang out, and steel whined as it tore free of scabbards.

"Stop," Demetrus said.

Though the king had not spoken loudly, the word vibrated through the room from the midst of the mob. His commandment stayed the coming battle.

"This is not treason," Demetrus said. "He strikes at my invitation and proves his valor. And for that, he is forgiven."

Kiereth opened his mouth to speak.

The king balled up his left fist and launched it into Kiereth's jaw hard enough to drive the younger man staggering back. The dagger came out of Demetrus's hand with the sound of sucking flesh, and blood sailed in a wide arc. The king grasped his wounded hand but did not cry out.

"I respect any man who faces his foe," he said. "But I will not fail to answer violence with violence. Let blood answer blood."

Demetrus cast his blood onto the floorstones. Through his focus, Regel heard the plink of the blood striking the stone, followed by a loud sizzle he needed no statue to hear. The sound spread through the hall like blood in water. He thought he could sense distant thunder, even if he could not quite hear it. At his side, Mask shrank back around him as though for protection.

"Necromancy," the sorcerer said.

Regel could only watch as the blood spread and shook upon the floor. Fingers reached up through the stone itself, and two hands pulled a body into the chamber. It wriggled like a worm climbing out of the earth, blood sloughing off in soupy rivulets. Within a moment, a gaunt man stood among the horrified revelers, his blood-drenched robes plastered to his skinny limbs.

"Vhaerynn," Regel murmured.

A dozen casters came up, but the necromancer waved his open hand almost idly in their direction. The wielders of those deadly murderpieces abruptly stiffened and cried out, and the casters twisted of their own accord. In a heartbeat, the noble warders aimed their deadly weapons at their own terrified charges, despite their attempts to pull their arms away. Kiereth stepped back, but Vhaerynn's magic seized him and he could not move. Veins pulsed madly in his temples, and blood trickled from his nose.

Behind his necromancer vizier, Demetrus clasped his wounded hand to his chest.

"No more arguments," Demetrus said to the room, his expression perfectly calm. "No more opposition. For five years, this has not been our city, but that changes tonight," he said. "Allow me to show you why the Summer Princes rule the Winter kingdom."

He motioned toward Kiereth, where Vhaerynn held him fast, and Prince Lan broke away from the throne on the dais, where he had been leaning casually. He drew his sword as he walked and pointed it at Kiereth's chest. Blood tinged the sweat rolling down the councilor's face.

"We have the will to rule," said Demetrus. "And you do not."

At Regel's side, Mask stiffened as though someone had stabbed her in the belly.

Lan lunged, and his blade burst out Kiereth's back, just under his left shoulder blade. A dark stain spread down his back around the blade. Lan pressed against him, as though embracing him like a brother. Through his focus, Regel heard what Lan whispered to Kiereth: "And so you learn your place, whore."

Hardened murderer that he was, Regel felt sick.

The King nodded to Lan, who stepped away. His sword slipped from Kiereth's body with a scrape of steel on bone, and the councilor fell to his knees, eyes rolling. He did not seem able to scream.

Demetrus clutched his wounded hand and spoke in a voice dark and powerful. "Tar Vangr has long been its own city," he said. "As of tonight, it belongs to Ravalis, body and soul."

Lan brought his sword around and halfway cut Kiereth's head from his shoulders. It flopped to the side and swung around on a hunk of flesh. Blood burst into the air.

The crown-prince severed the head fully with a second blow.

Somewhere in the crowd, a man screamed. The nobles of Blood Yaela started shouting, and a hundred voices rose at once, creating a cacophony of indistinguishable words. Two dusters appeared, flanking Demetrus, and they hustled the king out of the battle and away down a side corridor. In his wake, Vhaerynn smiled at the men held thrall in his magic.

Mask pulled insistently at his arm. "We have to move now."

As Regel turned away, Vhaerynn closed his fingers, and a dozen casters cracked.

~

Clad as a man, Serris watched Mask and Regel disappear out of the great chamber, which descended into chaos. She watched as Lan cut down Kiereth

Yaela, and though she would never admit it, her heart ached for a moment. The Heir of Yaela had been a good lover and, for all his faults, a good man besides. One more grievance to lay at the feet of Lan Ravalis.

All around her, nobles shouted and shoved at one another, lords and ladies shrieked or fled, and guardsmen drew steel to keep the revelers under control. Now was her chance to slip amongst them unawares, following Ovelia's hastily explained plan.

But Serris remembered the part she had to play—the warning from the masked man in the alley, and again, in her room with her daughter. If Davargorn could threaten her there...

Serris thought about the dagger sheathed against her spine—her favorite dagger. Regel's dagger. "No," she said under her breath. "Burn you, I won't do it."

But what choice did she have?

Serris made her way toward the dais, where Lan Ravalis stood over the field of battle like a triumphant general. She kept to the fringes of the fighting and passed unnoticed through the melee. If she could just catch Lan unawares, all this could be ended with a single thrust of her blade. She stepped behind him and drew.

Then her arm locked up, the muscles contorting into an impossible shape. The dagger turned in her fingers and pointed itself at her throat. She looked, and there stood Vhaerynn, smiling at her, owning her dagger hand with his magic. Raping her.

Serris managed to twist aside, and the blade only stabbed into her shoulder. She tried to recover, but Lan caught her, clasping her wrist in one hand and her throat in the other.

"A whore in a man's clothing." He laughed. "Do you want her, Vhaerynn? Or shall I—?"

But Vhaerynn wasn't looking at them. Instead, he had raised his head and was sniffing at the air. A smile of recognition spread across his face.

"Can it be?" he wondered aloud. "Have you returned, my old friend?"

He meant *Mask.*

Serris understood, of a sudden, what was going on. Davargorn's words filled her mind—his warning about a smiling monster. Mask's doll face. The warning she thought she could ignore.

Lan's fingers were tight on her throat, and the world started to crumble.

She had been wrong.

TWENTY-THREE

CLAD IN SERRIS'S DRESS and mask, Ovelia waited around a corner while the Ravalis guards hurried past toward the ballroom. She hoped Regel and Mask were able to evade the chaos erupting there. It didn't matter to her part, however, upon which she focused now.

Ovelia traced her fingers about the worn buckle of her black leather belt. The belt clashed with the rest of her garb and stank of old blood—not a surprise, since it was one of Mask's relics. Its ancient magic was not powerful but pivotal to this night. Ovelia had agreed to Mask's plan, but with those awful sounds coming from the throne room, she wanted to run back, to throw herself into the fray to—what? This whole mad scheme depended on her. She could only do her part, and trust Mask.

"Stop hesitating and just move," she said softly.

Calmly, Ovelia stepped down the corridor, raised a tapestry bright with Ravalis colors, and ducked into the dusty alcove behind it. The walls around her gleamed slightly silver in the diffused candlelight from the hall. No Ravalis came this way, and they sent no servants to clean or maintain this space. Ovelia had ensured it was so during her tenure as the Shroud, and it was good to see the Ravalis had overlooked it in the chaotic transition. She moved to a very familiar spot and ran her bare fingers over a glinting set of letters, which spelled out the name "Lenalin." Caressing the stone was almost like touching her dearest friend, and Ovelia had to suppress a sob. Perhaps it was merely the dust.

Powered by her touch, the silvery letters glowed brighter, and the glow extended in both directions, illumining the names "Semana" and "Darak" to the right and "Orbrin" to the left. The silver glow traced its way past Orbrin's name and illuminated first the name of the Winter King's long-dead brother Moritun, their mother Queen Aritana, and outward and past. The silver traced curling lines through the dusty stone, resolving into a stylized tree, showing the Blood of Denerre coursing through the ages. The bloodtree filled the alcove, around and above Ovelia, tracing the bloodlines that led back from Orbrin and Lenalin over a thousand years. Ovelia remembered long ago, when her father showed her this shrine. She'd thought at the time she had never seen anything so beautiful—except perhaps Lenalin.

Syr Norlest had told her the story of the name at the root of the tree, where the silver revealed the long-ago progenitor of the Blood. Queen Denes first led her people out of darkness to embrace the Prophecy of Return, centuries before the rise of the Empire of Calatan. They had found a world far darker than they had expected, but they had made the best of it, warding off the furious snows of appalling winter, beating back the barbarians and monsters of Ruin, and carving out a city-state they would eventually call Tar Vangr.

Every generation of the Blood of Winter had struggled and fought against the crushing tide of Ruin, and the last heirs of Denerre had proved no different. Ovelia owed a debt to the only family she had ever known to see justice done against the Ravalis, and she would honor it. She would not fail Orbrin, Lenalin, or Semana—the princess least of all.

Suppressing an unsettled feeling, Ovelia found the name of Orbrin's lost brother Moritun and pressed it. Ancient mechanisms whirred to life, and the lattice around Queen Denes's name parted to reveal a dark passage leading into the bowels of the palace. Five years as the Shroud, and she had never let on the existence of these passages. In truth, she hadn't known precisely why she'd kept them a secret, but it had seemed right at the time. Now, it proved essential to their plan.

"Halt!" A man stepped out of the darkness, caster leveled at her. "Stay and be known!"

Unless, of course, the Ravalis had indeed learned of the passages and placed unseen guards there.

If she'd had Draca in hand, Ovelia might have seen this danger in its guardian flames. But of course the Ravalis would have identified the sword at the door and captured her. She should have trusted her instincts. Ovelia saw her death in the guard's cocked caster, and with it the failure of their plot.

When the caster didn't erupt in doom, Ovelia remembered to breathe.

"Name yourself, woman," the guard said. "And why are you here? The revel is that way."

Ovelia saw a glimmer of hope. He hadn't recognized her.

"Old Gods!" She willed herself to weep. "Don't kill me. I ran away and now I'm lost. I didn't mean—oh Gods!" She clutched her stomach and bent double.

"For the Fire's sake, woman, don't blubber." The guard looked painfully awkward at her display. "I'm not going to—" A scream echoed up the corridor, and the guard looked away. His jaw tightened with trepidation. He didn't know what was going on.

On one knee, Ovelia pawed at his leg. "You have to help us," she said. "You—"

"I can't abandon my post," he said. "I—"

A dozen casters cracked, and cries of terror rose from the ballroom.

"You have to help," Ovelia said, willing him to go. "The king is in danger!"

The guard stepped around her, heading toward the source of the cries, and her heart leaped. Then he paused, his brow furrowed at her silver hair. Damn. "Stay, lady," he said. "You seem—"

Ovelia rose in a fluid lunge, seized the caster, and smashed it upward across the guard's face. Then, as the man staggered back, Ovelia slammed the butt of the weapon into his temple. He collapsed.

She slung the caster around her shoulder, put her hands under the guard's armpits, and dragged him into the hidden passage. The mechanism closed the entrance once more, plunging them into darkness. A heartbeat later, she felt the familiar drain of the nearby torches. Powered by an old magic, they drank a small portion of her body's warmth and kindled with blue flame. Abruptly, the corridor lit up around her, as far as her resonant heat extended, and sickly-smelling smoke crept up to the ceiling. Usually, the draining candles unnerved her, but she pushed it from her mind. Tonight she had other considerations.

Ovelia stood over the guard, the caster pointed at his head, considering. She'd given him every chance to go. He had been in her way, and he didn't deserve this: to be murdered, unknown and unmourned, in the cold secret halls. At the same time, if she let him live, there was always the possibility he would awaken and all their plans would be undone.

"Dammit," she said. "Why couldn't you just go?"

Why were her hands so calm? Had she fallen so far that cold murder did not trouble her?

Long ago, as girls, she and Lenalin had made these passages their secret kingdom. The corridors became vile dungeons for knights and princesses, ancient caverns for hunting Old Gods, or great crypts of the Deathless Ones. They explored together, side by side—the princess and her knight, two shivering girls whose hearts raced.

As she stood over the guard, considering his casual murder, Ovelia remembered.

~

"It's dark, princess," the young Ovelia said. "Are you sure you're for this?"

"Of course I'm sure, thinblood." Lenalin flipped her silver-blonde hair back from her face and raised her chin. "I am a Princess of the Blood of Winter." She made no move to approach, though.

Ovelia smirked at her. "You're not afraid, are you?"

"No!" Lenalin's voice cracked and undermined her wrath. "I mean… No, it's just… dusty. Dusty, and dank, and the like. It's not proper for—"

Ovelia giggled. "Her perfect highness, afraid of a little dirt." She stepped back into the corridor as though to leave Lenalin alone. "Or a little dark, mayhap."

"Wait!" said the princess, catching Ovelia's hand. "Won't you hold me?"

Ovelia blinked at her. "What?"

"I mean you can hold my hand." Lenalin blushed fiercely. "That is, if you want to."

"I…" Ovelia felt her heart thudding in her head, and warmth spread through her insides. Her tongue felt like a hunk of dead rubber in her mouth.

"Well, if you're going to be thus about it," Lenalin said with a sniff, and strode forward.

"Wait!" Ovelia's voice crackled.

"Aye?" The princess had made it three steps before she cast a dubious look over her shoulder. "Now who's afraid?"

Ovelia strode forward resolutely and seized Lenalin's hand. The blood raced beneath her skin. Their eyes met, and Ovelia lost her breath and could not find it. Her hand was calm, but her heart raced.

Lenalin laughed. "Come," she said. "We'll find an adventure."

～

Her hand was calm, and it felt monstrous. Did a man's life mean so little to her?

The memory faded as Ovelia heard murmuring words, one voice deep and male, the other smooth and female. They came through the concealed door—through the shrine of the Winter Tree—and passed quickly by. Some lordling with a lowborn evening-lass, perhaps. She ducked down and held her hand over the senseless man's mouth, in case he roused and spoke. As such, she could not see the newcomers as they approached and moved past. The voices were faintly familiar.

She wondered if the woman was one of Regel's Tears—perhaps even his squire Serris. The woman hadn't passed up a chance to glare at her since that first night at the Burned Man, and Ovelia well recognized that look. She knew what it was to be so protective.

Regel. Her hand drifted up to the carved necklace she'd worn beneath her lord's garb, and a fresh spasm twisted her midsection. She wondered again if she and Regel... But no. Surely she was too old for that. She sighed and massaged her aching stomach.

As a child at Lenalin's side, guiding the princess through the darkness, Ovelia had felt strong and confident. Even when they grew older and Lenalin married Paeter, yet had Ovelia known joy in watching her from afar and stealing occasional moments together. These last fifteen years since Lenalin's death, however, she'd felt hollow. She felt poorly made, as though her limbs fit only crudely. What reason had she to live, without the Blood she had sworn to defend? Without the warm hand she'd held so tightly?

"Semana," Ovelia murmured.

That was why her hand did not tremble on the caster. Come treachery, come murder, she would do her duty. She would slay the Summer King for Semana's sake. To her mind, a regicide was a powerful thing—but to her hands, it seemed a matter of course. One she had done before.

"Norlest taught you to slay men by steel, and kings are but men." She shut her eyes. "Orbrin taught you that well enough."

She squeezed the caster's trigger.

～

Regel opened the secret passage past the Winter Tree and led Mask through. The door ground on dusty stone, and Regel saw the blue flames of the candles already lit inside. "Hail, Tall-Sister," he said.

Ovelia appeared, a caster hanging from her hand. Her eyes seemed wet in the torchlight.

Regel looked around and frowned. "Serris did not follow you?" he asked.

"She is being me." Ovelia shook her head. "We have little time as it passes."

Regel nodded. "Weapons? I see you've appropriated a caster."

"Not a concern." Mask stepped past Regel and held out her hand. "The belt."

Ovelia unbuckled the ugly black belt Regel remembered seeing her wear in her guise as a lord at the revel. "Why did you have *me* wear it, and not yourself?" she asked.

"I couldn't know if they would have seers at the gate who would recognize it," Mask said. "And I thought it better for you to be caught than me."

"How compassionate," Regel murmured, but Ovelia only shrugged and handed over the belt.

Mask put on the belt, which struck an odd contrast with her sweeping white dress. She put out her hand, and Regel saw power flowing from the belt. The air shimmered above Mask's palm and coalesced into Draca. This, the sorcerer handed to a wide-eyed Ovelia. In a similar way, Mask then produced two falcata for Regel. All the while, the belt gave off acrid smoke as its magic worked.

Regel marveled. "Gauntlets, mask, chestplate, and now a belt. How many relics do you bear?"

"Turn away," Mask said. "I'm told this sight can be... disturbing."

Regel turned his back and gave the sorcerer her privacy. Casually, he put his hand in his pocket and grasped his carven focus, but the magic's smoke obscured his senses. He stole a glance over his shoulder, long enough to see the sorcerer's white garb burning away, replaced by her black suit. She tossed her porcelain doll's face away to shatter against the stone wall, and put on her favored black leather mask. Regel caught a glimpse of light-colored hair but that was all.

"The first task is done, and we are inside," Mask said. "The king was hurt in the battle, and they ushered him out, leaving the necromancer and many soldiers indisposed. We must strike quickly, before our absence from the revel is noted. Lord of Tears?"

Regel was looking at the shards of the smiling doll mask. He nodded. "I am with you."

"Good." Mask turned to Ovelia. "You know the castle, Bloodbreaker. Where would they have taken him? The healing chambers?"

Ovelia shook her head. "There is a room, down by the furnace, where he goes for privacy. He has a personal physician—Maure—who tends him."

Regel raised an eyebrow. "Lenalin's old nursemaid?"

"The same," Ovelia said. "She is loyal to the throne of Vangr beyond question. Far safer for Demetrus to use her than to trust Vhaerynn or one of his kin to tend him."

"Prudent," Mask said. "Where?"

"The king uses y—" She glanced at Mask and corrected herself. "Paeter's old private chambers. The passages lead there, but I do not believe they know the entrance."

"Lead on," Mask said. "But step warily. Legends speak of a guardian spirit in these secret halls. Perhaps we'll need Queen Denes to lead us, no?"

Ovelia gave Regel a knowing glance. "Not likely," she said, then disappeared into the gloom. As she walked, the torches lit along the path. Mask fell into step three paces behind her.

Regel lingered near the entrance to the passage. Perhaps Mask had not noticed it, but he did: a Ravalis guard lay hidden barely a pace from where Mask had discarded her doll's face. Regel knelt and touched the man's throat. "Hmm."

"Regel?" Moving quietly, Ovelia had approached within two paces of him. Mask lingered behind, deeper in the corridor.

Regel reached across and touched the carved necklace she wore. It was the dragon he had carved for her and hung on a leather cord—his gift to her, on what he had thought would be their last night together. "I thought you discarded that."

Ovelia's hand went to her throat. "I have not changed as much as you think."

"No, Tall-Sister," Regel said. "You have not."

She turned and passed back into the narrow corridor. Regel looked again to the unmoving guard. He checked the man's bonds, then left him breathing shallowly.

TWENTY-FOUR

A s THEY STOLE THROUGH the hidden passages within the palace of Tar Vangr, Regel saw Ovelia remembering. Her eyes might drift to familiar corners, or her fingers trail along one wall or another. He hoped her memories were fond—his own memories were anything but.

Long ago, he'd spent many lonely days prowling these passages to learn every twist and turn, to discover every potential hiding place. At the height of his skulking days, he could get from any chamber in the palace to any other in a matter of moments. The tunnels had been his kingdom, and stories of the palace's guardian spirit had not been so far-fetched as many believed. How many nights had he shadowed the Winter King himself through these passages, carving in hand, senses alert for any possible foe?

He had taken to following Semana and Ovelia—the princess and her warder-in-waiting—as they thought themselves alone in the darkness. He'd heard the words they'd shared: the secrets of girlhood and the stirrings of an enduring bond. He'd never been able to join them, of course, but could only remain the specter in the shadows, protecting them. It had not been right to intrude—he knew that—but he had been young, foolish, and in love.

"Lord of Tears," said Mask, her voice softly curious at Regel's shoulder. "Why do you call her Tall-Sister? She is no sister of yours."

He smiled wanly. "You would not understand."

"You think not?"

"I know enough of you to think so," he replied.

"And I cannot surprise you? Until yestereve, you thought me a man."

Regel looked down into the arrogant face shrouded in black leather. Mask's arms were crossed over her flat chest in a conceited posture. The illusion was quite convincing, though now that he knew the truth, he could see echoes of womanly movement in Mask. He wouldn't have believed it, but she seemed to be *pouting*.

"Very well," he said. "Ovelia was heart-sister to Princess Lenalin."

Mask looked at him quizzically. "Semana's mother?"

"Just so." Regel smiled. "Thus Ovelia named herself, as the taller of the two. Simple."

"A stupid choice," Mask said. "Her friendship brought her above her station, such that she earned a name as a child. And yet, she made such an asinine choice for her first name."

"No," Regel said. "She chose the name she did to show her devotion to Lenalin. That she wanted to live a life defined by her."

"But she betrayed the Blood of Winter," Mask said.

The humor drained out of Regel and his face fell. "We are creatures of duty,

Ovelia and I," he said. "I would not expect you to understand."

"It was *duty* to slay her heart-sister's father?" Mask said with a ragged chuckle. "I would hate to have her sworn service under me. Either of you."

Quick as a striking snake, Regel grasped Mask by the throat before she could react. He pushed the sorcerer against the wall. "You listen to me, and you listen well," he said. "Ovelia shed blood and suffered for Lenalin every day. None loved the princess so well as she did."

"Not even you?"

Regel hesitated. Ovelia had passed around a corner, leaving them alone.

"Oh come now," Mask said. "Do not deny it."

Regel clenched his jaw.

"Was she beautiful?" Mark smiled in her mask. "Was she sweet and demure? Was it her face or her body you loved? Did you dream of her by night or spy on her as she slept?"

"You cannot ask—"

"And yet," Mask said, heedless of his words. "You rutted the Dracaris whore because you could pretend she was your princess. Tell me I lie, Lord of Tears. *Regel.*"

Regel could not find his voice.

"You let her die," Mask said. "You let Princess Lenalin die because you loved her and she did not love you."

"Stop."

Mask's lips were close to Regel's now. "The hands that slew her were not yours, but you killed her just the same. And for what? Jealousy—"

The last ragged word choked off as Regel tightened his hand around Mask's throat.

"You listen to me, you Ruin-scarred hag," Regel said. "I loved Lenalin more than a wretch like you could ever understand. She died because she would not let me save her." His eyes narrowed. "And even that does not nearly match how *Ovelia* loved her."

Mask's mouth opened, but Regel crushed her back against the wall and stifled sound.

"If you question either of us again, I shall put an end to your words. I swear it."

He expected Mask to retort with irony, but instead the sorcerer only stared at him. Considering.

Ovelia's head appeared around the far corner, silver-blonde hair flashing in the blue torchlight. "What passes?" she asked, her voice dangerous.

"Naught." Regel eased Mask down.

Ovelia looked to Mask for confirmation, but the sorcerer waved. "Peace, Bloodbreaker," the sorcerer rasped. "All passes well."

Ovelia gave them an uncertain nod. "Make haste." She vanished around the corner.

Regel started down the corridor, but black-wrapped fingers brushed his ankle. He turned, eyes thunderous. Mask knelt before him, hands on his calves in the old supplicant's pose—a tradition as ancient as hospitality or honor. "What of Semana?"

Regel tightened his fists. "What of her?"

Mask's red-rimmed eyes were brighter than fresh steel. "Did you love Semana as you did her mother?" Regel saw her lick her chapped lips. "And does Ovelia?"

"What does it matter?" he asked.

"It matters," said Mask. "Answer me this, and that shall be the end of my questions."

A refusal came to Regel's lips but he held the words. He remembered Ovelia's plea that first night in the Burned Man tavern, and the ardor in her eyes as she knelt in the alley and promised her lifeblood in exchange for vengeance. She'd spent all of her resources on the hunt for Mask, even traded her body for passage to Luether. She'd committed treason against the Ravalis and thrown her lot in with a man who most had reason to hate her. All of this she'd done for Semana— just to *avenge* her, not even to save her. And now that they had some hope...

"Is there a heart that beats here?" Regel knelt and laid his fingers against the cold leather that wrapped Mask's chest. "For if there is not, then you cannot and will never understand what Semana means to that woman—or what they both mean to me."

Mask started at him, her eyes awed.

"Only know this," he continued. "If you are lying—and Semana is dead— then when I am finished with you, whatever scars or disfigurements you bear will be as lady's rouge on a beautiful maiden." He drew his hand away. "Do you understand?"

The sliver of Mask's mouth he could see twisted into something like a smile. "Promise?"

Regel turned, and they moved on.

~

They came at least to their destination: a private sitting room, windowless, buried in the heart of the palace where the Narfire rose. Regel understood why a scion of summer like Demetrus would favor the heat of the eternal fire buried deep in the mountain. Spyholes allowed Ovelia to peer through, while Mask hung back and leaned against the opposite wall. Regel stood between them.

"Is the king within?" Mask asked softly.

"I believe so," Ovelia said. "A woman is sitting by the bed, tending to him."

"Maure?" Regel leaned to look through the spyholes.

"Too dark to tell," Ovelia said. "But this one seems slender. Young."

"What does it matter?" Mask asked, her voice guttural. "You see his face?"

"No." Ovelia pulled away from the wall and met Regel's eyes. "What do we do?"

"We strike," Mask said. "The two of you. Go and slay him. The woman too, if needs be."

231

Regel and Ovelia exchanged glances. "Why not kill him yourself?" Regel asked. "Unless now is the moment you choose to betray us."

"No." Mask's eyes darted from Regel to Ovelia. "I am in earnest."

"Where are the guards, Mask—to take us prisoner and behead us for attempted regicide?" Regel kept his voice mild but he drew his falcat halfway. "What reward will you receive?"

"No." Mask's eyes lit with green fire and flame danced along her fingers. "Heed me—"

"I will do it," Ovelia said, breaking the growing tension. "For Semana, I could kill a thousand kings in a thousand bedchambers in a thousand cities."

When she spoke, it was not Regel she gazed upon, but Mask, who nodded slowly. Regel sheathed his scythe-sword.

"Very well," said Mask. "Go, Bloodbreaker. Bloody your hands with a second crown."

Ovelia reached for the latch.

"Wait." Regel seized her hand. "We do this together."

Ovelia's eyes widened. "But you just refused—"

"I do not trust her, but I trust *you*." Regel pulled Ovelia closer. "Let us be bloodbreakers together. There need be no other divide between us."

He kissed her lightly as Mask watched, eyes flickering in the candlelight.

"Draw your sword, Tall-Sister," Regel said.

"You cannot spill Demetrus's blood," Mask said. "Remember the blood ward summoning Vhaerynn to the hall."

"The sword isn't for the king." Regel nodded to the blue torches. "When this door opens, the light might disturb them."

Ovelia drew the Bloodsword, and immediately the nearby torches guttered and died in its devouring magic, plunging the three of them into darkness. The only light came from the crimson flames flickering along the blade and the simmering green magic of Mask's helm. In that dull illumination, Regel drew a cord of wire from his sleeve: the garrote he had used in Luether. Death by wire was ignoble, but this was not the time for honor.

"Watch the sword," Regel said. "We'll need its warning magic, if this is a trap."

Ovelia nodded.

"Are you coming?" Regel asked Mask.

"I can watch from here," Mask said. "And if all goes awry, I can destroy you all with a blast of Plaguefire. Thus, even in death, you'll succeed."

"How reassuring." Regel drew the carving focus out of his pocket. He detected guards outside the private chamber, but if they did their work in silence, all would pass well. He drew his senses out of the object. "One thing more."

Ovelia's eyes widened. "Regel, are you sure?"

"Sure about what?" Mask asked. "Why do you wait?"

Regel opened his hand to reveal the carving. Over the last day, it had taken shape, and though it was not finished, it bore a recognizable form. He had rounded its edges and carved three hollows like eyes and a mouth.

"A face?" Ovelia asked.

"A mask." Regel extended the carving toward Mask.

The sorcerer regarded him warily. "What is this?"

"There are moments worthy of remembrance," Regel said. "And they should be marked."

Slowly, not daring to break their shared gaze, Mask claimed the carving from Regel's hand. She looked at the dawnstone mask, small enough to fit in her palm, and Regel thought she trembled.

Time to move.

Regel gestured for silence, then pushed the latch up and slid the door open, making little more than a whisper on the stone. Silently, he stepped into the dark room, and Ovelia followed. He recognized the lionskins strewn about the floor, the roaring fire with its sickly heat, the sheets like liquid velvet draped across the grand bed. He'd come here five years ago, the night Ovelia had slain the Winter King.

"Please, Regel," Ovelia had said, tears rolling down her cheeks. "Please!"

He shook the memory away and crept forward, consciously relaxing his hands. He would need a tight grip on the garrote, but there was no sense causing himself pain. For the first time in years, he longed for Frostburn. Its chill would shield him from fear and hatred. The Blood Ravalis was a flame that had taken all he held dear: the Winter King, Ovelia, Princess Lenalin... He would not let it burn Semana away as well, not if there was a chance she yet lived.

He crept toward the woman sitting at the king's bedside and raised his hands. The wire gleamed between his palms. Would her death be necessary? It seemed like five years ago, when he had slain Paeter. Then, he had spared a woman he did not know, and she had become the first of his Circle of Tears. Would this one be different?

The woman turned toward him, and for the first time he saw her face: Serris's face.

At first, Regel thought his senses deceived him and he was lost in memory, but then Ovelia drew in a sharp breath of recognition. Regel saw the gag in Serris's mouth and her wild eyes. Her hands were manacled to the bedpost and she could not stand. She shook her head frantically. Regel reached forward and pulled her gag free.

"Run," she said. "Regel, you have to—"

The king's blanket tore back, revealing a gold-armored man with fiery red hair and a short, thick sword, perfect for close-quarters combat. His armor emitted a high pitched whine as the thaumaturgy imbued in its golden curves rose and burned the air.

"Welcome, Oathbreaker!" Lan Ravalis said as he stood, lightning crackling around his blade. "And the Dracaris whore, too. And to think, I thought you'd be too clever for this trap."

233

"Regel," said Serris. "Regel, listen to me. Sarelle. Her name is—"

"Shut up." Lan lashed his cleaver-like sword across and opened her throat before her next word, drowning her voice in a welling torrent of blood. Serris slumped off the chair, but the manacles kept her from falling to the floor. She hung from the bedpost, choking and gagging.

"Old Gods!" Ovelia gasped.

"I told you if you didn't still that whore's wagging tongue"—Lan shook blood from his sword—"that *I* would."

Regel attacked without thinking. It was the same blow that had killed Lan's brother five years ago, though Regel struck with his bare hand. The prince brought up his sword to parry, but the force of Regel's strike snapped off the prince's blade at the hilt. He might have carried through and flattened Lan's throat, but the lightning woven into the prince's armor discharged and smashed Regel against the wall. From the force of the blow, Lan stumbled off the bed, right into Ovelia's assault. Draca smashed into the power armor with a loud *crack*. The prince fell back, unhurt and laughing wildly.

The world shivered, and Regel felt pain shoot through his body. He could barely move, but he could hear wet wheezing near him. He managed to climb up the bed to Serris, who stared at him hard, as to speak to him with her thoughts. He reached trembling fingers toward her face, but her body jerked out of the way. She made one last gasp, then her eyes glazed and she was dead.

"Regel!" someone was shouting. Ovelia. "Regel, get up!"

Regel was stunned, hardly understanding. It had all come to pass so quickly. He saw blood bloom from the cut Lan's shattering sword had left in his hand, but he felt far away. He looked up and watched as the prince strode around the bed, caught Draca in his gauntleted hand, and hurled Ovelia back. The bloodsword's flames licked at Lan's armor to no effect. Ovelia was paying as much attention to Draca as to her opponent, but Regel saw what she saw: no warning shadows.

"Terrible, is it not?" Lan asked. "The power you thought would save you—failing."

"Regel!" Ovelia shouted.

Lan reached for her. Ovelia swung at him, but the prince ignored the blade bouncing off his shoulder guard, caught her by the throat, and raised her into the air. She managed to slap Draca against his armored hip, and a jolt of lightning knocked it tumbling from her fingers to clatter to the floor.

At that, Lan smiled madly in her face. "You think the Blood of metal and the forge cannot counter your little toy?" he asked. "That you could walk into this house and kill with impunity? Well?"

"R-Regel..." Ovelia managed.

"Whores never know when to shut their mouths, eh, Oathbreaker?" Lan put the jagged remains of his blade to Ovelia's face. "If you're so hungry, you can put this in your mouth. For now."

"Hold." Regel staggered to his feet, drawing his falcat. Serris's blood coated his hands.

"You're not angry about the scarred one, are you?" Lan asked from the other end of the bed. He dropped Ovelia to the floor and turned to Regel. "Really, I did you a favor. Now you don't have to pretend not to see that face."

A curtain of red fell across Regel's world. He drew a falcat, snarled, and lunged at Lan.

It would have been a deathblow, but Lan reached over and pulled the mattress up to block his leap. Regel tumbled over the twisted bed, kicked off the wall, and flew at Lan. The prince simply slapped his sword aside and lashed out with a lightning-enhanced punch, but Regel twisted in midair and jabbed a dagger with all his strength into Lan's thigh. The blade turned on the power armor with a shriek of parting metal. The prince staggered back, startled at the sudden pain.

"Regel, his blood!" Ovelia cried. "Don't—"

Regel barely heard her. He raised his dagger and sword. "No mercy, Lan Ravalis," he said. "This time, you die."

"You think so?" Lan felt at his bruised thigh. "Even if you *could* shed my blood, it would be your death. Vhaerynn wards all of us Ravalis. I think you are overmatched, Dead King's Shad—"

Regel struck before Lan could finish his boast. He moved with blinding speed, faster than any man should have been able to. The prince tried to block, but the blade eluded his gauntleted hand, darted in, and swatted him on the side of the head. Lan staggered aside, and Regel followed up with a dagger thrust to the base of the spine. It would have crippled or killed an unarmored man, and he struck so hard his blade shattered on Lan's armor. The prince cried out and stumbled to one knee, then to the floor.

"What have you done?" Lan strained, but he couldn't stand or even turn to unleash his armor's stored lightning at them. "Coward!"

"I won't shed any blood." Regel sheathed his sword and drew out his garrote. "I won't have to."

"You lose." Lan ripped off his left gauntlet and put his broken sword to his bare flesh, but Regel hurled his dagger and knocked the blade away. The steel screamed off the prince's right hand, which still had its gauntlet on to protect the vulnerable skin.

"Your necromancer can't hear you," Regel said. "You are alone."

With a desperate cry, Lan threw a pillow in Regel's face, but the slayer cut the soft thing aside with a flash of steel. Feathers filled the air, falling to settle in Serris's lifeblood pooling on the floor. Regel stepped through the rain of white, blade glimmering as he bore down on Lan who, unarmed, looked about desperately for a weapon—to cut at his attacker or to cut himself.

"Was this your plan?" Regel asked. "Face us alone? That was foolish."

Lan's terrified face split into a mad grin. "Indeed."

A thunderous crack split the room, and a casterbolt struck Regel just above the right knee. His leg shot out from under him and his sword skittered from his hand. When he tried to rise, his leg went dead and dropped him back to the floor.

"Regel!" Ovelia scooped up Draca, but doing so put her in Lan's reach. Lightning flashed from his gauntlet, and though Ovelia got the sword up in time to block it, the force still slammed her against the far wall. Draca clattered to the floor, and she slumped down after it.

Numbing pain shot through Regel's world, and he roared wordlessly. Blood fountained from the wound. Ovelia lay moaning and gasping, as much a victim of Lan's blast as the poison Regel himself had put in her. Where was Mask? Had she betrayed them after all?

"You're right." Wincing at the effort, Lan climbed back to his feet. His armor's thaumaturgy sputtered and died, but it had done its work. "It *would* have been foolish to face you alone."

The double-caster, pointed at Regel's face, still held its second bolt. Regel looked up along the line of the casterman's arm to his face shrouded in bones. His two eyes blazed—the one almost black, the other milky white. "Davargorn," Regel said, hardly able to breathe against the pain.

"The great Lord of Tears himself," Lan said. "Made careless through one slut's blood."

The prince dealt Ovelia a kick to the side and stooped to relieve her of her belt-knife. He grasped her by the hair and dragged her, kicking, over to where Regel knelt. Regel tried to move, but Davargorn tapped the caster against his head.

Lan jerked Ovelia's head back and put his knife to her bulging throat. "Shall we try that again?" the prince asked, his teeth bared like those of a bear. "I didn't spatter you enough with the first one. Perhaps if I aim better—"

"Hold, all of you," came a dark voice, one ragged as a wolf's cry.

The world slowed. All eyes turned to the doorway where Mask stood. The sorcerer stood tall, her jaw imperiously raised, seeming fashioned of steel rather than flesh. The room came alive with the green-black energy of voracious magic, and Regel felt it leech the warmth from the room.

Lan's eyes widened. "What by the Fire are *you*?"

Like a queen—like a *goddess*—Mask surveyed Lan and Ovelia, then looked to the blood gushing down Regel's crippled leg. Her gaze lingered over Davargorn, who averted his eyes. Regel knew he was a traitor to his mistress, and she would punish him for it. Soon.

"Lower your blade, Lan Ravalis." Mask spoke in a voice so deep and malevolent Regel hardly recognized the sound. He realized he had never had the full measure of this creature.

"Burn you," Lan said. "Shoot that thing, Davargorn." He jerked his head toward the man. "Why do you hesitate?"

The disfigured man in the bone mask stood motionless, staring at Mask.

"You've lost, Prince," the sorcerer said. "Yield."

"Why?" The prince sneered as he cut the tiniest crease into Ovelia's throat. Blood trickled down her white skin. "Why should I give you anything, Syr... *Thing*?"

"So you can salvage some honor, you stillborn wretch of a rotted Blood," Mask replied. "Release that woman and face me with some courage. Or do you have none?"

Regel was so tired. Dark blood poured down his leg to stain the golden bearskin rug, matting the fur as though the bear was still alive and wounded. Regel fought to stay awake.

Ovelia saw it too. "Please," she begged. "Help Regel, he's going to bleed to—"

"Silence, whore!" Lan wrenched her head back, cutting off her words. He turned again to Mask, his eyes glittering like daggers. "Who are you, that you *dare* question me—Crown-Prince of the Ravalis, the man who will be king of Tar Vangr, and Luether thereafter?"

"I am one that does not cringe behind a helpless woman," said Mask. "Or are you a coward, too?"

Lan bared his teeth. "Very well, creature."

He thrust Ovelia away, and her head cracked against the wall. She stumbled dizzily for a heartbeat, then sank to the floor near where Regel lay. Blood trickled down her cheek.

Bereft of his shield, Lan puffed out his chest and sneered at the sorcerer. "Strike, then, if you've the manhood," he said. "I fear none, however awful his mask."

Mask stood frozen, her hands crackling. Regel could do nothing about the two of them, so he reached toward Ovelia. She coughed at his touch—still alive.

"Strike!" Lan roared, and stepped toward her. "Or does that mask hide your fear?"

Mask hands were trembling. Her eyes shot to Regel as though for guidance.

"Strike," he murmured. Fading from blood loss, he could barely speak.

Still, Mask hesitated.

Somewhere, Regel heard shuddering blows falling on the door from outside. Ravalis guards. His world had come unpinioned. Regel looked up at Ovelia's muddled eyes. She was fading, as was he. The room suddenly felt so cold he shivered. Breath steamed up from his lips.

"Strike," Lan said, stepping almost close enough to Mask to touch her—to crush her in his embrace. "Am I not your foe? Strike, for surely if you do not, I will kill you. *All* of you."

Mask's entire body shook. She couldn't do it, Regel knew. Why couldn't she do it?

At that moment, the door burst wide under the boot of a guardsman in blue and red. Half a dozen men pushed into the room, stopping short as they saw their lord and master not half a pace from the black-clad sorcerer. They raised their double-casters.

"Highness!" Davargorn was a blur of motion as he leaped.

Two casterbolts crashed into him at the same moment. The first struck him in the belly, and the second exploded through his shoulder. The force of the bolts blew him off his feet and against the wall, where he slumped to the floor, a mess of blood and flesh.

Davargorn's disjointed eyes shot to Regel. They gazed at one another across three paces, two men caught in the same web. They both lay dying, of injuries they had suffered for the same purpose: protecting those they should hate. Davargorn gave Regel a tiny smile, shivered, and stopped breathing.

"Tithian!" Mask cried, in a voice that Regel had never heard her use before—a voice that was high and impossibly young. She looked to the castermen, who were taking aim with their second bolts. "Stop! I command it!" Her hands shot to the buckles of her mask.

"No," Ovelia moaned from the floor. "Highness, no!"

Mask unbuckled her leathern shroud and wrenched it free of her head. Silver hair billowed around her face. She smoothed it away from her creamy-smooth cheeks and delicate features. Regel gasped at her hazel-red eyes gleaming with a familiar fire and her jaw set in implacable, royal command.

"I am Semana Denerre nô Ravalis, Greatdaughter of the Winter King and Princess of Tar Vangr." Her eyes blazed with silver-blue flame. "I command you to stop!"

Darkness slipped in around him like a forgotten lover, and Regel's eyes closed.

ACT FOUR: MASKS

Five Years Previous—The Dusk Sea—Ruin's Night, 976 Sorcerus Annis

WHAT SAY YOU?"

Mask—the most horrible creature Tithian had ever imagined, let alone faced—had just asked him to betray the most important creature in the world: Princess Semana. In return, the sorcerer offered knowledge, power, training—all that he might ask.

Tithian squared his shoulders and faced Mask. "I've an answer," he said. "*Master.*"

His caster gave a mighty *crack*, and a fiery bolt sizzled across the deck of the skyship *Heiress*.

Almost lazily, Mask raised one skeletal hand, and its body blazed with green shielding magic. The casterbolt slowed and stopped in its flight. It vibrated, clanging against the shield like an angry hornet trapped against a sheet of glass.

"A poor choice, Davargorn," Mask said. "You must learn that choices have consequences."

The quarrel turned slowly in the air, then shot back along its course to strike Tithian full in the chest. Fire erupted through his middle and the force blew him back against the rail. He stumbled and fell.

"Tithian!" Semana cried, though he heard her only blearily.

Tithian somehow caught the rail and twisted in the air so that his feet stretched out into darkness, and he hung suspended in the air for an instant by the force. Ruin spread out below him—a great black sea of nothingness. He saw the harbor of Tar Vangr, toward which the far edge of the ship had started to sink, dipping away from him. The temptation to fall was vast—he would soar and find peace. But Semana needed him, and he would sooner suffer the pain of a thousand casterbolts than fail her.

When he came back down, he slammed into the side of the skyship hard. His vision blurred as he hung there, struggling to breathe. He fought to keep his grasp in a world slipping bloodily into nothing.

But he did not die.

Somehow, even as he hung over an impossible fall, a casterbolt in his chest, he still lived. The ship tipped lower, the tilt becoming more pronounced, and the rail became an angle he could lie on—steep, but easier to hang on. He held himself up, panting and wondering why he wasn't dead.

"Move," he said to himself. "*Move.*"

Slowly, fingers trembling, he reached over with his free hand and grasped the quarrel. Pain lanced through him from an epicenter in his chest, and he realized the impact had jarred the casterbolt loose, like a nail hammered halfway back through. The shaft was slick with blood and the tiniest movement sent such pain through his body that he almost fainted. But he clung to awareness with a stubbornness that would have made the dead Syr Sargaunt smile. Tithian seized hold of the bolt, braced himself, and wrenched. What seemed like a bundle of a dozen knives slid out of him. The casterbolt slipped from his nerveless fingers and tumbled end over end toward the black sea. Somehow, he managed to hold on.

Dimly, Tithian thought that he should have climbed up first before he dealt with the bolt, but at least he was still awake. He slithered back onto the heaving deck, if barely. His heart thudded in his head, and his body screamed at him, but he didn't care. Only Semana mattered.

The *Heiress* groaned, shifting to the side as it made its slow, shuddering way toward the sea. Its mage-engine damaged irreparably, the ship was sliding out of the air. Tithian knew his life would come to a shattering end within moments—if the wound did not kill him first. He touched at his chest gently. There was pain and a great deal of blood, but none of it seemed to be actively flowing. He almost thought the flesh had closed somehow.

He put it out of his mind and searched the smoky deck—*there*. There was Semana, but—Tithian's eyes widened—no Mask. The princess was sitting alone, knees drawn up to her chin, sobbing. She had something in her arms, but he could not make it out at this distance.

Tithian limped across the deck. "Princess?"

"Lost," she was whimpering. "All of them—lost to Ruin."

Hesitantly, Tithian touched her on the shoulder and Semana looked around. Black blood covered her face, and her eyes glowed in the light of the burning ship, so bright they sent him staggering back a step. They seemed almost red. He saw now what was in her arms: a suit of black leather, flattened and empty. The mismatched war-gauntlets lay discarded on the deck. Hanging from her left hand was a hollow black mask.

Semana stared at him for a moment that stretched, infinite, in all directions. There was pain in her eyes, and a terrible sort of purpose. It was almost like hunger.

"Princess?" Tithian asked.

Then the leathers fell to the deck and Semana threw herself into his embrace and put her arms around his neck. "Gods!" she wept, kissing his scarred cheeks. "Gods, Tithian! Are you well?"

New strength crept through him. Even now, bleeding and riding a crashing skyship to his doom, Tithian felt hope stir in his breast, the way it ever did when Semana so much as smiled at him. Then his eye fell upon Mask's discarded armor and his hope turned to fear.

"What happened?" he asked. "What of Mask?"

Semana pulled her face away and met his eye. "I... I killed him," she said.

Tithian blinked. "Killed him," he said. "How?"

But the princess shook her head. "He was using magic, and... it turned on him."

240

"Turned? From you?"

"He struck at me, and it was like he struck a solid wall," she said. "The magic turned back in protest. I don't know how, but I was stronger."

"Stronger." Tithian felt thick and slow.

"*Better.*" Semana looked down at Mask's armor. The black leather was flattened and empty, the body within entirely gone—turned to dust and scattered on the wind. Her hand stretched toward it, almost with longing. "A sharper blade."

Tithian winced at a niggling pain in his chest. He'd nearly forgotten his wound.

"Old Gods!" Semana drew away. "Your chest."

"Is it bad?"

"No." Semana sounded shocked. "It's barely there."

Tithian looked down and his eyes widened. Sure enough, while blood slathered his chest, the wound itself seemed like little more than a blemish on his skin. "But I felt the bolt go into me," he said. "I pulled it out!"

Even more wondrous, as he watched, the wound closed entirely. A thin silver radiance played across his flesh, and within a breath, even the mark vanished.

"Lifefire," Semana said. "You are an heir of Calatan—a wielder of true magic."

"How do you know that?" Tithian prodded at the wound.

"He—" Semana said. "He told me this would happen."

Tithian's gaze snapped to her. "He? Mask?"

But Semana was shaking her head. "We have to go," she said.

"Go?" Tithian looked around. The ship was still sinking toward the bay, which loomed larger. They had perhaps a hundred count left before it struck. "Go where? We are lost! Mask could fly, but—Highness? What passes?"

Kneeling beside the empty armor, Semana drew first one, then the other of Mask's boots over her bare feet. She stood, and the air rippled around her feet, distorted by magic. She floated into the air, and in her arms, Tithian drew up from the deck just as easily.

Tithian's face went white. "How are you doing this?"

"The boots." Semana looked back at Mask's armor.

Tithian clasped her arms harder. "Fly us to the castle, Highness. The king must hear of this."

"Yes," Semana said. "Yes, of course. I have to go there. If they attacked me, he might be in danger as well."

"Old Gods." Tithian hadn't even considered that.

But Semana shook her head. "First, there is something I must do." Slowly, they floated back to the deck, and Semana dropped to one knee beside the disembodied suit of Mask's armor.

"Highness—Semana," Tithian said. "What are you doing?"

He could see her impressive mind whirring, which had also seemed wondrous to him.

"Someone sent Mask to slay the Blood of Winter." Semana traced her fingers across the blasted iron gauntlet with the war claws, and its elegant silver twin. "If

I show my face, my enemy will know the sorcerer failed and be able to vanish. I cannot let that happen."

"What do you mean?" Tithian asked.

"This way, we can find him." Semana seemed not to have heard. "I must stop it. I *will* stop it."

"Yes, but—" Tithian's eyes widened as he understood, at last. "You cannot mean to—"

"If this is my destiny, then so be it." Semana began unlacing her scuffed and torn dress. "Will you stand with me?"

All hesitation fled Tithian's heart. He stood as tall as he could. "Always."

"Then give me your dagger."

Davargorn turned the bloody blade over. Semana reached behind her head, took up her luxurious braid of silvery hair, and sawed it off. Mask's blood smeared both the hair on her head and in her hand. She returned the knife to him, then held the braid in one hand, the mask in the other. She looked from one to the other.

"Princess," he said. "Are you certain of this?"

"Your princess is dead." Semana raised the mask to her face. "I am Mask."

Tithian smelled the leather's reek of ashes and of death.

TWENTY-FIVE

S *EMANA!*

The world came back in a rush. Ovelia woke coughing, her eyes streaming, and she had one shuddering breath to peer around at dark stone walls dancing with firelight. Her insides were on fire and she wanted to void herself or vomit up her guts. Then she felt pressure on her head as of two shields crushing her skull between them, and she lost the world again.

When light returned a moment later, it came around the edges of a cool cloth pressed to her forehead. She tried by instinct to pluck it away, but her hand wouldn't move. All she could do was moan.

"Peace, lass," said a quavering voice, and Ovelia relaxed.

The cloth drew away, and the light blinded Ovelia. After a moment, she could see well enough to make out the diminutive woman who sat beside her. A frown wrinkled the craggy face—one that held disappointment and pity in equal measure. Ovelia knew that face.

"Maure," she said. "So it was not a dream."

"Alas, no." Maure took the cloth from Ovelia's brow and wet it anew in a chipped basin. "Master would have you cleaned and mended. I'm to do both."

"Master?" But Ovelia already knew. "Lan Ravalis, you mean."

The old woman shrugged. "I serve him or her what sits upon the Winter throne, whoever they killed to climb it," she said. "However much blood is spilled, there's always babes to be birthed and sick tended." She made a sucking sound with her tongue between her teeth. "You've been both in your time."

Ovelia felt cold. Pain twisted like a knife in her stomach. She shivered with the need to eat, but the thought of food made her ill. She lay in the same inner chamber where they had fought Lan and Davargorn: Paeter's old bedchamber, where she had met him so many nights for years. She felt unstuck in time, drifting between then and now, uncertain if she was awake or dreaming. The furniture stood just as it always had, and the whole place reeked of death. The chamber showed signs of fresh violence: blood spatters and gouges in the stone. She focused on the blood: Serris's blood. Regel's blood.

"Lan Ravalis," Ovelia managed. "He is a good master?"

"No, but few are." As ever, Maure's face seemed compassionate and judgmental both at once. "I've had but one good master, and you killed him."

She couldn't deny that. It made her want to weep.

"I've served many a master," Maure went on, wringing a cloth in a copper

243

basin. "Lan is better than some and worse than others. At least I am an old nursemaid and hardly prey for his lusts. I am neither young"—she traced her fingers down Ovelia's cheek—"nor pretty."

"I guess we have that in common."

"Alas. You're still cursed with a good face." Maure clucked at her. "I remember birthing you of bright little Aniset as though 'twere yesterday, though it were nigh forty winters past. Aye?"

Ovelia flushed despite herself. "I'd not say, if it please you."

"Spare my feelings, I see." Maure grimaced. "Lass, I've seen you naked and held you weeping, so you need keep no secrets from me. I remember your *own* child—"

When Ovelia heard those words, her awareness sharpened. She grasped the old woman's hand, caught her gaze with a warning glance, and shook her head.

Maure patted her hand. "The murmurs of an old crone mean less than nothing." She laid the cloth back on Ovelia's eyes. "You should rest. He comes soon."

For the first time, Ovelia looked down at her heavy body, lying still as death upon the sheets. Maure or someone—she hoped it had been Maure—had dressed her in a silk slip of Ravalis crimson, trimmed with azure lace. Something a blooded courtesan might wear or—she realized with a shiver—something the would-be wife of a Ravalis lordling. She felt the cool weight of her carven necklace against her throat—at least that was her own. She willed her legs to move, and pain seared through her. Every muscle ached. Her body felt like rotting wood, with an unquenchable hunger in her middle.

"What of the others?" she asked. "When I was taken, there was a man with me, and—" She stopped herself. Clearly, Maure knew nothing of Semana, or she'd have asked earlier.

Maure scowled as though cursing inwardly. "I know of the man, and—"

"And?" Ovelia pressed, heart pounding in her throat.

"Nothing."

Lan Ravalis stood at the door, sheathed in a rich tunic of red and blue. Ovelia had seen no finer garments outside of court rituals. The triumph on his face glowed almost as hotly as his fiery hair and beard, and it made his handsome face look like a terrible caricature. Ovelia's world grew darker.

"Of Regel the Oathbreaker," Lan Ravalis said. "There is nothing."

TWENTY-SIX

A T FIRST, THERE WAS nothing.

Then he became aware of a long, long darkness.

From time to time, blue candles passed from above his head down toward his feet, then disappeared gradually. The world faded again, and he only woke fully when his bearers dropped him unceremoniously on the hard stone. Only then did he remember himself.

Regel was his name, and he was dying.

His head thumped against a stone surface. The soldiers who had dragged him down this long corridor left him to lie while they pawed at the wall.

"Around here—ah!" One of the soldiers found a seam around a door that looked just like the wall. He knocked on the seeming stone, which rang like metal. "Right here. Let's get the others."

"Hrm." The second man was smoking what smelled like cheap summerweed. Regel could see his dull features by the light of the glowing embers. "Why not just take the bodies to the furnace?"

"Orders, sodder. Prince Lan don't want these three to rest easy. Wants 'em buried as traitors."

"He's a harsh man, the prince." The man tapped his pipe on the wall a thumb's length from Regel's face. Ash sprinkled his cheek. "But well. Not like it matters to them where their bodies lie."

"Sure it do," the other man argued. His accent and piety marked him as winterborn, whereas the first man was clearly a summerborn atheist by his speech and indifference. "Don't give the body to the fire, and the spirit can't join the Nar. Its torment never ends."

"Will you forget that superstitious refuse and help me? These bodies are heavy."

Bodies, Regel thought. They thought he was already dead. And *three* bodies meant...

Something heavy landed on the floor to his left, and the men headed back up the hall. Confident they weren't looking, Regel risked a glance. Not a hand's length away, Serris's dead face was staring at him, her dull eyes wide. Below her chin was a mass of black, dried blood. It left a cold hollow in Regel's chest. The remarkable woman he had sculpted from a nameless girl into an angel of vengeance was gone, leaving only a cold husk. She had wanted to tell him something important. Now she never would.

The guards returned and let something fall with a sickly thud. "This all of them, true?"

"Aye, just the three."

As they labored at the door, Regel looked the other way, and there lay a distorted face he recognized as well: Davargorn. The features had a kind of nobility to them, as though death had finally brought the ugly man peace. The splintered ends of spent casterbolts still protruded from his chest.

"Ah," said one of the guards. Regel heard stone rattle. "Here it comes."

A whir of ancient gears made a door slide out of stone wall, then across. A scent of decay wafted into the corridor from the chamber, which Regel realized must be used for disposal. How many foes of Tar Vangr lay moldering in this charnel crypt, their spirits unable to rest easy?

The smoking man tossed his weed-ashes away—they fell burning on Regel's belly—and grasped Serris under the armpits. "Too bad they didn't leave this one alive, eh?"

"Don't matter," said the other. "Clean her up a bit as she is, and she'd do."

"Burn you!" The man sniffed. "Teats out of legend, though. Shame is what it is."

Regel felt something swell in his chest he recognized as grief and anger. Their callous words gave birth to rage, merely thinking of the dishonor they did to both Serris and Davargorn. Indeed, he wept for the boy. He had been a foe, yes, but Regel did not hate him. He had given his life to protect Semana.

Semana.

It happened without his knowing. A tiny whine clawed up his windpipe and rattled between his teeth. The sound was no louder than a rat's squeak, but it was there.

The men paused. "What was that?" said the one holding Serris by the shoulders.

"Silver Fire, that one isn't dead! See to him."

The soldier dropped Serris with a dead thump and bent low. His rancid, smoky breath beat on Regel's cheek as he drew his dagger with a scrape of steel on leather.

Davargorn's eyes opened—the one black, the other luminous white.

Steel flashed and the back of the guard's calf split open. The man was too surprised even to cry out, and he lost his breath when he fell. When he was down, Davargorn pounced. He landed on the guard chest to chest, and Regel heard the two bolts squish into the man's flesh. Davargorn smashed his forehead into the guard's nose, cutting off the man's scream of surprise in an eruption of blood between their faces.

The other guard staggered away from Serris's corpse, leaped past them, and ran.

Davargorn pulled away from the bleeding, sobbing man to snarl at Regel. "Strike!"

The guard's dagger gleamed as Davargorn tossed it skittering across the space separating them, and Regel caught it by the hilt. He forced his body up and almost fainted at the strain. Weakness filled him, but he did not care. He sighted after the fleeing man.

Semana, he thought. Ovelia—

"Strike!" Davargorn spat.

Regel threw. The blade scythed end over end after the stumbling guard. The man had the misfortune to look back at just the wrong instant, and the blade sank into his eye. He jerked up, erect as a lightning rod, and his hands flinched toward the blade. Then he fell to his knees and crashed to the floor.

Davargorn slammed his head into his own guard's face again, then put his arms around the man's head and twisted viciously. Regel distantly heard the guard's neck crack as the world turned to shades of gray and he sank to the floor. That was the last of his energy.

Davargorn knelt over him, his face smeared with hot blood. His white eye gleamed.

"You were dead," Regel murmured, or though he did. "I saw."

"Yes," Davargorn said. "Now, so are you."

"Can't—" Death was coming, and he could not fight it.

"Not yet, Lord of Tears." Then Davargorn put his hands on Regel's chest, and a silvery glow suffused his fingers. "You don't get to die yet."

TWENTY-SEVEN

OVELIA LOOKED UPON HER death standing in the door to the chamber, the grin on his face irrepressibly satisfied and cruel. She earnestly wished for the dark to return, if only to spare her those terrible eyes. They were like hands touching and burning her all over.

Maure rose immediately, wringing the wet cloth tightly. "Your Highness, she is not—"

"I know well what she is not." Lan's smile widened, his teeth becoming fangs. "And what she is."

The Crown Prince was a big man with a bear's face, its every line drawn into a powerful, slightly up-turned nose like a snout. Thick shoulders and an even thicker neck completed the image of a beast in a man's skin. She could not look at his huge hands without imagining them on her body—grasping her, choking her. It was not pleasant, though a part of her grew warm.

Not him, she prayed to the Old Gods. *Do not let him be as Paeter was.*

Ovelia looked up at the old midwife, whose face was stormy. "Do not ask this of her," Maure said. "Have you not hurt her enough already? She needs rest, not—"

"Please," Ovelia said. "There is no need, Maure."

She tensed herself to rise, but the midwife put her wrinkly hand on her shoulder. "Highness, I forbid this woman to rise. Do you understand? If she dies on her feet, what use is she to you?"

"What use indeed?" said the prince. "What do you know of it, hag?"

"Don't think my age makes me forget what men and women do," Maure said, her old voice burning with indignation. "I know what you want and why she's here. So listen to wisdom or be denied your spoils, prince."

"You amuse me, old woman," Lan said. "Very well. I will ask of her nothing but what she gives of her own will. Satisfied? On your way, now."

The midwife bent low to check Ovelia one last time. "Ward yourself, lass." Maure pressed her lips to Ovelia's forehead, and tears leaked down onto the younger woman's face, below her own, dry eyes. "Ward yourself."

Ovelia swallowed rising despair tinged with loathsome desire. "Yes."

Then Maure—midwife, wetnurse, teacher, Ovelia's oldest friend and mother to many—hobbled under Lan's arm as he leaned against the doorframe and was gone down the corridor. Lan peered after her as a lion at an elderly ewe that might fall behind the flock any moment.

"She knows naught of this business," Ovelia said. "Spare her."

"Spare her?" Lan laughed. "Why would I harm her? She is a good servant and loyal. You, however..." He let the words trail away and chuckled. "Well, I kept my word. I will ask of you nothing you would not offer. Willingly."

Ovelia's heart had slowed in its pace, as though her body accepted the inevitability of it all. "What I have done, I have done for love," she said. "Remember that."

Lan put his hand to his chest in mock offense. "My lady, you wrong me," he said. "I am motivated by much the same impulse."

"Love." Ovelia closed her eyes. She understood.

"For love of you, Lady Dracaris, last of your Blood," he said. "Or at least desire."

Ovelia touched her fingers to her brow and hid a mournful smile behind her hand. "No," she said. "No. It is not love or desire, Bear of Luether, but jealousy."

"Jealousy?" Lan sounded intrigued. "Whatever do you mean?"

"Paeter," Ovelia said. "You always hated your brother for having what you could not."

"As you say." Lan's face twisted. "Whether for love or hate, I have risked treason in allowing you traitors to live. The least you could do is offer me a kind word."

"Slayers—" Ovelia's heart leaped. "I am not the only survivor, then."

Confusion flashed across his eyes, then dawning realization, and she knew she had won a minor victory. "Indeed," Lan said, displeased to be caught in the truth. "I have spared Semana as well, of course. You did not think I'd throw away such a lovely thing—and so valuable."

Ovelia's blood cooled, and her mind turned back five years to another Ravalis speaking much the same words to her. She understood only too well. They would play the same game then as now, but would this Ravalis know it as well as Paeter?

"Am I to be your bride then?" Ovelia gestured to the Ravalis colors she wore. They were barely clothes—only bedchamber silks such as a courtesan might wear under her proper attire. "I think you are already married."

"I am." Lan stepped forward, eyes on Ovelia. "To a dried up old husk of a Vargaen who needs help sucking my blade. That thinblood creature has never been worthy of the Ravalis. But you." He held his hand just over her breast, fingers flexing. "Ah. You are more worthy of this honor than she."

If Ovelia had harbored any doubt, it vanished now. "What must I do?" she whispered.

"You *must* do nothing. But perhaps you *wish* to." Lan stood tall, his smile spreading ear to ear. "First, I should like to see what I've spared. Perhaps you wish to stand? I would enjoy that ever so much."

Ovelia tried, but her body screamed against her movement. Her stomach assured her it would kill her if she tried again. She managed to raise her head a hand's length before pain swept her and laid her flat once more. She lay back, gasping.

"I would stand, Shield-Whore," said Lan, "for Semana's sake."

"You'd not harm her," Ovelia said. "Surely you wouldn't be so stupid. She is the heir to Tar Vangr. The true heir. You cannot use her if she is dead."

"Nay," Lan said. "But she does not need all her fingers to sit the Winter throne—or such a pretty face. Who knows?" He gestured to the bearskin rug beneath his feet. "The pelt of a Winter pup might look as well as that of a Summer bear, and feel softer."

Ovelia closed her eyes.

"You've reconsidered, mayhap?" Lan asked. "Stand."

Her neck tensed and her shoulders heaved. Every muscle, bone, and sinew in Ovelia's body ground together. She felt like she was being pulled apart. She pushed.

She imagined Semana weeping alone in a dark cell. She saw Semana screaming as men forced her down and drew apart the fingers of her hand. She pushed.

She thought of the last vow she had sworn to Orbrin. She pushed.

And then she stood. The world shivered, but she had climbed to her feet.

"Excellent." Lan nodded, something like respect on his face. He put a hand to his chin, considering. "I see you've not forsaken your body these five years. I would see it fully, if you wish."

Under his cruel scrutiny, the darkest part of her stirred—the part of her that desired this. *Longed* for this. She had spent her life hating herself for it, but now she had no choice but to embrace it.

Trying to ignore his eyes—to distract herself from his desire and her need—Ovelia looked down at the bed. The sheets were still heavy with blood—Serris's blood—and there was no desire in that. Her stomach had merely hurt when she woke up, but now it contorted as though Lan had thrust an iron gauntlet into her guts and squeezed. Also, the bearskin beneath her bare feet was sticky with a dark stain: Regel's blood, shed for her and for Semana. They had given of themselves that she might live—would not Ovelia do the same?

But to surrender to that darkness—the scraping, creaking hollow that made her a monster among women—would that be death or would it be worse?

Lan saw the hesitation on her face and misjudged it. "Your choice is simple, Whore of Dracaris," he said, using Paeter's words in almost his own voice. "Do as I command, or your princess dies."

She almost pitied the poor man in that moment. She was not considering whether to rut him. She was considering if she would revel in it, and what that would make her.

Lan was right in one respect: the choice was simple. To resist would be to die, and to die was to let Semana die, and that she could not do.

"First," Ovelia said. With all her strength bent to standing, it was a bare whisper. "First, assure me that she is safe. Give me your word."

"You have it." Lan gestured to her crimson slip. "Now take that off. Slowly."

As she reached up to the laces of the silky gown, he drew from behind his back a set of red-stained manacles. Serris's blood, still fresh.

"My favorites," he said with a grin. "Can't let a little stain bother us, can we?"

Ovelia did her best to suppress a shiver.

"Best accept it, Lady," Lan said, chilling her. "Unless you believe in miracles."

She did not.

TWENTY-EIGHT

THERE WAS BLACKNESS.
Then there was fire.

Regel's body wrenched up from the stones, taut and screaming. Crimson light surrounded him. Pain tore through his veins like clear liquor set afire. His eyes burned and his sweat burrowed stinging trails down his cheeks. Smoke filled his lungs rather than air. His stomach churned and heaved. His leg—Old Gods, his wounded leg *blazed* as though molten steel coated his flesh.

Was this what his old master had promised? Was this death? If it was, then Regel despaired.

Then, of a sudden, the pain lessened. The fire ebbed and the world returned to his glazed senses.

He was back in the corridor, surrounded by the stench of death and fresh blood. Serris's pale body, her face twisted in terror, lay beside him. Davargorn sat against the wall, his unmasked face maleficent in the pale blue candlelight.

"Welcome back." Davargorn strained to pull a broken casterbolt from his chest.

"We're alive," Regel managed to say.

"So it would seem." He nudged Regel with his twisted foot. "Can you move?"

Regel forced himself into a sitting position, expecting pain but finding only a pale numbness. He looked at the torn breeches over his injured knee. Where there should have been a gaping hole, there was only new skin. "You restored me."

"I did." As Regel watched, Davargorn pulled one of the shattered casterbolts from his chest. It bled only a little before a dull crimson radiance surrounded the wound, which promptly began to pull itself closed. "Lifefire, my master called it. What a magic for a slayer to have."

Regel put his hand to his head—he still felt dizzy. Legends spoke of the healing power of Lifefire, but never had they described it this way—nor had they spoken of how much it hurt.

Serris lay slumped bonelessly against the wall, staring in terror.

"You restored me," Regel said blearily. "Can you aid her?"

"My magic has limits." Davargorn rose shakily to his feet, and Regel could see a silvery glow shrouding the wounds in his chest. As he watched, they vanished. "I cannot create life, only fan the flames. Her embers grew cold long before either of us woke."

"I see." Regel nodded. "Whose arms do you wear?"

"Pardon?" Davargorn stooped to search the guardsman whose face he'd broken for blades.

"Who is your master?" Regel asked. "In Luether, it was Mask... Semana." It was difficult to reconcile the two in his head, though he shouldn't have been so surprised at the revelation. The signs had all been there, even if he'd chosen not to see them. How she had reminded him of Lenalin, her intense dedication to the cause, and even her plan. Taking the identity of her own assassin to root out her enemies? It was the sort of cunning he expected of the Blood of Winter.

Regel began again. "When first we met in Luether, Semana cast you out, but then you sacrificed yourself to save her. So I will ask once more: whom do you serve?"

"It doesn't matter." Davargorn extended his good hand, but Regel eyed it warily. "Come now, Lord of Tears. If I'd wanted you dead, I'd have left you dead."

Regel had to concede that. "I must rest."

"Oh?" Davargorn said with derision. "The fatigue passes quickly—or at least it does for men not so old as you. One moment." He continued to pace anxiously, checking the felled guards every few seconds as though to make sure they were dead.

"A question," Regel said.

"Only if it's brief."

Davargorn dropped a Ravalis dagger at Regel's feet. A matching blade rode the younger man's hip, counterbalanced by a sword on his other side. The belt looked too big for his narrow frame.

Regel lifted the blade. The steel was inferior, but the balance was good enough. He tested the edge, watching Davargorn without looking at him. "In Luether, when we asked for proof, Mask—Semana—gave her finger. That was your magic as well. Tell me, did she make you cut off her finger, or did she do it herself?"

Davargorn stiffened. "That's no concern of yours."

"Well enough." Regel had his answer, then. Five years had turned Semana into a sharp blade indeed, if she could maim herself for a deception. "You restored her, too? Your magic is that great?"

Davargorn looked away. "We need to get moving."

Regel climbed shakily to his feet. His bad knee ached—he suspected it would ache for the rest of his life—but his leg would support him. They stood amongst the bodies, both fresh and old: Serris and the guards against the corpses hidden within the secret room. Regel knew exactly where he was. He himself had used this dumping place, in his service to the Winter King.

"I know these tunnels," Regel said. "I'll guide you, if you tell me the truth."

"Burn you," Davargorn said. "If you don't move, I'll leave you behind."

"Unlikely," Regel said. "These tunnels were built huge and winding, with only a single exit. You'll wander here the rest of your life, which won't be long without food and water."

Far off, they could hear a weeping moan: some damned soul kept prisoner in the catacombs, chained or—perhaps worse—left to stumble and grope in the darkness.

"You think I want to escape? You think I do not want vengeance?"

"Neither," Regel said. "The princess is too valuable to the Ravalis to slay, and too dangerous for them to hold openly. She lives still."

"Good for Nar-burned her." Davargorn bent to strip the tunic from the guardsman. "But what is that to me? She betrayed me in Luether. You saw."

"And then here in Tar Vangr, you sacrificed yourself to shield her from casterbolts," Regel said. "So I ask you again, whom do you serve?"

"Shut up." Davargorn touched the hilt of his sword to accentuate the point.

"When Semana ripped your face away, were you surprised, or had that been your plan? Was all that staged, or—?"

Davargorn whirled, sword half drawn. "I said shut your burning mouth!"

Regel regarded him calmly. "Tell me, or run me through right now. I'm in no state to fight you."

Davargorn's eyes searched him, considering doing exactly that. Finally, he sank down to the floor against the wall. A helpless smile crossed his distorted features. "I don't know."

Regel understood. The boy might not know his own heart, but Regel saw it clearly. He heard it in Davargorn's voice, and he saw it in his loose shoulders and the way he sat languidly. Davargorn simply *had* to help Semana, just as Regel had needed to help Lenalin. This boy and he were the same, albeit a generation apart, and so too were their respective princesses.

"Understand this." Davargorn leaned his head back and a deep sigh fell from his lips. "She has been Mask for five years. Five years, since that night on the *Heiress*, when Mask tried to kill her. We killed him instead, Lord of Tears, and Ma—*Semana* took his place. She donned his armor. If she had not—" He shook his head. "In all that time, she watched for enemies in every shadow. She let no one see her face. The princess had no one to trust. Not you, not her sworn shield, no one."

She had you, Regel thought, but he kept his silence.

"Then, a year ago, she learned the identity of the Shroud."

"Ovelia." It began to make sense now.

Davargorn nodded. "Can you imagine how that felt? The very traitor who had ended Semana's Blood—who had condemned her to a life unavenged and in hiding—had not only survived the fall of Winter, but had been *rewarded* by the Ravalis? We—*she* had to do something."

"She sent you," Regel supplied. "You were to lure Ovelia to Luether so Semana could kill her, away from her private army of Ravalis spies."

Davargorn nodded. "It was simple. All I had to do was let Mask's name slip in a few taverns and the Bloodbreaker surfaced within a day." He tapped his dagger on the floor, sending the ring of steel up the passage. "She made ready to flee the city, and I planted the seeds of her treachery to turn the Ravalis against her. All I had to do was breathe word of her to Lan, and he would chase her from Tar Vangr. Everything passed according to my plan."

"Until she came to me," Regel said.

"That was a surprise," Davargorn said. "Who could have expected the Bloodbreaker would go to the man who hates her most in the world? And that you would make an accord! Mask and I did not expect in a thousand years that would come to pass."

"You underestimated her as much as I did."

"So it seems," Davargorn said. "I could not warn Mask that you were coming, so I followed you to Luether and brought you both into our trap. You defeated us. That was when she—" He winced at remembered pain.

"Did she dismiss you out of anger, or because she knew what you would do?" Regel asked. "Return to Tar Vangr and the Ravalis, whom you had already turned into allies. Position yourself as Lan's personal guard, and draw close to the throne."

"She wouldn't—oh, burn me." Davargorn winced at the realization. "That's *exactly* what she did. Then, if you were to fail against the Usurper, she would have asked me to do it."

"And you would have," Regel said, "no matter what had passed between you."

"Yes." He shut his eyes. "She is brilliant. A queen among tyrants."

"That, I am beginning to understand." Regel nodded slowly. Lenalin had been so manipulative.

"I cannot understand why she did what she did, though," Davargorn said. "She had won. You and the Bloodbreaker both were doomed in Prince Lan's chambers. She had but to stand back and do nothing, and yet she revealed herself and lost all." He shook his head. "It seems so stupid."

Stupid, but noble. Again, Regel thought he understood something the boy did not.

They sat in silence a time, and finally Regel felt well enough to stand. He did not betray his strength right away, of course. First, he asked another question—one he could not leave unanswered.

"Serris," Regel said. "Did you mean her to die?"

"Who?" His gaze dreamy, Davargorn hardly seemed to hear him.

"A bit of wisdom." Without warning, Regel crossed the pace between them and pressed Davargorn back into the wall, his blade to the boy's throat. "Don't tell foes your weaknesses."

"Remember my magic." Davargorn scowled. "I do not fear you, Lord of Tears."

"You should," he said. "Weak as I may be, I can kill you beyond embers to fan."

Davargorn's face remained cool, but the fear that flickered across his good eye told Regel he believed him. "I am sorry for your squire, Lord of Tears, but this solves nothing—"

"I assume you threatened her," Regel said. "How long have you owned her loyalty?"

"Since that night Ovelia came to you. She was a weapon to use against you if I needed it."

"Against me?" Regel lowered his blade. "Would Semana not slay me anyway?"

"She—" A look of discomfiture came across Davargorn's face. "We need to move," he said. "You should leave your squire. We can't carry her."

The simple truth made Regel's chest feel hollow. Much as he hated to leave Serris, both he and Davargorn could barely carry themselves. He'd have to come back for her body.

"Just tell me this," Regel said. "Did you mean Serris to die?"

Whether he needed the ugly man or not, Regel knew he would kill Davargorn if he had.

"No." Davargorn shook his head as much as Regel allowed. "Lan brought Serris into this. She must have attacked him in the ballroom, but he and Vhaerynn captured her. Neither of us expected—"

"Or cared." With his face pressed close to Davargorn's, Regel felt the boy's breath on his lips. Finally, he stepped away. "Very well."

"Very well?" Davargorn rubbed at his throat. "That is all? *Very well?*"

"You saw only the need to help Semana. You did not care for the blood that was spilled. That makes you reckless, but not a murderer. Good enough for now."

Regel reversed the knife and offered it to Davargorn, hilt first. The mismatched eyes met his, wondering. "We need each other to rescue Semana and Ovelia," Regel said. "You need my knowledge of the tunnels, I need your magic. We work together, or we all die—them and us."

Davargorn eyed the proffered blade. "And you would trust me enough to disarm yourself?"

"We need each other," he said. "It makes no great difference who bears the steel."

Slowly, Davargorn took Regel's dagger and slid it into his belt. "So what now? Saving your red-haired whore, I wager."

That barb had been calculated to bring a rise out of him, and Regel ignored it so he could think. He thought of Semana, standing like a goddess in black leather, her hair flowing alongside her glowing eyes. She'd deceived him—deceived everyone— but he couldn't abandon her. And however confused he might be, neither could Davargorn. As to where... Regel knew of the most likely place, and that was down here in the tunnels. As for Ovelia, he suspected only an hour or so had passed since the battle with Lan, but even that might be enough for the poison he'd put in her belly to have slain her. Her body wasn't down here, so perhaps she yet lived, somewhere. But could he save Ovelia if it meant letting Semana die?

"We save Semana first," Regel said. "I know where they likely took her."

"What of your honorless lover?" Davargorn's voice betrayed loathing for Ovelia.

"She can care for herself. And she would want Semana saved first."

"Truly?" Davargorn sheathed the sword. "As you say, Lord of Tears. You know the Bloodbreaker better than I. No tricks."

"No." Regel grimaced when he moved his leg. "Do you still have the flying boots?"

Davargorn scowled. "Probably gracing the pink feet of some over-fed summerborn by now." He turned up the corridor. Rather than follow, Regel knelt, and Davargorn looked back. "What is it?"

"Naught." Regel swept his fingers up Serris's dead face and closed her eyes. He pressed his lips to her forehead, then rose. "We go."

I am coming, Ovelia, he prayed. *Wait for me.*

255

TWENTY-NINE

IT WAS IN THE waiting that she felt true pain.

Ovelia stood naked in the center of the room, her flesh chilled despite the raging fire on the hearth and in her middle. She wore only two things: manacles sticky with blood that bound her hands behind her back, which had already started to make her arms strain, and her carved necklace, which Lan apparently liked. She stood untouched and unmoving, feeling every tiny ache and bruise. Her head and her belly pained her the most, and it took all her energy merely to stand rather than swoon.

Lan Ravalis paced a circle around her, inspecting her body from every angle. Rather than cringe away, she kept her posture steadfast, not wanting to concede defeat. She stood proudly, shoulders back, dragon tattoo gleaming. Under Lan's eye, Ovelia felt like a horse at market, though whether he meant to ride her or chop her up for meat was uncertain. She didn't like how much she liked that feeling.

"You've aged well, Lady." Lan rubbed his meticulously shaved chin.

She averted her gaze and said nothing.

Her defiance seemed to amuse Lan. "The years seem hardly to touch you," he said, "though there are certainly creases."

His hand extended toward her backside, and her muscles tightened as though bracing for the thrust of a knife. His fingers were warm, however, and even gentle. She shivered, and that it was not out of loathing made her hate herself.

Is this not what you deserve? that other self within her asked—the one who had confronted her in the mercyhall in Luether, the one who spoke to her at night when she lay awake and refused to weep. *After what you have done, is this not what you have earned?*

"Mmm." He cupped her hindquarters, squeezing hard but giving no pain. "You've almost the firmness of my niece, and she's twenty years your junior."

Ovelia raged at the slur to Semana, but she knew Lan meant to bait her. "Thank you," she said without meaning it. She wanted to hurt him. Wanted him to hurt her.

Lan put his arms around Ovelia then, and pressed his chest and belly hard against her back. Ovelia caught her breath as his fingers found her bare breasts. She strained to keep her breath constant.

"I've always wanted you." His head craned around her neck, and his breath beat like burning summerweed on her skin. "The way my brother got to have you—how he used to gloat over it... All he needed to unlock your legs was his little slattern of a daughter."

Ovelia closed her eyes tightly. Her heart was racing despite herself—excitement

256

building where there should be only anger or shame. It was vile, but she could not help it. All her life, she could never help it. This was what she wanted.

"Lady Dracaris, you... By the Nar, I'd not expected *this*." He clasped her tighter, and she gasped. "You enjoy this. You . . . You are all my brother said and more."

"Please," she whispered, because she meant it and because it made the desire redouble. "Please let me go." Half of her—the half she wouldn't give voice—wished he wouldn't. She loathed herself for it. Old Gods, she was on *fire*.

"Why?" he asked. "Why does this please you?"

Ovelia could not explain. Lan was not like Paeter—he didn't recognize what was inside Ovelia, and so he did not understand what she was. Lan was a fledgling squire given a weapon he'd never seen and did not know how to wield. In that way, Lan was no better a lover than Regel had ever been.

"We have used each other before," Ovelia whispered. The awful hunger within her faded, replaced by a horrible yearning of another sort.

Lan was touching every bit of her, caressing and rubbing and scratching. He swelled against her back, the waistband of his breeches straining. She wanted to have him. She wanted him to take her.

Then he said it. "Why the girl?"

"What?" Ovelia's eyes snapped open and she stared at the ceiling. Snowmelt dowsed the fire inside her. Dark desire ebbed and faded, and she remembered the ache in her belly and the dizziness in her head. "What did you say?"

"Semana." Lan nibbled at her neck, but instead of maddening her, his teeth only sickened her. "Did you desire the girl for yourself? Dream of that silver hair trailing along your skin?"

Ovelia couldn't breathe. That image—like Lenalin, except...

"I could bring her," Lan said. "You'd enjoy that? Making love to her as I watched?"

Ovelia tried in vain to remain still and feel nothing. Her dark desire collapsed in on itself, and she was once again herself, standing in judgment, ashamed and terrified. Over and over, she saw Semana's face—judging, weighing, and condemning her. Semana, her— "No!" Ovelia gasped, and wrenched away.

She made it two paces before she fell gasping to one knee. Lan stared at her in smug satisfaction, thinking he had won something over her. And perhaps he had.

Ovelia caught a glimpse of movement—something red—across the room, and she looked. There stood a woman in the mirror, panting and rocking on one knee, her dragon tattoo sparkling in the firelight. Her eyes were puffy and her cheeks hollow from lack of real sleep. Her bound hands looked to be flushed red like blood. And her hair... Maure must have washed it clean of dye, for it was red like fire again.

"I am myself," she said. Down to the pit of her jet black soul.

Viciousness came into Lan's eyes, and Ovelia could offer no defense as he grabbed her by the throat and wrenched her up. "You are mine," he said. "Or I will flay that girl alive and dress you in her skin. I will rip out her entrails and adorn your wrists and throat. Or—" Now his face twisted terribly. "Or I will have that bloody Court Sorcerer enchant your limbs and make *you* do it. See if I cannot."

Ovelia hardly had the strength to respond. "I believe you."

"You are mine," Lan said again. "*Say it.*"

"Yes," she whispered, because she had no choice. "I am yours."

"You are my whore," he said. "Say the words, Bloodbreaker."

Ovelia met his eyes. "I am your whore," she said.

"You will do what I will of you," he said. "For I am your king."

"Yes. Anything you would have. You are my king." She willed herself not to think of Orbrin—she pushed his kindly face out of her mind. "Tell me your will."

"First." Lan's smile curled triumphantly. "First, prove that you are mine. Kneel before your king and pay him obeisance."

Ovelia hesitated. She, who had bowed to no man but the Winter King. She, whose honor was rubble and whose heart was stone. After all the insults he had paid her—after what he had said of Semana—it was more than she could endure. But did she not want this? Did she not *deserve* it?

Lan was smiling, oblivious. He pulled her into his chest and raised her eyes to meet his. "As you love that little Winter-slut," he said. "Bow to your king."

The words blew the years away like dust. She was once again young and desperate, defending Semana with her virtue and her life. Darkness stirred—the darkness that had been with her all her life.

Semana, Ovelia thought, and—fingers trembling—she sank to one knee. She bowed her head, and her necklace fell free of her chest and swayed where it hung from her neck.

Lan reached for the laces of his breeches.

THIRTY

REGEL HAD NOT EXAGGERATED the scope of the complex beneath the palace of Tar Vangr. Blue candles lit along the walls as they stalked through the metal lined tunnels that twisted in and around themselves like the skittering threads of a long abandoned web. One could wander the halls and passages for months or even years without finding an exit, unless one knew where to look.

The crypts had been ancient when the Empire of Calatan had been young. They spoke of a finer craftsmanship than the secret passages in the palace above, though years of neglect had turned the steel girders dark with age. Cleverly concealed doors, like the one that had opened to the secret charnel chamber, led to unknown rooms, most of which could never be accessed. The art of opening such doors had faded with the centuries, and no one living today could force one open. Regel had tried for some time in his youth to break into many of the chambers, mostly in vain. Only flawed doors like that of the charnel room would work, leading to anonymous chambers full of dust, their original purpose inexplicable. But even a handful of accessible chambers were enough to make the tunnels invaluable. Finding these doors was nigh impossible for the inexperienced, and the unexpected turns, sudden pitfalls, and nearly invisible nooks made the tunnels a perfect hiding place for treasures—or for prisoners kept forever secret.

Into this place the two men stalked, shadows carved out of the light of a lone torch Davargorn bore inside his warding cloak. They kept the light small and directed in their path.

"Leading me into some dark corpse hole, Lord of Tears?" Davargorn asked.

"There is a cell down in these depths, reserved for the most important prisoners. Here they can never be found, except by those in direct service of the Crown. Like as not, Semana is there."

"And if she isn't?"

Regel shrugged. "Then we will provoke the Ravalis for no reason, likely to our deaths."

"Oh very good." Davargorn sneered. "Just remember: I hold all the blades."

"Indeed."

Regel knew the tunnels well, though he had not been here in many years. As a child, he had made his home in the secluded corners of the palace, and the tunnels had been his refuge when guardsmen chased him from the kitchen or—later—after assassinations. Now, Regel himself had become an old shadow of a dead king, while Davargorn had become that graceful, ruthless boy from his memory: a vicious killer skulking the shadows, hopelessly in love with a woman he could never attain.

And if Davargorn was anything like his younger self, Regel knew he intended treachery at the first opportunity. Regel would not forget that.

Several times, they had to double-back to bypass a fissure that cut through the tunnel or a partially collapsed ceiling. The tunnels had changed somewhat from the last time Regel had been here, and his bad leg meant he couldn't skitter around them as he once had. As the King's Shadow, he had leaped from rooftop to rooftop and even scaled the thousand-foot sheer palace wall of Tar Vangr. Now, only five years later, he felt much older.

Regel could tell their constant backtracking grated on the younger Davargorn. Eventually, the man even spoke. "Who dug these, anyway? They look ancient."

"No," Regel said. "Vangryur miners delved deep and found them almost four hundred years ago. Thousand of years old at the time, sealed away by a long-ago cave-in." He peered around a corner, then motioned Davargorn on. "Legends credit the Old Gods of the Nar or the little gods of the earth."

"But the legends lie?"

Regel shrugged. "These tunnels date from before the Prophecy of Return. Perhaps from the Old World itself," he said. "Some say that when the folk of Denerre returned to this world, they passed through these tunnels."

"Ridiculous," Davargorn said.

"Spend an hour in this place, and you will feel the weight of ages on your shoulders."

Davargorn made a derisive sound. "Nothing here now." He kicked loose stones to skitter down the corridor. "Naught but dust."

"Aye, dust." Regel traced his fingers through the thick dust, which crumbled between his fingers and filtered to the floor. "Dust and shadow."

～

After a time in the dark, they heard the echoing sounds of boots and muted conversation that indicated waiting guards. A little further on, torchlight flickered along the walls ahead. Davargorn left his own torch to gutter against the floor, and together the men stepped into the muddy darkness with the grace of hardened killers. Ten paces ahead, two Ravalis guards stood on either side of a faintly glowing red sigil drawn on the stone wall. The image gleamed like still damp ink—or like fresh blood.

"Only two," Davargorn whispered. "I can deal with them both."

Regel restrained him. "That sign is a blood magic ward. If either of them touches it, an alarm will sound, these tunnels will fill with warders, and we shall never escape."

"I take one, you take the other. We strike at the same moment." He looked at Regel's knee. "You can't run at them, and I can't throw worth a speck of blood."

"I can." Regel held out his hand for one of the daggers.

Davargorn hesitated. "Can you kill a man from this distance with a throw?"

"The nearest one," Regel said.

Davargorn's good eye widened and a twisted grin split his features. "Oh, that is rich," he said. "I go alone, against two men, and I have to run *past* the first one?"

"Would you rescue your princess or not?"

"What if you miss? Or perhaps you'll not throw at all and just leave me to my fate."

"You'll have to trust me, it seems."

"Very well." He drew the knife at his belt and gave it to Regel. He paused, then handed him the second knife as well. "Two chances are better than one."

"I won't miss with the first."

"So you say." Davargorn reversed the sword in his hand, blade down, and ran.

Regel took aim, considering the moment. If he threw too late, the blade would not catch the guard before he touched the ward. Too early, and he would alert the other man before Davargorn could reach him... or hit the boy himself. Also, he had to predict how the guards would move in response to Davargorn's charge: which would draw steel, and which would go for the ward? Either or both?

Regel drew in a breath to steady himself. He raised the knife close to his eye.

The guards saw Davargorn falling upon them like death. The near one cried out and grasped the hilt of his sword, while the farther guard reached for the ward.

Regel found stillness and threw.

Davargorn shot right past the near guard and ran the second one through. He tried to pull the sword free, but it lodged in the man's ribs. The first guard whirled on his defenseless foe, but the hilt of his sword caught on his belt. He cursed and wrenched hard, and the sword sang free.

The point of Regel's dagger burst from the man's throat. His sword clattered to the floor and he reached up to clutch at his neck while his other hand reached for the ward. Davargorn slapped the reaching fingers away and shoved the dying guard across the hall to slump against the stone.

"Took you long enough," Davargorn called back.

Regel released the breath he had been holding and limped forward. Davargorn was pulling at his stuck sword to no avail. Regel bent to recover his knife from the dead guard's throat.

"Pitiful steel." With a wet crack, Davargorn wrenched his sword free. "Luethaar, probably. They make poor blades down south, no?"

Regel placed his palm on the center of the ward. Fire shot out from around his hand and wreathed the steel portal, circling in arcs around its edges. It tore along twin grooves carved in the corridor wall, shattering packs of dust, and raced down the tunnel wall. A low hum just perceptible to the human ear filled the air. It would be louder above.

Davargorn's eyes widened and his hand trembled on the sword. "What have you done?"

"Listen to me now, boy, for we have only moments before the Ravalis arrive," Regel said. "They have only to follow the line of fire and will come straight to us. We can escape before they arrive, but only all three of us. Do you understand?"

Davargorn's body trembled, and finally he uttered a curse. "You win." He pointed to the ancient door. "Open it."

"Blood magic," Regel said. "Blood calls to blood. Remember that."

Regel raised his knife to his hand, cut a red line through the flesh, then placed his bloody palm on the ward. The flames abruptly turned gold instead of crimson, and the stone ground against itself. In the space of a single breath, the wall opened, revealing a dungeon lit by a single flickering candle.

What they saw inside the chamber, however, caused both of them to stop breathing.

"Dust and shadow," Regel murmured.

Hanging before them—a taut black steel chain running from its neck to a hook mounted in the ceiling—was a very limp, very dead Mask.

THIRTY-ONE

WHEN SHE WAS ENDED—WHEN there was nothing left but darkness and defeat—it was Regel's words that came to Ovelia. "*Dust and shadow,*" Regel said in her mind, the words in time with passes of the necklace that swung like a pendulum. "*None of us are more or less.*"

There was strength in those words: a wild abandon of sense and prudence. Regel spoke them over the dead—whether they lay on a bier or were about to rush into doom. She'd never quite understood their meaning until now. Ovelia's eyes opened. "All of us die," she murmured.

"Eh?" Lan looked down at her. "What was that?"

Another of Regel's favored wisdoms came to her, and a tiny smile crossed her face.

"Two moments... when a man is weakest," she whispered. "When he makes love..."

Lan's eyes gleamed with lust. He reached out to her, but before his hand could touch her, a keening hum shot through the chamber and he cringed. An alarm ward.

"And when he thinks himself victorious," Ovelia said.

She leaned forward and bit him.

Lan shrieked. He shoved at her, but she held on and he only succeeded in making her bite harder. Something in him gave way, and she loosened her jaw rather than break his skin. If she shed Lan's blood, Vhaerynn would come, and she would die.

Blows fell on Ovelia's head and shoulders, and Lan finally succeeded in clouting her on the temple. Her jaw released and she fell to the floor, coughing. She spat blood onto the fur rug, but it must have been her own blood, for no terrible sorcerer appeared to end her life.

"Nnh—" Lan covered his loins awkwardly, but Ovelia could see the mass of bruises forming there. Lan tried to wrap the trembling fingers of his other hand around his belt dagger. "Whore... nnh!"

Ovelia got her feet under her and lunged at him with all the strength she could manage. She jarred his hand from his blade and they collapsed writhing to the floor. The prince cried out in incoherent rage and pain, but Ovelia slammed her forehead into his jaw, knocking him senseless for a moment. She brushed her head against his shirt to wipe away the blood streaming down her face—she'd felt his teeth punch through her skin. But it was her own blood rather than his, and so it would not mean her death.

She tried to rise, but pain ripped through her belly and she fell on top of Lan, her vision blurry and her head exploding. Had he stabbed her? She didn't know and couldn't see well enough to check.

The high hum burned her ears. A ward had been activated in the halls below them. Her heart started racing and her vision went blurry. The royal cell, far below: *Semana.*

And she knew, somehow, that Regel was the cause of the alarm. He lived yet.

She felt at Lan's pockets, but she could find no key to her manacles. She abandoned the search and gritted her teeth against the pain. Blood oozed from her cut wrists, but the pain was as nothing compared to the agony inside her. She couldn't worry about that. Semana needed her.

Ovelia tried to scramble off Lan, but his fingers tangled in her hair and yanked her head back. "Filthy whore!" Lan roared, his breath hot on her neck. She felt cold steel at her throat. "You—"

Ovelia slammed her head back into his face, and Lan moaned. His dagger slipped from her throat, leaving burning pain in its wake. She fell to the floor, wincing, and worked her shoulders to pull herself along Lan's rug. She forced one leg under her and tried to rise. Then a hand fell on her ankle.

"No," she said, panting. "*No.*"

Roaring, Lan wrestled her down. Without her hands, there was little Ovelia could do. She drove her shoulder into his chest, but it was like hitting a wall of stone. He punched her square in the face, and stars exploded across her eyes. Lan tackled her and they crushed a wooden chair, sending pieces skittering in every direction. Ovelia felt sharp wood cut into her bare flesh. Lan straddled her, ignoring his battered crotch. The prince's fingers wrapped around her throat and began to squeeze. "Whore!" he cried, as though that was the only word he still knew.

Ovelia thrashed, but she didn't have the strength to twist free. She could barely make herself move. The edges of her vision crumbled.

Semana *needed* her.

Ovelia put all her strength into her right leg. She shoved her knee up as hard as she could, right between his thighs into his bruised crotch. Lan cried out. His hands faltered and his fingers splayed like arrow shafts. He curled down, caving in on himself.

Heart hammering, Ovelia stood up, slamming her shoulder into Lan's jaw hard enough that he snapped back as though she'd struck him with a hammer. The back of his knees caught on the edge of the bed, and she staggered and fell heavily atop him. His dagger lay on the floor within easy reach, but it was useless. Even if her hands weren't still bound, a blade would do her no good if Lan's blood summoned Vhaerynn to slay her. Instead, she straddled his midsection and reached down behind her back, her hands trembling between his legs, and clutched his bruised blade hard in both hands.

"No king," she spat, and twisted.

Lan shrieked. Somehow, his agony gave him the strength to strike, and his fist caught her on the left side of the head. They tumbled dizzily onto the floor. Ovelia's hip exploded in pain on the bearskin rug and she almost bit through her tongue. Lan snarled, his eyes burning, but when he tried to surge toward her, he screamed in pain, clutched at himself, and let go of her leg.

From the floor she kicked at his head with all the force she could muster. Her bleary aim was off and she caught him in the shoulder, but it still hit hard enough to knock him on his back. Panting hard, she fought to rise and somehow succeeded. She wavered on her feet, balance hard to find.

"Whore!" His voice was pitched high and broken. "Wh—!"

She brought down her heel on his face. Then again. And again.

Finally, he stopped moving except to twitch feebly on the blood-stained rug.

Heart thundering in her head, she caught sight of herself in the mirror and stopped for an instant. The fight had left her face a mess of bruises and her own blood, with one eye swollen shut and her lower lip split in two places. This did not bother her, however, so much as her nakedness—modesty could come upon one at strange moments. As best she could with her manacled hands, she wrenched the blanket from the bed—a silk so deep crimson it seemed black—and wrapped it around herself. In the mirror, with her hair of fire and that mantle, she looked more like the Red Sorceress from legend than a Knight of Winter.

Ovelia shivered and looked over her shoulder just as Lan murmured and stirred. Had he made a noise that had drawn her attention, or was it the other way around? She couldn't say. It was almost like having Draca again, even though the sword was nowhere in sight. In all likelihood, the Ravalis had squirreled it away in a vault or melted it down by now. She wished she had the sword, with the simple clarity of its magic to tell her what to do. Draca did not lie, as her heart often did.

In any case, she turned to regard Lan where he lay like a wounded animal on the bloody rug, breath rasping through his throat. Still alive. She remembered standing over the unconscious Ravalis guard in the secret tunnel behind the Denerre bloodtree. Old Gods, how long ago had that been?

Ovelia sat down on Lan's chest, facing away from him, and wrapped her ruddy fingers around his throat. She found she didn't have the strength or leverage to strangle him. She tried to choke him with the manacle chain, but he could still breathe around all the pressure she could manage to exert.

"Burn the Old Gods," she cursed between clenched teeth.

Ovelia forced herself to rise, then knelt awkwardly on his throat. He coughed and struggled, as though his body refused to die even when his mind had no sense. She lost her balance and slipped off him, not once but twice. The second time she lay panting on the matted bearskin rug and tried to gather her strength. Her stomach felt as though a creature had burrowed in and was tearing her asunder from inside. She coughed, and blood spewed from her mouth as though from a wound deep down.

Ovelia looked to Lan, who lay beside her. The prince had sprouted a dozen awful bruises on his face and midsection, and matters only became worse as she looked down at his mangled groin. She could not tell if his chest rose or fell.

She had to choose: leave him alone and try to escape, hoping he expired on his own, or use the last of her strength to make sure Lan was dead, then collapse and die herself.

Semana needed her.

Finally, Ovelia forced herself up and padded away, limping where she'd slammed her hip into the floor. At the door, she turned, put her bound hands on the latch and fumbled to open it. Her hands shook.

The door gave way and she backed through it. The corridor seemed empty, and Ovelia stumbled against the opposite wall and panted in the darkness. Her heart thudded and her belly burned. Weakness seeped through her, as though she was bleeding from a dozen unseen wounds. Sweat poured down her face and breath came hard. Old Gods, her insides were on *fire*. She needed medicine. Herbs. Anything.

Ovelia could hardly think for the pain. She looked down at her belly, where she was sure she would find a ripped-open gash, but there was nothing—just smooth skin with no sign of injury. Old Gods, what if she had been right and she was carrying Regel's child? Was she even now *losing* that child?

The blanket shifted awkwardly. Automatically, she tried to reach up to adjust it, but with her hands still bound, she succeeded only in upsetting the blanket and making it worse. She thought to search for keys again, but her legs didn't have the strength to carry her back into that awful room. She slumped against the wall and slid to the floor, trying to breathe through her nose. Her mouth had closed tight.

The humming sound—the ward from the depths—faded and died away, but it had done its work. Guards would follow the ward through the tunnels to investigate the sound and, like as not, they would find Ovelia along the way. Even now, she heard footsteps down the hall, and she could do nothing more than sit, waiting defenseless outside the room of the Crown Prince she had maimed and possibly killed. At least she had managed to cripple him, before she succumbed to her own weakness. Perhaps the Ravalis would be merciful and kill her immediately. The thought gave her relief, but then she realized she would fail Semana all over again, and her heart ached.

Perhaps she shouldn't have fought back. Perhaps she could have used Lan, as she used Paeter years ago. Let him have his way with her and endure. Perhaps...

Ovelia sank fully to the floor, face pressed against the cold stone of the wall. She was so tired. Tired of the horror, tired of the pain, tired of all the blood...

"Hail!" Strong hands caught her about the shoulders. "Pass w—oh *Gods*. Lady Dracaris!"

At first, she thought it was Lan come to avenge himself upon her, or perhaps Paeter returned from the grave. But this face was thinner than either of those men—the eyes gentler.

Garin Ravalis wound the fallen blanket around her shoulders. "What happened to you?" He brushed at her sticky cheeks. His fingertips came away red with her blood.

Ovelia tried to speak but couldn't. She shook her head and nodded toward Lan's door.

Garin, his face writ with horror, looked toward the door, but Ovelia caught his hand. She willed him not to go. She didn't want to be alone.

"All's well," he said. "No more harm will come to you, Lady. I swear it. I just have to see."

Ovelia nodded limply. Her jaw was clasped tight. She wondered if her lips would ever open—if she would ever speak again. The horror seemed too real.

Hand on the warpick at his belt, Garin looked in the door. Ovelia watched him weigh the variables in the situation, see the implications, and determine his course. Now she imagined he would turn on her and draw his steel to make an end of it.

Garin turned his bright blue eyes on her. His jaw was set. "He attacked you," he said.

Ovelia looked at him numbly, then nodded.

"Old Gods of the Nar." Garin's fingers shook on the hilt of the warpick at his belt.

He was going to kill her, and there was nothing she could do to stop him.

"No," he said, as though he could hear her thoughts.

Ovelia blinked, confused, as Garin wiped away the blood and spittle on her face.

"My cousin is an animal. Whatever hurt you have dealt him, he no doubt deserves." Garin took her hands in his. "Now come, we must get you away. Someone triggered a ward in the depths. Your friend, the Lord of Tears? That creature in the mask?"

He didn't know about Semana. She wanted to tell him, but when she opened her mouth, blood trickled down her lips. Her blood. She was bleeding inside. Old Gods.

Lenalin my love, she thought. *I'll be with you straight.*

"Lady?" Garin asked. "Are you—?"

She spat gore on the stones and wiped her chin. "Silver hair," she said. "They both—"

Weakness overwhelmed her, the world went numb, and Ovelia collapsed into Garin's arms. He was shouting at her from an increasing distance and she was sinking, unable and unwilling to hang on.

THIRTY-TWO

M ASK HUNG LIKE A discarded doll, spindly limbs trailing. The sorcerer could feign death with astonishing veracity, but this hanging corpse was clearly nothing alive. Regel had only to look at the tongue bulging from its mouth-slit to know that. At the ends of its arms, the mismatched ensorcelled gauntlets dangled limply. The Ravalis had even replaced Mask's flying boots on the body.

The chamber was otherwise empty of prisoners. Withered chairs, a table, and a cot made it seem like a liveable space, but scattered rusty implements of pain belied this impression. Threadbare tapestries painted with the colors of blood showed scenes of men and women in agony. Numerous chains hung from the ceiling, where prisoners could be strung up—as Mask had been—for torture or as an example.

Pain erupted in Regel's head and he staggered away from where Davargorn had struck him with the pommel of the guard's sword. The blade clattered to the floor as two hands grasped Regel by the throat and shoved him against the wall.

"*Bastard!*" He snarled in Regel's face, sending flecks of blood and spittle onto his cheek. "You did this to her! *You!*"

Regel caught hold of Davargorn's arm and tried to pull it away, but to no avail. The younger man was far stronger, particularly in his fury.

"You *knew* they would do this! You brought her to her death!"

"She gave me no choice," Regel said.

Davargorn threw him to the floor and turned, but that put his eyes in line with the body and he uttered a moan from the depths of his bowels. He ran to the hanging body and pressed his face into its belly. Regel saw the hands tremble— the gauntlets slip.

"I cannot," Davargorn said. "I cannot heal her. There is nothing here. Only dust."

"Dust and shadow." Regel raised his chin. "I am sorry. I know she was in your heart."

"My heart?" Davargorn turned his face to glare over his shoulder. "How could you know *my* heart, old man? You do not even know your own! You do not know what power you hold!"

Breaths passed. Davargorn paced, alternately slicking his spindly hair or clapping his withered hand into his good one. "For nothing," he murmured, "all for this—for *nothing!*"

Again, he buried his head in Mask's stomach, his shoulders shaking.

"Tithian," Regel said.

"I see your gambit," Davargorn said. "You triggered the ward so I would defend the princess, and you would escape. Too bad for you she's past defending."

268

"Indeed." Regel regarded him levelly. "What passes now?"

Slowly, Davargorn turned to face him. His eyes gleamed in the blue candlelight that filtered in from the corridor, and from the red burning ward that beat like a heart. He held his sword raised, ready to plunge it into Regel's heart. "I should kill you."

"And will you?"

"No. It's beneath me to slay a worthless cripple." Davargorn lowered the steel. "There's no reason to take you along either. I'll leave you here, and you can die beside your princess. As for me—" He glanced out into the corridor. "I've a Blood to break."

Davargorn took all the blades they had taken from downed guardsmen, leaving Regel unarmed. He made to go, but Regel stepped into his path. "You could stay," Regel said. "Honor your beloved."

"*Beloved.*" Davargorn scoffed. "I suspect this is the last time we'll meet."

"I do not," Regel said.

"Best of luck, old man," Davargorn said. "I hope you die choking on your own blood."

With one last sneer—and a pained look at Mask's form—Davargorn was gone. Regel gave a deep sigh, then eased himself to the floor. He sat and breathed.

~

"Your princess is dead," he told himself. And laughed.

Davargorn stumbled through the winding corridors, biting his left hand to keep from screaming. The dead flesh—it had been scarred when he crawled from the womb—hardly felt his teeth, even though he could taste the blood. He could heal himself, but he would only heal himself back to his disfigured state. A cruel trick for fate to play, but fate had never loved him after all.

He laughed louder. "Your princess is dead, you ugly fool!"

Blearily, he followed the red light on the wall. Some dim part of him realized the ward would lead him up to the palace, and if he encountered any soldiers on the way, so much the better.

Abruptly the ward blinked out of existence, like a burning string that turned to ash as he watched. Something had ended it. He was lost. He tripped over his feet and fell. His knee and arm took most of the impact, and he felt bone give way. The sword he had been carrying skittered out of his fingers and was gone into the darkness. His milky white eye could see just fine in the dark, and he didn't need a sword to kill minions of the Ravalis.

He realized he'd tripped over his leg—his twisted leg, the one that had always caused him such trouble—the one at which everyone had laughed. Even the princess had laughed, he knew. Not that she'd ever done it in his hearing, but how could she *not* laugh?

Semana.

He rose despite the pain. Ignoring the protests of his flesh, he stumbled on through the dusty darkness. His lungs wheezed at the effort, but he would heal.

Even as he walked, his bones popped back into place with little more than loud itching. Life came back into his damaged body.

"Not hers," he said. "Not hers, though. She's gone forever!"

He saw a flickering light just around a corner and almost ran into two Ravalis guardsmen. Their torchlight dazzled him for a second. They must have heard him coming, but even so they backed away in surprise at his sudden, mad appearance. Too bad for them.

Davargorn caught the first one's head in his bare hands and wrenched him down with enough force to shatter his neck. He caught the man's caster and brought it up, just as the second man got off a cast. The thunder of the caster's discharge almost deafened Davargorn, but he hardly felt the bolt tear through his thigh. He raised the captured caster and put his bolt through the man's right eye from two feet away. The back of the guard's head burst and blood spattered the wall.

Dismissively, Davargorn tossed the spent caster onto the bodies, ripped free the bolt in his thigh, and pressed on. He made it only half a dozen paces before his wounded leg crumpled under him, and he dashed his forehead against the wall. It still needed time to heal. His head and neck pulsed in pain and his body didn't want to rise.

Damn guidance. Damn his body. Let them come to him. Let him make an end of it all.

"Come and face me, Ravalis!" he cried. "I will kill all of you. All of you!"

His shouts echoed down the corridor. Distantly, he could hear booted footfalls and loved that sound: it meant more foes for him to slay. Slaying was his purpose.

He settled into place, waiting while his leg healed itself. As he sat, his blood spread in a pool on the floor. The stone seemed so comfortable. But he could not let himself slip away.

"My princess," he murmured. "Princess Mask."

Torches flickered in the passage ahead of him. More guards were coming.

They rounded the corner, and he rose with a roar.

~

Regel breathed in deeply as he sat relaxed with his legs crossed, waiting.

When he was satisfied Davargorn would not return, Regel rose and deactivated the ward with another touch. The burning red light vanished. The ward had sounded for only a forty count, perhaps, but guards would be on their way. Likely, Davargorn would give them some trouble, but haste was needed.

Regel stepped to the hanging body and grasped it about the hips, much like Davargorn had. But instead—in a move that would have horrified the younger man—he shook the corpse. The chain creaked angrily and the body danced. He heard what he expected: two clangs of metal on stone as first one gauntlet, then the other slipped from the body's hands. Freed of the gauntlets, the purple fingers curled into ugly claws. He had thought as much.

That done, Regel crossed to the winch on the wall. He pulled the lever and the chain slithered upward. The leather-wrapped body slumped unceremoniously to the floor, its neck at an odd angle. The lifeless eyes stared and the dry, puckered tongue pointed accusatorily at him.

Regel knelt beside the corpse. There, he unbuckled the mask and pulled it off. Beneath the black leather was a bruised, seared face, fringed with ratty blonde hair, the eyes wide.

It was not Semana's face.

He had suspected as much when first they had entered the chamber. That the gauntlets did not fit had only confirmed the truth. Regel wondered who the wretch might have been: some poor boy who had run afoul of the Crown, perhaps, or else a stunted man brought down from the cells above for this cruel jest. It was yet another crime for which the Ravalis would answer.

He crossed deeper into the royal cell and pulled aside one of the ratty curtains that passed for tapestries in this foul place. Cut into the wall behind it sat a cage just large enough for a human being of small stature, if she sat huddled in a ball. The cell smelled of urine and dust and death. It was not an uncommon torment for a noble prisoner to be left alone for unknowable hours in cramped darkness, not knowing when next a light would appear—if ever.

The dark-skinned, angular creature lurking inside the tight hole looked at him, unafraid. Ragged clothes barely hid the creature's painfully thin body, and its bright red eyes gleamed. Regel gave it a considering look, and the prisoner bobbed its bald head in return. It grinned widely, yellow teeth clashing fiercely with skin like burnished darkwood, but did not otherwise move. It was not Semana.

Regel let the tapestry fall and moved to the second tiny cage. Empty.

The third contained only moldering bones and a fetid odor.

His heart quickened its pace, but he tried to remain calm. He had to be right.

He moved to the fourth and final of the cages. His fingers trembled as he reached for the curtain.

Within, arms curled around her filthy knees, hunched Semana. She wore a torn, ragged shift of some earthen color. Other than bruises on her arms, she looked largely unhurt. Her hazel eyes sparkled warily at him over a ball of cloth stuffed in her mouth. Despite her ignominious state, he allowed himself an exhalation of relief. She was alive.

"Princess," Regel said. "Wait one breath."

He drew forth the ring of keys he'd taken from the guard outside and found the key for the cell soon enough. He'd used this very key himself long ago, and he knew its grip.

When Regel drew the door open, Semana shifted back in the cell as far as she could go. She regarded him after the fashion of a cornered dog: distrustful and ready to pounce.

"No more harm will come to you," he said. "I swear it."

Regel reached for her gag. The cloth came out of her mouth bloodied at the end, and she retched onto the ground between her knees. As she coughed and panted, Regel examined her thin frame with increasing concern. Gone was the soft body of a young girl, and instead she seemed barely more than a skeleton. She looked as though she hadn't eaten a full meal in years.

Hands trembling, Regel tossed the gag away, then stooped again and extended his hand into the cage to Semana. She shook her head and curled tighter into a ball. "Mask," she said.

"What?" Regel had not expected she would say anything like that.

She extended one long-fingered hand. "Mask."

Regel looked, and indeed, he was holding the black leather shroud he'd taken from the corpse. "You don't have to wear this," he said.

Semana nodded to him. Her face was turning red. "Mask."

"Let me clean it, at least," Regel said. "A dead man wore it. His tongue—"

"*Mask!*" Semana screamed.

Regel extended the black leather mask into the cage. Semana snatched it from his fingers and held it over her face. She sucked in air with a nasal wheeze.

"Where—" Her thoat worked, swallowing hard. She looked around nervously. "Where is he?"

"Who?" he asked. "Davargorn."

With an uncertain murmur, Mask clutched her shoulders and shivered. "Where is Davargorn?"

Regel knew she had been asking after another, and it made him uneasy. He glanced back at the room, but other than the other hidden prisoner, they seemed quite alone. For the moment.

"Semana." He put his hand on hers. "We must make haste. Do you understand me?"

Finally, her eyes turned to him. They were so very different from Lenalin's— from either of her parents—that they took Regel aback. The mask's death magic made Semana's eyes look crimson.

"I understand," she said. "My armor. My gauntlets."

"It's all here," Regel said. "On the body of a dead man."

Semana's fine lips curled. "I took it from much worse."

He brought her the rest of her armor, and she donned it with practiced grace, flexing her limbs in each piece. He looked away, wondering why the Ravalis had left such a collection of ensorcelled relics for the taking. Were they truly so cruel as to leave it for a jest?

"Very well, King's Shadow," came a rasping voice. The princess had finished donning her garb, making her Mask, not Semana. "Lead me to Demetrus and let us make an end of this."

THIRTY-THREE

LIGHT CAME BACK TO Ovelia dully and she found herself in a soft world of white. She slept upon a feather pillow and heard the familiar creak of bed cords as she moved. Above, she saw an equally familiar ceiling of black stone, whose contours she had traced with her eyes many times. She turned and saw a mirror, just where she had expected it: her red-rimmed face stared back at her. Alive. Herself.

"My room," she murmured. "This is my room."

"Mine, actually," a voice said. "But then, I'm the new you."

For a heartbeat, she thought her reflection was speaking to her, as it had seemed in Luether. Then she saw movement at the edge of her vision: someone else was in the chamber with her. "Who—?"

Pain lit inside her: a fire in her belly that had burned to embers but roared back into life. She sat up and curled around her midsection, gasping for air. Strong hands found her shoulders. She struggled but the pain was too great.

"All's well, all's well!" said Garin Ravalis. "Lady Dracaris—Ovelia!"

"Water," Ovelia tried to say, but it came out as a choked rasp rather than a word.

"To give you water now would kill you," Garin said. "You're poisoned."

"What? I—" The words dropped a piece of the puzzle into place. "What kind of poison?"

"Thaldrin," Garin said. "Very advanced. The only way you could have survived this long is with small doses of sweet-soul, administered daily—"

"And over a long period of time," Ovelia finished. "Of course."

She understood. Regel had sneaked poison into her cup at some point—probably that first night—then kept feeding her enough of the antidote to keep her moving. But the thaldrin would keep working and ultimately, her body would grow tolerant of the sweet-soul and it wouldn't save her any longer. Regel had planned to betray her from the very beginning, and ensure that she would die if she betrayed him first.

"Quickly," Garin said. "I know what's wrong and how to help, but I needed you awake to ask this. Do you have a source of halanx?"

"Halanx?" She narrowed her eyes. "That's a poison."

"Just tell me you have it," Garin said. "I couldn't bring all my things from Luether without arousing suspicion, and you weren't much of an alchemist as a Shroud. Or were you?"

Ovelia forced her muddied mind past the burning in her middle. "Secret compartment." She patted her hand dizzily against the stone wall above her head. "I have sweet-soul—"

"Too late for sweet-soul. The thaldrin's done too much damage." Garin reached past her, but the angle was wrong. "Apologies, Lady. This won't be proper."

He knelt on the bed next to her head so that he could reach the compartment with both hands. It opened and he rummaged through the vials. Ovelia felt his wiry leg pressing hard against her shoulder. She glanced to her left, saw his hip close to her face, and recoiled.

"Sorry," he said, drawing several vials from the compartment.

"No, just—" Ovelia thought unsettlingly of Lan. "Your cousin."

Garin winced. "Sorry." He crossed to the table where he mixed precise measurements of the vials into a single cup. "This will taste awful. Should I make it in a tea to cover it?"

"No." Ovelia's stomach roiled. "No tea ever again."

Garin sat beside her and pressed the cup to her lips. She raised her hands as though to take the cup from his fingers, but the pain was too intense and she curled over again. Some of the potion spotted the blanket wrapped around her naked, bloody body.

"Drink, Lady," Garin said. "Feel free to gag. There is no one here but me—no one else to show your strength."

"Ahem." Alcarin—the man she had seen coming off the *Avenger* with Garin a few days ago—leaned against the far wall. He had sat quietly the whole time, his expression one of distaste.

Garin smiled. "Except my squire, that is."

"Is this wise, Master?" Alcarin said. "She is a vicious traitor. She will kill you the first chance she gets, and even if she doesn't, the second the guards find her—"

"Glad I have you to make sure that doesn't happen, then." Garin nodded toward the door. "You remember the plan we discussed. Get to it."

The sharp-faced young man pursed his lips, then stepped across to press his lips to those of Garin. "I'll do what I can. You take care."

"Always."

Alcarin left, and Garin looked back to Ovelia. "Well then." He swirled the liquid in the cup . "Don't think you get out of this."

Ovelia shook her head. "What are you having him do?"

"Redirect the guards, keep them away from Lan's little rut chamber as long as possible," he said. "Cover our tracks. The rest of my family can't know you're alive, much less that I'm helping you. That will lead to uncomfortable questions."

"Why *are* you helping me?" Ovelia asked. "Or is it in your noble heart to help anyone in peril?"

"Why does anyone help anyone else?" Garin's eye gleamed. "I want something from you."

"What? Secrets? Coin?" She glanced after Alcarin. "Obviously it's not sex."

"Something far more important, Lady Dracaris. But you must drink this first."

Ovelia smiled wanly. She let him pour the potion between her lips. It tasted like ashes, vinegar, and death. She choked on it, and it dribbled down her chin.

"Old Gods, what is this?"

"Vanarast, bolthan, and now halanx," he said. "That and another thing."

"Those are poisons," Ovelia said. "You just killed me."

"Only when given individually," he said. "Together, they cancel each other's effects and serve only to strengthen the body's response. If it isn't too far gone, your body will fight off the thaldrin."

"And if it is?" Ovelia asked, her voice barely a whisper.

"Then 'twas an honor all too brief to have known the great Bloodbreaker," Garin said. "You're far lovelier than the tales give you credit. And just as tough."

Ovelia smiled, then immediately choked and spat. The enormous pain inside subsided to a dull ache. Dizziness came over her and she felt dark oblivion coming again. She groaned.

"Pain?" Garin's earlier nonchalance vanished in concern.

"Hunger." She wiped sweat from her face. "I feel... shaky."

"Sweet-soul withdrawal," said Garin. "It'll take time to fight off the addiction."

Ovelia shook her head, wondering. "Thaldrin means 'inevitable dark,' and yet you found a way to cure it," she said. "Like magic."

"Chemics," Garin said. "I countered the thaldrin, but I can do little to reverse its effects. Nor can I do anything about the sweet-soul: You need rest to recover your strength, if you ever will."

"Not an option. I—" Ovelia tried to get up, only to fall back to bed. "What?"

"I thought you might feel that way," Garin said. "Hence I added a touch of something to put you to sleep. Just for a bit."

"You—" Weariness was claiming her. "You villain."

"Indeed."

Ovelia thought of Regel, and hoped he was faring better than she. Regel... She put her hand to her throat, touching only bare skin. "My things. Did you find them?"

Garin's face grew troubled. "If you mean your sword, Lady, then no."

Ovelia shook her head. It hardly mattered to her anymore. "My necklace?"

"I didn't want you to strangle in your sleep." He reached into his shirt pocket and pulled out the carved dragon necklace she had worn. "What is it? The dragon of Dracaris?"

"Something of the sort."

She took Regel's carving and ran her fingers over it. Then she reached up behind her and set the carving on the godshelf behind her pillow, next to half a dozen carvings done in the same hand. She smiled wanly as the waking world faded.

"Rest, Lady," Garin said, brushing an errant lock of crimson hair out of her eyes. He touched the warpick at his belt. "No harm will come to you in my care. I swear it."

"I believe you," she said, or perhaps she trailed off. "But Sem..."

Silence and sleep filled her.

THIRTY-FOUR

Regel led the way silently through the tunnels that had once been his
kingdom. When he had come this way with Davargorn, he had purposefully
led them along a confusing, circuitous path. The youth must have followed the
ward, as Regel had expected, for they found no sign of him. By contrast, Regel
led the princess on an indirect path toward the palace: a series of shortcuts and
sharp turns he had used in his youth. They ducked wandering Ravalis guards
twice, taking shelter in alcoves and secret hiding places Regel knew as well as his
own body. The soldiers apparently patrolled the tunnels, but they seemed just as
lost as Davargorn would be and could easily be eluded.

Wordlessly, Semana followed behind. She wore again the black leathers that
stank of decades of blood and death, the flying boots and shielding breastplate, the
storing belt, the gauntlets with their slaying power, and the death's head mask with
its Plaguefire. Arrayed like a warrior the night before a great battle, the sorcerer
strode toward Demetrus with a purpose that made Regel wonder if she had intended
this all along. Whether she had planned every step of this scheme from the start.

He had two irreconcilable images in his mind—one of Semana, one of Mask—
and whenever he tried to speak to her, they reared up and choked off his words.
In her armor, Semana didn't look quite the same as Mask had: the Ravalis had
stripped her of the bindings she'd worn beneath the armor before, so her breasts
swelled the leather just enough to betray her womanly figure. But in that armor,
beneath that mask, she was still the sorcerer to him—sexless and deadly. It would
take a will of iron to manipulate Regel and Ovelia and Davargorn as she had, let
alone take the place of an infamous sorcerer-slayer for five years. He wondered if
he had ever known Semana Denerre at all.

"Will you speak to me?" Regel murmured when they hid from a third troop
of soldiers. The summermen trudged on, pining for hearthfires and lovers that
awaited them elsewhere.

"About what?" She still spoke with Mask's rasping voice, even if the time for
deception had passed. He wondered if it was simply habit, or it had become her
voice for true.

They came to the corridor that passed the central chamber where Lan had
ambushed them. Regel found it ironic but appropriate their path had led them
this way. Ruin hung heavy about these chambers, and they had come to do its
work—or, at least, Semana had.

They had come to the uppermost of the crypts, and a short flight of steps led
to the secret corridors. They had come out, ironically, just below the furnace
room in which Lan had laid his trap. At the top of the stairs, the door stood
slightly ajar.

"Hold, Princess," he said, but Semana walked right past him.

The sorcerer slapped the door off its hinges with the magic of her silver gauntlet. Inside, she raised the talons of her fire gauntlet, ready to slay any attacker. "Empty," she said sharply.

The chamber was hollow as a tomb and devastated as though by a whirlwind. Overthrown furniture and the shattered bits of a chair lay scattered about the floor. Had their battle caused such devastation? Regel could not say for sure. Blood was everywhere: spattered on the walls, streaked across the sheets, pooled to mark where Lan had killed Serris. Had Ovelia suffered a similar fate in this very place? Regel saw no bodies, which was reassuring. There should have been soldiers here, though.

"My carving," Regel said. "Do you have it?"

Semana looked at him blankly. "Why?"

Regel shook his head. He stooped, picked up one of the pieces of chair, and focused upon it, searching for an image in the wood. His senses expanded, though they were not as sharp as they would have been with a nigh-finished carving. Ovelia had been here, and Lan as well. He could smell the particular tang of sweat and blood. He could follow the course of their battle through the destroyed room. All the blood was hers: Ovelia hadn't shed any Ravalis blood during the battle, which would have summoned Vhaerynn and meant her death. She could still be alive.

But where had they gone?

"Move on," Semana said. "Time wastes away."

"I'm searching for clues," Regel said. "We must be cautious. If we move too fast—"

"Burn your clues and sear your caution," Semana said. "Lead me to Demetrus."

But Regel shook his head. "No."

"No?" The word skirted the line between shocked and enraged.

"This vengeance is folly," Regel said. "You stand to gain nothing except your own death—and most likely mine. Better that we turn aside and live."

Semana seemed to grow taller in her indignation. "Says the man who sacrificed everything to seek vengeance for a dead girl."

"That was justice, and it is a different thing," Regel said. "You may not understand this, but vengeance will only make your emptiness the greater."

Semana looked at him long and hard, then reached back and unbuckled the fasteners of her mask, which she dropped carelessly. Her face was haggard—her eyes puffy—but her silvery hair was luminous in the furnace room. "I am naked without that mask." She quaked. "Look into my face."

Hers was the beauty of a winter's dawn. Regel saw the mother in the daughter. It was stronger than any magic she could have worked upon him.

"You cannot know how Demetrus has hurt me," she said, her eyes welling. "He took everything from me. Destroyed my family and stole my crown. I have spent five years planning this, and now, at the last, I need your help. You and I, avenging the Blood of Winter."

Semana averted her eyes and sank to one knee. Tears flowed freely now.

"Please do not take this chance from me." She laid his hands on his calves and looked up at him, her lips trembling. "Please, for my mother's sake."

In that moment, it was almost like Lenalin asking him for aid.

Almost.

"I told you yestereve," Regel said, "that I was done being manipulated by you."

Instantly, Semana's tears ceased their flow, and her pleading visage became as stone. She looked, if anything, disappointed. The transition was so abrupt, Regel felt a shiver at the base of his spine.

"You're as fine an actress as Ovelia," he said.

"Better." She rose, her voice a chill wind, and smiled without mirth. "If you'll not serve your Princess, must I force you to serve her Mask?" She raised her clawed gauntlet, which glowed cherry red with heat. She held her mask in her left hand.

"Semana." Regel was keenly aware he lacked a weapon. Davargorn had taken all the blades when he ran off. "I intend to help you. I merely wish to know how and why first."

Semana considered him, then lowered her talon. "Very well," she said. "Give me your word, and I will tell you whatever you wish to know."

"You have it," Regel said. "Demetrus will die this night."

Semana nodded. "Ask your questions then, and be quick."

"Was this your plan all along?" Regel asked. "To murder me?"

"What?" Semana reacted with a touch of surprise that lent veracity to her words. However great an actress she had become, she could not school her reactions perfectly. "I never wanted to hurt *you*, Regel. You were my greatfather's loyal man."

"How would you know?" he asked. "His own First Shield slew him. Why would you believe better of his shadow?"

"I..." She shook her head. "You won't believe me when I say this. You'll think I'm a fool girl."

"I know you aren't," Regel said. "Try."

"That night, five years ago," Semana said. "What you said to me, on the balcony outside the king's hall."

"That was you?" Regel understood fully, though: Semana must have become Mask before they'd faced one another outside the king's chambers. Scared and confused, because she'd just been attacked.

Semana nodded. "You accused Mask of killing the princess—killing *me*," she said. "The anger in your words, and the sheer hate in your eyes... I knew you were loyal. You had nothing to do with the attack. If we'd had another moment, I might have revealed myself to you. But—"

Regel nodded, but whether it was because her words were believable or because he wanted to believe her, he couldn't say. "And Ovelia? I might be loyal, but you would murder *her* in a heartbeat?"

Semana sighed. "Regel—"

"You sent Davargorn to Tar Vangr to lure her to Luether, that you might kill her," he said. "You expect me to believe that was your only plan?"

"Of course not," she said. "But I never expected she would bring *you*. You, who have so much reason to hate her. I did not know how she felt about Mask— whether she would think him friend, enemy, or the like—but I knew how you felt about her. Or, at least, how you *should* have felt—unless you were her accomplice." She put up her hands. "What else was I to think, but that you were a traitor as well? It wasn't until we faced each other, in the temple of Aertem, that I saw your loyalty to the Winter King and improvised this new plan..."

"To turn our steel against the Usurper," Regel said. "So that we would kill him or we would die, and you would triumph regardless."

"Just so." Semana nodded. "You were a means to an end, and I am sorry that I used you, Regel, but I had no one to trust."

"You had the boy," Regel said.

"Tith—" Semana's face grew dark. "Davargorn is none of your concern."

"Is he your lover?"

"That is *truly* none of your concern," she said.

Regel nodded. That was more than fair. "And what of Ovelia?" he asked.

"What *of* her?" Semana's eyes turned red, and Regel thought it was a mark of all the deadly magic she carried. She had become Mask, whether she meant it or not.

"You played her," Regel said. "That night on the *Avenger*, you showed her your face to win her loyalty. You played upon her love for you, and now you've played her to her doom."

She drew herself up. "I did as I had to."

Regel clenched his fist. "She gave up everything for you, and you would abandon her?"

"She killed my greatfather, Regel, and Paeter as well." Semana scowled. "I loathed the man, but he was still my father, and Ovelia slew them both in one night. You cannot imagine how I hate her."

"Semana."

"I hate her." Seemingly without her awareness, Semana had begun to float into the air, borne aloft by the smoking magic of her boots. "I *hate* her."

"But you do not understand—"

"No—*you* do not understand."

Invisible force danced from Semana's silver-wrapped fingers and seized his body, holding him fast and unmoving. Semana floated above him, and a storm was on her face.

"I am Mask," she said. "A blade forged for battle, death taken flesh. My hands are soaked in the blood of decades."

"You are not," Regel said, struggling to breathe. "Mask wouldn't have saved us."

279

"Saved you? Is that what you think?" she asked. "I never—"

"Right here, in Lan's chambers, when we walked into an ambush." Regel gasped. "You had won. You could have let us die... but you saved us. You could have killed Lan, but you did not. Instead, you showed your face and surrendered your chance for vengeance. Why?"

Semana floated silently, her fingers clutched into fists. The darkness in the chamber made her face look just as much a mask as the leathern one she'd left on the floor.

"Who am I, then?" she asked. "Who am I, if not Mask?"

"You are Semana Denerre," he said weakly. "Princess of the Blood of Winter. *My* princess."

The magic in her boots subsided, and she floated down to the floor. She bent to one knee, and at first he thought she would help him rise. Instead, her hand went to the fallen mask, and Regel felt Plaguefire claw its way into his middle. His guts felt like they were rotting.

"Names change, Regel Oathbreaker." She reclaimed the mask and rose. "The past falls to Ruin, and the world moves." She pressed the mask to her face. "Dust and shadow, no? Isn't that what you say?"

"Wait—" Regel said, lungs heaving, but it was too late. Semana donned the mask and fastened the buckles. The last princess of Winter was lost.

"I don't need you," she said. "I see you're just another broken tool."

Mask turned aside and touched a hidden catch on the wall to open the secret corridor. Of course she would know the palace as well as he did—it had been her home all those years, had it not? And Semana had ever been as adventurous as her mother. The same fatal flaw.

"Wait," Regel said. "I—"

Mask passed into the darkness, leaving Regel fighting for air on the cold stone floor.

THIRTY-FIVE

OVELIA CAME OUT OF the darkness to find Garin cleaning her bloody skin with a moist cloth. His touch was delicate but firm, with none of the awkward hesitation of a man touching a naked woman he does not know. It reassured her.

He saw her eyes flickering and smiled reassuringly. "You're awake—excellent."

"How... how long?" Ovelia asked faintly.

"A few moments," he said. "Long enough for me to collect supplies and to clean you a bit." He gestured at a tunic and breeches he'd laid over the foot of the bed. "I might have dressed you, but—"

"It wouldn't be *proper*?" Ovelia eyed him dubiously.

"Indeed." Garin grinned. "You'll need clothes, unless you plan to stagger around naked—not that I would object, mind. A Lady's choice must be respected."

Ovelia forced herself to sit up, which let the blanket that covered her fall away, and Garin averted his eyes politely as she slipped into the tunic he'd brought. There was a dull weakness in her belly—not pain, but she knew what it meant. Even now, her fingers were awkward—grasping and catching at the tunic like half-dead things. Part of that was the thalarin, though she suspected just as much was the withdrawal. "Give me the sweet-soul."

His mirthful expression turned suddenly very serious. "That's too dangerous. You're gaming with your life if you take this again." Garin turned but kept his eyes politely on hers. He had her vial of sweet-soul in his hands. "Alcarin will return soon and then we'll get you to a proper chiurgeon, at least."

She gave him a dubious look. "A healer for the Bloodbreaker, foe to Winter and Summer alike?"

"A healer loyal to me," Garin said. "I am the Shroud of Tar Vangr, after all."

"Until they find out about your treachery."

"Not the shortest tenure history has ever known," Garin said. "Two hundred years ago..."

"Enough." Ovelia tried her best to suppress her shivering. "Is my aid worth so much to you? You would turn against your Blood just for another sword?"

"Hardly that." Garin turned, his chin high. "That day in Luether, when I saw you and Regel—"

"So you *did* know us," Ovelia said. "I thought perhaps my disguise fooled you."

"Don't deflect." Garin smiled slyly. "I should have killed you both, but I did not. Why do you think that was?"

"You've a kind heart?" Ovelia shook her head. "What is it you want from me?"

"Hardly." He put his fists on the desk and leaned forward. "I love Luether. I saw in you—both of you—a strength that has nothing to do with Blood. You were otherwise engaged then, but now..."

281

"Now I can help you instead."

"Yes." Garin crossed to her and knelt to put her hand to his lips. "Come with me," he said. "Come with me to Luether."

"You're going back?" Ovelia blinked, stunned. "But you said yourself, you're the Shroud of Tar Vangr. Once I am gone, you can pretend you never saw me. You can go back to being a loyal fox."

"Loyal to a family that hates what I am? No." Garin shook his head. "I came to get more warriors and more weapons, and in you, I have all I need. Your magic, your skill, your heart. You are the one."

It all sounded fantastic, but Ovelia had witnessed stranger wonders. "Why would you trust me?"

"I am an excellent judge of character." When Ovelia frowned, Garin chuckled. "I have seen you fight, and I would take you at my side before I took a hundred of my uncle's Dustblades."

"Flatterer." Ovelia stretched, and her body protests with a chorus of aches. She felt thin and all but used up. "My body may not last the night, and I won't do you much good after."

"Let me worry about that," Garin said. "Say you'll come with me. Be my sworn shield."

Ovelia saw herself reflected across the room in the small mirror over the basin. Her hair burned like fiery blood in the silvered glass. She was young again, being entrusted with a great honor: another royal heir to protect, another city to redeem.

But beside the glass was a portrait she kept—a portrait she used to gaze on every morn. The woman was lovely and young, her hair silver and her eyes a deep, steel-gray. The portrait was of Lenalin, but in that moment she saw only Semana. Ovelia would never abandon her.

"Very well," she said. "But there is something I must do first. Something that is as important to me as redeeming Luether is to you."

"I thought it might come to this." Garin looked uneasy. "You need rest."

"There's no time." Ovelia held out her shaking hand. She could no longer hide her body's reaction to withdrawal. "Give me the sweet-soul."

Garin hesitated, but ultimately he held forth the vial. Not putting it in her hand—that was wisdom. She extended her tongue and he laid two bitter drops on it. A blissful softness chased the foul taste. She wanted to insist on more, but she still had the strength of will to resist. Quickly, her body started to relax.

"This will serve." She patted her breeches. "Turn around."

Garin did as she instructed. "I expected you would not listen to reason. I told you I was an excellent judge."

"And are you going to stop me?" Ovelia fumbled the breeches on. "Again?"

"I suspect that would be an exercise in vanity." Garin tapped the warpick on the nearby table. "I'm coming with you. To aid you on your task, and to protect my investment."

Ovelia nodded. "There will be fighting. You may have to kill your own kin."

"I will do what I must." Beside the warpick lay a sheathed sword and belt, which he took up. "It's not your Bloodsword—I don't know where they're keeping that—but you need steel."

"I may be too weak to wield it," Ovelia said.

"Regardless." Garin knelt to wind the belt around her hips. "You never know."

"No." Ovelia looked over his head at the portrait of Lenalin again. "You never do."

When Garin had buckled the sword belt on Ovelia, he crossed to the door. Before she followed, she laid her fingers on the portrait of her long-dead friend. "If someone had told me fifteen years ago that I'd be standing here, and you long gone," she whispered. "I'd have broken that man's nose, sister."

Garin paused at the door and looked back. "Ovelia?"

"Aye." She nodded to Garin. "Aye, I'm coming."

THIRTY-SIX

WHEN TITHIAN DAVARGORN AWOKE, surrounded in corpses, a dozen guards in crimson tabards trimmed in blue stood over him, swords drawn, staring down without comprehension. This was the third group, or perhaps the fourth. These men were Ravalis—the ones who had taken Semana away from him. And he would kill all of them.

They hesitated, and so he struck with impunity.

The first man went down to a twisted left fist that slammed into his ear, and Davargorn drew his belt-dagger to slash out the throat of a second before the others could even cry out.

Then they were on him, striking from all sides.

Davargorn felt the thrusts and cuts but didn't care. He slashed and wheeled amongst the men for position. One of the magically-charged blades hit hard enough to send him staggering with a burst of force, but he flew with the blast and let it carry him into another victim. He grasped the man's arm, ripped out his throat with his dagger—or was that his teeth?—and seized a sword that crackled with magic.

As he cut and hacked, blood sizzled across the ground. It flowed, seemingly of its own accord, into the pool of blood Davargorn had left against the wall. The pool shivered and began to swell upward into the corridor. He'd been fighting so long he'd taken to imagining things. He ignored it and fought on, cutting men down like a scythe cleaving grain.

Finally, Davargorn drew back to run a staggered guardsman through, and abruptly his arm froze in place. He looked around, snarling, but there was no one to hold him. His arm was not his own. Then the flat of his own blade smashed into his face and blood burst from his nose. The blade came in again, then twice more, before finally he sagged to the bloody stones below.

The guards tried to take advantage of his inaction, but they did not seem able to move either. They stood like statues with terrified faces.

Davargorn could only watch as a man rose from the blood pooled on the floor. He pulled himself out as though climbing from a hole in the stone and stood over Davargorn, gaunt but imposing, his eyes shot through with cords of coagulated crimson. He held the golden blade of the Aza in his hand.

"Did you think I would not remember the taste of your blood, Tithian Davargorn?" asked Vhaerynn the necromancer. "It makes me hunger."

Davargorn could not speak, only glare.

The necromancer turned to the guard Davargorn had wounded but not slain. Vhaerynn smiled as he laid his hand on the man's chest. "Peace," he crooned to the terrified guard. "This will end soon." In his other hand, he raised his knife.

Even Davargorn winced at the squelch of steel into flesh as Vhaerynn stabbed the wicked blade into the guard's chest. The man gurgled, and his flesh turned gray and wasted away like dust. His body shriveled into a skeleton in a heartbeat, as though he had been dead for years. Crimson mist leaked from the withered husk, which Vhaerynn inhaled like the aroma of a sweet wine.

"Not enough," Vhaerynn said as the man's body sloughed to the floor. "I need more."

The other guards who had survived Davargorn's assault burbled and cried out in terror, but they could not escape or fight back. Why had the necromancer left their voices free? Perhaps he enjoyed the sounds they made. Efficiently, Vhaerynn strode amongst them, killing each and absorbing their essence. When all were dead, the necromancer turned back to Davargorn with a smile like that of a satisfied hunting cat. His blood-smeared dagger gleamed in the torchlight.

"You've something to say?" Vhaerynn waved, loosing Davargorn's throat.

"Very well." Davargorn resolved to face death with courage. "Feed upon me, monster."

"Oh, I'll not kill you, Tithian Davargorn." Vhaerynn stretched languidly. "You might prove useful, and I would hate to waste you."

"Useful?" Davargorn said.

"I had thought you would stand beside your princess whore and her warders, but it seems not," Vhaerynn said. "How she needs you at her side."

Semana, Davargorn realized. He meant Semana. "But—but my princess is dead."

"She is not." Vhaerynn smiled. "The Lord of Tears knew she lived, and he tricked you away from her. Would you have your revenge?"

Davargorn struggled against Vhaerynn's magic, but the power was just too strong. "Free me," he said. "And I will strike as you command."

Vhaerynn looked upward, as though he could see through the metal walls and the tons of stone above the maze of ancient tunnels. "The king calls, blood to blood," he said. "But I will not answer."

"I don't understand," Davargorn said.

"Let there be an end to it," Vhaerynn said. "An end to Summer and to Winter. Let the Blood that rules the World of Ruin be that of *real* power."

Davargorn sensed the treachery Vhaerynn meant, but he couldn't put it all together. No matter. He was a threat to Semana and had to die. Davargorn would do what he asked, and betray him.

"Free me," Davargorn said. "I can help you. You said so yourself."

The necromancer wasn't listening. With all his will, Davargorn fought against the blood magic paralyzing his limbs. If only he could—

Then magic swelled, spreading across his whole body, and Davargorn gagged.

Vhaerynn glanced ruefully over his shoulder at him. "Come now," he chided. "You think I cannot feel your heart beat and know when you lie?"

Davargorn felt Vhaerynn's power lift him up against his will, like a giant hand closed tight around him. Over his closed fist, the necromancer smiled. The magic slammed Davargorn into the wall, then the ceiling, where Vhaerynn held him. Agony ripped through his limbs and he could not draw breath. The magic squeezed until he thought his eyes would pop from their sockets.

"I shall enjoy your princess's screams for mercy while I take her," Vhaerynn said. "Just as I have taken you."

"Se-Semana," Davargorn said, eyes leaking bloody tears.

Vhaerynn hurled him against the back wall, and he knew bone-splintering blackness.

ACT FIVE: BLOOD

HIGH IN THE COLD stone palace, he felt it.

He felt it in the press of the blood against the walls of his veins. He felt it in nearby bodies, pulses racing as if in sympathy with the blood-letting to come.

Vhaerynn, the last Necromancer and greatest sorcerer in Tar Vangr, loved it.

The old man paused in the corridor outside his prince's rut chamber, stopped in his tracks by a swell of hatred that saturated him like a draught of strong-wine. Delicious and deadly. Vhaerynn smiled.

Death stirred in the City of Steel this night, prophesying the disaster about to unfold. For those trained in the ways of blood magic, the anticipation of death was the sweetest of drugs, and it filled Vhaerynn with such pleasure he almost forgot how to walk. He caught himself on a nearby endtable and savored the sensation, not merely for the taste but also for the world it would usher in its place. He had experienced an expectant rush this powerful only once before in recent memory: ten years past, when Paeter Ravalis had sent his wife on a shattering jaunt through a mirror. That event Vhaerynn hadn't expected, but he'd savored the taste of her bloodletting all the same. And this time, it would be worse.

The best part was that no one else knew. This doom, which seemed so obvious to him, passed them all as a vague unease. The more sensitive folk of the city might experience the resonance as night terrors that woke them screaming, but they would not know until the funeral bells rang the following morn. The Blood of Winter was doomed, but not alone.

Since he was a boy over a hundred years ago, Vhaerynn had known instinctively when to stand back and let Ruin take her course, or to step forward and participate in spreading death.

The door to Paeter's chambers opened, and the prince staggered out. His tunic was only half done and his breeches disheveled, as though he'd dressed himself in haste. Pain wet his eyes, and wounded pride suffused his swollen face, deepening its golden cast to a ruddy brown.

"Necromancer." The prince drew up to his full height in a juvenile attempt to cover his moment of vulnerability. "What do you want?"

The blood beating in Paeter's face called out to him, filling his mouth with the tang of salt and a touch of rot. The prince was old before his time, and tired. Appropriate, for a man marching to his death.

"Your highness." Vhaerynn bowed. "I heard you were not well, and came to offer my services."

Paeter blanched, which amused Vhaerynn. As chiurgeon to the Ravalis, the sorcerer's skills surpassed anything else Tar Vangr might offer, but unsurprisingly his treatments often involved bleeding the patient.

"I'm well enough," the prince said. "Just off to buy a whore or three. Care to join?"

Tempting. Vhaerynn was hungry—the blood growing thin within him. He would need to feast soon, and a lowly coin boy or street girl wouldn't be missed. Well, at least she wouldn't when the Ravalis came to power. Inexplicably, King Orbrin cared about such things.

"Oh no, my thanks," Vhaerynn said. "Why not bring your playthings to the palace? It is warmer here." He laid one bony hand on Paeter's shoulder. "Safer."

"Not while Orbrin sits upon the throne." Paeter shook him off. "Should I give him cause to question me? To muddy the succession? He has already exiled one of my blood. Nay, while my late wife's father rules and I play nursemaid to that ill-gotten bastard Semana, I must be the dutiful heir."

"Oh, I doubt that will be a problem for long," Vhaerynn said.

The Winter King's power had waned, and soon Demetrus could move against Orbrin. Without Orbrin's last heir, the Ravalis would face no obstacle in their path to the throne. The Summer Princes would prove easy enough to manipulate. Vhaerynn himself would set the Diadem of Winter upon Demetrus's brow, and behind the Summer King, the necromancer would find a warm shadow in which to work his will. But even that was simply the next step in a long path he had walked for many decades.

What he did was needful. There was no honor or justice to it, but such things did not matter. Ravalis, Denerre... A thousand Bloods like theirs had risen, boiled over, and drained away to nothing, and nothing ever changed. Ruin continued its relentless assault, and the world slipped deeper and deeper into darkness. But all that would change. One day, Vhaerynn—the last true wizard, heir of the Sorcerer-Kings of Calatan—would inherit the last of the mage-cities for his own. One day *soon*.

Paeter was looking at him curiously, and Vhaerynn realized the prince hadn't left—nor had Vhaerynn done what he had come to do. "Was there something else?" the prince asked.

"Only this." Vhaerynn traced his fingers across Paeter's bare chest, and the prince staggered back with a hiss of pain. Vhaerynn's touch had drawn blood. "Gird yourself, princeling. The hurt is not deep."

"What is this?" Paeter demanded.

Vhaerynn smiled. "You are important, highness. I seek only to protect you."

Paeter narrowed his eyes. "Explain."

"This ward links your blood to mine," Vhaerynn said. "Should you be assaulted, I will know and come save you from harm. Your blood will summon me when—*if* it is spilled."

Paeter didn't look convinced. "I need no protection, from you or anyone. Leave me."

"Ah, but your highness," Vhaerynn said. "Have you made no enemies? None who might seek vengeance for... perceived wrongs?" He glanced at Paeter's door, behind which he sensed two hearts beating: one in shame, one in hatred. The prince had finally ruined himself.

Paeter nodded. "Fine. Do it quickly, if you must. But you had best not deceive me, necromancer, or you will find out exactly how little my father values you."

The threats of spoiled children meant nothing to Vhaerynn. He endured, timeless in his power and purpose, and often he had to clear his path of those less worthy. He would cast the ward, but he had no intention of invoking it. Tonight, when death came for Paeter Ravalis, the prince would not find the fabled protection of the wielder of the Golden Blade of the Red King, the savior of a dying world. Instead, he would find only blood.

"This will hurt only a little," Vhaerynn said with a smile.

THIRTY-SEVEN

REGEL LAY IN THE prince's rut chamber, dying in a room that echoed with death. He could sense the doom this room had seen—could feel it building within him and without. Caught in the grip of Semana's Plaguefire, sweating corruption from every pore, he became part of that ruin. He was both its victim and its perpetrator. The pain weighed on him like a shroud of ice. The world turned hazy, as though the magic had drawn a film across his eyes.

He wanted to roll over and die, but instead he fought. He had to find a way. Semana needed him.

Somehow, he felt warm.

The veil over his eyes parted. His scarred leg groaned, but he forced it under him. He clutched a tapestry, ripping it half from the wall as he pulled. It held, and he managed his feet.

He didn't have the time to consider. Semana needed him.

～

Unarmed, Regel limped toward the throne room of the palace. He prayed to the Old Gods he was not too late. He had to stop for breath every few paces, but finally he found himself at the base of the stairs that led up through the secret tunnels to the great chamber at the height of the palace. The door let a crack of light onto the stairs. He climbed step by agonizing step.

Finally, Regel staggered into the throne room, only to find Semana—fully masked and rippling with Plaguefire—standing a dozen paces from King Demetrus as he sat cross-legged on his throne, his posture meditative. Around them sprawled the bodies of a dozen guardsmen, choking and gasping as sickly magic held them down. The king seemed unmoved: he faced his imminent death without emotion.

Demetrus Ravalis had been old thirty years ago, and he was ancient now. Despite or perhaps because of his age, the Summer King seemed just this side of indestructible. His body had grown tighter than iron shackles, his leathery skin hardened to stone over the decades. His still-sharp brown eyes had sunk deep in folds of brown skin around a powerful Ravalis nose. Gray stubble dusted his cheeks and chin. He'd gone mostly bald but kept his remaining hair neatly cropped. A hard man with a falcon's face. He was a patriarch among men, his life a lesson of perseverance.

And today would be the day that he died.

The great Hall of Denes, crown jewel of Tar Vangr, towered around Demetrus. The stained glass holding the World of Ruin at bay misted with the chamber's warmth, while the sun—just kissing the distant horizon—painted orange shadows through the room. As though impervious to any chill, Demetrus wore a light robe bare at the shoulder in the classic Luethaar style. He had set the crown of Tar Vangr on the arm of his throne and every so often tapped it thoughtfully with three fingers.

By contrast, Semana looked not at all calm. Her body trembled as she stood erect before the throne, shaking with barely restrained fury. Fire coursed around her war gauntlet, and smoke rose from her silver glove. With her mask on and ablaze with Plaguefire, she had become an angel of death. Every bit of her armor burned, alight with power, fueled by her own rage.

"Say that again, Usurper!" she cried.

Regel inclined his head to Demetrus. "Majesty," he said.

"Ah." The Summer King gazed at Regel through clear hazel eyes untouched by the rheum of age. "Regel Frostburn, King's Shadow. The summers have been kind to you."

"And the winters to you. A moment to compose myself, if you will."

Demetrus waved indolently, ignoring the inferno of magic that stood not a dozen paces away.

Semana rounded on Regel. "Stay out of this, Lord of Tears!"

Regel caught his breath and bowed to the king. "You know why we have come, Majesty?"

Demetrus shrugged. "Ours has been a reunion five years overdue. Your loyalty demands nothing less, and I respect that in a foe as well as a friend. And you are both of these things."

"Speak not to him, but answer *me*!" Semana cried. "I am the one who shall strike you down, Blood-traitor. I, who am—!"

Demetrus continued as though she had not spoken. "How may I serve you, Syr Frostburn?"

"I have left that name far behind, Majesty. I am the Lord of Tears now, and the Oathbreaker."

"To me, old friend, you will always be Regel," Demetrus said. "Do you object to this name?"

Semana gave Regel a curious look, which he tried to ignore. He would not call Demetrus a friend, but the two of them had known one another many decades. He supposed Demetrus might as well call him that. "If I may ask, Majesty," he said. "Where is your vizier—your necromancer?"

Demetrus cleared his throat. "Vhaerynn and I spend little time together. He loathes me, to tell you true. Though if yon puppy strikes me, I assure you he shall be with you straight." He traced the marks of fingernails that cut through his chest tattoo. Vhaerynn's blood ward.

Regel saw Semana bristle at the king's casual dismissal. Magic swelled around her fists—putrid Plaguefire that sent wisps of foul smoke into the air—but of course she knew she could not strike. After he issued that warning, Demetrus ignored her entirely. Was he confident in his necromancer's protection, or was it something else? The king's courage staggered him, and Regel was not a man easily impressed.

"Do you sleep well, Regel?" the king asked.

"Not very, Majesty," Regel said. "Such is the curse of age, no?"

"I sleep poorly, myself." Awkwardly, Demetrus took hold of one leg and crossed it over the other, then leaned his elbows on knee and ankle. It made him look relaxed but also very tired. "I pass my nights in meditation, rather than sleep. The Vangryur claim it is age—that my mind needs less rest than that of a younger man, but I think you and I know the truth."

"Regret," Regel said.

"Just so," Demetrus said. "Regret is the curse of living in a dying world. The more evil one has done, the more plentiful his nightmares."

Demetrus pushed himself to his feet. For a moment, it seemed he might fall, but his eyes were grim and his footing secure. The Summer King was not a man given to weakness.

"I have spent these nights waiting for death, and I will not meet it sleeping. And now—" He turned the full weight of his majesty on Regel. "Now you have come."

Regel bowed stiffly on his injured leg. "Apologies, Majesty, but you err," he said. "I have not come to kill you." He nodded to Semana. "*She* has."

"She?" Demetrus raised his chin imperiously. "This thing is meant to be a woman?"

Semana's hands clenched. "Justice," she said. "After all you have done to me and mine."

"You and yours." Demetrus scoffed. "So says a nameless rogue."

"*Nameless?*" Semana loosed a cry of anguish and fury. "You presume to tell me you do not know this face? The man who wore this mask before me?"

Demetrus scoffed. "I know none with a face of leather, man or woman."

"You lie," Semana said. "Five years ago, you sent Mask to spill the Blood of Winter."

Demetrus narrowed his eyes. "Slay me if you will, but insult me not," he said. "Orbrin Denerre was my friend and ally. I would never have done him harm."

"Liar!" Semana cried, her rough voice breaking into her own, softer tones. "All your wretched life, you've done nothing but lie and betray. That ends tonight."

"Again, you insult me," the king said amiably. "Who are you to speak thusly to a king?"

"A queen, Usurper!" Her hands shot to the buckles of her mask.

"Wait—" Regel started, but he could not cross to her fast enough to stop her.

Semana cast her mask at the king's feet, where it bounced twice and lay still.

"I am a queen," she said again. "Your *rightful* queen."

~

As they came to the second hidden door that opened to the throne room, Ovelia pulled up short and raised a hand to stop Garin. The world lurched drunkenly, but she kept her feet.

"What is it?" he asked. "I heard nothing."

Ovelia shook her head. It was as though she had seen warning in Draca's shadows, but of course she was not holding the sword. She saw the thrust of a king's knife, a blinding flash of magic, and blood. So much blood. She gestured to the door, and Garin went to listen.

"Voices," whispered the Ravalis prince. "My uncle, and the Lord of Tears."

Ovelia's heart leaped. "Regel?"

"There is another, as well," Garin said. "A woman I do not know. Young— very angry."

Ovelia shoved past Garin as best she could and shoved at the door, but it would not open. Her weakened fingers were too clumsy to open the catch.

"What is it?" Garin tried to catch her arm, but she shook him off. "Lady?"

She drew back from the door and looked to Garin. "Open it!"

"But Lady Dracaris, who knows how many—"

Ovelia slicked her hair back from her eyes and drew her borrowed sword. "Open it *now*."

~

When Semana took off the mask, Regel might have expected many things to cross Demetrus's placid features—surprise, confusion, anger, or even an unlikely joy at seeing his greatdaughter alive—but the king's expression remained blank. He stepped toward her and observed her imperiously, searching her tight frame from the crown of her silvery hair to the toe of her blood-stained black boots.

Then he laughed, and the sound echoed throughout the vast, empty chamber.

"I am to recognize a pale-headed waif in stinking leathers as my equal? Or— even better—as my liege?" Demetrus stepped around her, scrutinizing her from all sides, and came to stand between her and the throne, as before. "Truly, girl, you offer a fine jest."

"Do you—" Semana's voice quavered. "Do you not know your own Blood?"

"Oh, I know *you*, Semana Denerre." The king put his hands on her shoulders and met her gaze with eyes sharpened of steel. "Blood of Winter, aye, but no blood of *mine*."

By the Narfire, Regel thought. He *knows*.

Demetrus grasped Semana tight enough to leave bruises through the leather. "You are no Blood of mine," he said. "And never will a whore of muddied blood sit my throne."

Semana caught his wrist in her hand and the king straightened. "It's not your throne."

She raised her left hand, with the silver interlocking mesh glove, and her discarded mask rose into the air and shot to her hand. As soon as she caught it, greasy smoke flared around the mask. Green fire coursed through Semana's hand and into Demetrus's arm, causing the flesh near her black-wrapped fingers to rot before Regel's eyes, turning green-brown and shrinking in upon itself. Gray veins crept across Demetrus's face and his throat convulsed in time with his racing heart.

"Stop!" Regel grabbed for Semana's right arm.

Fire blazed, burning Regel's bare fingers black, but he broke Semana's grasp. Demetrus sagged back into his throne and Semana fell back a step, hungry withering magic trailing from her fingers.

Regel followed, holding her arms. "Stop this, Semana!" he shouted.

"*Mask*," she corrected, black magic pulsing behind her eyes. Plaguefire bit into him, flowing into his arms and sucking at his life. "This man murdered my family, and tried to do the same to me," she said, her voice cold. "Now stand away, or you can die with him!"

"Enough of this." Demetrus drew a knife from under his robes. Regel stepped in front of Semana, but the king barely looked at them. Instead, he cut open the scabbed wound on his palm from the revel. His blood dripped onto the stone at his feet. "Vhaerynn Lifedrinker, come forth."

Regel tensed, ready to spring at the first sign of the vizier.

A moment passed. Demetrus's blood pooled at his feet. No sorcerer came forth.

"Treachery," Demetrus breathed. "I am undone."

"Treachery on all sides." Semana raised her burning gauntlet toward Regel where he stood, strength eroding under her magic's assault. "Stand away."

Despite the Plaguefire, Regel stood firm. His breath came in wisps and his heart thundered. "I will not," he said. "You could not kill Lan, nor Ovelia, nor me. You are *not* Mask."

"*Traitor!*" Magic boiled around her and green lightning roared forth to smite Regel. He felt the power pulling away at his heart, far worse than in the corridors below.

"Stop," he whispered. "Semana... you can't..."

"Damn your 'can' and 'can't'," the princess cried. "I will do as I must, and you have no right—*none!*—to tell me otherwise."

Regel sank to his knees. "Stop," he said. "Stop this now, you spoiled, *stupid* child!"

Semana's face went white. "You dare?" she cried. "By what right do you rebuke me?"

"I rebuke you"—Regel's lips parted—"as your father."

Semana's eyes went wide.

A shadow loomed over them.

~

The door finally opened and Ovelia staggered into the grand chamber, clutching her midsection with her free arm. She bit back the pain and looked toward the throne.

She saw what would happen before it came to pass. There knelt Regel and Semana, staring at one another, and there stood Demetrus, a naked blade in his hand. Where his guards or his court sorcerer were, Ovelia couldn't begin to guess. Semana's back was to him, her attention on the kneeling Regel, who seemed to be in the grip of her Plaguefire. The king's knife glinted as it rose high. She saw herself, falling to her knees, stabbed through, Semana in her arms.

The blood of Draca did not lie.

"Semana!" Ovelia ran toward them. The world seemed to drag.

The princess turned her silver-blonde head, and Ovelia saw her hazel eyes gleaming. Ovelia came between the king and the princess and caught Semana by the shoulders. She plastered herself over the young woman like a living shield.

The knife cut across the intervening space and plunged into Ovelia's back. She saw more than felt the point burst from her chest. She watched it stop before it could open Semana's neck.

She had made it.

The two women looked into each other's eyes—eyes of the same hazel hue.

Then the knife wrenched out of Ovelia's back and pain erupted in its wake. The king pulled the blood-smeared blade high to strike again—but Regel appeared and caught Demetrus's raised hand.

Ovelia slid to her knees, dragging Semana down with her, their eyes still locked. The princess tried to pull away, but Ovelia held her. One black-wrapped hand broke free to touch Ovelia's shoulder, a touch infused with joy and melancholy. At last, Ovelia thought. At last she had done it.

Semana's eyes turned red.

At that instant, there was a flash of light—sucking green radiance that stole her breath—and Ovelia was thrown backward to crunch against the wall. She arched taut against the stone, her flesh burning, and fell limply to the floor. Her feet sprawled, her legs like boneless rags, and her head lolled. Smoke rose around her vision, and the world crisped away. Her eyes were on fire.

There, over the smoke that rose from her numb body, Ovelia saw Semana standing in the center of the room by the throne of Tar Vangr, her outstretched hand wreathed in a green storm. Her stance was stricken, and her eyes terrified. To Ovelia's faltering vision, the fire grew brighter and turned silver as she became a mere silhouette, poised between the World of Ruin and its utter destruction or rebirth.

The world burned away.

THIRTY-EIGHT

As Ovelia took the blade for Semana, Regel moved without thinking. He caught Demetrus's arm as he pulled the knife back for another strike. It was easy—too easy—to turn the blade and bury it in the king's stomach.

"Betrayed on all sides," Demetrus said.

They stood together, he and the king, entwined in a murderous embrace. Demetrus smiled, his teeth fringed in spittle, his eyes wide and terrible. His insides shuddered, as though something had come alive around the wound—something not of his own body. Regel released him, and Demetrus sank back onto his throne.

"Did I not promise?" the king murmured. "Strike, and he would be with you straight."

There was a flash of green light over Regel's shoulder. He glanced back to see Ovelia thrown away from Semana, only to slump against the far wall, her face on fire. Semana gasped where she stood within a tempest of sickly green lightning. As Regel watched, Semana drew back her crackling hand and stared down at it, a mixture of shock and disbelief on her face.

"Semana," Regel said, reaching toward her. "It's—"

"No." She turned toward him, eyes blazing with uncontrolled magic. "*No!*"

Regel threw himself aside, and the bolt of force she sent toward him instead caught Demetrus on his throne. The magic split him apart like a butchered hog. Blood spattered the grey stone.

"No!" Semana looked down at her hands as though they weren't parts of her body at all. "I didn't mean—" Then she fell to her knees, struggling against sobs and against the slaying magic she could barely control. "Stop it! Stop!"

Not knowing what to say, Regel stepped toward Ovelia, but Garin Ravalis appeared between them, his warpick drawn. "Stay back!" he said.

"Why would she do that?" Semana moaned. "She hates me. She—"

Garin stood protectively over Ovelia. "I thought you were her ally," he said to Regel. "But now I see you were using her as much as anyone."

Regel might have spoken, but a dull laugh from behind caught Garin's attention. Regel lunged forward at the opportunity and smashed the pommel of the king's dagger into Garin's forehead. The Shroud collapsed and Regel turned back to the throne, blade up and ready to throw.

Demetrus's body was writhing on the throne. At first, Regel thought the king must have clung to some spark of life despite the destruction Semana's power had wreaked, but then he realized the movement was not from the king but from *inside* him. As he watched, Demetrus's chest parted to admit a pair of grasping, clutching hands. A man pulled himself free of the torn corpse and stepped down from the throne. He wore a black robe—now dampened by a sea of blood—and his black beard stuck to his chest. His fingers and nose dripped gore, as did a gold-bladed knife he held idly in one hand.

"Vhaerynn." Regel brandished Demetrus's bloody dagger between them.

"Regel Oathbreaker." The necromancer looked to the corpse of Demetrus strewn over the throne. "It seems the king is dead, and I think Ovelia Dracaris slew his heir. Alas, what a tragedy." He plucked up the Diadem of Winter. "But Tar Vangr shall endure. I shall see to it."

Regel understood his tone. "You wanted us to succeed."

"Did I?" Vhaerynn set the crown on his own head.

"You lured us here, and gave us the tools to kill Demetrus," Regel said. "That was why you left the armor for me to find. So that we'd assassinate the king and you'd keep your hands clean."

"Do they look clean, Regel Oathbreaker?" Vhaerynn wiped blood from his face and examined it on his fingertips. "My only crime was not answering when the first drop of his royal blood called to me. When more of it was spilled and the call grew louder, of course I came. Alas, I seem to have answered too late for him." He turned back, his eyes suddenly boiling red pits. "Not too late for you, however."

Regel started to throw his blade but Vhaerynn's magic was faster. The court sorcerer twisted his hand upward into the air and Regel froze, his arm craned back.

"That's my arm now, Oathbreaker," Vhaerynn said, flicking his fingers. "Or should I name you Bloodbreaker as well?"

Operating by its own will, Regel's arm shot around, aiming to bury the dagger in his own belly. He stopped it with his other arm, but the enchantment gave his limb impossible strength. Its force knocked him to the floor, where he strained to hold back from gutting himself.

"This is what you should have done when Orbrin died—joined your blood to his in the uncaring dirt." Vhaerynn stepped toward him. "You will not long outlive *this* king, however."

Regel clenched his teeth and fought against the invasion of his body with every ounce of his will, but it was not enough. Then he saw Semana stand up behind Vhaerynn, her gauntlets alive with magic.

Vhaerynn raised his head and sniffed, as though scenting the air. "A fine jest," he said. "Your blood tastes so similar to that of my old friend. But no." He shot out a hand, his fingers glowing red so that the bones showed through his flesh. "You are not Mask, little girl."

Semana cried out as her right arm—no longer under her control—jerked aloft and the jet of flame she'd meant for Vhaerynn instead cut into the darkened ceiling. Her legs slipped her control and threw themselves out from under her. She crashed heavily to the floor.

"Leave her be!" Regel cried.

"Hmm." Vhaerynn waved his free hand at Regel. Abruptly, his arm stopped trying to kill him. Instead, pain ripped through him as his blood thickened in his veins. With a gurgle, Regel collapsed and curled into an agonized ball.

"Fascinating," the necromancer said. "You are not Mask, yet you have his power."

"Was it you?" Semana demanded, sweat beading on her brow. "You know this armor—this magic. Did *you* send that creature to slay me?"

Vhaerynn looked nonplussed. "I know not your face or your tale." He swept his hand down, and Semana rose to her knees like a poorly directed puppet. "Why would I send a creature as elegant as Mask to slay a common slut who does not know her place?"

Semana's right gauntlet, boiling with fire, twisted toward her face, and Regel could see her struggle to control it. Veins appeared on her pale face, and cords stood out across her neck. Somehow, she took control of her left hand with the silver gauntlet, which she turned toward the necromancer. Desperately, she cut her hand across the air between herself and Vhaerynn—the way she had in the temple with her invisible blade. The necromancer waved the magic away like an irritating fly.

"Do you not know me, sorcerer?" Straining, Semana slashed again with her free hand.

"Should I?" Vhaerynn asked, countering her stroke without effort. "I know that you are stupid, if you would use a child's art against a master."

He snapped his fingers, and Semana's head jerked aside. When she turned back, blood ran from her nose and her lip—blood that danced under Vhaerynn's whim. She bore no outward sign of a strike, as though the blow had come from within her own body.

"I am Semana Denerre, your rightful queen," she said. "You owe me your—"

Another of those internal slaps sent Semana's face to the other side. Her ears were bleeding now, matting her silvery hair to the sides of her head. Her words cut off in a moan.

"I see no queen here—only a murdered king," said Vhaerynn, standing over her. "And though I hardly mind the deed, now you will die for it, you disgusting child."

"Idle threats." Semana fought to move her arm. "Is this your greatest power, burned one?"

"Hardly."

Vhaerynn's eyes flashed bright red. He raised his hands and closed his fingers, as though to crush her between them. Semana arched up on her toes, her whole body straining as though crushed from within. She moaned aloud and blood ran from her eyes like tears.

This was the end, and Regel knew it.

Ovelia lay unmoving two paces from him, her chest burned through by Semana's magic. Her blackened face was turned toward Regel, and her crimson hair fell across her features like a funeral shroud. He remembered her now as she had been: a spirited girl who would suffer no insult, either to herself or to her mistress. The day they first met, when he had known no name—before he had even been Regel—he and Ovelia had dueled. He had defeated her handily, but she had tackled him afterward and pounded blood from his face. He remembered her red hair hanging over her vivid eyes like copper suns...

Her eyes. Regel realized her eyes were open. They were glazed and sightless, but also alive.

"Ovelia," he said.

Her eyes blinked, and her lips formed a word he could not make out.

"I poisoned you," Regel said. "I am sorry."

Ovelia's head shook. Her hand grasped his, and she spoke to him in words that he could not miss, even through the sounds of the mageduel. "Help her," Ovelia said. "Help my child."

Semana, Regel thought. She meant Semana, the child she had loved and protected all these years—the one she would die to keep from harm.

"I cannot," Regel said. "The necromancer... Vhaerynn has us both."

Ovelia smiled wanly. "The moment comes," she said, her voice weary. "I see it. Semana—"

Then her eyes closed and she trailed off.

"Ovelia." Regel squeezed her hand tight. "Ovelia!"

A curse caught his attention. Vhaerynn had sworn by the Narfire. Regel looked around, and what he saw gave him pause. The court sorcerer was standing over Semana, one arm raised aloft to fuel his control of her body, but Regel saw sweat streaming down his forehead. A burst of magic struck him and sent him back a pace, and the Diadem of Winter flew from his head. Vhaerynn's expression was one of frustration and wonder. "Why do you not fall, girl?"

Blood running down her chin, Semana had raised her arm as though to fend him off. There was no hint of Plaguefire. She cast no magic at all, but simply faced his onslaught with her own force of spirit.

"Fascinating," Vhaerynn said. "I have never encountered a will so strong. What talent you might have. I would take you for my squire, if you were not a nameless wretch and already dead."

Semana panted, her chest heaving as she sucked in air, eyes locked to the sorcerer's face. Under her tattered cloak, Regel saw as she slowly raised her clawed gauntlet, fighting for every fraction of a thumb's breadth. If she could keep Vhaerynn's eyes on her face for one more moment...

"I have a name." Semana brought the gauntlet around. "I—"

Then Semana screamed as Vhaerynn twisted one hand and seized the fire gauntlet. Flames scorched a burning line into the floor. When the necromancer crooked his hand, the fire gauntlet tore from Semana's hand and flashed to his grasp.

"Treacherous little bitch, aren't you?" Vhaerynn asked, voice wavering. "All your magic bound up in devices—little tricks unworthy of a true sorcerer.

Mayhap you should taste mine..." His eyes welled with bloody tears and he smiled viciously. "All of it."

And with that, he brought the full force of all his power down on Semana.

It should have killed her then and there, but somehow she kept breathing. She fell to her back, screaming. On the floor, she writhed and arched as magic danced around her, blood trailing through the air like a whirlwind around her frail body.

"Does it hurt, Child?" Vhaerynn asked. "Do you beg for release?"

Semana moaned and wept.

Regel moved his arm. In turning all his power on Semana, Vhaerynn had freed him.

"*The moment comes*," Ovelia had said. "I see it."

He saw it too.

He pushed himself to his feet. His bones ached with every one of his forty-five winters. Despite the magic, it had grown so cold he could see his breath. He felt like a tired old man, beaten and broken, but he would not lie down and die yet.

Once more, he thought. Just once.

He drew up Ovelia's fallen sword and stepped resolutely toward Vhaerynn.

"You cannot defeat me," the necromancer said to Semana. "Your powers are nothing!"

Semana could not protect herself. She was going to die.

He thought of Frostburn, the sword he had once wielded, and the cold power trapped within: the power of death. He thought of its opposite, the power of life.

He thought of Lenalin, who had never wielded Frostfire, and the Winter King, who had.

He thought of Ovelia, of the moment she had promised. This moment.

"Vhaerynn!" Regel slashed with all his might at the necromancer's head.

Regel's blade didn't hit—it shattered in the air before it had even come close—but the damage was done. Vhaerynn's power caught Regel as he fell, strangling him with his own body. Regel knew the strike would slay him, but he had distracted Vhaerynn from Semana, who was even now climbing to one knee, then to her feet. As Regel watched, the Plaguefire died away, replaced by silver-white flames. Frostfire, the power of Denerre, passed down through the generations, awoke in Semana.

Before them, an unbound Semana burned with white flame. Hoarfrost danced across the floor, reaching out from where she knelt. The fires her gauntlet had lit turned abruptly to barbed ice sculptures. Power swirled around her, unknowable and unmatchable. She was life and death in a single force.

"Gods," the necromancer murmured. "Beautiful."

"Yes," Regel murmured. "She is."

"I have a name," Semana said as she rose. "It's *Mask*."

She thrust her arms toward them, and a storm of white fire burned into them with unearthly cold. It knocked Regel sprawling, his body shivering as white frost spread across it.

Vhaerynn took the full force of the blow. His body flew across the chamber to shatter against the great glass window that separated the throne room from the Tar Vangr night. Half the throne room exploded outward, bringing in a gale of cool air that fueled the icy flames.

The necromancer's scream—if he uttered one—vanished among the sounds of roaring flames and of shattering glass.

THIRTY-NINE

THE SUN WAS RISING. Regel could see the dim, muddy red light through the massive hole Semana's magic had ripped in the side of the palace. He turned over, coughing.

There Semana knelt, stained all over with blood, wearing a mantle of silver-white fire like a god's shroud from myth—like an angel's halo. She was looking at the silvery flame that wreathed her hands.

"I cannot deny it," she said. "No matter how I run."

Regel spoke, but it came out as a wordless groan.

Semana looked to him, then over at Demetrus. "He is dead. But I don't feel—?"

"Satisfied?" Regel asked, his voice rasping like Mask's had. "Vengeance is an empty cup. You'll ever be parched, however much you drink."

Semana seemed to consider, looking at her hands. "Yes."

Boots pounded on the stone outside the throne room, and Regel realized their battle must have drawn every Ravalis soldier in the place. He looked vainly for a weapon. "Princess—"

Semana waved her silver gauntlet, and Regel saw a translucent wall of magic spring up around the chamber. Silence descended as the wall blocked out sound as well as movement. Regel could see but not hear the doors rattling against the magic.

Semana reached toward the throne and King Demetrus's corpse stirred. For a heartbeat, Regel feared it would birth some other horror like Vhaerynn, but instead the Diadem of Winter wrested itself from beneath one of the king's arms. During the battle, the crown had flown from Vhaerynn's head and landed in the dead king's lap. Now it floated to the princess as though borne by an unseen footman. Semana plucked it from the air, considered it a moment, then tossed it at Regel's feet.

"I've seen the wages of rulership, and they are worse than those of vengeance." She looked coldly at Ovelia, who lay unmoving at Regel's side. "I'm quit of her— quit of you all."

She turned, but Regel reached through the Frostfire around her and caught at her ankle. His fingers went numb and ice spread up his arm, but he held firm. "Stay."

Semana looked down at him, considering. "My mother's garden." She turned her gaze to the smoky Vangr sky. "I'll wait for one hour."

She walked toward the glass-covered balcony. Semana paused a moment at the rail and looked down at her feet. Then she looked again into the Tar Vangr dawn, vaulted the rail, and soared away on the magic of her boots.

Regel heard coughing and looked around, heart in his throat. It was Garin, not Ovelia, who stirred. He sat up where Regel had stunned him, retching and looking about blearily.

Regel ignored the Ravalis prince and crawled to Ovelia's side. He took her hand, which was cold to the touch, and pressed his ear to her lips. He thought he felt the tiniest wisp of breath. She lived, though he could not say for how long.

"A healer," Garin said. "She needs—"

Regel started to move away, but Ovelia gasped awake and clutched his hand tight. Her eyes roved blindly to his face and beyond. She couldn't see him.

"Regel," she said, her voice fearful.

"Yes," he said, cradling her in his arms. "I am here."

"Regel—" she said. "I'll not ask forgiveness."

"There is nothing to forgive," Regel said. "Whatever he said—whatever he did to you to make you kill him, I do not care. Only stay with me."

Garin appeared, hovering over them. "I will fetch a healer," he said. "I can have one here in ten breaths." He started away, only to find the doors shut up with Semana's magic. "Silver Fire!"

Regel shook his head. It did not matter.

They lay in each other's arms, Regel and Ovelia—the last Knights of Winter, who had loved and hated and won. It was a cold victory, but a victory, and much remained to be done. Could Regel do what must be done without her?

He wondered, if he had trusted Ovelia from the first, whether today would have been different. If they had been honest with one another; if he had not poisoned her; if—

"I am sorry," he said, because he could say nothing else.

"Do not be," she said. "I cannot live, Regel. After all I have done..."

"Ovelia," he said. "None of that—"

Ovelia smiled weakly. "Kiss me," she said, tongue trying to wet her lips. "Once for last."

He leaned toward her, but she averted her burned mouth at the last moment.

"Kiss *me*," she said. "Me, not her."

"Always," Regel said, and kissed her on the lips. "Always."

FORTY

S THE SUN CREPT toward its zenith behind ominous clouds, Vhaerynn *burned.*
He could feel the blessed warmth on his frost-gnawed skin—and the agony
it brought to his torn and battered body. Rain fell on him—the scalding rain of
Ruin—and sweat dripped across his face like liquid fire.

It was not just pain—he was a necromancer, and he knew pain. It was *fire.*

He floated in a sea of shattered glass, gripped by a personal winter so cold it
seared flesh from his bones and crystallized his blood. Red-black jelly oozed from
thousands of cuts upon his flesh—each of which he could barely feel individually,
with the skin around them frozen into death. Horribly mutilated, cut so many
times, why was he not dead?

But he knew. He knew it was the magic of which he had been so proud. His
Gods-cursed *magic* was keeping him alive when he should be dead.

*The Denerre girl appeared over him, her face wreathed in a silvery halo. Rut her,
with her pompous whore's face—rut her good and bloody.*

"Please," he begged. "Please... kill... me..."

She paused at the railing around the balcony and looked down at him.
"Kill yourself."

Then she was gone, leaping over the rail and into the wide sky.

No. That was a dream. Or a memory. That had happened hours ago. How
long had he lain here?

Vhaerynn drifted.

There was a flash of silver radiance from within the chamber, and confused voices.
He tried to look and saw a multitude of people... No, all images of two, or perhaps
three people?

The Lord of Tears was one, and a red-haired man he could not name. And a
woman. A woman who had been dead, but now—

Another dream. He let himself go numb and senseless again.

Perhaps this was death, and if so, he welcomed it. The pain had long ceased;
he had pushed past it into a new world beyond understanding.

A sound caused him to stir. He lost that blissful otherness of the empty black,
and found himself once again in something that felt like his body. A woman knelt
over him—a woman in the sackcloth robes of a chiurgeon. Her fingers worked
with needle and thread, lacing his flesh back together.

The pain was welcome. He'd cut himself as a boy—for the pain, and for
the control.

"Ahh," he murmured, comforted.

She smiled down at him wanly. With her fine features, she might have been
lovely, were she not so tired. "My Lord Sorcerer, welcome ba—"

The court sorcerer reached out, took her head in his hands, and wrenched. Her neck snapped and she slumped bonelessly into his lap. Her body jerked its way into death atop him.

The dagger. Where was the Blade of the Red King?

He found it under his hand, eager for his touch, and he jabbed it into the healer's flesh as she quivered her way into death. She became a corpse on the instant, and turned to a layer of dust that coated him like a cloak. Her life essence flowed into him, bringing with it an ocean of pain such as he had never known. He felt every bit of his flesh drawing back together. Bones knit of their own accord and skin wrenched across his muscles—it was life and youth and he loved it. The glass felt like liquid fire in his flesh, cutting and ripping. The Denerre bitch must have nearly killed him, for it to hurt this much.

His eyes focused, and he looked around for another victim to feed upon. They were in the healing chamber, as he had expected, and the other chiurgeons backed away in terror. That was also not a surprise. Whom he saw amongst them, however, he did not expect.

"Cruel as ever," said a shaky voice from nearby. "Good."

There stood Lan Ravalis, covered in sweat. His eyes were wild and his teeth gritted like those of a beast. He held the Diadem of Winter in one hand and a naked sword in the other. The wavy blade was red and its hilt was shaped like a roaring dragon. Draca, the bloodsword of Dracaris.

"I see death has not changed you," Lan said. "Near-death, anyway."

Vhearynn coughed, which hurt. "Can you say the same, Summer Prince?" He doubted it.

Lan's face darkened. "I am no prince but your *king*, sorcerer," he said. "Bow to me."

So he had failed to remove the Ravalis from the throne, and he suspected the Blood of Winter yet endured as well. For now, on both counts. "I can hardly move, Your Majesty."

"Bow to me." Lan nodded to the chiurgeons. "And I will give you another to consume."

Vhaerynn smiled. That, as much as anything, indicated his proper path.

He pushed the crackling remnants of the dead healer off his lap, and the corpse collapsed into a cloud of dust when it struck the floor. The dust of her body stuck to his blood-soaked robe, garbing him in utter filth. His legs itched as he swung off the pallet, but he welcomed the pain. Bones crackling, sweat streaming like tears, Vhaerynn shifted to one knee.

"I live to serve my king," he said.

～

"Is it true?" she asked from behind him.

Regel looked up and around from where he sat on the little curving wall around the long-dried fountain. Rain had fallen in the last hour, but rather than

305

collect in the stone basin, it had drained through an old crack in the wall. He remembered that crack—he'd been here when the stone had split.

This had been Lenalin's favorite place, many years ago. The Narfire was close here, and it kept the garden warm enough to bloom through the winter when properly tended. Flowers and fruit trees used to grow out of season in this private grove Orbrin had reserved for his daughter, and Regel had known many gentle moments in this place: he, Lenalin, and Ovelia.

The garden had not weathered the passage of years well. Robbed of its caretaker when Lenalin died, it had begun a slow, inevitable slide into Ruin. Many had tried to maintain it over the years to no avail—Ovelia in particular, in memory of the woman she had loved.

"Is it true?" Semana stood amongst the leafless trees that marked the edges of the withered garden. "Are you—" She swallowed. "Are you my father?"

He looked at her evenly—scrutinized her face amid silver-blonde curls, peeking from beneath a rain-streaked hood. She still wore Mask's armor, though she only had the silver gauntlet. Regel remembered Vhaerynn seizing the fire gauntlet during the battle. Her bare right hand trembled on the fringe of her weathercloak. "Yes."

Semana stood silent for a moment, then slowly—seemingly without thinking—she drew her hood down to her shoulders, revealing her gnarled locks of silvery hair. They were still stained with blood, but they would wash clean.

"Why?" she asked, so softly he almost didn't hear.

"Because I loved your mother," Regel said, "and she loved me."

Semana smiled and even laughed—the laugh of a beautiful young woman, not the dry hacking chuckle of the creature she'd pretended to be. "I mean, why did you never tell me? Before five years ago, after Lena—after my mother died. That was ten years."

Regel smiled ruefully. "You were too young and it was too dangerous." He put out his hand and opened it, as though releasing dust to filter into the air. "Paeter suspected, and nothing could convince him otherwise. He... He killed your mother out of his jealousy. I could do nothing."

"Why not me?" Semana's voice broke. "Why not kill *me*, and spare her?"

Regel shook his head. "You were his power," he said. "Even Paeter was not so stupid as to put all his hopes on your brother. After Darak was exiled, you were his only heir." He shook his head.

"And so you let me believe that *beast* was my father," Semana said.

Regel wiped his brow with his fingers. "It kept us from war."

"For ten years!" Semana said. "Ten years of peace, to let the Ravalis consolidate their power—to exile my brother to his death, and then..." She balled up her fists, which crackled with magic—Plaguefire again, rather than the Frostfire of Denerre.

"I am sorry." Regel shook his head. "We were fools, as all those in love are."

Thunder rolled, and Regel felt the air grow heavy. He stepped toward Semana and pulled the hood over her head. "It will rain," he said.

"And we should hide my face," she said. "The Ravalis could have eyes anywhere."

Regel nodded sadly.

"What of the Bloodbreak—" Semana paused. "What of Ovelia?"

Regel looked away.

"Regel." She put her arms around him. "I did not mean to hurt her. I—"

Regel's eyes went to the smoldering palace, and through the mist to the bitter red sun. The light did little to alleviate the dark clouds over the city. The rain was increasing—going from a patter to a downpour—and the skies rumbled.

"All's well." He laid his hand on her silver-crowned head. "Peace."

He extended his cloak around her, saving them both from rain tainted by centuries of misspent magic. They stood, father and daughter, amongst the withering world.

"Ovelia." Semana peered down at her hands. "Tell me: does she live?"

Lightning split the stormy morn sky.

Silently, Regel drew her tighter into his arms and laid his cheek against her gleaming hair.

The rain fell burning around them like shards of molten glass.

EPILOGUE

THE SUN GLIMMERED ON the horizon outside the mighty glass windows of the throne room when Ovelia came to attend the Winter King. Ruin's Night was almost over.

Through the great window of the throne room, she thought Tar Vangr looked tiny indeed: like a tableau in a conjuror's looking glass. The City of Winter's towers barely scraped the infinite black tinged with stars. Gazing upon the scene, Ovelia felt at once insignificant and powerful.

"Do you know," asked King Orbrin, "why you are named Ovelia?"

She had not expected this question. Neither Paeter nor Regel had called her by her name tonight. The prince had named her "whore" and the other had needed no words to name her worse. After that, "Ovelia" hardly seemed like her name at all. She shook her head.

Orbrin wore a faint smile. "Norlest—your father—had no facility for names. And of course, your birth took him by such surprise as to muddle his wits."

The king brushed back his silver hair. That it was poorly groomed indicated he had risen from bed without servants to attend him. He wore a simple white robe, over which he'd draped the silver cloak of Denerre. He looked warm, though also old—tired.

"If not my father," Ovelia asked. "Then who named me, Majesty?"

A smile transformed his aging face into something beautiful. He was still handsome, though the ten years since his daughter's death had aged him terribly. His silvery eyes sparkled.

"You, Majesty?" she said. "*You* named me?"

He nodded. "And please, name me Orbrin. We know each other well enough, I think."

"Yes." Ovelia smiled against a sudden wave of anxiety—this night had shattered her, stripping two of the three constants in her life. Her sacrifice to be near Semana. Her last remaining friend in Regel. The Winter King was her third and most important anchor, bound with potent secrets. "We do at that."

"I gave you a name from the old Calatan tongue," Orbrin said. "I might have chosen a weapon, an exploit, or a hero of myth and legend. But yours was a different destiny I foresaw, in every speck of dust on your path. And thus did I name you."

"What destiny is that, Maj—Orbrin?" Ovelia asked.

308

He smiled. "*Shield*." He laid one gnarled hand upon her shoulder, and her body went taut under his touch. "Not just a simple disk of wood or steel—but *oveli* means *to* shield. It was the battle cry of my blood, long, long ago, when we carved Tar Vangr out of the frozen wasteland of this new, broken world." He put his other hand on her other shoulder and looked her in the face. "You are a protector, like your father before you. But while he chose this destiny, yours was written long before you first drew breath."

"I... I do not understand," Ovelia said. "Surely I chose my own path, Orbrin."

He shook his head. "I knew the moment when first you met my daughter, your eyes alight with wonder," he said. "I saw that your destiny had been written in the stars long before."

"The princess..." Pain woke in Ovelia's heart. "Lenalin is dead, Majesty. I failed her."

"We all failed her—I, most of all—but that is not how I would remember her." Orbrin continued unabashed. "When first you met, I saw how you loved Lenalin with a passion that would never fade—would outlast the stars above or the Narfire below. You loved her instantly and without restraint, far more than I ever could. And so I knew that you were destined to shield her—and her blood—with every breath and fiber of your body. You were her shield."

"I am *your* shield, sire," Ovelia said.

"Just so," he said. "But are you willing to do your duty, no matter the price?"

"Yes," Ovelia said. "Orbrin, I—I failed Lena, and now I have only you. And Semana, though she hardly knows me." Fearful understanding gripped the base of her spine like a cold talon. She fell to one knee, hand at her heart. "Semana is in danger."

"Yes, she is." The king nodded. "And it is not a simple danger, but one for which, I fear, you may not be able to do what must be done to protect her."

"Tell me, Majesty," Ovelia said, reaching forward to grasp his calves—the ancient gesture of supplication. "I'll do it on the instant. I swear by the Nar and the Old Gods, that I'll—"

"Be not so quick." He put a finger across her lips. "You can spare me half a word, no?"

Dutifully, she fell silent and nodded.

"Ovelia, this will be hard," said King Orbrin. "Perhaps the hardest task I've ever asked of you, harder even than..." He shook his head. "I must invest a great deal of trust in you—and faith."

"Anything, Majesty." Her voice trembled. "Orbrin."

"When you do this." He closed his eyes and clenched his jaw. "Once you have done it, you will have to protect Semana. You will have to give everything for her."

"Of course," she said. "Majesty, you know that I—"

The king put his fingers again to her lips. "You'll do it alone. No one else."

"I don't understand."

"You cannot trust the Ravalis," the king said. "Not Demetrus, not Paeter. No one."

"Not Paeter?" Ovelia remembered the prince's cruel smile and his hair like blood and fire. She felt his contemptuous words scratching at her ears. "Cruel oaf he might be, but he is Semana's father and your son by oath. She is his link to the succession. Why would he not protect her?"

"After tonight"—Orbrin returned her a tiny, bemused smile—"Only Semana matters."

"What do you mean?" she asked, suddenly very afraid.

He went on as though she had not spoken. "The Council cannot protect her. I do not expect they will have power for long—five years at the most, if Yaela's cowardice holds true and he does not move openly against the throne. What you do will prevent civil war, but no doubt the Council will have enough blood on their hands and daggers at their backs." He paused, as though considering whether to say more. Then: "And you'll not tell Regel."

"But—" Ovelia's eyes widened, but she had already lost Regel this night. "Yes, Majesty."

"You will be alone in this task," he said. "Understood?"

Ovelia nodded, then shook her head. "Majesty, he is loyal to you. He is as loyal as I—"

"If he survives what is to come, to draw him into this will only compromise your efforts," said the king. "He will hate you after this, and you will have to count him an enemy."

What was he asking of her? Ovelia was lost, her head aching with the bewildering flurry of his words. A single question formed, however, and she gave it voice: "What is to come?"

Orbrin shook his head, still smiling, and he looked suddenly very tired. "Ah, Ovelia, I've made such a mess of things. I am aware of a plot against my life—nay, nay, stay a moment." He waved her to peace. "It is a death of my own making. Too long have I struggled against these Ravalis vultures, and in the end, they prove the stronger. I cannot survive this."

"If they send slayers, I will kill them." Ovelia put her hand to the hilt of her family sword. "I will defend you to the last drop of blood in my body."

Orbrin touched her cheek, sending a cold thrill through her skin. "You are honorable, but you have no grasp of politics. That, you will have to learn: learn to lie and manipulate others to do what must be done."

"And what must be done?" Ovelia asked. "Just tell me, Majesty!"

The king nodded in the face of her wrath. "Draw your sword."

"Majesty?" Ovelia didn't understand. "Majesty, I don't—?"

"Do it now, if you love me." He opened his royal robe, revealing his thin, gray-furred chest. "If you refuse me, then I burn your eyes and name you Oathbreaker."

Now she understood. "Kill you?" Ovelia hesitated, her fingers trembling on the hilt of the Bloodsword. "Your Maj—Orbrin, there must be another way."

"There is not," Orbrin said. "Ovelia, Paeter is dead this night."

"But—" Ovelia stopped, her words evaporating. She'd just talked to Paeter—

warmed his bed, even. It didn't seem real. "You are certain of this? He is *dead*?"

"Or will be," Orbrin said. "And that is my mistake. Even if I could deny involvement in Paeter's death, the Ravalis will accuse me of it. You think any of my blood will be safe? There will be civil war, and you, me, Semana—all of us will die, and the Ravalis will take the throne. That cannot come to pass. For Tar Vangr to survive, the Ravalis cannot rule. The world will fall to Ruin." He shook his head. "I have to die, Ovelia, and yours must be the sword that kills me."

"Mine," Ovelia said. "I don't understand."

Orbrin grasped her hand on the sword. "By doing this, you will be the Bloodbreaker, reviled and hated by all in Tar Vangr, but so too will you prove yourself an ally of the Ravalis," he said. "Whatever you have to say or do to walk amongst them—to win their trust—that you must do. Violate your honor, lie through your teeth, kill any man they ask you to, only live and protect Semana. She has to ascend the throne, or our world comes to an end."

"Orbrin—"

"You know that I am right," Orbrin said. "Tar Vangr is the last mage-city of Old Calatan, the last bastion against the World of Ruin. One by one the others have fallen while the City of Winter has endured. Soon that will come to an end: the Ravalis will bring the city into calamity, and all the works of men will be swept away." He put her sword to his chest. "The Blood of Winter must spill for the Blood of Calatan to flow on. Let my death have meaning. Do it."

Tears rolled down Ovelia's cheeks. "I can't."

"Come, come, my nerve will not last forever." He grasped her hand on her sword and closed his fingers tightly about her knuckles. "I'd most want it to be you, rather than another."

"No," she said, her heart racing. "Please—don't—"

Ovelia didn't see what happened, but of a sudden she was falling backward, her cheek ringing with fiery pain. Orbrin had struck her. "Strike," he said. "Or must I do that again?"

Ovelia tasted blood where her lip had split. "Do it again and again," she said, "I'll not kill you. Name me Oathbreaker, but I'll not do it."

Veins stood out on Orbrin's forehead, and his eyes welled with tears.

"Can you not see I am dying anyway?" he asked, slamming his fists down on his knees. "The Ravalis lurk all around my throne, and I have driven all my blood away. I could not protect my queen, nor could I save Lenalin from Paeter. Darak is gone these five years. There is no hope left for Winter but Semana. If I go on, what will become of her?"

"So death is your answer?" Ovelia asked. "Are you such a coward?"

His hand rose and she dared him to strike her again, but Orbrin touched her face tenderly. He teased a lock of her red hair between his fingers.

"A single mistake, and Lenalin grew to hate me," he said. "A single mistake, and the Blood of Winter drips to an end. All but a single last light, across a great rift."

It was that, then. The sin that lay between them—the one Ovelia had never told anyone.

He rose and drew her to her feet. Ovelia's body trembled throughout, her fingers shaking.

"This rift—we can mend it," Ovelia said. "I will tell Semana. *We* will tell her the truth."

Again Orbrin shook his head. "She must never know," he said. "Never know what has been done for her sake." He closed his eyes, regret drawing them tight. He seemed ancient. "I have been so selfish, Ovelia. I forced this pain upon you, and now I must let you pay a greater price than mine. I am so sorry."

"No." Ovelia laid her hand upon Orbrin's cheek—his tears ran over her fingers. "Do not apologize. What I have done, I have done for love, not duty. Always."

His frown turned to a gentle smile. "Strike quickly, as you love me."

Ovelia's sword rose between them like a barrier. Flames leaked around the steel, warning her of the death to come. She saw herself running Orbrin through, and saw herself surrounded in a ring of Ravalis steel. And Draca did not lie.

Above her, Frostfire wreathed Orbrin's face. How like a king he looked—how like a god.

"Strike then." He smiled. "Strike, and be my shield."

Again she was young, and he strong and beautiful. Years evaporated in the silver-white flames that surrounded them and Ovelia knew again what it was to love and be loved, as no one since her princess had been able. Then Orbrin pushed toward her, or else she pushed toward him. Whichever moved first, they came together, and the blade sank into his chest—through his heart—and out his back.

They breathed as one: a single, resonant breath that shook them both.

The Frostfire of his blood faded around Orbrin, last King of Winter, and he fell to his knees. His face, raised toward hers, was serene.

Ovelia's lip trembled and she touched his cooling face. Then she screamed in sorrow and in hate and in despair. She fell to her knees, catching his face between her hands, and begged him without words to wake. She begged him not to leave her. The world vanished and she was rocking back and forth, the body of a dead king in her arms.

She must not have heard the doors to the chamber shake, or the booted feet trample inside, because when she looked up, Ravalis guardsmen in red and blue surrounded her and she could not explain how they had come. Their weapons were drawn and they stared, bewildered, at the dead king and his champion, clad in Denerre silver and white silk but dyed Ravalis red with blood.

Ovelia rose, drawing Draca free of the king as she went. The finely-honed steel parted from the dead flesh with a wet slitting sound. She gazed around the circle, challenging each and every one, but the guards could not face the blood-smeared angel who stood in their midst.

Her eyes strayed past the ring of Ravalis red to the balcony, where stood a forbidding figure all in black leather. And beside it, blue-steel drawn, was Regel, the Winter King's Shadow. They two stood and stared at Ovelia.

Slowly, she raised the Bloodsword to her eye and saluted.

Then the guards rushed her and the old world was gone.

Present Day—The Throne Room of Tar Vangr— The First Day of 982 Sorcerus Annis

As the sun rose, light crept across the cold floors of the throne room to where Regel knelt beside Ovelia as she lay still in a spreading pool of blood—his, hers, Demetrus's. Everyone's.

Semana had bade Regel follow her, but he could not simply turn away. Not yet.

"Lord of Tears," Garin was saying. "Regel—Regel, we have to go."

Semana's wall of magic was faltering as Ravalis guards pounded upon it from all sides. Regel knew he had only a moment before all would be lost. All that Ovelia had fought for, and all that she had died for. He had to move, if he was going to honor her. And yet...

"Regel!" Garin grasped his shoulder and shook him. Regel felt it only distantly. "I mourn her too, but we must away, or all this is for naught."

All blood was alike, Regel realized. All of it hot when fresh, cold when aged, and spilled whether in vain or to a greater purpose.

It all came back, then.

He remembered Ovelia's words, that day on the *White Dart*, about his healing hands. He'd hurt her shoulder so badly, but he'd healed her despite it.

Then again he had touched her upstairs in the Burned Man, soothing her hurt wrist.

He felt again when Davargorn had forced new life into his body.

"*How could you know my heart, old man?*" Davargorn had demanded, tears in his mismatched eyes. "*You do not even know your* own! *What you are! What power you hold!*"

He remembered forcing himself to rise in the corridor, even as Semana's magic should have killed him. New strength had entered him, as if by magic.

He remembered holding Ovelia's hand when the necromancer was killing him, and she had awakened. "*Help her,*" Ovelia had said. "*Help my daughter.*"

"I have been wrong," Regel said.

He knelt, laid his hands on Ovelia's chest, and closed his eyes.

"What are you doing?" Garin knelt at his side. "She is gone and will not come again."

"I have always been wrong." Regel smiled.

He embraced his new path.

And a miracle came to pass, on that first day of the year, when Ruin's sway lifted. In that place of death, a man sent healing life into a woman, and it changed them both.

In that moment, one bright light shone forth and changed the destiny of a once-dying world.

THE NAMED AND MARKED OF RUIN

Ravalis, the Blood of Summer ("Summer Lasts a Day"): Outlander Rulers of Tar Vangr, City of Winter

Cassian Ravalis (892–961): Last King of Luether (City of Summer), elder brother to Demetrus, father to Garin, perished in fall of Luether.

Demetrus Ravalis (894–present): King of Tar Vangr, younger brother to Cassian, father to Strevon, Paeter, Alistra, Lan and others.

Ansa Ravalis nô Dorane (889–938): Wife to Demetrus Ravalis, perished birthing daughter Alistra.

Anthien Ravalis nô Vultara (916–961): Mistress and eventually second wife to Demetrus Ravalis, perished in the fall of Luether.

Toblius Ravalis (910–present): Younger half-brother to Cassian and Demetrus, husband to Alcha Varas.

Strevon Ravalis (930–961): The Hawk of Luether, first son of Demetrus, perished in the fall of Luether.

Paeter Ravalis (933–976): The Jackal of Luether, second son of Demetrus, husband to Lenalin Denerre, father to Darak and Semana, slain under mysterious circumstances.

Nameless (935–937): Third son of Demetrus, perished nameless.

Alistra (938–present?): The Spider of Luether, only daughter of Demetrus, imprisoned in the tunnels for unknown crimes.

Dorian Ravalis (940–961): The Wolf of Luether, son to Demetrus, perished in the fall of Luether.

Garin Ravalis (943–present): The Fox of Luether, former crown-prince of Luether, only son of Cassian.

Alcarin Summer (954–present): Smallborn squire to Garin.

Lan Ravalis (944–present): The Bear of Luether, son of Demetrus, husband to Laegra.

Laegra Ravalis nô Vargaen (940–present): Daughter of house Vargaen, neglected wife to Lan.

Alcha Ravalis nô Varas (930–present): Wife to Toblius, wed after Fall of Luether.

Boulis Ravalis (948–present): The Hound of Luether, son of Toblius.

Tolus Ravalis (951–present): The Falcon of Luether, son of Toblius.

Vhaerynn the Necromancer (unknown–present): Blood sorcerer and vizier to Demetrus.

***Denerre, the Blood of Winter* ("Justice In the Storm"):** Extinct Former Rulers of Tar Vangr

Aritana Denerre (885–932): Former ruler of Tar Vangr (910-932), youngest ruler of Tar Vangr in centuries, mother to Mortiun and Orbrin.

Moritun Denerre (911–936): Former ruler of Tar Vangr (932-936), elder brother to Orbrin, perished suddenly and unexpectedly in battle.

Orbrin Denerre (916–976): The Winter King, former ruler of Tar Vangr (r. 936-976), father to Althar and Lenalin and a third nameless child, perished at the hands of Ovelia the Bloodbreaker.

Matir Thorass (914–961): Wife to Moritun, political bond to Orbrin, mother to Althar and Lenalin and a third nameless child, perished in the fall of Luether.

Althar Denerre (937–955): Former Crown Prince of Denerre, perished in a duel.

Nameless (938–942): Second son of Denerre, perished in the cradle without a name.

Lenalin Denerre (940–966): Wife to Lan Ravalis, perished under mysterious circumstances.

Darak Ravalis nô Denerre (961–971?): Son to Lan Ravalis and Lenalin Denerre, exiled to Ruin for treason at a young age.

Semana Denerre nô Ravalis (963–976): Last Heir of Winter, daughter to Lan and Lenalin, perished in a skyship tragedy.

Tithian (963–976): Smallborn winterblood pageboy to Semana, missing, presumed dead.

Dracaris, the Blood of the Dragon ("Eternal, Unyielding"): Treacherous Sworn Shield to Denerre

Norlest Dracaris (917–961): Sworn Shield to Orbrin, father to Ovelia, perished in the fall of Luether.

Aniset Winter (922-942): Smallborn mother to Ovelia, perished in childbirth

Ovelia Dracaris the Bloodbreaker (942–present?): Sworn Shield to Lenalin, missing since slaying the Winter King in 976.

The Circle of Tears ("Ever Weep, Ever Watch"): A consortium of Spies in Tar Vangr

Regel Winter the Oathbreaker (936–present): The Lord of Tears, formerly the Frostburn, Shadow of the Winter King, sworn slayer in service to Orbrin Denerre, spymaster of the Circle of Tears.

Serris (960–present): Smallborn squire to Regel, First of Tears.

Erim (961–present): Smallborn thief, occasional lover to Serris, bastard son of a Dolvrath noble.

Vidia (946–present): Smallborn baker.

Nacacia (957–present): Smallborn warrior.

Daren (955–present): Smallborn warrior.

Krystir (955–present): Smallborn spy.

Meron (940–present): Soldier, bastard son of a Vortusk noble.

ABOUT THE AUTHOR

Erik Scott de Bie (tip: "de Bie or not de Bie, that is the question") grew up in the smoggy central valley and verdant mountains of California. He has been writing fantasy and scifi novels since before he could drive, and has been published since before he got his degree from Willamette University. He lives in Seattle with his wife Shelley and a menagerie of cuddly dire animals.

Erik's work has also appeared in the Forgotten Realms D&D setting, Pathfinder's Golarion, the Iron Kingdoms of Warmachine, the Traveller universe, and countless anthologies, both shared world and original. He is also the author of the multi-media Justice/Vengeance superhero series.

Check out World of Ruin updates, lore, deleted scenes, and behind-the-scenes features on erikscottdebie.com, as well as Erik's ever-growing bibliography. Find him on Facebook at www.facebook.com/erik.s.debie

Made in the USA
Monee, IL
10 February 2021